A Wild Blue Wonder Press Novella Collection

ISBN: 978-1-7341685-8-7

This is a collection of works of fiction. Names, characters, businesses, places, events, locales, and incidents are either the products of the authors' imaginations or used in a fictitious manner. Any resemblance to actual persons, living or dead, or actual events is purely coincidental.

Scripture quotations in the stories "If I Knew You Were Coming" by Bailey Gaines, "The Tussie-Mussie" by Katja H. Labonté, "Fear Not Tomorrows" by Erika Mathews, and "Courage to Stay" by Kellyn Roth are taken from the King James Version (KJV). Scripture quotations in the story "The Cottage on the Hill" by Andrea Renee Cox are taken from the New King James Version® (NKJ). Copyright © 1982 by Thomas Nelson. Used by permission. All rights reserved.

Cover Design by Hannah Linder Designs

Copyedits by Andrea Renee Cox

Formatting by Kellyn Roth

Wild Blue Wonder Press
P.O. Box 1156
White Salmon, WA, 98672
admin@wildbluewonderpress.com

Introduction

Welcome to *Springtime in Surrey*, the first-ever anthology published by Wild Blue Wonder Press. The creation of this collection has been a mighty work for all the authors and other people involved, and we're immensely proud of it.

The following eight stories are, of course, set in springtime in County Surrey, England. They span a wide variety of decades—both contemporary and historical. Some stories are romances, some are not. All of them are explorations of a woman's relationship with God.

We hope this collection blesses you!

Kellyn Roth
Founder of Wild Blue Wonder Press

Jesus, I Am Resting

a novella by Faith Blum

Chapter One

Epsom, County Surrey, England
March 1914

Elinor Chapman was alone.

The sun shone too brightly for a funeral. But when did the weather cooperate in this town? The green grass covering all the other graves stood in stark contrast to the somberness inside her. Only the pastor and gravediggers were there to hear Psalm 23 read. Cold comfort for someone who no longer had any friends or family. All she had were her mother's clients, and she didn't want to make her mother's death public knowledge yet. She'd even chosen to not announce her mother's death in the paper.

And all her money went into the ground with her mum. She had finally saved enough money to pay a doctor to help her mother, but that same day, her mother died, leaving Elinor alone at seventeen with a list of clients who might never accept her as a laundrywoman. She had convinced the clients to stay on as her mother's cough grew worse, but now Mum was gone. Elinor would need to act like nothing had happened.

After the Psalm, the pastor said a short prayer, and the gravediggers shoveled the dirt on top of the plain pine box. The three men left Elinor alone, and she knelt next to the dark mound, letting the tears fall for the first time.

Her whole life seemed full of tragedy. Her father had been killed in the second Boer War when she was three, and now her mother was gone. How was she supposed to survive without her?

Elinor wandered home in a daze, thinking about all the laundry she had to do back home. The soap, the water, the constantly being wet. She went past the large, beautiful buildings without seeing them. Her steps clicked on the cobblestones, and when she reached the house, she realized it was a miracle she hadn't been run over by an automobile or horse and buggy. She'd crossed four roads without registering a single one in her memory. How had she not been killed? Perhaps it would have been a simpler …

No. She shook her head. She couldn't think that way. She had to move on like her mother had when Elinor's father died.

Though, what was the purpose now that she had no one to live for?

Day in and day out, Elinor did laundry. Washing, rinsing, hanging the clothes to dry, ironing. When she wasn't doing laundry, she delivered it and looked for other people who needed laundry washed. Two clients per day was plenty to keep her busy but barely enough money to live off of. She needed to push to try to find three clients for some days. If the amount of clothes was low enough per person, she could still manage to keep up with it. Or she could just work into the night like her mother had done when Elinor was younger.

Every time the work brought up memories of her mother, she couldn't tell if the burn of tears was from the lye in the soap or her own grief. It didn't matter. She had to work anyway, tears or no tears.

On one of her regular delivery runs, the door was opened by a stranger. The man was handsome with dark-brown hair and brown eyes you could get lost in. A little older than her, perhaps, but only by a few years.

"Hello there," he said. "You must be the laundry lady."

She nodded briskly. "Hello. I have Mrs. Carmichael's laundry."

He held out his hands. "I'll take it. No reason you should carry it any farther than you already have. I'm Andrew, her son. You must be Elinor."

"Yes." So this was the Andrew her mother had always talked about. Apparently, both Elinor's mum and Mrs. Carmichael had believed Andrew and Elinor might marry—a silly thought now, as differing as their circumstances were. Of course, he was a decent young man, but he wouldn't be interested in a working girl like her. She handed the basket off to Andrew.

He took the basket but didn't close the door. "Mother has talked about you a lot. She said something about not having seen your mother for a while. Is she all right?"

Elinor stiffened. "No. She …" She took a deep breath and willed herself not to let the tears escape. "She died over a week ago."

Andrew stepped outside and set the laundry down on the front porch and turned toward her, grief on his face. "I'm sorry. I didn't know."

"Few people do." Elinor's stomach roiled. She wanted to keep it that way but just told one of her clients. Would he blab it all over town?

"Do you need anything?" Andrew's concern seemed genuine. "Help with the house? Food while you get yourself established?"

"More people who are willing to pay to have their laundry washed." Elinor tried to keep the mood light so she wouldn't cry. Again.

Andrew's concern turned into a slight smile. "That might be doable. I have a couple friends who live on their own and don't have wives yet. I can ask. I'll talk to Mother as well. Between us, we'll find a couple people for you."

"Really?" *Is he really willing to help a near stranger?* They had just met. Sure, their mothers knew each other, but Andrew and she didn't. Her heart warmed.

"Of course. You and your mother have been such a help to us over the years. It's time we do a little extra to help you out. And as a Christian, it is my duty to help the orphans. And I truly want to. I don't want to see you have to do something else to make money. Not when you have a legitimate job to do. I lost my father recently, too, so in a small way, I know how hard it can be sometimes."

Elinor smiled. "Thank you."

"Did Mother already pay you?"

"Yes. She is one of the few clients who pays me before I do the work."

"I'll bring this in, and the next time Mother or I drop the laundry off, I'll be sure we have a couple people who are interested."

"Thank you."

May 1914

Andrew somehow ended up always being the person who dropped the laundry off and usually found a way to talk to Elinor for a couple minutes when she returned the cleaned and pressed clothing. Two months to the day of meeting Andrew, he came with the dirty laundry as usual but seemed different.

"What's wrong?"

"Huh?" he asked. "Oh, nothing's wrong. Why?"

"You seem nervous."

"Bother. I didn't mean to be. But I guess it's only natural." He cleared his throat. "Elinor, I've become smitten with you. I'd like to come calling. If you'd prefer I ask a male relative or friend first, I can. But I didn't know who to ask."

Elinor's breath stopped. Someone wanted to court her? A well-liked young man wanted to get to know her, a mere laundrywoman, better? "I … I don't have any relatives or male friends. Besides you, and you can't well ask yourself."

Andrew chuckled. "True."

"Your mother is agreeable?"

"Definitely. How did she put it?" He looked up for a moment. "She said, 'Of all the girls I know in this blamed city, she's one of the best I know of. Hardworking, attractive'—she gave a wink there—'and if she's anything like her mother, a good Christian girl. She could work on Sundays but doesn't. She could do immoral things to make more money but refuses. And she can handle herself without being cruel about it. She's the type of girl any woman would want for a daughter-in-law.'"

Elinor's mouth dropped open. "She said all that?"

"What's more, I agree with her. You are all of those things."

Elinor took the basket from him and set it in the small patch of grass next to the pots of water. "I would be honored for you to come calling. I don't know if I am smitten yet, but I'm willing to give it a try. I am rather busy every day except Sunday, though. And I can't make myself unbusy any other day."

Andrew smiled. "Our short talks on laundry days and then some longer talks on Sundays will work for me. Smitten or not, I am willing to take things slow so we have plenty of time to get to know each other."

They chatted some while Elinor finished up the laundry she had been working on before he came. By the time he left, Elinor felt she could become smitten—or even fall in love with Andrew. She had seen too many awful men in Epsom that she never dreamt she would ever find someone she could even remotely like. Was it possible she could actually marry someone someday?

Sunday, June 28, 1914

Elinor didn't stay up on the news, but she couldn't miss it this day. Archduke Ferdinand of Austria-Hungary was assassinated. A knot filled her stomach as she hoped nothing would come of it. But she knew that England rarely let something like a country in trouble go by without going into war. The knot stayed in her stomach for days after the news.

On Wednesday, Andrew came by with his and his mother's laundry. "Good morning, Elinor. I …" He paused "We need to talk."

Elinor stood and set the laundry aside and took the basket from Andrew. "About what?"

"I enlisted."

Elinor's breath caught in her chest. She stumbled and gasped for air. Enlisted? No. He couldn't. He wouldn't. Had she heard wrong? An image flashed in her mind of the one picture her mother had of Elinor's father. Her father in uniform. She shuddered and gasped again.

"Elinor?" His words sounded like they came through a tunnel. "Take a deep breath for me."

She somehow managed an almost-deep breath.

"Good. Now another."

She took another breath, and her chest loosened some with each breath Andrew coached her through. When she had calmed down a little, she sat on the front step.

Andrew knelt next to her. "Now tell me why you reacted like that."

"My father died in the Second Boer War," Elinor stated.

Andrew didn't respond, and she looked at him.

"That isn't enough of an explanation, is it?" She sighed. "I was three when my father died. I don't remember him, but I know it was really hard on my mother. I can't lose another man to a war. Someone I care about."

Andrew rubbed her hand with his thumb. "I didn't think about how my enlistment would affect you. I'm sorry about that. I don't even know if there will be a war. And if there is, everyone is saying it will be over by the end of the year."

Elinor pursed her lips. A lot could happen in a couple months. He could be maimed, killed, horribly disfigured. "There is no way to rescind your enlistment, is there?"

Andrew's head dropped. "No."

Elinor crossed her arms. "What happens if war is not declared?"

"I signed up for three years or until the end of the war. Whichever is longer. I will be going to training soon but still have a couple weeks before I go."

Elinor nodded. "I'll try to be patient. And not worry too much. But it will be hard." *Harder than you will ever know. War is too hard on everyone. Why does everyone love it so much? And how am I supposed to trust God when I know Andrew's in danger?*

"I know. And I am sorry. I'm sorry I didn't talk to you first. I'm sorry that you lost your father to a war. And I'm sorry that another war might be coming. I acted on my belief that God was leading me to enlist. When God leads me so directly and clearly, I act quickly. I didn't question it."

"You're sure it was God leading you?"

"Absolutely. I don't like war. Or fighting. Or the possibility of dying and leaving Mother and you alone. This isn't something I have dreamed of or even really thought about before war started in Germany. I did talk to Mother briefly, but she agreed with me."

"I bet she hated it, too."

"She isn't a fan of me being in danger, but she supports my decision."

Elinor straightened her back. "I will, too. I don't like it at all, but I'll support your decision. But you need to promise to write me as often as you can."

Andrew stood. "I promise."

Chapter Two

August 4, 1914

War. A word Elinor never wanted to hear after her father's death. But even more so after Andrew's enlistment. It had been over a month since the assassination, and Elinor had hoped that meant England wouldn't go to war. The news about England joining the war spread quickly through Epsom, and Elinor heard about it before noon. When the client dropped off his laundry and told her of the declaration, a sob escaped her as he left her home.

She couldn't lose Andrew. Did that mean she was in love with him? How did one know if they were in love? Not that it was important to think about right now. She had other things to contemplate. With war declared, her clients would slowly disappear. Should she go overseas and do laundry for the army? No. She couldn't be so close to the terror of the war. Not knowing Andrew could be out there being wounded or killed.

She needed to talk to Andrew but had a pot full of soaking clothes that needed to be washed, rinsed, wrung out, and hung up to dry. With a resolve that came from pure determination, she forced herself to put her hands in the scalding water and scrub a shirt on the washboard. Up, down, up, down. Andrew would be shipped off soon. Elinor knew that in her heart. He had enlisted. He was fully trained already. If a month of training counted as "fully trained."

Dunk the shirt in the rinse water, wring it out, scrub again. How many men would go to France to fight alongside their allies? Surely they would send plenty of men. But the whole army? Perhaps

Andrew would be left here to defend England from a surprise attack. She plopped the shirt back into the rinse water, splashing herself.

A growl escaped her throat. Like she needed to look more like a slob. If Andrew made it back to Epsom today, he would come here. Unless he didn't have time. If that happened, Elinor needed to hurry and finish this laundry so she could go to Andrew's mother's house in case he made it home but not to Elinor's house.

As she scrubbed the last of Marcus' laundry, another thought came. Many of her clients were young men. Young men who would probably answer their country's call just like Andrew had. What would she do then? What could she do? She had nursed her mother as she became sicker and sicker. Perhaps she could do some nursing. It would allow her to help with the war effort without being too close to the actual war.

She finished rinsing and wringing out the clothes and hung them up to dry. She had to go to Andrew's home even if he wasn't there. She had to talk to someone, and his mother was the only person she knew who would be willing to give her sound advice. Elinor slipped out of her wet dress and found a plain, but dry, dress to put on instead. Now all she needed to do was get to Mrs. Carmichael's home before dark.

Elinor rushed down the busy streets, past newsboys hawking their papers all about the declaration of war, and dodged horses and automobiles. She would get there just in time. Maybe even before dinner.

The door opened before she knocked. Andrew stood there in his uniform, his brown hair tussled from having removed his hat. "Andrew," was the only word she could form. Was she breathless from the quick walk or the sight of him? She couldn't say for sure.

"Come in," Andrew said. "Mother told me to go get you. I planned to spend as much time as I could here, but she didn't want to keep me away from you."

"That was sweet of her. I'm so glad you're here. I wasn't sure I'd see you before you leave."

Andrew looked down. "I leave tomorrow afternoon."

Elinor's heart skipped a beat. "So soon?"

"The commanders have been planning for this declaration for a while. All enlisted men are shipping out tomorrow or the next day for extensive training."

"Where to? Or can you not say?"

Andrew took her arm and led her to the parlor, where his mother sat by the open window.

"Elinor! You must have had the same idea I did. Welcome. Come, sit down. I'll get the maid to bring us some refreshments. Unless you would like to stay for dinner."

"If it isn't an imposition."

"Not at all," Mrs. Carmichael said. "Not at all."

"Mother, Elinor had the same question you asked before suggesting I go get her."

"About where you will be sent?"

"Yes," Andrew replied. "All I can say is that I will be in France. I don't even know where yet. I do have an address for you two to send letters. From there, the letters will find their way to me somehow. Eventually."

Elinor sat on the settee next to Mrs. Carmichael, and Andrew sat across from them. Elinor soaked in their time together that night, knowing it would likely be months before she saw him again. She didn't end up talking to Mrs. Carmichael about anything besides Andrew and his antics. But she felt better anyway. She would figure things out somehow on her own.

August 17, 1914

Elinor pulled on her light-gray skirt, then smoothed the white apron over it. The color scheme for nurses didn't make sense. She would be working with wounded soldiers. White and light gray stained easily. But she wasn't in charge of anything, let alone the uniforms. She needed to leave so she could arrive on time for her first day. A quick glance around the one room house showed she hadn't forgotten anything.

She wasn't sure she could see wounded soldiers all day every day without thinking about Andrew, but she had to try. It was the only job she could find that she would be any good at. Nursing came second nature to her after nursing her mother for the last few months of her life.

She made her way through the slightly emptier streets. The war had changed Epsom. Women were less chatty. The sidewalks held less foot traffic. There were fewer cars on the roads. Female constables stood on street corners. The main thing that stayed the same was the children scurrying around. Elinor dodged a mud puddle. She couldn't go in with splashes of mud on her dress.

She reached one of the racecourse buildings that had been converted into a hospital. She straightened her head covering, feeling like a nun with her long, white covering but knew it was important to keep her hair out of the way when tending the wounded.

Elinor stepped into the large stone building and almost gagged at the smell of alcohol and blood. She took a minute to adjust to the darkness inside as well as the odors. Then she rolled her shoulders back and strode in to find a doctor who might be able to direct her where to go for the first day.

A man in white pants and white shirt stepped into the hallway. His blond hair almost blended into his pale face and clothing.

"Doctor?" Elinor said.

The man turned her direction, and she was struck by how handsome he was, though in a different way from Andrew. Andrew was tanned, dark haired, and obviously spent a lot of time outdoors. The doctor was thin, but his features were pleasing to look at.

Elinor gave herself a mental slap to stop thinking that way and concentrate on what the doctor was saying.

"You must be the new nurse. Elinor Chapman?"

She nodded.

"I'm Doctor Hathaway. Follow me. You can shadow me for now and then I'll pair you with a nurse until you are comfortable with your duties. The nurses mostly check on the patients to see what they need or assist the doctors. Are you comfortable around blood?"

Elinor nodded her head.

"Good. We finished treating a soldier a couple hours ago, and I should check on him. His bandage will have some blood on it, and you can help me change it." The doctor crooked a finger, telling her to follow him, and she did. He walked fast down the hall and into a small room, where four beds lined the walls. "This is where soldiers go after surgery. There are a couple more rooms, but we don't have enough for each man to have his own room." He stopped at the last bed on the right. "This young soldier had his leg partially amputated. The bandage on his stump is what needs to be changed."

Elinor nodded. "Right now, or do we talk to him first?"

"He is unlikely to wake up until this afternoon. But yes, you should check to see if he is awake and needs anything first."

Elinor went to the head of the bed and checked the man's forehead with the back of her hand. It was warm but not hot. He seemed fine. If he wasn't here, she would have thought he was simply taking a nap. But she knew better. "Not awake and no fever."

The doctor raised an eyebrow. "Well done. Thank you for checking that. Do you know how to change a bandage?"

"No."

The doctor taught her how to change the bandage and then told her to check on the soldier again later. Elinor followed the doctor around until noon, when he passed her off to one of the older nurses, Mrs. Berkshire. Together, they went to the after-surgery room. Elinor headed straight to the amputee's bed.

At the head of the bed, she looked right into his pain-filled eyes. "Hello. You woke up. Can I get you anything?"

"Something for the pain. My right foot is killing me."

Elinor blinked. "I'll see what I can do." How could he feel pain in the foot that was missing? Surely he had to be mistaken. She went to Mrs. Berkshire. "He feels pain in his missing foot. Is that possible?"

Mrs. Berkshire sighed. "Unfortunately, yes. There is little we can do about it either. We can give him a little morphine, but it won't help the phantom pain except to dull it. I'll come with you."

Elinor tried to smile but failed. There was a lot to learn in this job. She hoped she was up for it.

Mrs. Berkshire gave the young man morphine.

Elinor put her hand on the soldier's, hoping to distract him. "What is your name?"

"Malachi."

"I'm Elinor Chapman. Do you need water?"

"Not right now. Just someone to talk to."

Elinor looked across at Mrs. Berkshire, who nodded. "I need to check your bandage, but I can listen while I work on it. What did you want to talk about?"

"My fiancée."

Elinor almost missed a step. "What about her?"

"I don't know where she is. I know she is in Epsom but not where."

"How is that possible?"

Malachi rubbed his face with a hand. "Hattie and me grew up as orphans. We got engaged before I shipped out. Then this happened. She planned to stay at the house we found empty one day, but I've written her there and not gotten any responses."

Elinor finished changing the bandage before moving closer to him. "The post is slow, so maybe she did write but it hasn't caught up to you yet. I'm still waiting to hear from my beau, too. He's in France somewhere fighting, and I don't know if he's still alive or not." She found a chair and brought it over. "Maybe I can help. Where is this house? If I have time, I can walk past it on my way home."

"You would do that?"

"Of course I would. I'm an orphan, too. More recent than you and your fiancée, but I know how hard it is. I've been thinking I should find a way to help the other orphans join the war effort and stay busy without getting into trouble. I just don't know how."

"I can help you figure that out."

Elinor smiled. "Thank you. I'd like that. Now tell me about this fiancée of yours."

Malachi spent the next thirty minutes talking about his fiancée and where they lived for the two months before he went to France. Elinor finally took her leave of him to get back to work, but her mind kept working on ways to help the other orphans.

Chapter Three

"You are a natural at nursing," Doctor Hathaway commented.

Elinor's cheeks warmed. "Thank you. I had some practice nursing my mother."

"What did she have?"

"I don't know. We couldn't afford a doctor to find out. She had a nagging cough that eventually became almost constant. And then she became too weak to continue doing laundry for her clients. So I took over for her and nursed her as much as I could."

"Without having seen her, I can't say for sure, but it could be consumption. A lot of laundrywomen get it."

Her stomach clenched. Consumption? And laundry could cause it? Why? Was she in danger? "Why didn't I?"

"You weren't doing laundry as long as your mother, I assume."

"Correct."

Doctor Hathaway nodded. "That would be why. I would avoid doing laundry every day, if you can."

"I won't be doing it again until after the war at least, so I should be safe for a while." *And now I know and can avoid going back to that trade, if at all possible.*

"Good. Now check on the amputee and make your rounds. Ask someone if you run across something you don't know."

"Yes, sir." Elinor went to Malachi. She could see him from the doorway and paused. He was awake. She took a fortifying breath. Every time she talked to him, she thought of Andrew. What he had to be going through. The threat of his being maimed or killed was too much for her some days. Then she would see the doctor and realize she had more she could hope for. If Andrew died or she decided she didn't like him, the doctor could probably be another option.

"Miss Chapman," Malachi said as she approached. "You made it back."

Elinor smiled. "Of course I did. I do have some bad news. I didn't find Hattie."

Malachi's smile faltered. "Thanks for trying. I have some good news."

"What is it?" Elinor checked and changed his bandage while he talked.

"I came up with an idea on how the orphans could help the war effort and make a little money."

Elinor finished the bandage. "What is it?"

"Uniforms. Especially for winter. You'll need to check with someone about colors and styles, but if you know how to sew, and other orphans know how to sew, it could work. You could sell them to the army."

"And the army needs lots of uniforms," Elinor stated.

"Yes. It would help your beau as well."

Elinor looked away. The last letter from Andrew had upset her more than she cared to admit. His insistence that she stay safe when he was in a danger zone. His concern for her spiritual life. She felt smothered by him sometimes.

But she also liked how much he cared for her well-being. Even if she was convicted by what he said. She didn't have time to read her Bible and barely took time for short prayers. "Yes," she finally answered Malachi. "It would assist Andrew and his army buddies. Too bad we can't make them shell-proof."

Malachi forced a laugh. "That would be handy but unrealistic. You should be able to find some people who could donate material or blankets to make the uniforms out of. And store owners might donate thread and needles to the cause as well."

"Good idea. If we have enough orphans helping, they could go door to door to get the donations."

"Exactly," Malachi said. "The older girls can sew, and the younger ones and older boys can get the materials."

"Now I just have to gather some orphans and get them working. I have a day off soon, so I can gather people and supplies and get the orphans started sewing even while I'm here. This job pays better than my last one, so I can buy some materials as well."

Malachi grinned. "Sounds like we've got it all figured out."

"So far anyway. Now to actually get it organized. But for now, do you need anything else?"

"No. Just come back later so I can see your pretty face again."

"What would your fiancée say if she heard you right now?"

Malachi winked. "She'd be happy I could see well enough to know you're pretty."

Elinor laughed and worked her way through the room to check on the other soldiers.

It was Elinor's day off, and she spent it scouring the streets for orphans. The search was harder than she expected. Lots of children roamed the streets, but the only ones who talked to her were children who had parents. The orphans scurried away before she could say more than "Hi."

All she needed was one orphan to talk to her so she could find out if her plan was feasible or not. A young woman came her direction. She had golden hair that was speckled with dirt Elinor wouldn't have noticed if she didn't know how hard it was to clean her own hair.

"Excuse me," Elinor said. "Do you have a few minutes?"

The young woman stopped and stared at her with wary eyes. "One minute. I have a job to go to."

"I don't mean to be rude, but I am looking for orphans who can help me with a long-term project. Do you happen to be an orphan?"

"Yes. You are the laundrywoman's daughter, aren't you?"

Elinor smiled while trying to keep the tears at bay. "Yes."

The young woman took a step closer. "She was always kind to me. What kind of long-term project are you wanting to do?"

"Make uniforms for the army. I thought some of the older girls could do the sewing, while others gather donations of material, needles, and thread."

"Where would we work? Most of us don't have homes."

Elinor's smile grew. "I do. You could sew there."

The young woman looked her up and down. "You won't find anyone else while looking like that. You look too clean to be an orphan. I'm happy you have a good job as a nurse, but if you want this to work, you should have someone else find the orphans who want to help."

Elinor swallowed hard. "I hadn't thought of that. You're a wise woman. What is your name?"

"Mary."

"Mary, would you be willing to find other orphans who would be willing to sew or gather supplies?"

Mary grinned. "I'd love to. I have to go now. I really do have a job I need to do. But I will start looking for workers tomorrow."

"Thank you."

"Happy to help. I'll gather as many orphans as I can. When and where can we meet with you?"

"Next week, Tuesday." Elinor gave her address, and Mary waved as she left.

Elinor watched Mary with a smile. Her plan was in place.

Three weeks later

Elinor had orphans sewing in her home and gathering donations on a consistent basis. She stayed up late to sew and woke up early to get things ready for the girls who would arrive. Her letters to Andrew grew shorter and shorter, but she didn't think he would mind. She was staying busy and helping people. What more was there to a wartime life? She couldn't get married and have children right now, so she would do the next best thing: support the children of the parents who had died.

Then she got two letters from Andrew in one day. After work, she sat and read them instead of sewing.

Dear Elinor,

I am happy you found something you enjoy doing in helping the other orphans. I'm sure the uniforms will be appreciated as well. But, darling, I am worried about you. Your penmanship is getting worse with every letter, and the letters shorter. These two things make me think you aren't getting enough sleep. I want to make sure you are okay. Please get some sleep.

If you are having trouble, go to my mother. She will assist you. I know she will.

Elinor stopped reading. This again. Sleep was for the people who had money. Or time. She had neither. She needed to keep going. And going. Keep working until she could make it out of the poor side of town. Or marry out of it. Both options were unlikely to happen. She also couldn't help the orphans as much if she didn't live near them.

She sighed and started sewing. She sewed until her eyes refused to focus on the material and thread. Then she climbed into bed and slept until her alarm clock woke her.

Elinor woke with a start. The buzzing and rattling of her clock pounded through her ears. She groaned and rolled over to hit the alarm clock, only to remember she'd put it across the room so she had to get out of bed to stop it. Another groan.

She flung the blankets off and set her bare feet on the cold wood floor. A shiver ran through her body, and she quickly dressed, lit a candle, and cooked up some breakfast. Maybe someday she would be able to live somewhere with a more easily heated house. Or better wood so it would stay burning all night. She had to get out of this squalor somehow. Someday.

Elinor sat down and started sewing a shirt. She sewed until the first of the young women showed up to take over.

"Up already?" Mary asked.

"Yes."

"Do you ever sleep?"

Elinor looked up. "Of course I sleep. I may work hard, but I know my limitations."

Mary narrowed her eyes. "Do you? Because I can see the bags under your eyes even in this dim light."

"I'm fine. I can survive on only a few hours of sleep per night."

"Just don't wear yourself out too much."

"Yes, Mother."

Mary smiled. "Now get ready for your nursing job. I've got the sewing handled. You do know we've got plenty of help with the sewing and you don't need to do it when you get home or when you wake up. Right?"

"I know."

"But you have to feel useful."

"Yes."

"You are. You gave us something to do. And a way to make a little money. That is useful. Now go to work and consider going to bed, instead of sewing, when you get home tonight."

Elinor ignored her suggestion of sleep as she left for work. Mary's words rang through her head all day. Could she be right? Yes. She was even likely to be right. But that didn't mean Elinor could, or would, do anything about it. Rest was not her strong suit.

Chapter Four

Sleep sounded so good, but Elinor couldn't give in to it. She still had to work another half-day. Checking in on Malachi was no longer a necessity every day, which she was thankful for. She knew he would notice her exhaustion and mention it, and she didn't want to deal with that.

Elinor went from bed to bed and room to room without any thought. It was all by memory. Any conversation she had was forgotten as soon as she said it. Anything someone said that was out of the ordinary was not replied to, because she couldn't comprehend it. She probably seemed uncaring, but today, she didn't mind. She was too tired to mind.

After her shift ended, she somehow made it home. She had no idea how. Besides apparently through a mud puddle as her hem was stained with dark splotches. She decided to take Mary's advice today and go to sleep right away. After she washed her dress, at least, to get the mud out some.

Mary and a couple of the girls were there sewing and kept her company while she washed her dress.

"How are the soldiers doing?" one of the girls asked.

"Fine," Elinor answered. "I think anyway. No one complained loud enough for me to notice."

"Would you like us to leave early tonight so you can get some sleep?"

Elinor hated that question. If she had a larger house with more than one room, she could say no. But her bed was in the same room as the living, kitchen, and dining areas. And she knew she wouldn't be able to sleep with the lamp on. "Yes. But only tonight. I will sleep more tonight so I don't need to have you leave early again."

"It's fine," Mary said. "By the time we have to use lamplight, it gets harder to sew anyway."

"But if this continues, that means less sewing will happen in the winter months," Elinor protested.

"I didn't say it was impossible," Mary stated. "It is harder and slower but doable. We will find a way to make it work. We'll meet the quotas and have some time to spare. Now go hang your dress and sleep. You need it."

Elinor didn't have the energy to argue with the young woman. They were gone by the time she hung her dress to dry. She stoked the fire, hoping the wood would burn until morning not only to keep her warm but to dry her dress faster. The last thing she needed was to get sick from wearing a wet dress in the cool morning. She could always wear her second uniform, but she had hoped to only wash clothes once a week.

"Nurse Chapman, you seem unwell," Doctor Hathaway said.

Elinor forced a smile. "I'm fine. A little tired but fine."

"It wouldn't do to get our nurses sick. Make sure you get enough sleep at night. I know we work you hard here, but you need sleep, too. What do you do when you get home?"

"Help my fellow orphans."

"With what?"

Elinor cleared her throat. "We're making uniforms for the soldiers."

Doctor Hathaway shook his head. "That is commendable, but there are others making the uniforms, correct?"

"Yes, sir." What was with the interrogation today? She needed to get to work.

"Then let them do the sewing. You can only do one job at a time and still remain healthy. As I already said, we need our nurses to be rested. We cannot help the soldiers who come here if we ourselves are not well. Part of being a nurse is keeping a positive outlook. A tired nurse will never be able to provide that for the soldiers."

Elinor nodded. "I will try, Doctor."

"Thank you."

How dare he tell her what she should do? The next instant, she knew he was right. But she couldn't get ahead unless she made some sacrifices to herself and her health. She plastered on a smile she hoped would fool the soldiers and provide some of that positive outlook Doctor Hathaway wanted his nurses to provide. What arrogance. To think she was ever attracted to him. He was the opposite of the mild-mannered, humble Andrew.

Which then brought to mind Andrew's latest letter. Tears pricked her eyes as she entered one of the rooms lined with dozens of soldiers. Andrew had asked her what she was reading in the Bible. She needed to get back into the Bible. But she needed time to read. Which meant less work, but she didn't have time or the ability to do so. It was a vicious circle and one she had to leave in the back of her mind until the end of the day.

"Good morning," she said as she approached the first bed. "Do you need any water or food?"

"No."

"I will change your bandage."

"No."

Elinor started. "A little company?"

"No."

Elinor raised an eyebrow. Someone with less to say than her. Unusual. "Are you sure?"

His sad eyes gazed into hers. "I lost everyone. How am I supposed to live with that?"

Elinor felt like he'd punched her in the stomach. "I ... I don't know. I've lost nearly everyone myself. Sometimes you need to find someone in the same boat to help. Maybe one of your fellow roommates."

He shook his head. "I can't. I can't get attached again. I can't let myself care only for them to be ripped away. Sometimes into pieces." He buried his head in his hands and sobbed.

Elinor sat on the bed next to him. "I don't have any answers for you, but I do know that even with all the loss, caring for people again can hurt, but so often, you get much more joy from it as well. I have a beau over in France. Every day, I am in agony over possibly hearing from his mother that he is dead. But every night when I hear nothing, I know he's survived another day. It's hard. Especially after losing both my parents, one to a war. But it helps me to pour into some orphans who are even worse off than I am."

The soldier's sobs slowed, and he looked up at her with a slight gleam in his eye that wasn't from a tear. "You have a way with words."

Elinor smiled. She had no idea where they came from. Besides God, of course. He was the only reason she could say what she had. Even after she had stopped reading her Bible and praying consistently. Guilt gnawed at her. She had let work take over too many parts of her life. "I hope they helped. Do you need anything else?"

"Thank you, no. There are others who need help more than I do."

Elinor went to bed after bed and helped any of the men who needed it before moving on to the next room. And the next one after that. Faking her way through every movement, smile, and conversation. But she made it through the day.

Once home, she sat down and sewed until the other girls left. She didn't have energy to talk to them and barely registered that they chatted amongst themselves. When they left, Elinor set the sewing aside and dressed for sleep. She tossed and turned until she somehow fell asleep.

Her alarm woke her again what seemed minutes later and she jumped out of bed, crossed the room, and got dressed. She had to try something else to wake up. She needed something. Anything to stay awake. She boiled some of the coffee she had for the orphans who liked it, and cringed at the thought of what her mum would think if she knew. When the coffee finished, she gulped it down and pretended she hadn't almost burned her insides. She didn't have much hope of it waking her but had to try.

She stumbled out the door and made it two streets over before realizing she would get to work early if she went now. Where was her brain today? Did she have to go back home to find it? No. That was crazy talk. Brains could be suppressed but not left behind. All she had to do was work her brain to get it started again. She walked random streets heading toward the hospital and quizzed herself on what Andrew looked like, math problems, and other things to stimulate her brain. It helped some but not as much as she'd hoped.

By the time she arrived at the hospital, she felt a little more awake and like she could finally start her day.

Chapter Five

The next day, Elinor woke up with a stuffed nose and sore throat. She groaned and rolled over with a shiver. Her fire was dead again. She shouldn't go to work, but she had no choice. She had to, or she might lose her job. On the other hand, if she went feeling sick, she could lose her job, too. What choice did she have?

She got out of bed and staggered around the cabin. She took a home remedy she knew her mother would have suggested: garlic crushed into her tea with some honey. It tasted horrible but took the edge off her sore throat. If only it would stop her nose from running and getting clogged, causing her to sneeze all the time.

She dressed and drank three more cups of tea. They helped her feel a little better, but she knew it wouldn't last long. She had to go anyway. No matter what, she had a job to do.

Elinor sneezed four times before arriving in front of the hospital. Her handkerchief was taking too much abuse. And her nose already hurt from being chafed by it. She knew she looked like quite the spectacle. The nurse in uniform looking like she needed nursing herself. It was ridiculous. She couldn't be sick; she was supposed to heal the sick and wounded, not be the one who needed to be nursed to health. But here she was.

She took the first two steps up to the door and stopped to let a cough escape her chest. The cough was followed by a violent sneeze she barely caught in the kerchief.

"Bless you," a male voice said from near her.

"Thank you," Elinor replied after she finished blowing her nose.

"Are you really coming in to work?"

"I planned to." Elinor looked up at him. It was Dr. Hathaway. Of course.

"I don't think that is a good idea," he said. "You sound pretty sick, and we can't afford letting our soldiers get a cold on top of everything else they are dealing with."

Elinor sighed. "I can't afford not to work, though."

"You can today. You will be a better nurse if you get over this cold before coming back."

Elinor slumped. This doctor was one of the most dedicated men she knew, and she'd hoped he, at least, would be impressed by her own dedication. But no. Instead, she was being sent home like an errant schoolchild. "I can't change your mind, can I?"

"No." He kept his distance from her. "Go home. Get better and then you can come back."

"Yes, sir. I'll do that." She turned around and wandered home. It took longer than normal, because she didn't pay attention to which streets she turned down.

Once home, she stumbled through the door, and Mary caught her before she could fall on her face.

"What is wrong? Why aren't you at work?" Mary asked.

"I'm sick. They don't want me."

"That makes sense," Mary answered. "I wouldn't want a sick person working in a hospital either. Come. Lay down and let me get you some tea. My grandmother had a tea she claimed could cure death if God would allow it."

Elinor tried to laugh but ended up doing a sneezing cough instead.

Mary stared at her a minute, then turned. "Girls, I think it best you go home today. Come back in the morning. Unless you don't want to risk getting the cold, which no one will judge you for. I'll stay here to nurse our nurse."

Elinor tried to protest, but Mary put a hand on her shoulder.

"No protests from you, ma'am. You are in no condition to contradict me."

Elinor groaned but snuggled in under the thin blankets. Mary was right.

Mary hummed while she sashayed around the kitchen area, stirred up the fire into a warm blaze, and set the teapot on the grate. Elinor almost drifted off before the tea arrived.

"You didn't have two of the ingredients, but I did my best. I'm sure this will help even if it isn't the exact recipe."

Elinor sat up and took the cup from Mary. "It smells horrible."

Mary grinned. "I know. But it works."

Elinor wrinkled her nose and took a sip. "Ugh. It tastes worse than it smells."

"I know. Gulp it all down. I made sure it was cool enough to be drunk quickly."

Elinor took a deep breath and gulped the tea down as fast as she could. "Guaranteed to kill or cure, I suppose."

Mary patted her head. "Maybe that's what Grandmother used to say. I forget. Now, lay back down and get some sleep. I will stay here to make sure you do."

"Yes, Mum."

Elinor woke up with sun blazing in her eyes. She sat upright. How had she slept in so late? Where was her alarm? Why hadn't it gone off? She was going to get fired. She swung her feet over the edge of the bed and ... sneezed.

Her cold. She wasn't late. She wouldn't get fired. She had a cold and had been sent home. She buried her head in her hands. Why hadn't she rested more like everyone had suggested? If she had, she wouldn't be in this predicament. She would likely be healthy and at work. But no, she always had to push herself. She never slowed down. She couldn't. It wasn't in her nature.

Even now, all she could think about was the work that needed done. The sewing and nursing. Making sure the orphans had food and clothing. That she could write her letters to Andrew and read the few he sent back. That she could survive until he returned. A sob escaped her.

"Elinor?" Mary's voice broke into her thoughts. "Are you all right?"

Elinor looked up. "I'm sorry. I guess I'm not a very good patient, am I?"

"You slept half the day, so I'd say you are an excellent patient so far. But now I'm worried about you and what made you start crying."

"It's nothing. Nothing important."

"You don't ever cry, so I think it must be important. To you, at least. If it's private, that's fine, and I won't pry. But you are welcome to share with me."

"I miss my beau. We hadn't courted long before he was sent to France."

"Seeing the soldiers at the hospital doesn't help, does it?"

"No."

"I'm sorry. I'll let you be. You got some rest, and I did some sewing. I think you can be trusted now to rest when you need it. Right?"

Elinor tried to smile. "Yes. And that tea seems to have helped. Do you have some more?"

"Staying warm by the fire. Drink it as often as you can choke it down."

"I will. And I will sleep when I need to."

"I'll see you tomorrow morning, then. Good-bye, Elinor. Get well soon."

"Thank you for staying."

Mary left, and Elinor let herself off the bed slowly. Her head felt less stuffed, and she knew she had to brave the tea again if she wanted to get back to work anytime soon.

She went to the fire and found the pot of tea. With a deep breath, she poured some in a cup and gulped it down with a shudder. Maybe it was her imagination, but she thought it might be tasting a little better. It had to be her imagination. She couldn't start liking this stuff.

Elinor sat on one of the wooden chairs and picked up the uniforms closest to her. At least she could sew without harming anyone. Or passing the cold off on them. It would keep her fingers busy, too, which she hoped would prevent her mind from wandering far afield. But she doubted it. Her mind wandered even when it was busy caring for soldiers.

She would need to quit one of these jobs once she felt better. She couldn't keep doing both things in a day. The smart thing would be to quit nursing and concentrate on helping the orphans and making uniforms. But then, how would she make enough money to pay for everything? The army paid well for the uniforms, but it was only just enough for the materials and food for the orphans who helped her. If she quit nursing, she wouldn't have any money for her own food and clothing. Not that she needed much, but she needed something.

By mid-afternoon, she finished sewing a shirt and decided to take another nap after gulping down more tea. She needed to prioritize rest today.

Elinor slept until the girls arrived the next morning. Embarrassment flooded her when she heard the door open, but she pushed it away and greeted them with a smile.

"Good morning, ladies. Ready for a full day of sewing?"

"Only if you are willing to rest when we tell you," one of the girls said.

"I will. I also really need to learn your names today. I know you lot told me once, but I only remember Mary. Who isn't here today?"

"No," the tallest of the girls said. "She will be here later but needed to take care of something else first."

Elinor nodded. "And your name is?"

"Hattie."

Something niggled at Elinor's memory, but she couldn't think well enough yet to make the connection. The girl's name was familiar in some way, but how?

Each of the girls introduced themselves again and sat down on the chairs to sew.

Elinor dressed and stoked the fire before joining them. She knew she should eat but would wait a little longer. The least she could do was sew in her own home on her own idea before feeding herself. And this way, maybe the other girls would eat when she did. She hated eating alone.

The morning went by while the four girls chatted amongst themselves, with Elinor butting in once in a while. They talked about the war and what each had read in the snippets of papers they had gotten their hands on. It seemed the war was doing poorly. Elinor had wondered about it, since they had so many soldiers in the hospital, but hadn't heard definitively. And if the papers were saying the war was going poorly, it had to be actually going poorly.

Which meant Andrew wasn't likely to survive the war this winter, let alone if it went longer.

Elinor shook her head and concentrated on the conversation.

"I just wish I knew he was still alive," Hattie said.

"Who?" Elinor asked. "Sorry, I got lost in thought."

"My fiancé," Hattie replied. "His name is Malachi. I don't know where he is."

"Malachi?" Elinor asked. "Did you two have a shack on Mason Street?"

Hattie stared at her. "How did you know?"

"Malachi is alive and at the hospital I work at."

Hattie gasped and stood, the uniform falling to the floor. "Can I go visit him?"

"I can ask Dr. Hathaway," Elinor said with a smile, "but I don't see why that would be a problem."

"Thank you, Elinor. How is he? What was injured?"

"Oh." Elinor's sewing faltered. How did she tell Hattie that Malachi was missing part of a leg? Should she leave it up to Malachi to tell Hattie? "He had an injury to his leg. I'll let him tell you exactly what."

Hattie's smile faltered. "Are you sure?"

"Yes."

"How bad is it?" Mary asked.

"I'll let Hattie tell you after she sees him," Elinor said.

They finally stopped asking questions, and Elinor didn't continue in their conversation. She couldn't risk blurting out the truth. She only hoped Hattie would accept Malachi's injury.

Chapter Six

Elinor only missed five days of work at the hospital. But she loved every minute she had at home. And felt more rested. She knew Dr. Hathaway would want to talk to her today about her plan going forward, whether she would try to do both jobs or quit one. She knew what she had to do. What she should do. No matter how hard it would be.

She rolled her shoulders back as she approached the hospital. She could do this. Elinor walked into the hospital, and a genuine smile made its way onto her face. She would miss this place. It was hard work physically, but she would still miss it.

Elinor went to work right away and kept working until one of the nurses stopped her.

"I heard you were out sick."

"I was. I'm better now."

The woman looked her up and down. "Perhaps. But you should still have a doctor approve you being here."

Elinor raised an eyebrow. "Any idea where a doctor is?"

"No. But you go to the exam room, and I'll find one for you."

Elinor sighed. "Yes, ma'am." She knew the woman was looking out for the patients, but it irked Elinor to be ordered around like this. She had as much right to be here as that nurse did. She wouldn't have come back if she were still sick. She knew better than that. Especially after being sent home last time.

She went to the room the woman suggested, and waited. Thankfully, Dr. Hathaway came only a minute later.

"Miss Chapman, you must be feeling better to have come back."

Elinor nodded. "I am. You were right to send me home. I needed the rest and was able to get it."

"Did you do any kind of work?"

Elinor cringed. "Yes. I did some sewing."

"Ah. But that is low-energy work compared to nursing or laundry. I approve of that."

Elinor let out a long breath. "Good."

"You look to be better," Dr. Hathaway said after listening to her chest. "A stuffed nose yet, I imagine, but otherwise in near perfect health. I would like you to consider quitting one of the jobs you do currently. You cannot keep the hours you do. I know it is hard being an unmarried young woman without a family to help you."

"It is. But I have been thinking about it as well."

Dr. Hathaway looked at her expectantly.

Elinor stood. "I'm going to stop being a nurse. I can stay on until you find a replacement for me, if that is helpful."

Dr. Hathaway looked down. "You are sure?"

"Yes. Why?"

He looked up again and shrugged. "You are a natural at nursing. I hoped you might stay here."

Elinor's stomach clenched. All she needed to do was change her mind. She could have everything she ever wanted. Perhaps even Dr. Hathaway as her husband, if she tried. But she had a duty. "I can't. The orphans need my help more than you do. There are other women who can nurse. No one else is helping the orphans."

"That is logical. I'll talk to the other doctors and let you know by the end of the day whether we would like you to stay for a couple weeks or go now."

"Thank you."

As she followed the doctor out of the room, she saw Hattie being led to Malachi's room by another nurse. She followed at a distance and peeked into the room as Hattie approached Malachi's bed. Their joy could be felt all the way to the doorway, and Elinor smiled. If only she could see Andrew again. But not yet.

She needed to work on learning to rest. Talking to Dr. Hathaway was the first step toward choosing rest over torturing herself for a little bit of riches. She could live without new clothes for a year at least. And she could live on beans and water, if needed.

Peace filled her as she went back to work, possibly for the last time.

"I'm done nursing," Elinor announced as she entered her house later that evening.

Every set of eyes turned her way.

"You're what?" Mary asked.

"You heard correctly. I will be joining you four in your sewing. And also the younger children, once in a while, in gathering donations."

Hattie jumped up and hugged her. "Thank you."

"For what?"

"For being a nurse while you were able to. And for not telling me about Malachi's injury. It was better to hear it from him."

Elinor sat next to Hattie. "I'm glad you think so. I couldn't decide whether I should tell you or not."

"You made the right decision. I am sad he lost a leg, but he is in good spirits despite the loss, so I think we'll still be good." She grinned. "And we decided that as soon as he leaves the hospital, we are going to the courthouse to get married."

Mary squealed. "Can I come witness the wedding?"

"Of course," Hattie said. "I want you all there. It wouldn't be the same without you."

Mary clapped her hands together and bounced up and down on the chair. "I love weddings!"

Elinor laughed, the first she'd let loose in a while. "Who doesn't like a wedding?"

"Very few people," Hattie said.

They were all quiet for a while.

"I suppose I should either start helping you lot sew or do something else."

"Probably," Mary stated. "We might have to fire you otherwise."

"I'm the boss," Elinor said. "You can't fire me."

"Watch me," Mary replied, hiding a smile.

Elinor shook her head. "I'll get to work, then. Do any of you read the Bible?" She paused. "Can any of you read?"

Mary raised her hand, needle and thread attached. "I can read. And I read the Bible when I am able."

"I can read," Hattie said. "I don't read the Bible as often as I'd like, though."

"What do you say we all take turns reading the Bible aloud while we sew?" Elinor asked.

"Love the idea!" Mary said.

"Good. I'll start for today, since I'm not sewing yet, and then we can take turns. Each girl for each day. We don't have to read the whole time, just part of it. Then we can discuss it and pray over the uniforms as well."

Hattie spoke up. "Can we start by praying over the uniforms?"

"Of course," Elinor responded as she sat down. "Who wants to start?"

Chapter Seven

March 10, 1915

Six months had passed, and the winter snow slowly turned to slush as the rains started slowly coming. The war lasted longer than "until Christmas" and had started to drag on indefinitely. But Elinor had expected that. Andrew's letters were a balm to her heart. The prayers and Bible reading helped to pass the time as well. She avoided reading the papers. They were too expensive and depressing.

Midday, Elinor got up and put together a small lunch of bread and cheese. Simple lunches were best for the girls and her, so they could keep working. Especially with Hattie gone to visit Malachi more days than she was there.

The bread and cheese were on the plate, and Elinor was about to set it on the small table when someone knocked on the door.

Elinor looked toward it and set the plate down before going to see who it was.

"Elinor," Mrs. Carmichael said, a pained look on her face, "Andrew is injured."

Elinor's chest tightened as the breath went out of her. She sucked in some air. "How bad?" She paused. "Wait. Come in and sit down. Then you can tell me."

Mrs. Carmichael came in and sat on Hattie's chair.

Elinor got her a drink of water before sitting down herself.

"Thank you for the water, Elinor." Mrs. Carmichael set the cup aside. "I got a letter from Andrew's nurse. He was hit in the abdomen. He isn't out of the woods yet, but she is hopeful."

Elinor wrung her hands. "Can we see him?"

"Not yet," Mrs. Carmichael said. "But she also said he would come here soon to recover."

Elinor's eyes widened. "Home?"

Mrs. Carmichael smiled. "Yes, home. You are welcome to come visit whenever you can after he gets back."

Elinor slumped on her chair. This woman was so kind and caring. "Thank you. Would you like to stay with us and chat for a while? If you aren't too busy?"

"Thank you, dear. I would love that. And give me a needle, thread, and garment. I can sew and chat at the same time."

Elinor smiled and handed the older woman the garment she had been sewing and went to find herself a new one.

Elinor approached the house, her mouth getting drier the closer she got. Why was she so nervous? She had to get control of herself. It was her beau she was seeing. She should be excited. So why wasn't she?

Because she had changed. And she was afraid he wouldn't like the change even though she knew he had wanted it. Irrational. Completely irrational. She took a deep breath and let it out slowly.

Mrs. Carmichael opened the door before she got to the last step. "Andrew's been asking for you ever since I told him you were coming today. I told him I'd watch for you. Come in. Please."

Elinor smiled. "Thank you, ma'am. I appreciate you letting me visit."

"He's almost as much yours now as he is mine."

Elinor stepped into the house and followed Mrs. Carmichael to Andrew's room.

"I'll leave you two alone." Mrs. Carmichael ducked away.

Elinor's mind raced. Would he still want to see her after today? After the decisions she had made the last few months? Or had he wanted to see her to end their relationship? What if he was hurt more than his mother let on? What if he'd been sent home to die? She made her way into the room and to the bed. Andrew's face was pale and poorly shaven as if someone with little experience had done it for him.

"Elinor," he said, "I've missed you so much."

Elinor took his hand. "I've missed you, too. When your mother said you were injured, I prayed you would survive. I've seen so many who are badly wounded. I couldn't bear it if you were one of them."

Andrew tried to smile, but it faltered. "It's bad over there."

"I know."

He stroked her hand. "Let's not talk about the war or injuries. You look beautiful. And rested."

Elinor's cheeks heated. "Thank you. Your encouragement helped me decide to quit being a nurse. As much as I was able to help there, other women can be nurses, but I don't know of anyone else helping the orphans, so this was a better choice."

Andrew's smile stayed this time. "I'm so happy to hear that. Mother said she's been stopping in to help sometimes, too."

"Ever since she got the letter about your injury. She stayed with us and chatted and helped sew. It's been fun having an older woman there. The girls have opened up more, and our conversations are going deeper."

"Mother was always good at that, so I'm not surprised."

They were quiet for a while.

Elinor smiled. "I've had so many things I wanted to talk to you about while you were gone, but now that you're here, I can't remember anything. Not a single thing."

Andrew chuckled. "Me either. It's like I can't think around you."

"Is that a good thing or a bad thing?"

"I'm not sure. We talked a lot in our letters, so maybe we simply said everything we needed to in them. Or it's been so long since we were together, we're not sure how to talk to each other anymore."

"Will that change?" Elinor sat on the chair.

"I hope so. In the meantime, let's just sit here and talk if we think of something. I enjoy looking at you, if nothing else. It's been a long time since I saw something so pretty."

Elinor's lifted her hands to her warming cheeks. "Stop making me blush."

"You look even prettier with red cheeks, though."

Elinor's face got hotter, and she shook her head. "Of course I do. What can I do to embarrass you?"

"I don't know. I don't think I get embarrassed."

"I'll find something."

The rest of the visit was spent rehashing stories they had told each other before Andrew left for the war. Elinor went home just before dark fell over the city.

Chapter Eight

April 22, 1915

Elinor hurried through the muddy streets to the Carmichael house. Every afternoon, she left her girls alone to go visit Andrew. He wasn't quite healed yet, and she didn't want to waste any of the time they had together. He would go back to the front soon enough. And today, he promised to tell her about some of his time fighting. She knew it would be horrible, but she wanted to know so she could better help him recover.

Once in the house, she went to the parlor where he'd been the last week when she arrived. He stood as she came in. He didn't wobble as much this time, and Elinor rushed to him. "You are getting stronger."

"Yes, I am. My legs don't shake as much, and I even walked down the hall today without holding on to anything or anybody."

Elinor took his arm. "Would you care to try walking more? It's a gorgeous day today. We could go sit in the garden."

"Let's."

Elinor walked as if on a cloud. Having Andrew home even for a short time had been a balm to her soul. If only he didn't have to go back to the war. Maybe then they could get married. "And I'll be right here if you need me to help you."

"Yes, ma'am."

Elinor held his hand while they went to the back door. They made it to the bench before his legs buckled slightly, but Elinor didn't mention noticing that. No need to injure his pride.

"This was a wonderful idea. It's been a while since I got some fresh air that didn't come through a window. Mother insists on having a window open for me as often as she can, but it isn't the same."

"Nothing ever beats the real thing."

Andrew put his arm around her waist. "I said I'd tell you about what fighting in the war was like."

Elinor's chest tightened. "Yes, you did."

"Well, it was horrible. The men around me were getting bombed and shot, never being able to make any progress to go forward. Everyone was so optimistic about the war being over quickly. The army is losing their morale. We don't have much hope the war will be over anytime soon. I don't know when it will end or if it will end. England has always come out on top of a conflict. We were overconfident getting into this war."

"England doesn't always come out on top. They lost to the colonies in the 1780s and in South Africa during the First Boer War."

"I know. But they don't remember things like that. They only remember the wars they win."

Elinor rested her head on Andrew's shoulder. "Not everyone forgets. I know we supposedly won, but I will always remember that the Second Boer War took my father from me and that it was a totally pointless war that lost many lives. I only hope this war isn't the same. I couldn't handle that."

Andrew pulled her close. "I'm sorry. I hope this isn't another useless war, too. But I don't know. Right now, we're in a stalemate."

"Are you going to be okay after seeing so many people die?"

"I don't know." He pulled away slightly. "I think so. God has been gracious to me so far. I've learned that resting in Him can get you through almost anything. Have you heard the hymn, 'Jesus, I Am Resting, Resting'?"

"I don't think so."

"I hadn't either until one of my trench mates started singing it once." He cleared his throat and started singing, his voice starting out low and growing louder.

Jesus, I am resting, resting
In the joy of what Thou art;
I am finding out the greatness

Of Thy loving heart.
Thou hast bid me gaze upon Thee,
As Thy beauty fills my soul,
For by Thy transforming power,
Thou hast made me whole.

Simply trusting Thee, Lord Jesus,
I behold Thee as Thou art,
And Thy love, so pure, so changeless,
Satisfies my heart;
Satisfies its deepest longings,
Meets, supplies its ev'ry need,
Compasseth me round with blessings:
Thine is love indeed!

Jesus, I am resting, resting,
In the joy of what Thou art;
I am finding out the greatness
Of Thy loving heart.

Tears filled Elinor's eyes as she listened to Andrew sing. Those words described her life the last few months completely. Trusting in Jesus had satisfied her deepest longings and her heart. She had finally found peace and joy after learning to rest.

"God has certainly compassed me 'round with blessings," Andrew said. He turned slightly to face Elinor better. "Many blessings. One of which is you. You came into my life at just the right moment. I needed you more than you'll ever know. Especially now, in this time of war. I need something ... *someone* to live for. More than my mother." He cleared his throat. "What I'm trying to say is, Elinor, will you marry me?"

Elinor's heart skipped a beat. "What? I mean, yes." She laughed a little at herself. "Of course, I'll marry you. I was not expecting you to ... ask that now. Today."

Andrew cleared his throat. "I wasn't either. I wanted to ask you soon, but ... It seemed natural to do it now. Except that I don't have a ring for you."

Elinor waved a hand in the air. "I don't mind. My girls won't like it, but I don't care much for jewelry."

"Good. Shall we tell Mother?"

Elinor hopped up. "Yes. And can we have a short engagement? Get married when you can stand longer but before you have to leave? I don't want to be the fiancée who got left behind. I'd rather be the wife of the soldier instead."

Andrew took her hand and pulled himself up. "Yes, let's get married."

May 15, 1915

It was a small ceremony at Andrew's church. His family, the few who were able to come, and all the orphans Elinor had helped, were the only guests. Elinor couldn't stop smiling all day. She had found the love of her life and married him. Could life get any better? She knew it would be harder once he went back to war again. But she also had more resources now as a married woman. And Andrew and Mrs. Carmichael were on board with her moving their sewing to the Carmichael house and away from her shack. It would be farther for the girls to go, but they would find a way to make it work.

But first, Andrew and Elinor would have at least two weeks all to themselves in a family friend's cottage in the country. Elinor looked up at her husband in his khaki uniform. The buttons shone in the sunlight as they left the small church to the shouts of their friends. Young orphans ran around outside, throwing rice and wreaking havoc. Mrs. Carmichael and Hattie tried to get them to settle down, but they didn't listen, and the two women finally gave up.

"Be good to her," Malachi said to Andrew as he leaned on his crutches. "She's a good woman. She brought Hattie and me back together again. And helped a lot of soldiers at the hospital."

"She's told me some of the stories," Andrew replied. "I will take good care of her."

"Good."

"I do have a favor to ask of you," Andrew said. "While I'm gone to the war, be here for her if she needs a man around."

Malachi straightened. "Yes, sir. I will gladly do that for you."

"Thank you. It will ease my mind to know she'll have a man—a brother—to watch out for her."

"And mine," Elinor cut in. "Thank you, Malachi."

"My pleasure," Malachi said. "Now, you two need to go off on your little getaway before the army comes knocking their way in here."

Andrew grinned. "Yes, sir." He turned to Elinor. "Milady, our carriage awaits."

Elinor turned to the group of orphans crowding near them. "Ready to catch the bouquet?"

They all shouted, "Yes!"

Elinor turned back to Andrew and threw her bouquet behind her. She looked back again in time to see Mary catch it, her face growing beet red as she did. Elinor laughed with the other girls and waved as Andrew led her to the carriage, and they sped off as a married couple for the first time.

Epilogue

It seemed fitting that Andrew's return would be on the first day of spring. Elinor and he had first met on a spring day, married in the spring, and now they would see each other again in the spring for the first time in nearly four years of marriage. She hopped from one foot to the other on the train platform. The Spanish flu had gone through Andrew's camp starting just before the war ended in November. It raged on, and Andrew stayed to help nurse his army buddies and so he wouldn't spread the flu to anyone in England, especially not his family.

Elinor stopped shifting her feet on the depot's platform and put a hand on the top of her son's head. Matthew had turned three nearly a month ago and had never met his father. Elinor told him about Andrew every day, but it wasn't the same as actually seeing him. She wasn't sure what she was most nervous about. Seeing Andrew for the first time in four years or his meeting his son for the first time.

A train rattled and squealed to a stop. The other women crowded the train, but Elinor hung back. She wanted Andrew's and her reunion to be less public. Until she saw him—gaunt and worn but so handsome—stepping off the train. Her husband. The father of her child. Elinor picked up Matthew and ran through the crowd to Andrew.

Andrew opened his arms and pulled them into a hug. "Elinor," he whispered, "you look so beautiful."

Elinor's heart caught in her throat. He was actually here. Touching her. Hugging her. She melted into his embrace. "You do, too. I missed you."

Andrew kept hugging them until Matthew wiggled too much for Elinor to hold him.

She set him down and crouched by her son. "Matthew, do you remember how I told you about your daddy?"

Matthew nodded, his thumb in his mouth as he stared up at Andrew.

"This is your daddy." Elinor waited for Matthew to smile, but he didn't. Matthew was a cautious child.

Andrew knelt down to Matthew's level. "Hey there. I've been so excited to meet you. Mum has told me so many things about you. Do you still like trucks?"

Matthew nodded, but held back.

Andrew put his hand in his pocket and pulled it out again. "Good. I made you a truck. The wheels even go around like they're supposed to."

Matthew took the small, wooden truck and rolled the wheel with his finger. "Tank you."

"You're welcome. Shall we go home?" Andrew looked up at Elinor.

"Yes, please." She grinned back at him.

"Can I carry you, Matthew?" Andrew asked his son.

Matthew nodded.

Elinor followed alongside them with happy tears filling her eyes. She had waited for this day for four years, and although Matthew was a little wary of his father yet, he still trusted him enough to let him hold him. "It's hard to believe you're actually here."

"I know. Maybe this will help." Andrew stopped walking and pulled Elinor close to him with his free arm.

Her heart raced as he put his lips to hers and kissed her like a starving man.

"Mum?" Matthew's voice cut into their bliss.

Elinor pulled away. "Yes, Matthew?"

"Why Daddy kiss you?"

Elinor laughed. "Because Daddy loves me. It's what we do."

"And I love you, too, Matthew." Andrew gave Matthew a kiss to his cheek.

Matthew giggled.

Elinor threaded her arm around Andrew's, and they made their way home to see Andrew's mother. And spend the rest of their days resting in Jesus.

A Note from Faith Blum

Thank you for reading this novella. I hope you enjoyed it. This is my first completed work in the WWI era. It has been fun dipping my toes into this setting. I usually write Westerns, so the research, though challenging, was also interesting. The spring at Epsom was believed to have healing properties and the water was found to have a high concentration of minerals. Those minerals were found to contain magnesium sulphate and are now made into Epsom salts. There was at least one hospital in Epsom, but the one I described may or may not have truly existed.

World War I isn't an era that is written about much, so I'm trying to change that a bit. At the time of publication, I am editing a different WWI novel that is not connected to this story at all except for the setting (England) and the era.

If you like the WWI era and/or Westerns full of adventure and a hint of romance or would like to connect with me on a more personal level, follow me on Instagram (@faithblumauthor) or subscribe to my monthly newsletter: http://faithblum.com/newsletter.

The
Cottage on
the Hill

a novella by Andrea Renee Cox

Dedication

To the One Who catches my every tear and fills my heart with boundless joy.

Thank You, Yahweh, for Your great dreams for me; they far surpass my own.

"To everything there is a season,
A time for every purpose under heaven:
... A time to weep,
And a time to laugh;
A time to mourn,
And a time to dance;"
Ecclesiastes 3:1,4 NKJV

"Those who sow in tears
Shall reap in joy."
Psalm 126:5 NKJV

Chapter One

Teatime again, and there was no change in her circumstances, no chance of reacquiring her dreams. Moira curled a hand around the warm cup before her on the wrought iron table as a breeze danced through the soft curls of honey-brown hair near each of her ears.

Danced. *Dancer.*

That was a term that no longer fit her. Not so long ago—less than a year, in fact—it had been the moniker she'd most cherished. Now she had but one: her own name.

Not that it was a poor thing to be called, but it wasn't *prima ballerina* or *dancer* or anything close to the like. How *could* she survive without marvelous words attached to and often announced before *Moira Wood*?

Emotion swelled in her chest and pricked her eyes, but she wouldn't let the tears fall. Not again. She'd cried far too much over this, and giving another drop of her heart would only dig an even deeper chasm for her to climb out of.

Enough dwelling. Surely there's something else you can think on, Moira.

She straightened the sage-green cardigan she wore over a cream-colored blouse and glanced at her pale-yellow skirt to make sure it hadn't fluttered up to expose her knees. Then she forced herself to look at her surroundings as she drew the cup to her lips and took a sip of the tepid brew. Her lawn was perfectly manicured. Pink and purple flowers beautifully speckled the beds beneath the front windows of her little cottage tucked well beyond a low stone wall that was aged with lichen and smoothed by the winds that buffeted the land in spring. Today's light waft was only a tease of what would be present in the coming weeks.

If she could grasp an elusive thread of hope, such beauty could transform her downcast spirits. She hadn't gotten anywhere in her career without the gem of an optimistic outlook, but those doctors wanted to strip it directly from the marrow of her soul. After getting secondary opinions aplenty, she was beginning to let them. How could she help it after many months of disappointments and failed attempts to get back on the path from which her career had veered?

Once upon a time, she'd not only raced to the stars but was London's guiding light. She'd headlined numerous ballets and traveled the world, dancing with only the best leading males. Her most long-standing partnership had seen the creation of new lift combinations and a couple of daring throws, of which she was most proud. Now it looked like her dreams of a lengthy, much-acclaimed career on the stages of every major country on the planet were set firmly in the past.

The china cup *tink-tinked* as she set it back on its saucer. Nothing but bitterness had brushed across her taste buds with each gulp, and none of the vegetables on the tray, also bearing a teapot, looked appealing. She wouldn't touch the scones Mrs. Cook insisted on tempting her with.

This time, Moira didn't try to fight the sting in her nose. The future was bleak without plans, yet her heart longed to secure one. The whole of her life had been planned since she was three and begged her parents to let her study ballet. If she didn't have that set before her now, then she needed to find a different purpose.

Being a normal, non-dancing person was challenging for her. In the city, she'd been gaped at and whispered about for what she could no longer be, so she moved to her holiday cottage in County Surrey to get away from all reminders for a while. Here in the countryside, she could have things delivered without a fuss and didn't have to speak to anyone, if that suited her. But what purpose could rural living hold?

With an attempt to salvage what was left of teatime, she picked up a small carrot disc. Munching it proved she had little appetite, so she nudged the saucer away from her a mere inch. Her picturesque lawn and small cottage held no potential opportunity to pour her work ethic and heart into.

The sobs took over then. She wasn't supposed to be left without options for success. She wanted to find a path to take her life back, to return to that stage …

Maybe it was time to face the blunt facts the doctors presented. Perhaps it was impossible to extend her career or at least have one last, glorious coda that would permit her to retire on her own terms.

If she was to be receptive to what other plans God had for her, it was imperative that she accept the excruciating death of her grandest—and only—dream.

Teardrops dripped off her chin and plopped into her now-cool jasmine tea.

The tune Adrian Davis whistled as he toted a crate of foodstuffs and a case up the lane was a jaunty one that made him want to tippy-tap his way along, but he had two left feet if anyone ever did. It'd be much better if he just kept walking. Surely he'd do himself an injury if he gadded about like a twinkle-toes sissy boy.

Leastwise, that was what the neighbor kids had called him as a lad when he tried to put rhythm to the music singing through his soul.

Nothing in town had changed much since the last time he'd been here. Small shops lined the main lane, and houses followed the wending streets spreading out from there. It was quaint and cozy, but walking into the countryside filled him with a strong sense of *welcome home*, and he couldn't help but take in several deep breaths as he traveled suitcase in hand and crate under arm, toward his uncle's farm.

The song wilted on his lips as his thoughts wandered into his secret goal's territory. He'd much rather be heading to his own slice of property right now, but that hope hadn't materialized. There wasn't a reason why it shouldn't be attainable, but life hadn't gone in that direction. Every time he inquired of God as to why not, only silence returned to him. He'd heard that wasn't a *no* necessarily, but after dreaming of owning an expanse of land since he was a little kiddie, it felt like he was getting the brush-off.

Only, that wasn't the way God worked. He didn't just brush off someone's desires. He might lead them down a different path than they wanted, but He didn't ignore the cares of a person's heart. Every Bible story proved that God cared about the details of one's life. With that in mind, Adrian decided right then and there to not let the silence steal the music from his soul.

On he whistled.

He didn't dare sing. Nobody—not even the birds flittering from tree to low stone wall and across the sky—would care to hear that.

An unexpected sound floated on the breeze. He wasn't certain what it was, but it wasn't of nature. Birds twittered and crickets chirruped, but he couldn't recall any critter that made a light yet jagged noise like that.

As he kept moving up the slight slope of the grass-edged lane, he kept an ear tuned to the utterance. He didn't stop whistling, but he lowered his pitch. Going completely quiet would likely allow him to hear clearer, but it would also alert whatever was making the sound to the fact that he had taken notice of it. His experience told him that startling critters of all types didn't often grant positive results.

Around the bend that curved beneath the broad, budding canopy of a large tree, the sound became stronger. Now he could tell that it was crying, and not from an animal either. It wasn't the soft, tender tears of a long-held sorrow. No, these were the harsh, ragged sobs from deep in the gut that were only produced from a bitter sting of the heart. He'd had his fair share of that feeling and those wails but never released them when out of doors. Rather, he saved them up to dampen his pillow when whichever relative he was living with at the time was either asleep or out of town. It'd been many years since he last needed to let loose a bout of melancholy over his future. These days, he put his hands to work and coaxed his mind to follow suit.

The crying got louder, and he looked to the right. On the side of a gentle hill was a small cottage that looked like it had belonged to the land for a few hundred years and was the only building for as far as the eye could see. A short wall made of stones that likely had been pulled from the ground when it was first claimed guarded the place in a weary but stately fashion. Beyond that, the grass was neatly kept, and a few beds of bright flowers looked to have bloomed early this year.

Off to the side, out a little ways from the cottage but not so far as to be separated from it completely, sat a table and a couple of chairs. One of those was occupied by a woman whose bowed head and shaking shoulders belied the cheery colors of her simple outfit.

She startled and looked up, and her sobs cut off mid-sound. Surprisingly, she didn't swipe at her tears but rather tilted her chin upward.

That had him quirking his brow. Who was this woman, and why was she crying into her tea? More than that, why wasn't she embarrassed? Most people would be if caught in such a state.

After setting down the suitcase, he lifted the cap from his head.

She returned his salute with a nod that was regal and barely perceptible from the distance the land and wall between them created.

He replaced the cap, then retrieved his aged, brown suitcase and headed farther up the lane. Uncle Royston's farm was a stretch beyond the hill's crest, and Adrian couldn't wait to check out the flock of woolies he'd be helping with.

At the peak, he paused to look back. He couldn't see much from here, but he was almost certain he heard a humming that mimicked the tune he'd been whistling before he stopped to observe the woman.

A smile eased across his lips. Staying at his uncle's farm might not be so bad after all.

Chapter Two

Finally, he'd escaped. The chemist's had been busy, unfortunately, and every person in the place seemed to want to catch up with him. If Adrian had to hear one more "my, haven't you grown!" comment this week, he might have to wring a neck or two. Eventually, he'd made his way to the counter and gotten his uncle's medication, which he added to the large, brown sack he'd gained at another shop. Now that the door was closing behind him, Adrian took a breath of air that wasn't saturated in the variety of scents the little old ladies thought made them smell good. They clearly didn't realize how cloying all those florals were to a man who was used to earth and dung and sheep and horses.

Yet, flowers had their merits.

In fact, he ambled in the direction of the aubergine-hued cart that spilled over with rainbows of petals. He'd noticed the cart on the way into town this morning to run a few errands for Uncle Royston, but Adrian hadn't thought he needed anything from it. Now he reconsidered. If the ladies in the chemist's shop preferred that scent, surely there was hope that a small bundle of blooms might be well received.

Once he arrived, he returned the greeting of the young lady who tended the cart. Thankfully, she was busy helping a harried-looking woman select a few flowers. That gave him time to see which color or type he might want to purchase. Without knowing anything about the recipient's personality, other than she bore a regalness that contrasted with the sorrow of her tears, it was hard to know if she'd like the blue or the pink, the dainty or the complex. Simple would be good, with a few shades of bright pink and a complementary sprig or two of baby's breath.

"What is it that you're wanting today?" The lady came over to help him.

He pointed out a few different flowers and told her how many, then asked her to tie a ribbon around the bunch. Once he swapped money for the bundle, he headed out of town and back toward his uncle's farm.

The sheep seemed to like him well enough when he met them yesterday, but there were a couple that skittered away from him. It would take some time to win those over. Likewise, Uncle Royston claimed the hard bout of the bronchitis he was recovering from didn't mean he needed help tending his own farm. Even though he retained a telling, rumbly cough, he played the grump and sent Adrian out of the house as soon as the sun came up this morning. The host of random errands he was commanded to complete meant nothing, save for collecting the medication. It wasn't like Uncle Royston *really* needed a pair of light-blue woolen socks with no dark streaks in them.

Next time Adrian received such specific instructions, he'd tell his uncle to fetch the items himself, that his dad had sent him out here to help *on the farm* not away from it.

Even if Adrian didn't mind the tasks, he wasn't going to let his uncle run him over. He'd prefer, of course, to work with the animals. But he wasn't one to be sent on fools' errands simply because his uncle wouldn't admit he needed assistance for a short span.

When Adrian got near the bend in the lane, he couldn't help but whistle a jaunty tune. Maybe the woman would come and greet him today. It'd be nice to talk at the picket gate for a little while. He'd learn her name and what type of work she did. A hitch in his thoughts nearly tripped him.

Was she married?

She'd seemed so alone yesterday. However, the table had been far enough away from the path that it was impossible to tell if she was wearing a ring.

He looked down at the pink flowers with bits of white sprinkled throughout. This was a bad idea. A fellow could come blasting out of the house and knock his teeth in. *That* was something to look forward to, wasn't it?

Gathering a breath, he decided to launch back into the wordless song and walk confidently to her gate and see if she was outside again.

Prior to reaching the pickets, he saw the woman clutching a stringy bundle. Her shoulders shook, but this time, she didn't make a sound, though she did occasionally swipe at her cheeks. She hadn't done that yesterday. She probably thought she'd been alone but now suspected he could be coming along. Alternatively, somebody could be home, there inside the cottage, and she didn't want them knowing she was upset.

Adrian gave a sharp whistle, one he usually reserved for working with his dad's dogs as they corralled sheep together.

She lifted her head and turned in his direction.

He waved with the flowers, for he held the paper sack with the other hand. "Nice afternoon, isn't it?"

"Sun's peeking out anyway." Was that a smile or grimace on her face? She didn't try to hide whatever her expression was. While she'd responded to his inquiry, she didn't come near so they could chat awhile.

He tried not to let that bother him. Perhaps there was someone inside after all. Well, he'd purchased the flowers for her, and there was no point in bringing them to Uncle Royston's. The man would think he'd gone soft in the head.

Instead, Adrian waved them again, then stepped forward and laid them gently atop the stone wall. Surely she'd pause her crafting and fetch them before too long.

Either that or Adrian would be receiving a visit from a very upset husband.

Moira couldn't smile, though the man likely wanted her to. This knitting thing Mrs. Cook suggested wasn't working. As much as Moira wanted to keep her hands and mind busy, learning this skill only frustrated her. Since it had nothing in common with her now-former career, she struggled to find passion for it. She moved the heap of yarn and needles from her lap to the table next to the tray of tea things and swiped at the moisture on her cheeks.

Determined to at least drink more today than she had the day before, she lifted the cup to her lips. She managed only three sips before deciding against finishing the remainder of the spoiled liquid. This habit, one she wanted to grow accustomed to, wasn't normal for her.

Normal wasn't attainable.

That thought wasn't helpful. She forced her gaze to roam over the land, searching for anything to capture her imagination. Butterflies fluttered over the green grass and around the blooms near the cottage. The red squirrels chasing each other in a territorial battle were entertaining enough, especially when they dashed up the tree at the bend and ran circles around the thick trunk, pausing to chatter at one another every now and then. Whispers of something teased the edges of her mind, giving her hope that God was trying to filter a seed of an idea into her soul, but it wasn't yet tangible enough to understand. In the meantime, she'd rely on Mrs. Cook's attempts to teach her another craft or two.

Since there wasn't anything to be done now, other than utter more prayers for guidance, Moira chose to indulge in a luxury that was certain to add strain to her nightmares. She shut her eyes and imagined gracing the London stage once more.

After only a few moments of wind whispering through the trees and birds chattering amongst themselves, she could feel Henrique's arms around her as they swayed back and forth. Soon, she pirouetted away from him with a swirl of her skirt, letting the orchestral tunes flow through her in silky movements that mesmerized the audience until they were rapt and eager for her return to her partner.

When she faced him again, he was gone.

Her brow creased and spirits tumbled when she found herself still sitting at her patio table with a cup of salty jasmine tea and purple broccoli florets before her. For a while, she listened to the sounds of nature, wishing a different form of beauty would come to mind. She ate a few bites, but they struggled past the lump in her throat. If her tea wasn't tear-filled, she'd take a gulp for some moisture. Even so, it wasn't a bad idea.

As she consumed a small drink, she peered at the wall that hemmed her in. What was that blob the man with the windswept brown hair and strong physique had left behind? Clearly, it had been a gift intended for her. He had no way of knowing she couldn't approach the wall to fetch whatever it was he'd left behind. Much as she wanted to, it simply wasn't possible.

The gesture was thoughtful; he deserved credit for that. Too bad she couldn't tell him. Was there a way she could? She didn't know where he lived, but her closest neighbor, surly Royston Davis, might. Once she procured the information, perhaps she could invite the young man to tea one of these days.

Then again, she didn't know him from anyone. What if he were a journalist out to pilfer her secrets to sell them for a steep price? She fiddled with the small fork she'd ignored until now. If he were truly a journalist, wouldn't he have helped himself to her property, waltzing right up to her with a notepad and a bevy of inquiries? He hadn't imposed himself upon her land, for which she was grateful, but the distance between them wasn't helpful for ascertaining his intentions.

Maybe she'd have Mrs. Cook move the table toward the wall. Not so far from the cottage to be obvious, but perhaps a few meters to Moira's right would work. Then it would be easier to invite him in. A small wave and kind word ought to do well. If he were willing to join her, they could entertain the idea of getting to know one another.

Unless he wasn't sticking around for long. It wouldn't do to make a friend only to be forced to say good-bye in a few weeks. She wouldn't know anything until she spoke with him, but it was a risk. The question was, was she willing to take that leap not knowing whether or not she'd land safely? One of her favorite things was perfectly executing the most complex connection of steps, twirls, leaps, and lifts with a soft landing that defied the odds and showcased her mastery over the discipline she'd delighted in her entire life. Those special combinations and the on-stage camaraderie she'd delicately cultivated with her dance partner were what had made them famous, what led to shocked gasps and resounding applause, which never grew old.

While performing, expectations were clear. Hours and hours of rehearsals made a surety of that. But this? Reaching out to ask a newcomer if he was settling here in County Surrey or leaving soon—and beyond that, if he wanted to become acquainted or was after her story—provided little assurance and even less confidence.

It had been a long time since she'd had friends outside of the ballet, and she wasn't sure how to begin. Assuming the best about the man would help, and she'd seek God's wisdom to aid her in discerning the truth. Moving the table closer, by a small degree, to the wall held merit. One thought gave her pause.

What type of man would purposely pursue her when her heart held regrets and sorrows she couldn't conquer?

Chapter Three

Another batch of meaningless errands occupied the morning. This time, his uncle wanted toffee. He probably wasn't supposed to have any, but who was Adrian to argue with orders from the man he was trying to win over? After ticking off the lengthy list of other tasks to accomplish in town today, he popped into the sweets shop and selected candies for Uncle Royston and himself. Afterward, he chose 400 grams of random chocolates and gumdrops to fill a small, white sack.

Surely the woman who lived at the cottage on the hill would enjoy the treats.

Outside the shop, he got stopped by a plump woman who couldn't have been over four foot eight. He set down the larger of his packages and shifted the others to one arm. Before he could bend down to give her a hug, she poked her cane against his calf.

"Why, if it isn't Royston's nephew. How is the old codger? Has he given you the boot yet?"

"Now, now, Mrs. Brown." Adrian couldn't help but grin, even as he abandoned the idea of embracing her. Clearly she wanted to chat first. "That's enough sass from you. How're your grandkids?"

"Getting into trouble every day, but that doesn't stop me from spoiling 'em, now does it?" She motioned to the shop behind him. "Did you get some of their buttercreams? You still like those, don't you?"

"Couldn't change my sweet tooth if I tried."

She held up a hand to the side of her mouth but stage whispered. "I get the chocolate-fudge centers for myself; the caramels stick in my dentures! You will stop by every once in a while, won't you—

like you used to do on summer afternoons? Things do get lonely without my Maury, you know." The twinkle in her eyes dimmed, confirming her claim.

"Your quiver is the fullest in town, what with your having thirteen children. Surely they've all had a passel of kiddies themselves. Have you been blessed with any great-grands?"

A trio of fingers popped up, and her smile became prouder than he'd ever before seen. "Three!"

"See? You don't need me." He winked.

She blushed and waved at him. "Go on with you, of course I do. You come on by the next time your uncle sends you to town. And don't let him get away with that too often! He's got to be handled with a rough hand, if you ask me. Say ..." She edged closer to let someone scoot by more easily. "Have you met the young lady who's taken up residence in that little cottage on the way to your uncle's place? Good Christian girl, that one, but she's hit a rough patch, I do believe."

"Has she?"

"You didn't hear that from me, now." She tugged at his sleeve, and when he stooped down, she kissed his cheek. "You behave yourself on the way home."

He straightened, but his forehead wrinkled. "Now, why would you say that, Mrs. Brown? I haven't gotten into trouble since I was ... oh, at least as far back as Tuesday."

Her cackle was music to his ears as he picked up the largest package and shifted them all to be better settled in his grip. She scooted past him and slipped into the shop, and he pointed himself in the direction of the farm.

When Adrian reached the low wall, he was disappointed to see the flowers, now wilted, remained. How had he missed that on the way to town? Had the young woman taken one look at them and scoffed at his meager offering? Or had she merely forgotten to fetch them after she finished her tea and crafting?

He looked up and saw that her table had been moved a bit closer. Now he could make out most of her expression. Tension tightened the look she half aimed his way. Since she hadn't begun crying, maybe there was a chance of staving off her tears for the afternoon.

With the flowers abandoned, would she favor the chocolates?

Perhaps she was a recluse. But why, then, would she scoot the table closer to the outside world? Wouldn't she keep it near the cottage, to make a quick escape if the world pressed too close?

Deciding to invite himself in, Adrian set down all but one sack of shopping and opened the gate. There weren't paving stones or a pebbled path, so striding across the lawn was his only recourse. Upon approaching the woman, who wore a light-colored frock with lavender flowers sprinkled across it, he bowed slightly at the waist, though he couldn't fathom why, and extended the sack of treats.

"Delicacies for the lovely lady on the hill." He took in her gentle beauty as he waited for her response. Though her face was delicately radiant, her sparkling blue eyes with depths to explore were what caught his attention most, and that had little to do with the shimmery shadows intended to emphasize that feature.

After giving a shy smile, she tugged open the sack he still held and peeked inside. Then her gaze sharpened and her mouth pinched. If he wasn't mistaken, the stiffening of her already perfect posture was meant to brush him off. "I don't eat sweets." She retracted her hand and returned it to her lap. "Ever."

A more crestfallen young man she'd never seen. Oh, he was polite and didn't run up the hill at her proclamation, but Moira could tell she'd wounded his pride at the very least. She had to fix that.

She motioned to the other seat. "Would you care for tea? I could have Mrs. Cook bring a fresh pot."

When he dropped onto the chair with a saucy glint to his eyes, Moira wondered for a moment if she'd just invited a member of the press to join her. One more look at the white sack, now sitting on the table, removed all doubt. Any journalist worth his byline would know she wouldn't accept sweets.

"Nix the tea. I haven't a lot of time."

Moira caught sight of stout-framed Mrs. Cook, tray in hand, retreating from the cottage's doorway. Cheeky woman probably heard church bells the second she'd taken in the man's deep voice. Moira shook her head.

The man leaned his elbows on the table. "Have you lived here long? I just moved up the road. Royston's my uncle."

"Is he? I thought he might know if you've moved out his way. Never imagined you'd be staying there on his farm."

"That's the place. He needs a bit of help just now." The wink he gave her could only be interpreted as conspiratorial. "Not that he'd let on, mind. A prideful one, he is."

This fellow's jovial spirit intrigued her. He'd brought her gifts two days in a row, and that was quite endearing, if unnecessary. "Thank you ..." The unfamiliar words nearly stuck in her throat. "For the sweets, I mean. I'm sorry I can't ..."

He glanced at the tray with veggies and scones. "Seems I was only half wrong."

"Mrs. Cook insists on trying to fatten me up, but I usually feed crumbs to the birds and squirrels."

"They must love you." He snatched up a scone and tapped the sack. "I know just the woman to give these to. She'd tan my hide if I let them go to waste, and besides, she's got more kiddies than she can count, though she knows the number and don't let her fool you."

"Ah. Mrs. Brown."

"You know her, then?" He tore off a chunk of scone to eat and another to toss toward a warbler that serenaded them from halfway to the wall.

"Who doesn't?" Moira reclined elegantly against the chair's support, taking care not to slump in the process. "She comes by, though not as often as she'd like, she tells me. Honestly, I know God probably sends her to visit for a reason, but sometimes I wish He wouldn't."

He tossed another crumb before speaking, almost as if he were weighing what he wanted to say and how she might take it. How could her reaction mean that much to him? "Must be a story there if you don't want to chat with our good Mrs. Brown."

She dipped her head and ran her thumb over a fingernail. Did she dare utter her thoughts? They pricked her heart, but saying them aloud would expose a piece of her inner pain. The man seemed sincere and of solid character, despite his use of the word *story*.

Finally, she whispered on the breeze. "She sees too deeply."

Again, he didn't answer right away.

The silence was comfortable, like he was giving her room to contemplate her feelings as he sorted out his own thoughts. It made little sense that she waited with bated breath for how this fellow with an uninhibited smile and an apparently caring personality would respond to her vulnerability. Her stomach tied itself in knots just as it had minutes before her first solo dance.

"What are you afraid she'll see?" He grabbed a second scone to shred, and she realized he was doing her a sweet favor.

Should she tell him what she wouldn't confide in Mrs. Brown? Unlike her, he didn't seem the type to spread every bit of gossip he gathered, so it was less of a risk—especially when Moira considered he wasn't going to be around very long. "I'm not sure which direction God's leading me now that I can't … Now that my life is different. Aren't little girls supposed to be able to pursue impossible dreams?"

He watched her with gentle eyes and nodded. "I'm no expert, but from what I can tell, God tends to know what's best for us—even when we can't see it."

The reminder was what she needed to hear, but it brought a spritz of tears to her eyes. *If I'm no longer a dancer, who do You want me to be?*

A soft ray of peace sifted into her soul, and she thought she sensed *I'm giving you a new title* being pressed into her heart. Moira soaked in her Savior's presence but wondered what He meant. She had no business opportunities, nor could she bear taking on a non-dancing role in the theater. Could there be something equal to or— dare she hope?—greater than her previous pursuit? Had she missed it for being intently focused on building her own legacy? Her pulse quickened at the prospect of venturing away from all familiarity, but the peace that surpassed understanding appeared to be nudging her into the unknown.

She tugged at the three-quarter sleeve of her dress and eyed the man across from her. Since he'd already skirted around the protective wall she usually kept firmly in place, what could one more audible thought hurt? "Could a new path mean the old one was wrong?"

"I don't think so, necessarily." The fellow dusted off his hands, then folded his arms on the table. "Change is inevitable, and it wouldn't surprise me one bit if the Lord saw fit to use that fact to set your feet toward a fresh way of bringing Him glory."

As she processed his response, he looked toward the lane. Then he jumped up with a start. "Say! I ought to get back and check on Uncle Royston." He scooped up the last of the scones and grinned before taking up the white sack. "Sure you won't change your mind? I've heard women like to eat chocolate when they've got deeper topics to think through."

A smile tickled her lips as she shook her head. "Not this woman."

He shrugged. "I hope it wasn't a bother that I invited myself to tea." Before she could answer, he sauntered across the lawn. She liked that he took care with her gate. It probably wasn't polite to watch him fetch his shopping and walk up the lane, but there was something about his demeanor and kindness that wouldn't let her look away.

Would he come back tomorrow?

After the way she'd nearly cried all over him, she wouldn't blame him if he didn't. Surely he didn't need an emotional woman cluttering up his afternoons. Nevertheless, she hoped he would return.

When she remembered what she'd said about Mrs. Brown, Moira covered her face with her hands. What if Royston's nephew thought she felt that way about him, too?

This time when tears cascaded, it was for an entirely different reason than mourning her lost career and broken body. Her heart sent up a prayer she had no words for. Oh, that she could tell Mr. Davis he wasn't a bother to her at all!

Chapter Four

Moira adjusted her skirt. She liked the way the powder-blue material with indigo swirls settled into an elegant drape. The red blouse she'd chosen today was a bold selection with its short, capped sleeves and tailored cut that fit her form. It was one she'd had made especially for her last tour, but she hadn't had much chance to wear it. Her hope for it now was that it would make Mr. Davis smile.

When Mrs. Cook brought out the tea things, Moira noticed there was an extra setting. When she inquired about it, the woman pinched her lips and beamed as if she held the world's grandest secret before ducking back inside, where she made more noise than necessary in the accomplishment of her mid-afternoon chores.

Moira lifted the teapot and poured liquid into the cup before her, then replaced the pot on the silver tray. The platter of garden vegetables and scones she left untouched. She'd wait for Mr. Davis to come. Surely he would. Unless he held grudges, but she dearly hoped and prayed he wasn't that sort of fellow. The way her heart tripped and pranced, she would have thought she was up for the biggest production of her life. Instead, she was merely realizing there might be more to life than crumbling into a breakdown every afternoon.

That was different. Last week, she didn't think she would get to that point anytime soon. However, there was now a bright spot to look forward to in her days. She hadn't had that since the accident. She didn't want to think about that, but she ought to attempt to process it, to work through what happened and how it still deeply affected her. Would that final performance always be her greatest regret?

She sighed. If not for her unusual lack of focus that once, she'd be dancing with Henrique today. He'd visited nearly daily at first, but shortly thereafter, he'd claimed to be too busy to come often. She could never begrudge him a continuation of the career they'd shared. She was well aware of how many dozens of hours per week were put into rehearsals and keeping one's skills sharp as well as the demands of a performance schedule. What he'd said was true even if his tone and expression had indicated that it was too difficult to see her this way, broken and unable to be the winged sprite she had been upon the stages of London and the world abroad.

Light on her feet was no longer the perfect analysis of her. Neither were *butterfly of the stage* or *angel in toile* or *legendary* or *prima ballerina*. All her titles had been stripped away with that one tumble. She retained the accolades she'd earned, the awards she'd been presented. None of those could be taken away. She was especially grateful that the Queen Elizabeth II Coronation Award for contributions to ballet and dance couldn't be stripped from her. It was her most prized possession, yet it guarded her mantle with no power to reinstate her as the *queen of the ballet*, as her worst critic had finally complimented her last year.

That comment in the leading newsprint in London meant the world to her. She suspected the pride that inched through her veins at those words from that particular critic had caused her accident the very evening after that review had been published.

How had she been so daft as to let high praise launch her into the stratosphere?

As moisture stung the corners of both eyes, she cast her gaze out at the lane beyond the wall. No one, not a shepherd or postman, was in sight. She grabbed a small piece of cucumber and popped it into her mouth.

The man wasn't coming, and she couldn't blame him. If she couldn't hold on to the hope God had given her yesterday, why should she be blessed with a second chance to build a relationship with a strong man who challenged her to more substantial heights than she could ever reach on her own?

Mending fences with Uncle Royston was all the entertainment Adrian could want. The man had an endless supply of stories, most of which were unlikely to have ever started in truth, and the laughter they shared bridged the gap the elder Davis had intentionally kept between them the first few days of Adrian's being on the farm.

The tail end of the current story petered off into a hacking cough that seemed to have no end.

Adrian paused in his work to come over and whack his uncle on the back a few times, hoping to help dislodge whatever was sticking in his chest.

Once Uncle Royston had calmed down, he looked at his nephew and winked. "This cough's going to be the death of me."

"I hope not." Adrian grinned as he returned to the other post, where he hammered in his end of a piece of wood that would serve as one crossbar spanning between posts. "Is this the last of the places where the woolies have been getting loose?"

"Nah. We got"—a cough overtook Uncle Royston again but didn't last nearly as long—"eight more to go. At least."

Adrian's shoulders sagged before he put his hands back to work. The woman would think he'd forgotten her. Worse, she'd worry she'd come across as being bothered by him. He'd left in a hurry yesterday, but only because he was sure Uncle Royston needed him on the farm. Adrian was still proving he was worth his weight in chores and assistance, and he couldn't shirk that duty for long stretches of time, or he might not have a place to put his head come nightfall.

Even if he did enjoy the meaningful discussion the woman and he had shared.

His attempts to bring her joy might have missed the mark so far, but at least they'd garnered him an introduction of sorts. Maybe he'd been wrong to step foot on her lawn without permission. She had plenty of opportunity to shoo him away, but she hadn't. That implied she was interested in engaging in another lively conversation, didn't it?

The woman's reticence in having Mrs. Brown visit made sense to him. The pint-sized woman had coaxed out plenty of tales about his hurts and wounds during his summers spent on Uncle Royston's farm. Back then, it had been that he was too little to help, he was in the way, his hands weren't big enough, back not strong enough … any number of excuses Uncle Royston had given him when all Adrian wanted to do was grow up to be a sheep farmer just like him.

He wondered what paths his neighbor felt God was nudging her away from and toward. What would it be like to be the one to mine the caverns of the young lady's heart? He appreciated the vulnerability she'd shown him during their chat. What would she say or do if he searched for its source and attempted to mend it as he was doing with the fence before him, finding and fixing the broken gaps? Would she let him or instead throw up a wall between them, similar in style but taller of stature than the one that barred most strangers from her property? Hopefully she'd be willing to hear his reasons for being unable to stop by today. Oh, how he hoped she wasn't upset by his not being there!

That was solid motivation to figure out a way to make it up to her. Not only for his absence today but also for his gaffe in bringing a gift she couldn't put to use. He'd honestly thought that all women loved chocolates and other treats. How was he to know she'd be the one lady in County Surrey who wouldn't touch the trifles? Now he did. That was one mistake he certainly wouldn't make again. If Adrian was anything, he was a man who learned from his errors and did better next time.

"You're not near as bad at this as I'd imagined."

He looked across at Uncle Royston, who'd already finished his part of the job despite the wild tales and hacking cough interrupting his work. "What do you mean 'near as bad'? What am I doing wrong?"

"Your head's in the clouds. Gotta be present and accounted for if you want to make sure nothing sneaks up behind you."

Adrian glanced over his shoulder, halfway expecting to see some crazy beast similar to those that peppered his uncle's stories.

Nothing but a spread of grass and wildflowers, with a forest well beyond, greeted him.

Uncle Royston chortled long and loud, smacking a hand upon his thigh. His laughter dissolved into another fit, but once that calmed to a wheeze, he tugged at his cap and eased into an untethered grin. "Gotcha that time, didn't I?" He moseyed forward and patted Adrian on the back as he passed. "When you're done dilly-dallying, grab my toolbox and come on. We've got miles of fence to check yet."

Relief swept through Adrian as he tapped in the final nail and then gathered up the ancient wooden tray filled with tools and wire and an extra pair of gloves. He followed behind his uncle, not worrying about catching up. If he dawdled a bit, he could think all he wanted until he arrived at the next spot they would mend.

It was unlikely, at his uncle's pace, that they'd get "miles" accomplished before sunset. Adrian prayed quickly that they'd miraculously manage to finish up this project today. Much as he wanted to work on the farm, his heart was starting to hum a different tune. He wanted now to find a way to cheer up the tears-in-the-tea girl. Maybe someday she'd share her name with him. Of course, he hadn't offered his either, though if she knew Royston's surname, she could surmise Adrian's own. The woman and he had slipped right into an intriguing discussion, and names hadn't seemed important then.

He wasn't overly successful in lifting her spirits yesterday if the twinkle he'd detected just before he left had been a mist of tears, but that didn't mean he couldn't be tomorrow. There was something about the challenge of it that called to him in a way not much other than the dream of a farm had in years. If it weren't for Uncle Royston's insistence that he felt fine enough to tackle the fence mending today, Adrian would drop everything and race down the hill a stretch and find a way to get himself invited back to tea.

Besides having a piece of land and a flock of woolies all his own, enjoying an afternoon picnic with her was the only place on earth his heart seemed to want to be.

He caught up to Uncle Royston and set the kit at his feet, then hurried back to fetch more boards from the truck parked nearby in the field. After lowering them to the ground, he snatched up a plank, handed one end of it to his uncle, and walked the other to the far post.

This chore was going to take forever, but now Adrian was more determined to finish the task today. He had a different job to do starting on the morrow. Another prayer winged upward in hopes that the woman would have an open mind for his next attempt to bring her a full-blown smile.

Chapter Five

Shortly after Moira was situated at the table out of doors, with the tea things spread out before her, the gray clouds opened up. Seconds later, the tea in her cup and the upswept hairstyle she'd labored over for a half hour were completely ruined. Still, she waited and watched.

The man didn't come.

"Are you sure you want to be sitting out in the rain, Miss Wood?"

Moira looked over her shoulder at the large woman with frazzled, brown curls, who peeked out from the doorway of the cottage. "Go on with you. A bit of rain never killed anyone."

"That's debatable." But Mrs. Cook ducked back inside and shut the door.

Moira eyed the tea but then ignored it. That wasn't the point today. Would her neighbor come by? It was unlikely when it was raining kitties and pups, but one never knew. She'd wait for hours if she had to, just to catch a glimpse of him so she could apologize.

The way she'd implied his company was unwelcome was inexcusable. A little self-analysis didn't reveal a pretty picture. Not only had she let pride puff her up in the twilight of her career, but she'd let her frustration with the doctors and their ridiculous diagnoses bleed into her outlook until she was nothing but a pessimistic grump.

Today, that would change.

She put on a smile and eagerly awaited the opportunity to make her regrets known to the man. He deserved the apology, and she'd make good on it.

If only he'd show up.

The rain created a mesmerizing dance of splashes on the tea tray and the wrought iron. It speckled her outfit until the material darkened and she gained a chill that didn't seem to want to leave. That was likely bad, but she wasn't about to admit to Mrs. Cook that she'd erred in coming out here. If her neighbor showed up, it wouldn't be a mistake; it would be a chance to invite him into the quiet world she'd reluctantly carved out for herself here on the gentle hills of rural England.

She understood why he hadn't come yesterday. She fingered the teacup's handle as she felt a pinch brush through her chest. Her rejection of his gift hadn't been kind, never mind the fact she wouldn't use it. She could have given the treats to Mrs. Cook to take home to her children. It was a wonder Mr. Davis stayed to chat as long as he had afterward. Had it been awkward for him? It had been hard to tell, but she wouldn't be surprised.

How she wished she could take it back!

She peered up and down the lane, yearning for the man to appear from either direction. The compassion he'd shown in his thoughtful responses had sparked a thread of hope in her that hadn't been there in months, one she'd like to explore and see where it might lead.

Surely God was up to something if He had reawakened these feelings of anticipation and a longing to fully live. They didn't completely shove aside her yearning for getting back to her career, but they nudged it a slight distance away from the center of her heart. That gap filled with peace and comfort and the promise she didn't yet understand, and Moira couldn't help but wonder what God was choreographing. Was He carving out space so she wouldn't wallow in her inability any longer? Her grief likely wasn't finished, but perhaps this was a beginning of sorts.

Could that be true? Could there be more to life than ballet?

More rain slid down her face, and her breath caught. Was it possible that her time on the stage was truly over now? Would she come to a place in her mind and heart where she actually accepted that?

What would that acceptance look like?

This was the first time her contemplation of embracing her lot in life had gone deep enough to potentially stick. It rankled, but there was a lining of desire settling in about the edges. She wasn't quite sure what to do with that, but she bowed her head and prayed that

God would show her how to adjust to this different and hard restriction that had abruptly been placed upon her.

Through her career, she'd wanted His best plan for her, though she'd likely not listened to Him well enough to know which engagements she should have turned down. Now she had the same choice: seek His direction or rely on her own.

It took only a breath to decide. *Lord, please direct my steps, metaphorical as they are at this point. Help me know what You intend for me with this infusion of anticipation. What is life now supposed to look like for me? And what is the fulfillment of Your promise going to be? You've got me curious, You know.* She looked up, blinking rapidly to avoid getting raindrops in her eyes. Radiance swept over her face, and her heart stepped into a gossamer dance she hardly recognized but was glad to get to know.

Maybe things would be all right after all.

She barely felt the lightest of pinches at that thought. That was a surprise indeed.

Much as Uncle Royston tried to dissuade him, going so far as to predict he'd catch his death for a gallivant, Adrian couldn't let the woman believe she'd been forgotten. She faced enough, he was sure, on the daily that he daren't permit her to think he'd been offended by her reaction to the sweets. He'd had work to do yesterday. Would have again today if not for the rain.

He had nothing to bring along, as those fences took all his time and he couldn't even carve a simple flower or sheep to leave on the wall for her. Or to take to her. It still wasn't clear whether or not she was agoraphobic, though his presence hadn't seemed to irk her.

So he approached the top of the hill from the direction of his uncle's farm rather than from town. Would she be crying? The one thing he could offer that might help was laughter. He'd been told he was humorous at times, but that would certainly be put to the test this early afternoon.

He slowed his steps as he crested the hill, bending over the closed umbrella he used as a walking cane. His uncle's old, raggedy coat nearly swallowed Adrian's broad shoulders and thick torso, and its ratty tails slung rainwater with every stumbled step. A jaunty tune came out on a whistle as he approached, and he was delighted to see her perk up and twist a bit to see him coming.

Continuing at the slow pace took him longer to get down the lane and to her gate, but he was happy that she didn't look away. Her hair was plastered to her head, and she wrapped a soaked cardigan more firmly around herself. Had she been waiting on him despite the elements? The way she gave him her undivided attention made him think she'd been out here just for him.

When he finally arrived, he pretended to stumble over a rock and teetered forward until it looked like he would tumble to the ground. At the last second, he got his feet going in an old-man scurry-step that made use of his momentum to glide himself against the gate. He patted the soft-green-painted wooden pickets a bit as if he were trying to catch his balance and breath, then reached up and grasped the scuffed and broken top hat on his head. When he lifted it high in a salute to her, water sluiced down and splashed against his face.

She covered her mouth, and he prayed that wasn't a frown she hid. Hopefully she recognized him. He purposely hadn't changed his face with grease paint or anything similar—he was no music hall performer, after all. The whistling to alert her to his presence had also been intentional; it was the same tune he'd had on his lips when he'd first passed by her cottage.

After settling the hat atop his head, he hooked the curved handle of the umbrella over a forearm and fished out a rather large, white kerchief. He shook it out dramatically and used it to mop the water from his face. More rain replaced it swiftly, but he simply tucked the material back into his pocket and took the "cane" back in hand.

He waved and then pointed forward, asking permission to enter.

From afar, she lowered her hand to her lap and nodded.

After a moment and a smile, he grabbed the gate and pulled dramatically. It didn't budge. After leaning the umbrella against the wall to his left, he took the gate in both hands and gave it a shake.

It remained closed.

He looked at her and shrugged with upturned palms.

She motioned that he should push it, but he mimed that he didn't understand.

Instead of following her clear instructions, he picked up a different tune to whistle, something lively with a bit of an Irish flair. He snatched up his umbrella and twirled it around as he hop-stepped forward a little. He tapped the "cane" against the wall a few times, then turned and dragged it against the stones as he pretend-stumbled down the hill past the gate. The *chink-chink-chink* accented the heavy patter of the lightning-free rain.

When it looked like he would topple over from the higher rate of speed, he planted the pointy end of the "cane" onto the lane, coming to an abrupt stop that sent his free arm wheeling. He righted himself and shook out his coat, then brushed a few spots as if he were cleaning it.

A small bit of laughter reached his ears, and he grinned to himself. If she was on the upside of emotion, he'd take that as a big win. It would be the accomplishment he'd imagined when he gathered this get-up and set out to entertain her.

He eyed the pointy end of the umbrella and brought his hand up to his cheek and exaggeratedly gasped, mouth wide and eyes huge. Then he shook the umbrella, which didn't remove the pretend mud, so he opened the prop, revealing that only one panel of material was attached. The rest was only a metal frame.

When she didn't react, he brought the canopy down to aim it at her and gave it a bit of a spin. Surely now she could see that there was nothing blocking her view of him, or very little anyway.

Her laughter skipped across the rain-drenched lawn.

He gave the umbrella a shake, then a hearty whirl. Finally, he nodded and leaned the thing against his shoulder to "protect" his head from the rain. He stopped and removed his top hat and swept it down in a wide arc as he bowed in the most gallant way he could manage while remaining in character.

Her applause peppered the moist air.

He beamed, feeling his heart lift in grand accomplishment, as he righted himself, set the hat on his head once more, and gave it a pat to knock it more firmly in place. Afterward, he saluted her with a lift of the umbrella and headed home, making sure to keep up the old-man steps until he was hidden by the hill.

Would it always be so easy to make her laugh? He truly hoped his act had bridged any gap she might feel her rejection of the sweets had created. The last thing he wanted was for her to feel bad about that and think he was holding a grudge over it because he hadn't shown up yesterday. While he regretted that she'd felt obliged to sit out in the rain for him, he was glad in a way. The atmosphere had been perfect for his show, and it had aided him in tickling her fancy.

Laughter, in his opinion, was much better than tears that spoiled a good cup of tea.

Chapter Six

No matter how miserable Moira now was, laid up in bed with covers tugged over her lap, she couldn't regret sitting out in the rain. Right when she had been about to call Mrs. Cook out to help her back inside with the tea things, she'd heard that whistled tune from a few days earlier. Her heart had danced allégro, so she felt it had been worth biding her time in such a muck. Then the way Mr. Davis had entertained her with a wild, unencumbered spirit had melted her remaining regrets about her career.

The performing arts had always set her free, and she was glad to see that there was still something about them that captured her heart, even if she was no longer able to take part in the production.

Now, she wasn't exactly ready to attend the ballet, but it might be a possibility one day. This was the first time she'd thought of that in a positive light since the accident. She grasped her handkerchief close to her chest and sighed, absorbing the realization that perhaps she was beginning to heal. Not physically, mind, as that was apparently not an option, but emotionally. This truly was profound for her, and she whispered praises that God had brought her this far in a short span.

Ever since she'd caught sound and sight of the young man, God had easily used him to help Moira take new strides in her journey. It was awfully kind of Him—of Mr. Davis, too—to readily forgive her when she'd shown less than gratitude. *Thank You, Father. Your ways surely are mysterious and perfect, and Your mercy generous.*

A sneeze blasted out, but she managed to get the handkerchief in place in the nick of time. She mopped her nose, then folded the material over. It would certainly be put to good use again shortly.

The cold that pressed against her sinuses because of the damp a few days ago wasn't much fun, but that was the least of her worries.

It was nearing teatime, if the whistling kettle in the other room was any hint, and she was certain the young man would miss her today. Would that he would understand! There was little hope of that. How could he know unless he was told, and that was unlikely without her sitting out there, able to speak up for herself. She could send Mrs. Cook out to tell him or to at least leave a note on the wall for him, but those options seemed impersonal. Besides, she wanted to tell the man herself what had happened.

Perhaps he would knock on the door.

Or he could presume she was away from her cozy cottage.

As she coughed past a little scratchiness, she leaned up off the fluffy pillows between her back and the headboard. Once the fit was over, she reclined again and inhaled deeply. The change in her breathing from ragged to smooth reminded her of how her dream was shifting. It was a wonder how God could use a thing as small as a young man's kindness to spark a large chassé, or transitional step, in her life.

She wasn't sure where the nudge was leading, and the unknown future the Lord spread before her was intimidating. Somehow, she experienced an eager uplifting of her spirits.

Mrs. Cook brought in a tray of tea things, gathered up several soiled handkerchiefs to launder, and subsequently left without any response to her prattle, since Moira's voice hadn't fully recovered from her minor illness.

When Moira's mind wandered to the many stages worldwide upon which she'd danced her heart out, the prick of longing and the sting of regret weren't as deep or long as they used to be. That came as quite a surprise, for she thought this specific grief would be her mantle for the remainder of her life. That the cloak of melancholy was evaporating and her old dream was fading into the background of memory were unwarranted gifts. She hoped and prayed whatever came next would be even more gratifying. Presently, a sense of peace and contentment settled into the essence of who she was.

That had to be from God, for she knew no other source.

Nevertheless, she wished she could explain her absence to Mr. Davis, who was surely out looking for her now. A sneeze interrupted her, and she dabbed at her nose with the soft cloth, then took a sip of tea. Hopefully he would return on a day when she could be outdoors again, for she longed to learn more about him—and to let him get to know her as well.

On the way back to the farm, Adrian felt weird carrying a single flower, one that had dozens of butter-hued blooms at the end of the stalk, but he had to try again with the woman and see if the bouquet he'd left before had been ignored because of the proximity to the outside world. Surely she liked flowers! Every female relative he'd helped in the past had enjoyed a good cluster of petals. This particular woman was quite the mystery to him, but maybe he'd chosen too bold of colors last time. She often wore pastels. Perhaps the gentle breath of sunshine would be just the thing to make her smile.

Hopefully she'd understand his having to finish patching fences before he could make another visit.

Upon reaching her part of the hill, he looked about but saw no one. The table sat without the teacups, pot, and tray he normally saw. The chairs were unoccupied. The flowers looked brighter and the grass a little greener from the recent rain, but his chest felt heavier. He scratched his head and looked at the sky. Not a cloud to be seen. Why wouldn't she be out on a fine day? He waited there for well over several minutes. Then he sat on the low wall for a while.

She never came out.

Should he leave the flower on the wall? She hadn't come to get the last bunch from that location. The truffles hadn't been appreciated, but the show he'd performed had been well received. She'd even laughed. During none of his visits had she sent him away with a demand he never return.

Why the absence now?

He kicked a pebble. It bounced up the lane. His thoughts felt just as rocky as the hillside across the path. It wasn't like this woman had a legal hold on him. Yet, there was something about her that drew him in and made him want to be a better man. More than that, she made him want to put down roots here in County Surrey.

He wasn't planning on being here long, just until Uncle Royston got that cough taken care of and could manage things alone. After that, Adrian didn't have a direction. He prayed about it often enough, many times a day in fact, but the answer always came the same way: a relative needing help on their property. Some had farms, others a home in a small town, but they all needed him at just the time when he had no idea of his next step. Would he never have a place to call his own? For so long, he'd aimed to raise sheep and create a place where he could bring home a wife and raise a quiver of children. Would that forever be nothing but a wisp of wind floating through his mind, perpetually beyond his grasp?

He twirled the flower and considered his options again. He was definitely leaving it for her. The question was *where*? Atop the wall was out, as that hadn't worked before. He stood up and looked at the mint-green picket gate. That was out, too, as the proximity to the outside world was the same as the stone wall. Should he knock on the door? Surely she wasn't home if she wasn't outside for teatime. That seemed to be her routine. He could leave it on a windowsill, but she might not see it there.

He carefully pushed open the gate and headed toward the furniture. He couldn't leave it where he wouldn't be certain she'd discover it. What would be the point? She used the patio table nearly every day, so that was likely the ideal spot. He placed the light-yellow flower on the table directly in front of the chair on which she always sat. The wind wiggled the clusters of miniature blossoms. What if his offering blew away?

In only a few moments, he selected a chunky stone from around the flower bed and placed it on the stem so the wind couldn't get away with his gift. Hopefully the blooms would stay put. It wouldn't do for the woman to show up to an empty stalk because of something he couldn't help.

He'd have to leave that part to God.

With a glance at the house, he prayed that nothing was wrong, that the woman was simply putting away the weekly shopping. Then he tapped the table with a couple of fingers, walked back down to the gate, and gently closed it behind himself before heading the rest of the way up the hill. He needed to get back to the farm to check on Uncle Royston and let him know that the order of wire would be in late next week. There were also the sheep to look after and more projects to complete. The life of a farmer was one he enjoyed, but he sure wanted to know if the young woman was all right or not.

Father, why wasn't she outside today? Adrian tried to whistle, but his heart wasn't in it. The landscape he normally savored didn't hold the same appeal. As he approached the lane leading to his uncle's farm, he berated himself aloud. "What have you done, Adrian? Fallen in love with the woman after barely settling into village life again?" He shook his head, closed the distance, and ducked inside his uncle's house.

Chapter Seven

The weight of the trunk pressed on Adrian's shoulder as he walked down the hill. Why his uncle needed it repaired today when he was too sick to go anywhere made little sense, but it gave Adrian a great excuse to check in on the tears-in-the-tea girl. He only hoped she wouldn't think he was leaving town. It was easily explained, if she were home to listen.

He came over the peak of the hill that brought him into view of her cottage. Everything looked quiet from this angle. Although he wasn't sure if she'd be there today, he couldn't stop hope from zinging into his chest. It was like God was adding an angle to the goal, but Adrian wasn't sure how the two fit together. He didn't have a place to settle and call his own. How could he think of romance when he had no roots, no home to give her?

Father, what do You want for me? A farm with lots of sheep, a couple of horses, and room for a family? Or the girl who cries into her tea every afternoon? You know I've proven I can bring her joy. But what dream is the one You designed specifically for me?

His steps hitched. He hadn't thought of it like that before. The Bible told him that God had good plans for him, but Adrian hadn't considered that he'd have to choose between two really great things, that only one might be right for him. One pursuit didn't seem better than the other, except the fact that he'd be less lonesome with the right woman by his side. In that way, pursuing a deeper relationship with the lady of the cottage was definitely superior to raising sheep.

Laying down the idea of owning a sheep farm wouldn't be easy. It was the one thing he'd always wanted since he was a little boy romping around the pastures with his papa's puppies and sheep. In the summers, it was Uncle Royston's woolies. Now that Adrian was grown, every time he helped a relative on their property, hope settled deeper into his bones. He didn't know who he was if he couldn't keep this objective. Who would he be if he didn't end up with a farm of critters?

You'll still be My son.

That whisper had him stopping right in the middle of the lane. Could it be that his purpose wasn't defined by where or with whom he lived his life but to Whom he belonged? That made the decision tougher, because it meant that either path was acceptable. His gut wrenched at the thought of having to choose between the two. Maybe if he got to know the woman better, the choice would be made clearer, if not easier.

He walked on, trying to keep himself from staring at her cottage until the table and chairs came into view. That moment arrived soon enough, and when it did, his pulse lurched.

The tea things were spread on the table, but one of the chairs was tipped on its side. The lady sprawled on the ground, skirt, sweater, and hair mussed and spread about her, with a shattered teacup not far from her outstretched hand. He didn't sense any movement, and there was no telling how long she'd been in that state, especially since none of her neighbors—including him—were within shouting distance.

Immediately and without a second thought, he dropped the trunk with a clatter and launched himself over the wall. There was no time to fool with the gate latch. He sprinted across the lawn and then knelt next to her. Lightly, he touched her side, and she flinched, her eyes fluttering open.

"Oh, thank the Lord you came! I've been praying I don't know how long for assistance to arrive." She pushed up slowly onto an elbow. "I'm glad you've come to my rescue."

"What happened? Are you injured?"

Moisture welled in her eyes as he helped her sit up the rest of the way. There was something odd about her legs, which didn't move.

He softened his tone from *panicked* to *concerned*. "Does anything hurt ... Miss ...?"

"Moira." She let go of his shoulders, which she'd used to steady herself, and placed one hand on the ground. She lifted and straightened her legs, then fiddled with her skirt.

"That's a pretty name. Mine's Adrian, Adrian Davis." He didn't dare move. She was like a skittish lamb, and he didn't want to startle her any more than he already had. At least now he wouldn't have to keep thinking of her as *tears-in-the-tea girl*. As endearing as he considered it, she might think it unflattering.

"Will you help me up?" She looked up at him without lifting her face. "My carer had to fetch one of her children from school. She apparently came down with a bug of some kind—I certainly hope Mrs. Cook didn't carry my cold home to the little ones. She wanted to take me back in before she left, but I insisted I'd be fine out here. She was in such a fluster, she forgot to bring out my chair, not that it does much good on the terrain."

His brow crinkled as he eyed the tumbled piece of furniture.

After a sneeze she covered with her lifted arm, she motioned toward the broken teacup. "My mind wandered, and that cup slipped right out of my hand. I leaned over to catch it and lost my balance instead."

Adrian took her hand and bent her arm at the elbow to get a look at the skin near it. "Have you an aid kit? You're bleeding here. Scraped the skin pretty good, looks like."

She nodded but hadn't looked away by the time he glanced back at her face. "You'll have to carry me."

He tipped his head to the side.

Before he could ask the question, she answered. "I'm paralyzed from the waist down."

"Oh." That made things make more sense. Why she hadn't pivoted on the chair to get a better look at him that first day, when he wasn't quite in her front-view range of vision. Why her legs didn't move when she sat up. Why she hadn't gotten up after falling. The reason she'd need a different chair.

The fragility of her inquiry, though due to sheer necessity, was beautiful.

She smiled timidly. "If you'd rather not, I understand. But it isn't catching, you know."

He smirked. "That wasn't what I was thinking." Once he angled his arms to lift her, he hesitated. "May I?"

After giving a graceful nod, she wrapped an arm around his shoulders.

He scooped her up, then slowly rose, careful to keep his balance. It wouldn't be kind to toss her back to the grass. He stepped around the fallen chair and settled her on the remaining upright one.

She offered her thanks, and he nodded but quickly righted the other seat and picked up the largest pieces of the shattered cup. He'd ask for a broom and dust bin to take care of the rest after he saw to the blood on her arm.

She reached cupped hands so he could place the pieces of porcelain against her palms. Then she set the mess next to the teapot on the tray.

"It won't take me a minute to get that scratch cleaned up."

She motioned toward the chair he stood behind. "The flower was lovely. Thank you."

"Good, you got it. I wasn't sure where to leave it." After sitting, he wondered if he should fetch his uncle's trunk. It likely needed a bigger repair now that Adrian had dropped the thing, but he'd cover the cost out of his own pocket rather than expect his uncle to pay for his carelessness. He was keen on avoiding the almost-certain lecture, but there might be a good laugh in whatever story came out of today.

Not that Adrian considered the woman—Moira—simply a story.

But he did want to find out what the rest of hers was.

He cleared his throat and shifted on the chair—something he realized belatedly that she was unable to do. That thought made him go still as a fence post. "Do you mind my asking how you came to be paralyzed?"

In an instant, she looked down at her hands, which she moved from the table to her lap.

Maybe he shouldn't have asked. If the paralysis was a recent development in her life, that could explain why she was emotional each afternoon, but it also might be difficult for her to talk about.

She looked into the gaze he held steady. If there was one thing he did well, it was wait out skittish critters until they were comfortable with his presence. He was more than happy to sit here the rest of the day if that's what it took. The trunk and his uncle and the sheep could wait.

Chapter Eight

His gaze reached too deep. Moira wished she could squirm to satisfy the urge to do so. The question Adrian posed was the main reason why she secluded herself here at the cottage. To face her public and their inquiries was overwhelming, particularly when she had no answers to give even herself. No satisfactory ones anyway.

Yet, this man had proven trustworthy and compassionate. If Mrs. Brown hadn't caught wind of what Moira had divulged to him before, it wasn't likely he was given to having loose lips.

Kissable ones perhaps.

"Would you like some tea?" Blushing, she reached for the teapot, but as soon as she felt how cool it was, she knew the liquid inside would never do. "You'll have to help yourself to my kitchen, unless you'd be kind enough to carry me inside."

For several moments, he seemed to take her measure.

She tried to hold his gaze and managed to succeed, feeling bolstered by the easy comfort he exuded in that calm expression.

"A cup of tea would be lovely." He rose and stepped toward her.

With gentle, steady movements, he lifted her back into his arms. She braced herself with one arm around his shoulders again and felt rather secure against his chest. When they approached the cottage door, he paused long enough for her to turn the knob and nudge the door inward.

He must have given it a heartier push with his foot, because it swung farther and smacked the wall.

"Oh, sorry." He gave her a bashful smile. "Sometimes I don't know my own strength."

"Feels just right to me."

A diffusion of pink filtered up his neck. "Which way's the kitchen?"

She guided him through the sitting room and into the cozy kitchen with a bank of windows to let in natural light. During this time of day, no other forms of light were needed.

"Where would you like to sit?"

"Grab that stool"—she pointed to the tallest chair with a sturdy, straight back, which was tucked next to the icebox—"and set it between the sink and stove."

When he hesitated next to the stool, she realized he didn't have a hand free. "Hold your grip."

"Excuse me?"

She moved her arm from his shoulders, twisted her torso, and began to lean over the slightest bit. Then she paused as his grasp tightened a little. Upon feeling stable again, she reached out and lifted the stool. Together, they got it in place, and he set her on it so that she sat parallel to the counter.

Adjusting her legs by hand, she set her feet, encased in flat shoes that mimicked the look of soft-pink ballet slippers, on the higher of the two rungs of the stool. Afterward, she arranged her skirt to drape prettily over her knees and swish against her calves.

Not that she could feel it, but at least she could look charming for her guest.

"Do you need me to fetch anything for you?" He motioned toward the cabinets to his right.

"Everything's within reach." Once she had the kettle filled and heating on the stove, she fetched a tin of tea from a shelf and two mugs from the row of hooks attached below.

Adrian eased against another section of the L-shaped counter. "You've got a great place here. It's comfortable."

"Thanks. It suits me." She grabbed a spoon from the canister next to where the teakettle had been. "The unusual arrangement took some getting used to, but my carer showed me how to group things in ways that help me retain a façade of independence."

"Should I fetch your wheelchair?" He looked around. "Why don't you use it outside?"

"It's a rigged-up kitchen chair. None of the standard ones would fit through the narrow doorways of this ancient cottage, and I haven't the heart to change her bones."

He seemed to take in his surroundings with deeper appreciation.

Did he regret hearing her situation? She hoped he wouldn't be discomfited by it. "I didn't mean to deceive you." When he looked back at her, she reached toward him, wanting to reassure him with a light touch to his hand, but pulled back before he could react.

"You don't think your being paralyzed changes my opinion of you, do you?" He leaned toward her, invading her space with an earthy scent and a tender smile. "You're still beautiful, Moira."

Her heart fluttered, but she didn't know what to say to that. Thankfully, the kettle whistled. She busied herself with preparing the tea, but she couldn't get his words out of her head. *Lord, did my accident really not change me as significantly as I supposed?* She'd never walk or dance again, but maybe that wasn't the only thing people would see when they looked at her. Deep down, she'd believed the stacks of newsprints Henrique had brought her as she recovered in the hospital after that fateful performance. The articles surmised that her star had fallen, that she'd become irrelevant overnight.

But this man in her cottage thought her beautiful.

And you're still My daughter.

That sweet whisper from God slipped directly into her soul, and she felt like a whole and cherished woman again.

"This is who I am now." She absently handed a cup of tea to Adrian, took up the other one, then focused on him. "And I'm all right with that."

He grinned. "I'm glad."

Telling the truth hidden in her heart didn't feel like a big risk but rather a simple choice since he'd come to mean something to her. She didn't even need a bracing breath to calm her nerves as if for a grand pas de deux before the Queen, because Moira *wanted* him to know what happened to her.

She looked directly at him. "Once upon a time, I was a ballerina."

His eyes went a little wide, and he slow-nodded. "I should have known you were in the performing arts."

The heat surging into her cheeks wouldn't be stopped if she tried, so she ignored it and kept entrusting him with her story. "My last performance was exquisite. Every step, every arch of my back, each pirouette … my partner, all the other dancers … From the opening of the curtain through the intermission and after, everything went off without so much as a hiccup."

The following bit was the bane of her afternoons, if not all other hours of the day. But now she faced it as she'd done throughout her career: with the gumption of the prima ballerina she longed to become, the hard work and dedication that got her there, and the grace that made her outshine the competition.

She set the cup of tea on the counter and slid it slowly away from her until it rested beside a jar holding the yellow flower he left for her.

He smiled, clearly noting the care she'd taken with his gift.

"In the middle of the ballet's coda—that's the finale—my partner ..." She paused to contemplate how she wanted to explain the next part.

Adrian set his cup down but kept his hand around the ceramic. "What happened during the coda?"

Moira glanced down. When she met his gaze again, the only things she sensed there were encouragement and compassion. He didn't even know the details of what happened. Moisture stung her eyes at how incredible this man was, but she pressed on.

"We had a daring lift near the end. Henrique lifted me high above his head and transitioned me to a single hand, held firm on my hip. One of my hands braced on his shoulder, while the other one extended up, as if I were reaching for the stars." Her heart pounded with remembrance. "The thing that made this move extraordinary was how close we were to the edge of the stage. It never failed to garner gasps as we toured the world. This particular show was at our home theater in London, and the crowd was enthralled when he lifted me."

Adrian stepped closer but relaxed against the counter again, this time barely on the other side of the sink.

"He was supposed to take eight steps forward, along the edge of the stage. From the vantage point of the seats, it looked as if we were on the verge of falling, but his footing was sure and steady the whole time, precisely planted a few inches in from the very precipice."

"Did he lose his balance?"

Moira shook her head, and the feelings of that frightful moment vaulted back. "I did." A tear raced down her cheek. "One minute we were gliding along, but I must have lost count of his steps, because before he was ready, I shifted my weight for the exit into a one-armed embrace, during which he would slowly spin so that my extended leg swept over the orchestra before he placed me back on the stage. A mistake like that hadn't happened to me during any of our previous performances and only in the first few practices long before the first show ..."

Her breath hitched, and she bit her lower lip to retain her composure. Something about his gaze, intense and tender at the same time, silently asked her to continue sharing her memories.

"The next thing I knew, he reached for me but found no purchase. My momentum sent me beyond the edge of the stage, and I crashed into one of the music stands in the orchestra pit before landing with a hard thump amongst dress shoes and chair legs. The concussion had me a little dazed, but I needed to get up and finish the dance. When I tried ..." She clasped her hands together and tucked her chin against her chest. "I couldn't ..." Slowly, she raised her gaze to meet his. "My legs didn't do anything, and I couldn't feel them."

"Wow ... Moira ..." He reached out and nearly touched her elbow, but at the last second, he merely rested his hand on the edge of the sink. "I cannot fathom how devastating that must have been for you—for both of you."

"My partner—Henrique ... He leaped down into the pit, immediately knelt next to me, and asked questions I don't remember as he cradled me close. He probably shouldn't have moved me, but the doctors later told us that it hadn't made any difference." She went silent, having reached the end of the story.

Is it?

The whisper twisted her nerves. Every day she still breathed was another opportunity to add to the tale of her life's journey. Instead of remembering that, she let herself wallow in pity at all she'd lost. That was no way to live. It wasn't how she'd been raised, nor was it how the Bible instructed her to behave.

Tears surged forward, but she blinked hard, then closed her eyes for a few seconds to hold them back. She'd wasted enough emotion on what she couldn't change. From this moment forth, she'd live with courage and determination, for she knew God would desire nothing less.

Boldly, she looked back at Adrian. "Henrique visited regularly at the beginning, but he hasn't returned often since. It must be too hard for him to see me in this condition."

He opened his mouth, but Moira rushed the rest of the words out.

"I don't blame him; how could I? And I won't hold it against you either, if you feel the same." She gave him a playful grin. "Though I will be highly disappointed."

If Adrian decided to walk out of her cottage and, therefore, her life, the ache would reach great depths, as it had with her dance partner's distance. Such separation was survivable, especially since her Lord was shoring up her confidence once more. With Him beside her, she would learn to overcome the difficult feelings that tried to press her down. She'd pursue opportunities to add a sense of beauty to the world around her, for there must remain ways in which she could be creative and artsy and bring joy to the hearts of the people in at least her own community.

Without moving his hand from the sink, Adrian eased toward her, making her own heart trip an allégro. His gaze never wavered, while one side of his mouth lifted, etching endearing lines into his cheek. "I'd like to stay, if that's all right with you."

Chapter Nine

The rose-petal blush coloring her cheeks and the grin that accompanied it sent joy straight into Adrian's chest. If he could make her smile like that more often, his life might just be complete. It wasn't a farm of his own, but it was significantly better.

Moira lifted her arm in a smooth, graceful way and reached out. In the space it took for him to breathe, her hand lightly touched the back of his. The moment felt monumental.

Fresh tears welled against the lower rims of her eyes, but they didn't fall, nor did they seem melancholic. "Thank you. For staying, I mean. It's good to know I'm still worthy of having a friend."

His heart plummeted. Did she really think the entire world was so superficial? He turned his hand over and held hers with a firm but gentle grip. After only a second, he rubbed his thumb over her smooth skin.

He could offer any number of platitudes. *You're always worth it. If Jesus wouldn't leave you, why would I? A true friend would never abandon you.* But they all sounded inadequate. Furthermore, he didn't want to accidentally besmirch her dance partner's intentions without knowing what they were. She clearly held him in high regard, and it wouldn't be smart of Adrian to imply that he would stay even if this Henrique fellow refused.

What he could extend to her was reciprocity.

"If you've got enough time before your carer—Mrs. Cook, was it?—returns, I'd like to do a little sharing of my own."

Moira broke their physical connection and picked up her cup. "I'm sure she'll see to her ill child before returning, since she knows

I usually enjoy a leisurely teatime." She sipped the tea that had to be tepid by now. "Will you be at your uncle's long?"

"Until he doesn't need me." He slipped his hand into his pocket. "You see, I'm the family fix-it. Ever since I was a mid-teen, I would spend summers with relatives who needed help around the house or farm. Though I had skills suited to indoor work, I much preferred the farms. Something about being outside and working with the animals called to my soul."

Moira set down the mug and rested her hands palms up, cradled one against the other, on her skirt-covered lap. Keeping her back straight while seeming at her ease was probably a habit ingrained from years of repetition in her balletic career. Still, he appreciated the elegance about the way she held herself. "Do you have a preference of animal, or have they all been the same species?"

"I've worked with everything from goats and sheep to horses and mules, but my favorites are the woolies." They were veering off topic, so he took a breath and redirected. "Since I was a lad and visited Uncle Royston on holiday, I wanted to have a farm just like his when I grew up. Over the years, that dream carved into a detailed goal. I've sketched out plans for the house and barns and fields, and I know exactly which sorts of animals I want to raise." He sighed, though it carried less weight than it would have a season ago. "Yet God has never provided the opportunity for me to begin building such a haven."

"No?"

He shook his head.

"I'm sorry." Without seeming to think about it, she lightly touched her thigh. "I know what it's like to have dreams torn away from one's grasp. It's hard for me to imagine what it would be like to hope and wish and never obtain the goal in the first place. 'Devastating' comes to mind. Just the thought makes my heart ache for you." The slight tilt of her lips further expressed her sorrow on his behalf.

He embraced her empathy. That was something he could get used to. Everything he learned about her made him think she was the one woman on earth God meant for him to meet for a reason he hardly dared to contemplate, let alone say aloud. Perhaps he should. If there was one thing this exquisite woman had already taught him, it was that every day mattered and the next was in no way promised.

If he came on too strong, he risked frightening her away. That would be completely unacceptable. She already added much to his days. Hope and anticipation coupled with daily challenges to make her smile and, if possible, laugh had become his central aim of late. If he didn't have that, he'd feel empty again. Furthermore, this felt *right*. It was as if God had imprinted her onto his heart, and separation was to be found no longer.

"When you know, you know." The whisper was more to himself than to her.

She tilted her head slightly, and her eyebrows quirked, which only made her features more endearing. "What?"

Reaching out, he faced her and took a step closer, then another until he stood directly before her.

With no hesitation he could detect, she placed her hands against his and craned her neck a little so she could look up at him. Her eyes sparkled, but plenty of questions circled their depths.

"For years, I've wondered what God was waiting for." Adrian cleared his throat. This wouldn't be easy, as speaking these words was symbolic of snuffing out the desires of his past. "Why wouldn't He let me have my dream? Everyone around me seemed to be living theirs. It didn't seem fair. Now I see that I had the wrong vision in mind the whole time."

"Really?"

He gave her hands a light squeeze. "I didn't understand that any goal I might have could be made valueless if a better one came along. The *right* one. I thought I was stuck in a weird cycle of wasting my skills on other people's property when I could have had my own—not that I truly saw the work for my many relatives as a complete waste, but ..."

"I know what you mean. You want to carve out space for yourself."

"Yes!"

She swept an arm out to the side. "What do you think this place is? I wanted a haven away from the city, a small, intimate corner of the world where I could hide away and recuperate for a few days after an especially hard series of shows. Little did I know at the time of purchasing this cottage that I'd need it for a very different reason."

"Hiding away from the world in shame?"

Quietly, she nodded. "Something to that effect, though I realize now it was unnecessary for what was only an accident."

He cupped her cheek. "I'm glad you're letting it go."

"I'm unsure what my new dream might look like ..." She took his hand from her face and pressed a light kiss to its palm. "But I'm beginning to get an idea ... because of you."

Her words couldn't have struck the mark any closer. *Could this be real, God?* Could Adrian really have found the woman he was meant to spend the rest of his life with? A brief prayer for wisdom revealed a layer of peace that hadn't accompanied him before.

"You are"—he gently brushed the back of a finger along the curve of her jaw—"without a doubt, the most intriguing woman I will ever know. When I first walked by your place and witnessed you crying into your tea, I wondered why. In the span of a breath, a deeper compassion than I've ever felt was awakened. This urge in my chest made me seek ways to turn those tears into giggles."

A small laugh spilled from her mouth. "Why, you *are* Mr. Fix-It, aren't you?"

He clapped a hand over his chest. "Since then, God has given me the most authentic desire I've ever had, the only one I'm meant to pursue now. It has nothing to do with having my own farm or a flock of woolies and everything to do with making my tears-in-the-tea girl experience unfettered joy. Moira ..." He cocooned her hand between his palms. "Your laughter is magical, and I want—if God allows, of course—to be the cause of that magic for a lifetime."

He shook his head in amazement. "I don't know why I never saw this before." There was way more to life than building up a farm. If God wasn't in that hope, why on earth had Adrian held on to it for so many years of his life? "He had romance in mind for me this entire time." Taking a half step back, he plopped a hand atop his head, mind whirling. Had Moira and he missed years together because of his ignorance or stubbornness? Or was this the perfect time? Had she not been weeping into her afternoon sustenance, which wouldn't have happened without the accident during that final performance of her career, Adrian might never have run across her or been intrigued by what he saw. Although, he liked to think that anything about her would have sparked up his interest; everything about her certainly did now.

She leaned forward, not enough to be unbalanced or risk falling, and curled her hand around the side of his neck, then gently tugged him close. Those large eyes watched him with rapt attention. "What are you trying to say?"

"What if we could, the two of us together, create a life that's worth chasing—with working legs and flocks of sheep or otherwise?" Adrian lowered himself to one knee, gladly looking up at her for the first time. "I've known you less than a full spring, but when the heart speaks—when *God* speaks to one's heart, that is—a man knows what he should do—and does it."

Her gasp preceded by seconds the words he never thought he'd have the chance to say.

"Moira, will you marry me?"

Chapter Ten

The rest of the season flew by in a whirl of courtship and laughter that made up for the surprise Moira had experienced upon hearing his proposal. She'd given him an enchanted *yes*, because she felt God whispering to her heart that *Adrian's wife* was indeed the title He had in mind for her. She had never felt more at home—not even on the stages she'd felt so alive upon over the years—as when Adrian and she had shared their deepest hurts and highest hopes in her small kitchen that afternoon.

Over the past couple months, they'd spent time with his uncle and the sheep and visited Mrs. Brown weekly. They enjoyed her grandchildren's antics during the picnics Moira helped prepare. Adrian had gotten to know her carer as well, and Mrs. Cook now happily set out a pair of cups every teatime.

Adrian built her a new wheelchair with a slim profile and sturdy wheels that would get her around in and out of her hillside cottage. That was his most thoughtful gift but one she didn't want to use on this momentous day in the last week of spring.

It was finally time for Moira to launch into the next act of her life. In the little anteroom near the foyer, Mrs. Cook put the final touches on Moira's hair, which was pinned so that a few curled bits accented the cluster of small yellow flowers secured in place a couple inches above and behind her left ear. The remaining waves cascaded down past her shoulders. The cream-white dress she wore was created by her favored costume designer, who had been delighted to receive the request for a toile-and-satin ensemble, complete with pale-yellow pointe shoes that mimicked the color of the sash tied around her still-trim waist and the brighter hue of the flowers in her hair. Since she would hold no bouquet, as she would be carried down the aisle, she wanted an entire array of blooms that represented springtime in Surrey arranged around the altar at which she would exchange vows with the man God had used to reestablish her joy.

She did her own makeup, just as she had thousands of times before. This was, by far, her most exhilarating performance, only this time it was as real as could be. She kept the powders and creams as subtle as she could, but she made certain the effect was flawless, leaving her skin looking like glazed porcelain. The final thing she did was highlight her eyes with mascara and eyeliner as well as three different, complementary shades of shimmery eyeshadow—light gray, pale yellow, and gold. She couldn't help but be dramatic with this, but using the right touch completed the look of elegance she was going for.

When she was perfectly satisfied and had washed her hands free from any makeup that had dusted her skin, she tossed aside the cloth that she'd used to keep her dress fleck-free and smiled at Mrs. Cook. "I'm ready."

"Oh, that you are, my dear girl. I think I might cry! You just see if I don't." The older woman dabbed at the corners of her eyes with a handkerchief before tucking it back into her sleeve and coming forward. "Are you sure about this? I'm happy to walk you down the aisle, but isn't there anyone else you want to do it?"

For several seconds, Moira's grin faded. There was one regret she hadn't dealt with in the last few weeks, but that couldn't be helped now. If God had plans for a resolution there, He would lead her to it. In the meantime, she'd simply move forward with Adrian and see where their Heavenly Father led them next.

She lifted one arm, naturally extending the reach all the way through her fingertips in a graceful pose. "Carry me to my groom, Mrs. Cook."

"Yes, Miss Wood." The carer came forward and scooped her charge into her arms.

Upon reaching the doorway to the foyer, Moira widened her eyes at the sight before her. Only a few paces into the cozy room lit by an overhead light fixture as well as daylight streaming through the wide-open doors, Moira held up her hand and mumbled for the woman to stop.

Thankfully, Mrs. Cook obeyed, because Moira couldn't believe who stood before them. The tall, athletic man with blond hair combed smoothly into place wore a tailored white suit coat over a pale-yellow vest and white shirt. His trousers were light blue, and the color was present in his ballet slippers. Of course he would wear those, rather than dress shoes, to her wedding. The highlight of his appearance was the delightful sparkle in his eyes.

Surely the costumer had been busy these last few weeks if she'd not only designed Adrian's suit and accouterments and Moira's wedding dress and pointe shoes but had additionally fitted her partner for this extravagant occasion. Moira sent up silent thanksgiving to God, for He was the Master Choreographer of her life and all its surprises—whether she perceived them as bad or good.

"Henrique!" Though she was overjoyed to see him, the word came out a mere whisper. "You came!"

From behind his back, he brought his hands, one of which held an invitation she had posted with a hopeful prayer. She'd never received a reply.

"You didn't think I'd miss this red-letter day, did you?" He motioned to a couple of chairs that were set against the wall nearby. "May we sit a minute?"

At her nod, he brought the chairs over. Mrs. Cook positioned Moira on the closer of the two and helped arrange her skirt, then excused herself, mumbling about forgetting something in the anteroom.

As soon as Henrique perched on the chair facing her, she reached out and grasped his hands, the invitation fluttering to the floor.

"I'm thrilled to see you."

"I'm sorry I wasn't there for you after the accident."

Their words tumbled over one another, and they laughed lightly in tandem, as they'd done so many things on stage over the years prior.

He let loose an anguish-filled sigh, and his eyes filled with unshed tears. "I should have been there for you, Moira. I didn't know what you needed, how I should behave, to come or not come visit ..." While their hands remained connected, he shrugged, moving her arms as well as his. "I don't know who I am as a dancer without you either. I've tried partnering with a few other ladies, and the chemistry isn't the same."

She reached up and pressed her palm against his cheek.

He leaned into her touch. "If only I could go back and catch you or lift you more firmly, to better balance myself beneath you." The pain of regret in his gaze begged her to understand how deeply he ached at having played any part in her life-altering injury. "Would that I could change places with you that day."

"You would have *me* lift *you*?"

His smirk was duller than normal.

Leaning forward, she hoped her smile fully expressed the oceans of gratitude she felt toward this man. She clutched close to her bosom one of his hands with both of hers. "Henrique, no ... You mustn't blame yourself, for it was I. *I* moved too soon out of the lift. I miscounted your steps. They were behind me, as I faced the direction of your wake, but I had never done such a thing before, not since that first week of rehearsals and never on stage. My shifting—I've replayed it innumerable times in my mind, and it was unrecoverable—for both of us. Neither of us could have halted what instantly became inevitable."

She pressed her lips to his knuckles, knowing full well she'd leave behind a stain of burgundy rose. She didn't think Adrian would mind, for this very instant was what he would wish for her.

Henrique blinked away a sheen and held her gaze when she lifted her head once more. "Still ... I should have been there as you transitioned to this new style of life."

"You are welcome into my life at any time, Henrique. Surely you know this."

He squeezed her hand and gave her one of his dimple-inducing grins that had pleased many an audience.

"Promise me one thing, though."

"What's that?"

She gathered his other hand and gently pressed both. "You mustn't give up your career; you must keep trying until you find another partner."

"She won't be you."

"But she can still be great. Believe me, I know how much better you made me look than when I danced alone. You'll do the same for her, whoever she is." She relaxed against the chair's backrest, letting her hands glide gracefully onto her lap. "And I'll be the first one in line for tickets."

He tapped her knee as a broad grin spread across his face. "With your presence to anticipate, how could I not promise to carry on?" Then his smile waned, though his eyes didn't lose their dance. "If you'll allow me …"

Her heart pitter-pattered in the style of the tiny steps she used between consecutive leaps when dancing upon a stage. Whatever he had in mind, whatever he said next, she sensed by his expression alone that his own heart hung on the precipice of whether or not she said yes to his request. Barring a reversal of her role as bride to Adrian Davis, she couldn't imagine denying the man before her anything. He'd done so much throughout their journey together to ensure she had a spectacular career. Everything she became upon the stages of the world she owed in great part to him. She'd repay that debt in any way possible.

He slipped off the chair onto one knee and held one of her hands. "I know I wasn't there for you after the accident, not as I should have been, but if you'll be gracious enough to permit me, it would be my great honor to be there for you now. May I carry you down the aisle and give you away to the man who was there when I could not be?"

Her spirits soared, and she hugged him. She must have lunged forward quicker than she'd meant to, because, though she couldn't feel it, her derrière slid right off the chair and onto his knee, jostling her slightly.

His arms came around and steadied her, just as they often had before.

After she lingered in his embrace, she pulled back to peer into his eyes. "I can't imagine a more exquisite moment than being carried by you once again on the way to exchange vows with the man who will carry me from now on."

Henrique scooped her up easily and rose to his full height. Then he whirled around in a controlled, fluid motion that made her skirt swirl and her heart swell. It felt like the two of them were back on stage for a grand reprise. She hardly noticed when Mrs. Cook tucked the chairs back against the wall, fetched the forgotten invitation, and scurried forward to open the door leading into the sanctuary, for being held by Henrique once again was more than Moira could have dreamed of, especially on this of all days.

The guests rose and watched Henrique and Moira's progress down the aisle. Numerous relatives of Adrian's, most of whom he'd helped in some fashion or other through the years, were clustered around his parents, who she'd met a few weeks ago. Many of the other faces smiling back at her belonged to friends and competitors from the ballet companies of which she'd been a part throughout the years. The companionable love shining out from every pair of eyes was more than she could take. Joy filled her own with a mist she blinked away so as not to mess up her makeup prior to saying her vows and taking commemorative photographs.

Her now-clear gaze landed on Adrian's as he stood at the end of the aisle, waiting in his forest-green suit and pale-yellow bow tie and loafers that matched her sash. His hair was just as unruly as ever, but he'd at least tried to tame it with a gel that glistened but did very little to calm his locks. It was a good thing she adored that windswept look. The broadness of his grin hinted at something, but she merely soaked in the beauty of this moment.

For only a millisecond, she looked up at the ceiling, but her vision saw well beyond. *Thank You, Father, for this sweet reunion, this upcoming union, and the path You've set before us. Keep guiding us, because only You know just what steps the ballet of life will require from here on out.*

Henrique must have taken the relaxing of her neck as a sign, or perhaps he had this planned all the while. He shifted his hand to the middle of her lower back, and she immediately tightened her abdomen while taking a deep breath. When he hefted her up above his head with a straight arm, she arched her back, dipping her head in the same direction, as her arms came up and around in graceful arcs until they formed one of her favorite lift poses with one hand reaching beyond her head while the other stretched out to the side. She had no idea how her legs fared, but if she knew Henrique, he'd likely planned for a couple of the ballerinas in attendance to slip from their aisle seats and maneuver her legs and feet into the proper positions, with one straight and the other bent with the pointe shoe tucked behind the locked knee. In the edge of her vision, she saw her partner's other arm sweep out into a pose that granted him additional balance while looking elegant.

The remainder of the congregation—what felt like an audience to her—gave the grandest ovation of her life, one she cherished more than any other for what Henrique was giving to her—to the two of them—with this daring move: one final performance that would end with the most magnificent of codas.

After several strides down the aisle, he carefully lowered her into a basket lift. When Moira draped her arm around his shoulders once more, she nodded to the two ballerinas who had helped her legs do their job for the consecutive lifts. They smiled sweetly and glided back to their seats.

Just as Henrique and Moira reached the base of the aisle, Mrs. Brown from the left and Uncle Royston from the right brought forth tall, straight-backed chairs and settled them into place before the minister. Then they returned to their spots while wearing the broadest, most impish grins she'd ever seen on either one's face.

Henrique walked around one chair, and Adrian moved around the other until they stood facing one another in front of the stools. Her groom spread his arms into position to receive her, and Henrique carefully transitioned her from his grasp into Adrian's. Moira did her part and swept her right arm around the latter's shoulders while removing her left from the former's.

Before letting her go completely, Henrique whispered across her while looking directly into Adrian's eyes. "You're her dance partner now. Don't drop her like I did."

Adrian nodded. "I won't. That's a promise." His gaze shifted to her and held steady.

Moira couldn't help but laugh. They'd orchestrated this spectacular moment just for her. It was the most poetic, exquisite thing they could have done for her, and she treasured every second.

Her groom settled her on the tall chair on the left and arranged her skirt to its best appearance before sitting on the stool to her right and taking her hand in his and lacing their fingers together.

As the minister began the official ceremony, Moira looked at Adrian with all the love bursting forth from her heart. "You asked him to come, didn't you? When he didn't R.S.V.P.?"

His smile turned mischievous. "That's just my first wedding present to you, my love." He kissed her cheek and then her knuckles. Afterward, he turned his attention to the minister.

For a short while, she watched Adrian through glazed eyes. She squeezed his hand and sent up praises to the God Who granted her such a considerate, compassionate man. God truly had taken her broken pieces and reshaped them into something beautiful.

Her gratitude spilled over in the form of tears.

In a blink, Adrian pulled an empty teacup from a secret place beneath his stool and held it in the air beneath her chin. "We'll save these tears for your next cup of tea, my sweet tears-in-the-tea girl."

She giggled and leaned against his arm. Oh, how she was going to love being made to laugh for a lifetime by this man. "I have a wedding gift for you too, Adrian."

"What's that?"

"How would you like to add sheep to the fields behind our cottage on the hill?"

His head whipped around so that they were nose to nose. "Are you serious?"

Her nod was quick. "I can't be the only one having her dreams fulfilled today. Besides, you've waited long enough already."

Despite the minister's droning on, Adrian kissed Moira square on the mouth. A round of laughter and a few piercing whistles spread behind them, and the minister cleared his throat.

Moira and Adrian sheepishly turned their attention back to him.

"I haven't arrived at that part yet, you know."

Adrian moved to tuck the cup back beneath his seat, but Moira grabbed it and set it on her lap. It felt right to hold close the item that had first brought them into one another's world as they said the vows that bound them together until Jesus eventually called them home.

A Note from
Andrea Renee Cox

This story is my favorite romance (so far) that God has given me to write, and I thank Him for entrusting me with it. Furthermore, I thank You for helping me find the right words to make it beautiful. May it be the story readers need in their lives when they read it, dear Lord. You are the Master Orchestrator, and I thank You for bringing the following people into my life.

Daddy and Mother, thank you for teaching me about kindness and compassion throughout my childhood and teen years. I pray that I have learned these lessons well so that God's light may shine brightly through my every interaction with the people who step into my daily life. Thank you for the excitement you have about my stories. That helps me on days I doubt my skills.

Kristy, thank you for playing Barbies with me all those years. That precious time was where God planted the seeds of storytelling in my soul and watered them until they finally blossomed into this whole novel-writing gig. You, my dear sister, played a huge role in His work, and I thank you.

Kellyn Roth, thank you for sharing your Wild Blue Wonder Press dream with me and inviting me to submit a story to your company's debut collection. Who knew through our years-long friendship that we'd finally get to be published together? Thank you for your notes that made a world of difference for the romance in this novella, your encouragement through this publishing process, and even more, for your enduring friendship.

Cate V. and Claire Halter, thank you both for beta reading this story. Your comments challenged and encouraged me in the early stages of revisions, and I'm grateful.

The friends and fellow book lovers who have encouraged me over the years, thank you for that! Whether you were someone I met in person or online, years ago or more recently, I cherish your enthusiasm for my stories. Hopefully this little tale makes you smile. That's truly the least I can do in return for all your support.

Readers, thank you for choosing to read *Springtime in Surrey*. I hope this collection brings you many hours of enjoyment. If you'd like to read a few of my complimentary short stories, please explore my website and blog at andreareneecox.com.

If I Knew You Were Coming

Coming

a novella by Bailey Gaines

Dedication

To Rena Henderson and Wanda Gaines.

Chapter One

Guildford, County Surrey, England
May 1941

Joan Masterson opened a kirby grip with her teeth and heard the tiny telltale *click* that meant it had twisted. She pressed her lips together and let go of the last section of hair that dangled down her neck. After pushing the tines of the grip back into place, she rolled up the section of hair again and pinned it.

Success.

The last curl joined all the others on her head in routine rows.

She exhaled and reached for one of her scarves, selecting the brightest one with the most flowers. Sophie loved flowers.

Joan peered into the mirror at the far corner of the room, where Sophie lay in her little bed. Still sleeping. No moonlight could get in through the blackout curtains, so her daughter's sleeping form was just a shadowy bump in the light from the candle. She looked at herself in the mirror again as she tucked the point of the scarf under the two ends and tied a knot. Pulling her housecoat around her, she got up and padded over to the bed to throw back the covers.

The jangling of the phone shattered the stillness.

"Heavens!" She propelled herself out of the room and down the darkened stairs to the parlor. None of the children needed to be awakened by such a loud, harsh noise at this time of night. Snatching the receiver off the hook, she yanked her scarf off one ear and held up the receiver.

"Hello?"

"Joan!"

Joan dropped the receiver, which swung on its cord and clattered against the wall. Heart pounding, she grabbed the receiver and held it to her ear again. "L-Leo? Leo?"

"It's me, love." Her husband's endearingly-reedy voice floated over the line.

Joan sank onto the chair beside the phone. "Gracious ..." Tears took away her words, and she covered her eyes with her free hand.

Too many months had passed since she'd heard that voice. Too many months she'd spent imagining it in the censored letters that had gotten through to her. Her imagination had gotten mangled, with gaps in her mind blacking out the memory of his voice.

"Joan, I need you to listen, all right?" Leo's voice wavered slightly. "You listening, love?"

"Yes—yes, Leo, I'm listening." She pressed the receiver so hard that her ear flattened against her head.

Leo's exhale crackled. "I'm at Haslemere, Joan."

"Haslemere!" she echoed, incredulity making her head spin.

"I—I wanted to be home for Sophie's birthday."

She choked back a laugh and leaned back on her chair. "Yes, it's tomorrow. Oh, Leo! She'll be so excited when I tell her. And I know you'll love Oliver and Lottie." Her voice rose, and she moved her hand over her mouth to hush herself. "When will you be arriving?"

"There's the rub, love. They're not sending trains to Guildford at the moment. I was going to ask you and Sophie to come get me if I couldn't get to you in time, but I forgot about Oliver and Lottie. I can't ask you to spend that much." Disappointment sank his voice into a lower register.

Joan's brow furrowed. Still dizzy, she replayed Leo's words. "No trains to Guildford?" How did the army expect their soldiers to spend time with their families on their already too-short leaves if they couldn't get back home?

"Not from Haslemere, at least."

"But ..." She scrunched the fabric of her housecoat up in her fist. "There's got to be some way to get you here for tomorrow. I'll think of something. I promise I will."

"Well, don't think too hard. I don't want to keep you awake." An amused note crept into Leo's voice, although disappointment still oozed over the line.

"I should get to bed. I've got to be up early. Get the children ready for school, and Sophie goes to stay with Mrs. Rowland. And then out to Chilworth."

"Chilworth?"

"The Land Army assigned me there to help out a farmer. Didn't I tell you?"

Now Leo chuckled. "I'm sure you tried. I seem to remember a gap in that letter when you told me about the Land Army."

"Oh. Well, I suppose that's sensible." Now disappointment twisted her own stomach. What other things had Leo missed? Did he even know how much she was contributing to the war effort?

"I—" Leo broke off as a jumble of unintelligible words drifted through the receiver. "Half a minute!" he protested, his words muffled. "Joan, I've got to go." His voice was closer now, clearer. "I'll try to find a way to get home in time."

Joan gripped the phone cord tightly. "I'll think of something. Please don't worry, Leo."

"I'm not worried. I'll see you soon, one way or another."

Something in his voice drew her brows back together. How could he be so sure he'd even make it back home before his leave was up?

Well, it was good one of them was confident he'd get back.

She sighed. "I love you, Leo. Take care of yourself until I get to see you."

"Love you, too, Joan."

Click.

Joan rolled out of bed and pulled open the blackout curtains. She blinked to adjust to the gentle light after the complete darkness and pressed her nose against the windowpane. If her bedroom faced east like Oliver and Lottie's did, the first rays of the rising sun would have stabbed her eyes.

But here in her west-facing window, an oak tree soaring outside blocked most of her view of the sky. The tiny bits of space visible through the leaves were tinted a grayish mauve.

Too early to tell what the weather would be like.

Joan grabbed her Bible from her bedside table and sat cross-legged on the bed, then flipped the Bible open to the green ribbon she'd stuck in as a bookmark. Isaiah. So many prophecies. Sometimes it was hard to understand them all.

She ran her finger along the page, searching for the chapter break where she'd stopped the day before. There. Chapter 58.

The first part of the chapter focused on fasts. Fasts that the Lord would not pay attention to and those He would. The ones He would were always more pleasant to read about, even if carrying out the Scriptures would not have been easy.

Joan leaned forward and tilted her Bible in her hands to make better use of the natural light from the window.

> *Is not this the fast that I have chosen? to loose the bands of wickedness, to undo the heavy burdens, and to let the oppressed go free, and that ye break every yoke? Is it not to deal thy bread to the hungry, and that thou bring the poor that are cast out to thy house? when thou seest the naked, that thou cover him; and that thou hide not thyself from thine own flesh?*
>
> *Then shall thy light break forth as the morning, and thine health shall spring forth speedily: and thy righteousness shall go before thee; the glory of the LORD shall be thy reward.*
>
> *Then shalt thou call, and the LORD shall answer; thou shalt cry, and he shall say, Here I am. If thou take away from the midst of thee the yoke, the putting forth of the finger, and speaking vanity;*
>
> *And if thou draw out thy soul to the hungry, and satisfy the afflicted soul; then shall thy light rise in obscurity, and thy darkness be as the noon day:*

Joan paused and closed her eyes, letting the words wash over her. *Then shall thy light break forth as the morning.*

Her cheeks warmed. Such a beautiful promise, and a beautiful picture of the Lord's favor.

Lord, help me to choose the fast that You would choose today. Grant me an extra measure of wisdom as I try to see Leo today.

"Mummy?" Sophie's sleepy voice slid into Joan's thoughts.

Her brief time of solitude was over.

Joan closed her Bible and pushed it back over to her bedside table. She rubbed her hands over her eyes and got up to check on Sophie, who was sitting up, rubbing her own eyes.

"Good morning, Sophie." Joan bent down to kiss Sophie's forehead. "Are you hungry? Come help me wake up Oliver and Lottie and then we'll all go down for breakfast."

"Hurry, Sophie. Just because it's your birthday tomorrow doesn't mean you can dawdle." Lottie tapped the side of Sophie's bowl of porridge, pursing her lips primly.

Joan smiled at Lottie's bossy-mother voice. Children really were imitators. Six-year-old Lottie, the baby in her family, had somehow perfected a mother persona. Maybe by watching her own mother back in London, or maybe by watching the multitude of women Lottie would have seen during the evacuation from London.

Joan bent down to lace up her boots, her arms brushing along the ridges of her corduroy breeches.

Sophie banged her chubby hands on the tray of her high chair. "Birthday!"

Lottie held up Sophie's spoon with a blob of porridge on it. "Porridge. Then birthday tomorrow. Open up."

Sophie opened her mouth and stuck out her tiny red tongue. "Ehhh ..."

"There!" Lottie deposited the porridge into Sophie's mouth and sat back down at the worn wooden table, smiling in triumph as Sophie smacked her lips.

Joan opened the cupboard door and pulled a loaf of bread out of the bread bin.

"You're one to talk, Lottie." Oliver scraped his spoon around his bowl. It clinked against the edges over and over again. "You've not finished yours either."

"But I'm going to. And I'm going to do it quietly."

Joan glanced back at the smug tone in Lottie's voice. The little girl had her nose in the air as she daintily cleaned out her bowl.

Oliver rolled his eyes at his sister and, holding his spoon between two fingers, let the utensil swing from side to side, grinning at Lottie as the clinking became louder clanking.

"Stop it! It's loud!" Lottie's smugness crumpled, and she looked every bit the upset six-year-old she was, her lips and eyebrows puckered.

Joan turned fully around and lowered one eyebrow to give Oliver the universal motherly look that she knew by now he understood.

"Sorry, Mrs. Masterson." He dropped the spoon into his bowl with another loud clank. "Sorry!"

Joan let her face relax. "It's all right. Just bring your bowl to the sink."

Oliver slid off his chair and set the bowl gingerly in the sink, then put his arms behind his back. "Thank you for breakfast, Mrs. Masterson."

"She told us to call her Joan!" Lottie gestured with her spoon like a teacher pointing out an important fact on a chalkboard.

Joan glanced at Oliver's stubborn, sticking-out lip.

Poor boy.

He was so stiff and formal, even after almost a year with her. She spread jam on her bread and shook her head. "It's all right. You can both call me whatever you'd like. Lottie, if you've finished, go get your schoolbooks."

Lottie clambered off her chair, plopped her bowl in the sink on top of Oliver's, and ran upstairs. Her shoes thudded on each step and even through the upstairs hallway, allowing Joan to track her progress to the bedroom.

After a little tidying up of the kitchen, Joan herded the children outside and pulled the door closed behind her. As they headed along the cobbled walkway, Lottie and Oliver flanked her on either side, and Sophie perched on her hip.

Just as she stepped onto the road, a sparrow darted past her into the yard and settled in the hazel tree in the corner.

"Bird!" Sophie pointed, almost tipping herself out of Joan's arms.

Joan laughed and tightened her grip on Sophie. "Yes, it's a bird. It's a sparrow." She glanced up at the spring sky. A few wispy, white clouds floated overhead, but it was clear otherwise.

That'll mean we can get the potatoes planted today.

"I like sparrows." Lottie hopped over a crack in the asphalt. One of her Mary Janes scuffed on the road, leaving a dark scrape on the light-brown leather. "They're like fairies but birds."

Joan ducked her nose down into Sophie's hair to keep from chiding Lottie about her shoes. Those had to last her. But humor also bubbled up in her. How were fairies like birds, besides the fact that they flew?

Oliver scoffed. "That's just all birds."

"Birds are nice." Sophie bounced a little, surveying the hedges that lined the road like a grand general.

God bless whichever general gave Leo leave. A smile broke out on her face, and she kissed Sophie's forehead to keep from blurting the news. It should be a surprise to all the children.

Her smile faded. It was better if she didn't tell them. What if Leo couldn't make it home in time? What if he got shipped out before he could get on a train to Guildford?

"Joan?" Lottie tugged at her hand.

Joan looked down at the girl. "What is it?"

"You've a frown. We're not supposed to frown." Lottie's lips, although not frowning, were close to it.

Joan puffed out her cheeks, exhaled the air forcefully, and raised her eyebrows to shift her expression into a more pleasant one. "Right you are. Stiff upper lip. Show me yours."

Lottie sucked her cheeks in to make her top lip flip upwards.

Joan felt a smile forming. "Good girl."

Oliver peeked around her to gape at Lottie. "That's not what that means!"

"That's what it means to me." Lottie's hair bounced as she tossed her head. She held her chin high and adjusted her pink cardigan over her flowered school dress.

Oliver scoffed again and kicked at a rock. It skittered across the road, struck a fencepost, and bounced halfway back.

Joan switched Sophie to her other hip and nudged Oliver. "Show us your stiff upper lip, hm?"

"Oh … all right." Oliver scowled, then straightened up as if someone had whacked his spine. The scowl lines disappeared from his face except for a dent between his eyebrows, and his mouth flattened into a sober, almost grim line.

"You look scary." Lottie's eyes had widened, and she dropped back behind Joan.

Joan gave her hand a reassuring squeeze and turned back to Oliver. "Well, that certainly is a stiff upper lip. But Lottie's right. If we dropped your picture behind German lines, they'd retreat straight away." She grinned down at the boy.

Oliver rolled his eyes, but as he followed the flight of a bird across the road, the ghost of a smile smoothed out the last little wrinkle between his brows.

When they arrived at Mrs. Rowland's house, Joan stopped and let go of Lottie's hand. "Say good-bye to Lottie, Sophie!"

Sophie waved a chubby hand at Lottie. "Bye!"

Lottie stood on her toes to kiss Sophie's cheek. "Good-bye, Sophie. See you after school! Then it'll only be one sleep until your birthday!"

"Birthday!" Sophie echoed, clapping her hands.

Joan laughed, kissed Sophie's forehead again, and smoothed Lottie's curls before nudging her back onto the road. "Don't be late for school."

Lottie scurried after Oliver, who had shoved his hands back in his pockets and started ambling down the road.

"Good-bye, Oliver!" Joan cupped a hand around her mouth and stood at the gate of the nursery yard.

Oliver didn't turn around. The little tufty bits of hair that he could never get to lay down stuck up at the back of his head.

"Bye, Oliver!" Sophie's echoed good-bye was softer.

Joan adjusted Sophie on her hip one last time and pushed open the gate. After catching up on a condensed version of the latest gossip from Mrs. Rowland and kissing Sophie good-bye, Joan hurried back to the house to grab her bicycle.

Not having the children to talk to on the way back left her mind open to worries that Leo's call had awoken.

Did they have enough rations this week to make a birthday cake? Would she even have time to make a birthday cake?

There was so much work to be done already at the farm. Not only was it contributing to the war effort—albeit indirectly by feeding Britain and keeping the country's morale up—but it made up half of the money she needed to keep everyone fed and clothed. Ration books, even with her added allotment as part of the Women's Land Army, and clothing coupons only went so far. Even Leo's salary as a non-tradesman private and married man was barely equal to her own twenty-eight shillings a week.

"We work just as hard as the men did," Joan muttered as she swung onto her bicycle and pedaled down the road toward Chilworth. "You'd think we'd be worth thirty-eight shillings to the powers that be, but no."

"Not in wartime" was the phrase that got tossed around. And while that was a valid reason, the inequality still stung. Some of the girls had a saying, "Not in wartime, not in any time." If the government wouldn't ensure that women farmers were paid a wage equal to the men for equal work when the men weren't even around, what would happen when they came home?

She pedaled faster and shook her head, leaning forward to make better headway. The sooner she got to Farmer Gould's, the sooner she could find something to do with her hands that would take her mind off the worries of the day.

Chapter Two

"What're you doing for Sophie's birthday, then?"

Joan placed a potato piece into the furrow she'd plowed the day before, then glanced up at Tilly Pritchard, who was working one row over.

Joan reached into the canvas bag at her side and pulled out another potato piece. "Just a cake, if I can manage. And then ..." She put the potato in the trench, frowning. Her eyes darted to the chain around Tilly's neck, where she wore her engagement ring. Her fiancé likely wouldn't be getting any leave. Not as a pilot. It would be cruel to tell her that Leo was coming back.

But Tilly stopped what she was doing, put her hands on her knees, and leaned forward. "Then what?"

Joan exhaled and forced the words out. "Leo is coming." Saying it made her go lightheaded. It was really happening. She'd be able to hold Leo again, to have full conversations without the censors butchering them.

Tilly squealed, jumped the furrow of dirt between them, and plunged to her knees beside Joan, then wrapped her in her arms. "Joan, you're so lucky!" When she pulled away, her eyes glistened, although her smile shone brightly.

Now that was a stiff upper lip.

Joan smiled as some of Tilly's giddiness began to rub off on her. Leo was coming! "He's trying to make it back for Sophie's birthday tomorrow." She grabbed Tilly's gloved hands. "I didn't want to just blurt it out."

It seemed selfish to talk about her good fortune when Tilly didn't have any good news to share. But was it really? There were so few good things that happened nowadays.

"You goose! This is exactly the sort of thing you should blurt out!" Tilly squeezed her hands fiercely. "You're meant to shout it from the rooftops so everyone can share the—the joy of it!" She narrowed her eyes and turned to the farmyard, where Farmer Gould stood tossing forkfuls of hay into a trough. "Did he not let you off for today?" Disapproval dripped from her voice.

"What? No, I didn't ask him." Joan fidgeted with the strap on her potato sack.

"Why not? You silly!" Tilly shoved her. Disbelief radiated from her telegraph-pole straight spine to her high cheekbones, all the way down to the sharp angle of her arms propped on her hips.

Joan hurriedly steadied herself with one hand in the dirt. "The world can't stop just because my husband is coming back on leave, Tilly." No matter how much she wished it would stop, so that Leo would have enough time to make it back to her, so that he could celebrate Sophie's birthday, the world went on.

"Oh yes it jolly well can! And it should!" Tilly stood, reached out her hands, and pulled Joan to her feet. "You're going to march over there and ask Gould for the day off, or I'll do it for you!" She shoved Joan again in the direction of the farmyard.

Joan's boots caught on a furrow. She stumbled, but Tilly steadied her, grinning. "Go on," her friend urged, catching her hand to squeeze it reassuringly. "He's not an ogre."

"I know, I know!" Joan pressed Tilly's hand in return. "Thank you, Tilly." She picked her way across the furrows to the farmyard fence, hanging her potato bag on one of the fence posts.

"Mr. Gould?" Buoyed up by Tilly's exuberance, Joan had been confident. But now, standing in front of the older farmer, who had turned around to stare at her with his bushy, gray eyebrows raised, all that confidence vanished, replaced with a nervousness that made her stomach turn over like the dirt Tilly and she had plowed.

"Aye?" Farmer Gould leaned on his pitchfork and wiped his brow. "What is it, Joan?"

Joan took a deep breath. "My husband ..." Farmer Gould's face crumpled in sympathy, and she shook her head. "No, no, not that!" Her words caught in her throat, and she bit her lip. "Just the opposite. He's come back on leave, and I was wondering if … if you could let me have the day to prepare."

The farmer's eyes crinkled. "'Course, Joan. You ought to have asked me first thing. Go home, be with your husband. How many days has he got?"

Joan broke into a smile. "Oh, thank you, Mr. Gould!" She pushed open the gate and embraced the farmer, planting a quick kiss on his weathered cheek before pulling back to gaze up at him. "I don't know how long he's got, but I'll be back just as soon as he goes."

Farmer Gould's already-ruddy skin flushed darker as he patted Joan's back. "Aw, go on, love. Hurry home to him."

"I will!" Joan raced from the farmyard to the stone walk up to the house, scattering the small flock of chickens in her way. After grabbing her bicycle's handlebars, she wheeled it for a few meters and then hopped on, narrowly avoiding two chickens on her way to the road.

This time, she rode straight and tall, letting the wind dry the sweat on her forehead and ruffle the sleeves of her blouse.

The whole day! The whole day to prepare for Leo's arrival and Sophie's birthday celebration.

She glanced up, slowing down slightly and shading her eyes with one hand. What a beautiful day. A few round, puffy clouds floated above her, and the sky shone a brilliant, paint-set blue.

After skidding to a stop at her front door, Joan took just enough time to prop the bicycle against the wall before running inside. After scuffing her boots on the rug in the hallway twice, she pounded up the steps and into her bedroom.

Her panting huffed loudly through the quiet house as she stood staring at herself in the mirror. If she was going to ride the train to Haslemere to get Leo, she should look her best. But to get to the train station as fast as she could, she'd need to ride her bicycle. And for that, a skirt suit wouldn't do.

"Just a pair of nice trousers." She flung open the door to the closet, grabbed a pair of brown twill trousers, and perched on the bed to take off her boots. Then she peeled off her belt and dungarees, slipped into the trousers, and did up the buttons unsteadily.

Her fingers betrayed her again as she laced up her oxfords over her socks. She paused to take a few deep breaths and steady her hands, then stood up to yank the scarf off her head.

Forcing her nerves to behave, she pulled each of the pins in her hair out. Ringlets came springing down around her face. She combed her fingers through the curls, brushed furiously without caring about how the waves fell, then wrapped the scarf over the top of her head and tied it under her chin.

"Last but not least, lipstick." She grabbed the tube, twisted it until the red, waxy stick appeared, and traced the curves of her lips with it. She blotted it and took one last glance in the mirror. "Lovely."

She pounded down the stairs again, burst out the door, and hopped onto her bicycle. Worry and hurry kept her head down as she pedaled through the streets to the train station.

A church bell rang out a half hour as she propped her bicycle against a wall. As she pushed through the doors, her shoes clunking, she pasted on a smile for the woman at the counter. "I'd like a return ticket to Haslemere, please."

The woman's lips, bright red like Joan's own, puckered. "To Haslemere?"

"Yes, please." Joan rested one arm against the counter and tried to catch her breath.

The woman leaned over a book and traced the print with a well-manicured, oval-shaped fingernail. She raised her head and shook it. "I'm sorry, dear, but there are no trains to Haslemere today."

Joan's knees wavered. She clenched the counter to keep herself up, frowning in bewilderment. "N-no trains?"

"I'm sorry," the woman repeated, her eyebrows furrowing. "We've had word there might be an air raid today, so we've shut the trains down." She stared at Joan. "Are you all right?"

Stiff upper lip. You're not the only woman this has happened to.

There were other people in the world who might need to get to Haslemere more urgently than she did—although what could be more urgent than going to see one's husband on leave? But still, it wasn't the end of the world.

Even if it felt like it.

Joan took a deep breath and nodded, pushing herself away from the counter. "I'm all right. I'm sorry. Thank you for your time." No amount of self-control or makeup could disguise the dullness in her voice.

"Of course, dear." The woman's smile was sympathetic and pitying, as though she could read Joan's mind and knew the exact circumstances that would prompt her to want a train to Haslemere when none were running.

Emptiness spun in her head, and a heavy numbness weighed Joan down as she trudged away from the counter. The door to the station stuck, and she had to shove it to open it. The nearest bench presented her with something solid to sink down on.

She swallowed hard against the scratchy tightness in her throat, gulped a breath of air, and stared out at the street. The sun reflected off the body of a bicycle and into her eyes, which finally released the pooled-up tears they'd been storing.

I can't get to him.

A sob escaped, but she quickly covered her face in an attempt to muffle the sounds of her crying from others.

Was this what wartime did to people? Made them feel guilty for giving in to grief? Someone was already going through a more difficult time, but what could be worse than knowing your husband was just twenty miles away and not being able to see him?

A tear slid through her fingers and splatted softly on her trousers.

What if she never saw Leo again? What if that phone call was the last time she'd ever hear his voice?

That thought broke the dam of self-control, and she bent double beneath the weight of her sobs.

Gradually, her sobs gave way to sniffles, her gasping turned to slower inhales through her nose, and her ears began letting sounds in again.

The church bell was ringing. She'd sat there for almost a quarter of an hour.

Raising her head, she gingerly brushed her fingers over her eyelids to wipe away the last of her tears.

Was this what Leo would want her to do? No, he wouldn't want her to go to pieces just because they couldn't see each other. He'd want her to keep going, regardless of what happened.

"I can keep going." Her scratchy voice wavered, but she held her chin high, allowing herself one last sniff before retrieving her bicycle from the wall and pedaling back toward her house.

But as she passed the road to Mrs. Rowland's, she skidded to a stop. If she could manage to find a way to get to Leo, there would be no one to pick Sophie up at the end of the day.

She wheeled the bicycle around and sailed down the road. Her goal, the bright green of the yard gate, sat stolidly at the end of the lane.

"Joan!"

She stopped again, glanced behind her, and broke into a smile as Ruth Harper strode toward her. Ruth's steel air raid warden helmet obscured her face, but nothing could cover up the woman's confident walk. Even in the daytime, when her job entailed nothing but making sure no one was getting into any mischief, Ruth was always on full alert.

Joan walked her bicycle in a semicircle and squinted into the sun as Ruth neared.

"What are you doing out at this time of day?" Ruth tucked her hands into the pockets of her black wool trousers, her dark eyebrows showing beneath the brim of her helmet. "Aren't you meant to be out at Chilworth?"

"Indeed." Joan flashed the woman a smile. "But I've gotten word that Leo is coming back on leave. I'm picking Sophie up early."

Ruth's face, normally taut with the weight of her duties, relaxed into amazement. "No one else's husband from here's had leave! You lucky girl!"

Just like Tilly's excitement, Ruth's awe rubbed off on Joan. A shiver ran down her spine at how truly fortunate she was. Why had the Lord chosen Leo as the only soldier she knew of from Guildford to have leave?

At the same time, why had He chosen Leo's leave at a time when there were no trains to or from Guildford?

The reality of who she was standing in front of hit her, and she gasped.

Ruth frowned. "What …"

Joan grabbed Ruth's arm. "You know they stopped the trains today?"

Ruth nodded. "Possibility of an air raid." She glanced up and down the street.

"I can't get to Leo because of it." Joan inhaled so fast she nearly choked on her next words. "Do you know—is there another way I can get to him?"

Ruth's brows furrowed, and her face twisted. She tilted her head up to the sky and hummed thoughtfully. "No ..." she murmured, "no, not that either. Yes!"

Joan jumped as the lines in Ruth's face smoothed out. "Yes, what?" She held her breath, tightening her fingers on Ruth's arm.

Ruth locked eyes with her. "There's a supply lorry going down that way around half five."

Joan's mouth dropped open. She tilted her face to the sky as gladness sang its way through her veins. "Oh, Ruth!"

"Look at me, Joan." Ruth's sober tone snapped Joan out of her euphoria.

She looked back at the other woman, whose gaze bore into hers like a shovel into freshly turned earth.

"I'll ask the driver if he'll stop by your house for you, but he's on a strict schedule. He should be by around half five, and if you're not waiting for him ..." Ruth nodded once, her raised eyebrows a punctuation mark that questioned whether Joan had understood.

Joan breathed out shakily, nodding and holding Ruth's gaze. "I'll be there. I won't keep him waiting."

Ruth smiled suddenly. "No, you won't. He won't wait on you. Maybe a few minutes on the return trip, but that's all."

"I understand. I'll be ready. Thank you, Ruth! Thank you." The bicycle clattered as Joan threw her arms around Ruth, who stiffened and then relaxed into the embrace—for a moment.

"Just doing my part, you know." She gave a short laugh and shrugged her shoulders to escape Joan's arms.

Joan grabbed the handlebars of her bicycle and propped her foot on one of the pedals. "You do so much for us, Ruth. Thank you again."

Ruth waved a hand dismissively in the air, although her cheeks pinked with pleasure. "Go on, then. Go get Sophie."

Chapter Three

The boiling water on the stove sang its bubbly song, signaling Joan to dump the potatoes into the water. As she chopped up two carrots, the rhythmic *smack-smack-smack-smack* of the knife on the wooden cutting board combined to make a kitchen symphony.

Into the water went the carrots. She tossed a bone in to give the stew more flavor, added some barley, and covered the pot with a lid and turned the gas down as low as it would go. Oliver and Lottie, though unable to cook a whole meal by themselves yet, could be trusted to turn off the gas, and Oliver was tall enough to move the pot from the stove when the stew was done.

She tiptoed up the stairs and poked her head inside her room. Sophie lay curled up on her small bed in the corner, one fist bunched up under her chin as she dozed.

Joan nodded as satisfaction warmed her stomach. She descended the stairs into the kitchen and went to the pantry, stopping at the radio first to turn on the evening's orchestra recording.

Brahms's "Lullaby" floated into the room and followed her as she set out the carefully-hoarded ingredients that might be enough to make a cake.

Sugar and flour, some margarine, and an egg. She cradled the egg in her hands as she carried it over to the cake pan. Eggs were precious but easier for her to come by, thanks to Farmer Gould who always sent eggs with her if he had any extra. Consequently, the children and she often had more eggs than most.

The house shifted with a creak as the front door opened.

Joan brightened, depositing the egg carefully in the pan before going into the hallway.

Oliver and Lottie stood by the door.

Joan approached them, dusting off her hands on her apron. "Hello, dears. How was school?"

"It was school." Oliver shrugged out of his jacket and pulled an envelope from his pocket. "We met the postman on the way home. This was the only thing for you."

Joan took the envelope and knelt on the floor, her stomach turning uneasily. Before the war, letters were just letters and telegrams just telegrams. But in wartime, everything changed. A letter meant hearing from someone you'd not seen in more than a year. A telegram meant someone had died.

But this one was just a normal envelope. No telegraph markings or ministerial address. Just a street in London.

The paper fluttered in the wake of her breath as she flipped it open and read the signature.

She looked up at Oliver and Lottie. "Do you know a Mrs. ..." She glanced down at the paper. "... Mrs. Jernigan?"

The children's faces brightened.

"She's our neighbor," Oliver said with a nod. "Lives in the flat across the hall from us."

> *Dear Mrs. Masterson,*
> *I understand that Oliver and Lottie Fairburn are in your care. I deeply regret to have to tell you that Mrs. Fairburn was killed in a bombing this Monday.*

Joan's breath caught in her throat. She glanced up at Oliver, who was still watching her.

His eyes narrowed. "What?"

Joan hesitated. The children had just come home from school. They didn't need news of their mother's death right away. She breathed in slowly and swallowed once to make sure her voice would be waver-free. "Let me finish reading the letter, Oliver." She rose unsteadily and groped for the back of the chair beside the telephone, then propelled herself up the stairs and into her bedroom, her mind whirling.

Not only were there the children to consider, but there were Leo and Sophie. If she broke the news to the children now, what did that mean for Sophie's birthday celebration? What did that mean for her trip to Haslemere to get Leo?

If she told Oliver and Lottie about their mother's death, she would be obligated to stay here with them tonight. Children didn't deserve to be alone after hearing news like this.

But if she stayed here with the children, that was yet another day of Leo's leave gone. Another day ticked off the uncertain calendar of life. No one knew if Leo would get another leave before the war ended or if he would even survive until the end of the war.

Only God knew whether her husband would ever return safely, and He wasn't in the business of telling the future anymore.

Tears pricked her eyes, and she sat down heavily on her bed, letting the letter flutter onto the mattress beside her as she covered her face with her hands.

How could she be so callous? To put her own daughter's pleasure and her husband's presence before the feelings of the two children she'd cared for, for the past year and a half?

Had the war sucked all her generosity and feeling from her, that she would put her own comfort before the children's?

What should I do, Lord?

Joan exhaled through her fingers and lifted her face to stare at the closed door. Oliver and Lottie were out there, waiting to see what the letter from their neighbor said. Oliver would have realized something was wrong by now.

She picked up the letter again, then traced the words she'd already read.

> *... killed in a bombing this Monday. She was on the street when it happened. Her flat is still intact. I'm a widow with no children, so I've given up the lease on my flat and moved into the Fairburns' for the time being. If there should ever be a time when the children need to return to London and their father has not returned, please know that they will find in me a caring guardian, such as I pray you have been since the evacuation.*
>
> *Sincerely,*
> *Clara Jernigan*

The last phrase of Clara's letter stabbed Joan's already-tender conscience. The paper rustled as she gripped it tightly and turned her head away, squeezing her eyes shut to keep the tears from falling.

She had cared for Oliver and Lottie like they were her own, hadn't she? They had wanted for nothing while living with her. She'd been as kind and loving to them as she was to Sophie.

And yet …

She slid off the bed and went to Sophie's in the corner. She got to her knees and rested her cheek on the mattress, watching the rise and fall of her sleeping daughter's body.

If it were Leo who had died—tears came into her eyes again—would she tell Sophie right away? Would she put it off for a while, grieve out of sight until she knew she could give Sophie the comfort she would need?

It was different with Sophie, though. She'd been barely four months old when the war began and wouldn't remember Leo the way Oliver and Lottie would their mother.

And if Leo spent the majority of his leave waiting on a train from Haslemere, the time he could spend with Sophie was miniscule.

A tear slid down Joan's face and into her nostril. She pushed her arm under her nose to wipe it away and sniffed.

Sophie's lips puckered, and she whimpered as she turned on her side. Her eyelids fluttered, but she curled up her toes and flexed them, then sighed softly as her eyelashes stilled.

Joan exhaled gratefully and pushed herself away from the bed.

No matter how hard or uncomfortable it was, if it was news of Leo's death she'd been reading, she would want Sophie to know right away. Oliver and Lottie deserved no less.

She opened the door and descended the stairs. Her shoes dragged at her feet on every step, and her head felt like someone had loaded it down with a ton of dirt.

"Oliver? Lottie?" Her voice caught at her throat, but she swallowed and gripped the banister tightly.

Oliver poked his head out from the kitchen doorway. "What did Mrs. Jernigan say?"

Lottie's head joined his, her eyes wide with curiosity.

Their eager expressions turned Joan's resolve to slush, but she clenched her fists and held her hands out to the children. "Come into the parlor, dears."

She led the way, turning on the light as she made her way to her chair by the fire. Oliver and Lottie perched on the couch across from her, their faces expectant.

Oliver leaned forward, holding his cap in his hands. "Well? Did the Germans get our flat?"

Oh, if it were only that. Joan bit her lip as her insides twisted in anguish. "N-no, Oliver. Your flat is still standing."

Lottie sighed and sat back against the couch, her limbs splayed every which way. "He said I wasn't to cry about my toys." She nudged Oliver, who was still leaning forward and watching Joan's face.

"Toys can be replaced," he said. "If that wasn't it, what did she say?"

Joan licked her lips and got on her knees on the braided rug in front of the children. She took Lottie's hand first, then Oliver's. "I have to tell you both something very difficult. Can you be very brave?"

Oliver's intake of breath was harsh and sudden. "Not Dad!" He jerked his hand away and leaped off the couch. His hat tumbled onto Joan's lap.

Lottie sat up slowly, hanging on to Joan's hand. "D-dad?" Her voice wavered, and dampness pooled in her eyes.

Joan glanced back at Oliver, who stood facing the fire with his hands shoved deep in his pockets. "It's not your dad." She forced the words out even though her throat burned. "Your mum. She was—was killed—in a bombing."

A choked cry came from Oliver, but Joan's attention was snatched by Lottie, who flung herself into Joan's arms with a strangled scream of "Mummy! Not Mummy!"

Joan wrapped her arms around Lottie, pulled her off the couch onto her lap, and cradled the girl, rocking her back and forth. Tears streamed down her own cheeks and dripped into Lottie's hair. Joan maneuvered herself around to put her back against the couch and hold a hand out to Oliver. "Oliver, come here."

Oliver shook his head fiercely as his hands clenched into fists, and he turned back to the fire. "Sti-stiff upper lip," he muttered. "That's w-what she always told us." His voice wobbled and caught as a sob escaped him.

Joan's throat got tighter, cutting off any comforting words she might have been able to give him.

I should go to him.

But her legs wouldn't work, and her arms seemed glued around Lottie, who was still crying. The girl's body shook with the strength of her sobs, and her breath started to come in hiccups.

Joan exhaled to try to get rid of some of the tightness in her chest and forced her hands to move up to Lottie's back. She stroked the girl's shoulder blades and began to rock from side to side again. "Shh-shh." The sound came out shakily, like a flow of water disrupted by someone turning the handle of the waterspout down and then up again. But once it was out, her vocal cords and lips worked more freely.

She held Lottie like she would Sophie if her daughter woke up from a bad dream, humming softly when her voice would allow it and making soft shushing noises when it would not.

Oliver's boots appeared in her vision, and she glanced up at him. His nose was pink, and his eyes glistened with unshed tears. "C-can I sit down?"

Joan nodded, sniffing and wiping her nose on her arm. She let go of Lottie with one arm and patted the rug next to her.

He trudged over and sank down beside her. His back was stiff, shoulders hunched, and he crossed his arms as if to hem himself in and keep himself from touching her.

The ache in Joan's heart returned, stronger this time. Strong. Oliver was trying to be so strong, trying to take the news like a man when he was just a boy. But even men cried at times like these.

She squeezed her eyes shut, trying to block out thoughts of Leo. If the war had aged Oliver so much, what had it done to Leo and all the rest of the soldiers?

Leo.

The lorry!

Moving as little as possible, she glanced at the clock on the mantel. Only a quarter of an hour until the lorry would arrive.

Her pulse picked up, and her brain sent a signal to her foot to start jiggling. Ignoring it and keeping her foot still, she bent over to kiss Lottie's forehead. Lottie's sobs had faded into occasional sniffs and hiccups, but she showed no signs of lifting her face from Joan's blouse.

Maybe ... maybe she could set Lottie aside and make sure she was ready when the lorry arrived. When Joan shifted her legs as if she were going to rise, Lottie clutched her tighter and whimpered.

Joan closed her eyes. One phrase from her prayer book came to mind.

God our Father, you see your children growing up in an unsteady and confusing world.

The children's world had just become even more unsteady and confusing, and for the time being, Joan was their only source of stability. She could not leave the children now.

Lord, give Oliver and Lottie Your comfort in their grief. Wipe their tears as only You can. Use me as Your instrument to comfort them and give me the words I need. Be with—

Oliver's sniff broke into her prayer. When she glanced sideways at him, he swiped his sleeve across his face, gulped, and scooted a tiny bit closer to her. She slid one arm around him. Instead of pulling away, he nestled into the space at her side.

Pain seared her heart as she pulled him closer and started shushing again. Her mind drifted back to Leo.

Be with Leo as I ... I won't be able to see him today. Be with him as You are with me and the children. Abide with us and keep us in Your arms, just like I'm holding Oliver and Lottie now, Lord.

Oliver drew in a shuddering breath, wiggling under her arm but still not pulling away. Joan loosened her arm but kept it draped over his shoulder.

What had comforted her when she'd received news of her father's death in the First World War? Having her mother had helped, but her mother had been just as distraught as she was ... at first. A day after the news came, her mother had started humming. Lowly, shakily at first, as her vocal cords were still raw with grief, but the tune had slowly solidified into the hymn "Abide with Me."

As Joan had listened to the hymn and watched her mother's face, she'd felt a chill. Although her mother did not become immediately happy, the song somehow filed away at the sharp edges of the grief in her mother's eyes. Her mother, who'd sat in front of the fire for a whole day, had gotten up to wash her face after that.

Joan inhaled deeply to pull herself back to the present, repositioned Lottie's head, and started to hum the hymn softly. Her voice wavered at first, the high note on the first line disappeared, and the odd note on the third line was out of tune, but she made it through the tune one time.

Lottie let out a long, stuttering breath. She turned her head sideways, and Joan felt the little girl's ear pressing against her own chest. Heartbeats were comforting. She kissed the top of Lottie's head, then wet her lips and started to sing.

"Abide with me; fast falls the eventide;
The darkness deepens; Lord, with me abide.
When other helpers fail and comforts flee,
Help of the helpless, O abide with me."

Her voice faded away, leaving only the crackling of the fire. Then the muted roar of a lorry engine sounded from outside.

Joan stiffened.

She couldn't leave now. It would be wrong to have sat here with the children and then suddenly leave them, just as Lottie was beginning to calm down. Even moving might be enough to start her crying again.

Forgive me, Leo.

The lorry's horn blared. Once, twice, and then a long, drawn-out third time.

Both Oliver and Lottie jumped. Lottie grabbed onto Joan's clothes and whimpered. "What's that?"

Joan stroked Lottie's hair and started rubbing her back. "Ssshhh … it's all right. Nothing to worry about." She stared up at the ceiling and gnawed her lip as she listened to the puttering noise of the lorry engine.

Just leave, won't you? I can't go.

Finally, the lorry roared, and the sputtering engine noise faded away into the growing darkness.

Oliver shifted next to her. When she opened her eyes, he was sitting up straighter. "That's right, Lottie. Nothing to worry about." His voice had stopped wavering, but his eyes were still red and his nose still pink.

Lottie buried her face against Joan's chest again, sighing. She sniffed once and then yawned, wrapping her arms around herself.

"Are you tired, Lottie?" Joan kept her voice soft and calm.

"Mm-hm." Lottie nodded, and Joan's blouse wrinkled underneath her head.

Joan's knees popped as she scooped Lottie into her arms and rose to a kneeling position. "Oof."

She tried to stand up, but Lottie's six-year-old weight made her too unwieldy. She moved the girl carefully onto the couch, but Lottie clutched at her sleeves, grabbing Joan's skin in a grip that made Joan wince.

"Joan, don't!" Lottie's wide eyes filled with tears. "Don't let go!"

Joan jumped up as quickly as she could and reached out for Lottie at the same time as the girl leaped into her arms. The impact made her spine twinge, but she wrapped her arms around Lottie and stepped over Oliver's feet on her way to the stairs, watching the ground to see where to put her feet.

The stairs seemed twice as long as they normally did, and each step had to be made with extreme caution in the growing dimness, but she made it into the bedroom Lottie and Oliver shared and somehow managed to sit down on Lottie's bed without falling over or dropping Lottie.

She started to lay Lottie down, but the girl grabbed at her again. "No!"

"Ssshhh." Joan closed her eyes, willing herself to be patient. Lottie had just lost her mother. She needed comfort. Kissing the top of Lottie's head, she began to lay down on the bed, pulling Lottie with her and cradling her close to her chest.

This time, Lottie didn't protest but nestled close to Joan with a noise somewhere between a whimper and a sigh of weariness.

Joan stared at the wall where Oliver's bed sat as the shadows from the open window deepened. No one had shut the blackout curtains, but there were no lights on in the bedroom at the moment.

And frankly, the blackout curtains were less important than Lottie.

Joan blinked as the thought formed itself fully. The blackout curtains were part of the war effort, and she'd always striven to uphold the war effort as much as humanly possible.

Wasn't this part of the war effort? Wasn't comforting the evacuee children as important as sheltering them and caring for them?

Yes. Yes, it is as important.

Mr. Churchill might not see it that way, nor might the Air Raid Precautions units, who handed out fines for the most minuscule light shining from windows, but even if no one else saw it that way, she did.

When Lottie's breathing settled into a steady pattern that *whooshed* softly from parted lips, Joan untangled herself from Lottie one limb at a time, slid off the bed, and tiptoed over to the window to draw the blackout curtains closed. The door creaked as she pulled it shut behind her, but the noise didn't appear to have wakened Lottie.

Oliver sat at the kitchen table, staring into a bowl in front of him. Joan glanced at the stove, where the stewpot sat with the lid off.

Poor lad had to serve his own stew.

She sat down beside him, casting one more glance at the pot. Her stomach murmured at the thought of food, but the idea of holding a bowl of stew and bringing the spoon repeatedly to her mouth exhausted her.

Oliver looked up at her with dull eyes like some soldiers in newsreels had. "Lottie asleep?"

Lord, help him.

She nodded.

"That's good, at least." Oliver's voice was dull, too, with no inflection on the word *good*. There was nothing to make it good. "Thank you for supper."

She nodded again. Finding words required effort, and there was no energy in her veins for that.

Oliver stood up and put his bowl in the sink, then came to stand beside her chair. "Joan?" His voice had lost a bit of its dullness and taken on a higher, more vulnerable tone.

She turned to see him standing awkwardly. With no stiff upper lip anymore, he looked younger than his nine years. Young and lost. "Can-can I hug you?"

Tears flooded her eyes, and she nodded, holding out her arms. He hugged her hesitantly at first, keeping his body rigid, but then he slowly began to melt against her until she was cradling him in her arms the same way she'd been holding Lottie.

Oliver didn't cry. He sniffed a few times and once swallowed hard, but he didn't cry while she held him. She smoothed his hair and stroked it, holding him tightly.

After a few minutes, Oliver pulled away and swiped his hand across his eyes. "I'm going to go to bed now."

Joan nodded and leaned forward to kiss his forehead. "Good night, Oliver." What else could she say in a situation like this?

"Night." He trudged out of the kitchen, his footfalls on the stairs hollow.

Joan pulled herself off the chair and lugged the stew pot over to the icebox. After shutting the door, she leaned against it and rubbed her hands over her face.

Weariness made her eyes blurry, and she blinked several times to clear them before dragging herself up the stairs. Undressing and putting on her nightgown floated by in a flash. As she pulled the covers over herself, exhaustion weighed her eyes closed.

Chapter Four

Joan's limbs still felt leaden when she woke the next morning.

She squeezed her eyes shut. Sophie's birthday morning. They'd have to celebrate without Leo.

As she dragged herself out of the bed, she cast a glance to where Sophie still lay asleep. How could they even celebrate after the news about Oliver and Lottie's mother? Was it wrong?

Joan took off the scarf covering her hair and grabbed a snood, moving in front of the mirror to make sure all her hair got tucked into the loosely crocheted net.

Lord, help me to be a comfort to Oliver and Lottie today.

She changed into a housedress and laced her shoes, then went down to the kitchen, taking care on the stairs so as not to wake any of the children before they had to get up. It was Saturday anyway, so there was no need for them to waken early, but if they all slept longer, it would give her time to figure out what to do.

As she brewed herself some tea and cooked an egg on the stove, she prayed.

Thank you for Farmer Gould and Tilly and their kindness to me. Bless them for their hard work on the farm and let the harvests be plentiful. Thank you for Leo. Be with him as he's not able to be here on Sophie's birthday. Be with Sophie and me as we celebrate without him.

There was that word again. Wasn't it wrong to celebrate when something like Mrs. Fairburn's death had happened?

The kettle began to sing, and she poured the boiling water into her teacup and sat down at the table while the drink steeped.

Sun seeped in through the windows, but its light was hesitant, like it was being threatened by storm clouds in the sky. Likely it was—it had been a few days since the last rain—but they didn't need any rain to make them all gloomier.

The children needed to be allowed to grieve, but they oughtn't be allowed to wallow in their sadness. That helped no one, least of all the children.

Joan sipped her tea and closed her eyes in relief at the comforting warmth of the liquid. While Oliver and Lottie were still young enough that they would recover eventually, there needed to be someone or something to pull them out of their sadness.

Maybe having a quiet celebration for Sophie would help with that.

It would be a hard line to walk. The celebration must be discrete, with feeling for Oliver and Lottie's loss. They mustn't be made to feel excluded, but they also mustn't be forced to participate if they didn't feel like it.

But if they wanted some cake, there would be cake.

Joan's teacup rattled as she bumped against the table in her haste to rise. She turned on the radio and put on an apron, then turned on the oven and started gathering everything she would need to make the cake.

Strains of Schubert's *Trout Quintet* followed her around the kitchen as she went back and forth from the pantry to her recipe book.

This wouldn't be just any old tea cake with currants and sultanas in it. It would be a proper cake for a birthday celebration.

Struck with inspiration, she peered all the way to the back of the cupboard. "I know it's here somewhere …" The spice containers rattled and clanked against each other as she pushed things aside.

Finally, a little packet fit into her palm. "Eureka!" she whispered, a smile slipping across her face as she pulled the packet out. Blancmange powder. And it was the pink packet! Perfect.

As the fast bit of the *Trout* piece began, she mixed the sugar and margarine together. The twinkling, racing piano part made her heart beat faster and sent an urgency flooding through her veins, but one couldn't rush cutting margarine into sugar. The same urgency tensed her muscles as she turned the handle of her eggbeater furiously.

What was it about orchestral music that let it express and evoke so many emotions? It had no words. She shook her head in wonderment and mixed the flour and blancmange powder with the eggs and sugar-margarine mixture.

The batter took on a lovely, light-pink color as she poured it into two sandwich cake tins.

The light-hearted Schubert music and the physical effort had somehow eased her heart and mind so that when she bent over to put the cakes in the oven, she smiled. Then she shut the door and straightened up.

A low roll of thunder drained the smile off her face and down through her body until it landed in her already-heavy shoes and weighed them down even more.

Rain streamed down the windowpane and enveloped the house with a curtain of rushing-water noise. Noise that ordinarily comforted her but now felt oppressive and isolating.

Lord, why today? I was so happy until You sent the rain.

Guilt immediately clenched at her heart.

The weather should not dictate my feelings. Forgive me, Lord.

She shook her head and exhaled forcefully as she picked up her teacup and drained the last of the tea from it, then grimaced. It had grown cold in the time she had spent on the cake, and cold tea never went down well.

Another roll of thunder rumbled over the faint noise of the slackening drizzle, and she glanced at the clock on the wall. Nearly seven. The children would be waking up on their own soon, if the storm didn't waken them.

A hammering knock from the front door pounded at her ears. Who was trying to break down her door, and why wouldn't they stop?

Irritation made her shoes clack loudly on the floor as she rushed to the door and threw it open, preparing a tirade for the intruder. Her hand froze on the door handle, and the rain faded away to a whisper.

Leo's face, filled with such eagerness that he looked as young as Oliver, swam before her eyes.

"Joan?"

The crack of Leo's reedy voice brought sound, sight, and sense rushing back.

Joan tried to stifle a shriek of disbelief. She licked her lips and managed to shakily form his name. "L-Leo?"

He pitched forward and enveloped her in an embrace so tight her spine popped. She gasped, and somehow her arms worked, wrapping around him.

His lips found hers, fumblingly at first, as if they'd forgotten how to kiss. But when he remembered …

Joan leaned into him, breathless with the overwhelming flood of feelings that enveloped her. Tears leaked out from her closed eyes and onto her hot cheeks. She was really holding Leo, really being kissed by him.

Wet patches dotted the thick wool of Leo's uniform underneath her hands, and she finally broke the kiss and looked up at Leo. The longer top portion of his hair flopped over his forehead as she ran her fingers through it. Damp.

"How long have you been out in the rain?" she choked out.

"Long enough." Leo gestured behind him at a horse and wagon that stood by the gate. The farmer tipped his hat and slapped the reins on his horse's back, hunching his shoulders against the rain as the wagon rumbled away.

Joan gaped at him. How far had he ridden in the storm? Surely not all the way from Haslemere! She pulled away to get them both inside.

But as she ran her hands down his arms, one palm caught on something smooth and wooden. She stepped back and looked at him, really looked at him this time and let her gaze take in everything, not just his face.

Her eyes locked on the crutch tucked underneath his left arm and followed the wood down to his leg.

What was left of his leg.

It ended just below the knee, and his trousers leg hung limply, almost the way it would on a clothes hanger.

Her throat choked off her breath, and her stomach turned a queasy somersault as her eyes flicked up to his. "Leo?"

His cheeks had gone pale. He snatched her hand and squeezed it. "I'm fine. I'm all right, Joan."

She put her free hand to her mouth to keep from sobbing. That wasn't all right. That was … horrific.

"Joan …" Leo's eyes and mouth tightened like he'd tasted something rotten. But something else lurked in his eyes. A gaunt look. Eyes shouldn't be gaunt, but his were. "Joan, please, let's go inside."

She nodded, keeping her hand over her mouth. Now his leg was all she could see. His poor leg.

She gulped as she held the door open and watched him hobble straight into the parlor. He did move quite smoothly, but it wasn't his normal gait she was used to.

Leo eased himself onto his armchair by the fireplace with a grunt, propping his crutch on the chair's arm.

Joan sank onto her rocker across from him and stared at him. She'd known she would cry, but this ... it was too much. How could God expect her to know how to respond to this after yesterday?

Leo met her eyes and then looked away, gazing steadily at the fire. Although his expression was calm and set, the corners of his jaw poked out a little and the vein in the side of his neck was pulled taut.

Say something.

Joan squeezed the fabric of her apron in her fists. Finally, she cleared her throat. "How-how long?"

His eyes darted instantly over to her, his eyebrows drawn together in a harsh angle. "How long what?" The normal reediness in his voice had turned into something rawer and sharper.

She nodded toward his leg. "How long ago did it happen?"

Leo's brows knotted even closer together. "A month. No, almost two. They kept me in bed for two weeks before they'd let me get up and learn to use this." His fingers brushed over the crutch, like an owner absentmindedly rubbing his dog's head.

"And then it was another week or so before they shipped us all home and I could get to a telephone." He shrugged and relaxed a little, his body molding itself to the chair.

"Two days ago." She exhaled slowly and glanced up at the ceiling.

"I meant to write, Joan." The crack in his voice and the gaunt, haunted look in his eyes were apology enough.

"Hush," she said quickly. "You're here now. That's what's important. You're here for Sophie's birthday."

"I'm here for good. I'm—unfit for service now." Leo shook his head and then smiled. It had pain and resignation behind it, but it was a smile. "I told you I'd see you soon, didn't I?" He grabbed his crutch and leaned forward. "Where is she?"

Joan felt her eyebrows knit together. Home for good. She blinked at the realization. Of course he was unfit. That was why no one else had gotten leave. They couldn't spare anyone unless he was useless.

That was why he'd been so sure.

"Joan?"

She blinked again and cleared her throat. Leo had levered himself off the chair and into a standing position.

"Sophie's sleeping. I'll go up and get her."

"Nonsense." Leo was already propelling himself toward the stairs. "I can manage stairs."

She hurried after him and brushed past him, standing on the bottom stair to block his way. "It's not that, Leo."

He frowned, tilting his head to the side and pursing his lips. "What is it, then?"

"It's Oliver and Lottie." She propped one hand on the banister and the other on the wall. Leo had always appreciated frankness, so it would be better to come out and say it. "I received a letter yesterday ... Their mother's dead."

Chapter Five

Leo's face froze. He blinked, but his eyelashes fluttered as if he was flinching. His nostrils flared, and his Adam's apple bobbed as he swallowed. Shifting his weight on his crutch, he nodded slowly and repeatedly. "Right," he said finally. "Right. How did ... how did they take it?"

She stared at him. "Take it? They're children. They were devastated."

Leo blinked again. "Of course. Of course." His voice softened. "Ought we not to celebrate, then?"

Joan dropped her arms, confident now that her husband wouldn't go barging up the stairs like a one-legged elephant, and shrugged. "I thought it would be all right if we had some cake and celebrated quietly. I planned to let Oliver and Lottie sleep as long as they wanted, and if they feel like joining us, having some cake to eat might help them."

A muscle in Leo's cheek jumped, and he turned his head away from her. But she had already seen the flash of scorn that narrowed his eyes and drew his brows together.

Suddenly, her idea seemed ridiculous. How could cake soothe the hurt of losing a parent?

She wiped her hands on her apron, which probably dirtied them with flour more than cleaned them. "I suppose that must sound awfully silly, Leo." He'd teased her before and laughed at her, but he'd never scorned her.

But of course things were different now. He'd seen things, done things, that probably made even birthday celebrations seem trite and meaningless.

Leo looked back at her and shook his head. "No," he said, his voice cracking again. "It's not silly." He swallowed hard and hopped backward. "I'll put on some tea." As he limped to the kitchen, he glanced back and made a shooing motion with his hand.

Joan watched him go, then turned to tiptoe up the stairs. Her eyes and throat burned, so she blinked and massaged her throat to dispel the tension.

Once inside the bedroom, she closed the door and leaned against it. Leo's homecoming had not been the joyous event she'd envisioned. Yes, she was glad he was home, but that flash of frustration in his eyes had dampened the spark of her excitement. What else had changed about Leo?

She sighed and massaged her face, closing her eyes. Maybe he just needed time. Time to adjust and maybe to forget the things he'd seen—if they could be forgotten.

Maybe they could pretend things were normal for today.

Inhaling deeply, she went over to Sophie's bed and scooped her up into her arms. "Sophie, wake up."

For a moment, Sophie's head lolled against Joan's shoulder, but then Sophie scrunched her eyes together, making a little mewling noise as she opened her mouth and yawned.

Joan broke into a smile and kissed Sophie's forehead. "Happy birthday, Sophie."

"Birthday?" Sophie blinked sleepily and then opened her eyes wide. "Birthday!"

"Yes, birthday!" Joan chuckled and brushed a few errant strands of hair away from her daughter's forehead. "And I have a birthday surprise for you. Your daddy's come home ... just for you."

Sophie's forehead puckered. "Daddy?"

Joan's chest twinged, and her stomach knotted up. "Yes, your daddy." She kissed Sophie's head again and started down the stairs. "He's the handsome man in the picture frame by my mirror."

"Ohhh." Sophie leaned her head back against Joan's shoulder and yawned again. Her head bumped against Joan's arm with every step she took.

Joan looked down at her daughter. How much should she tell Sophie? For now, the most important thing was that Sophie was not afraid of Leo. "Your daddy loves you very much, and he wants you to love him, too."

"I love him." Sophie smiled and stuck her thumb in her mouth.

Well, once Sophie had determined that she liked something, it was hard to dissuade her. So much the better. Joan shook her head with a smile. If only everything in life was as simple.

When she came into the kitchen, Leo was staring into a teacup and leaning on one elbow, his fingers gripping his hair.

"Leo?" she said softly.

His head jerked up, and his eyes, which had been filled with pain, widened and softened. He held out his arms. "Sophie." His voice wavered as a small, uncertain smile played around his lips.

Sophie looked up at Joan. "My daddy?"

Joan nodded, not trusting her voice.

"Hello, Daddy." Sophie waved a chubby hand.

The legs of Leo's chair scraped the ground as he scooted it forward, still reaching out. "My, you've gotten big."

Joan transferred Sophie gently from her own arms to Leo's, giving him a reassuring smile. "She has grown, hasn't she?"

Leo held Sophie out at arm's length and looked her up and down. "You look just like your mother." He smiled up at Joan, his eyes shining, and pulled Sophie close to his chest, burying his face in her hair.

Joan picked up Leo's cup from the table and took it over to the stove, where the kettle was just beginning to steam and make the wheezing sound that proceeded its whistle. She found another cup for herself and readied the tea bags, then turned around.

Leo had sat Sophie on the table and held out his hand solemnly. "Hello, Sophie. I'm your daddy."

Just as solemnly, Sophie reached out and put her hand in Leo's. "Hello, Daddy."

As they shook hands, Leo broke into a smile. It almost made the corners of his eyes crinkle but not quite.

Would that shadow in his eyes ever go away?

Leo jumped as the kettle began to whistle but laughed it off and gave Sophie a sheepish smile. "Just the kettle, Sophie. Here, come sit on my lap."

Sophie smiled and wiggled off the table into Leo's arms. "Today—today is my birthday."

Leo chuckled. "Yes, it is. Happy birthday to you. Did you know Mummy's got a cake in the oven for you?"

"Cake!" Sophie bounced, her whole face lighting up.

So far, Leo was doing wonderfully with Sophie. Joan smiled and finished pouring the boiling water over the tea bags. She set a cup in front of Leo, who nodded at her and laid a hand gently on her back.

Joan leaned in to kiss his forehead, then pulled away to check on the cake. As she opened the oven door, a rush of hot air made her eyes water, but as soon as she blinked to clear them, two tins of pale-pink cake glowed in the darkness of the oven.

She glanced back at Sophie, who peeked over Leo's shoulder with a smile, and grabbed two oven mitts to protect her hands from the hot cake tins as she set them out of the oven to cool.

Sophie's eyes widened, and a gasp broke from her tiny lips. "Cake!" she exclaimed again.

Joan laughed as she hunted in the cupboard for the strawberry preserves. "It's a pink cake." She found the preserves and set them out by the cake, then joined Leo and Sophie at the table.

The lyrics of "Ode to Joy" ran through her head as the triumphant streams of Beethoven's Ninth Symphony pounded through the kitchen. The sound of the rain slacked off, and Joan's heart quieted as she sipped her tea. Everything was all right.

A stair creaked.

Joan set her cup down and glanced through the kitchen doorway, her heart in her throat.

Lottie appeared, still dressed in her nightgown, and Oliver followed a few steps behind her. Both children stopped when they saw Leo, who quickly set Sophie on a chair and grabbed his crutch.

"You must be Oliver and Lottie," he said as he picked himself up off his chair. "I'm Leo."

Lottie took a step back behind Oliver, but she poked her head out. "Sophie's daddy?"

Leo smiled at her and stopped a few feet away from the children. "Yes, Sophie's daddy."

"My daddy!" Sophie waved at Lottie, a smile wreathing her face.

Lottie's smile was more timid, but she stepped out from behind Oliver, who was staring at Leo with a blank expression. Fiddling with the ruffle on her nightgown, Lottie said carefully, "Hello, Sophie's daddy. What should we call you? Joan told us to call her Joan."

Leo's mouth quirked up as he glanced back at Joan. "Then you may call me Leo." He leaned forward on his crutch, bending his good leg, and held out a hand. "It's good to meet you, Lottie."

Lottie shook his hand, some of the timidity leaving her face. "And you, Leo." She let go and retreated behind her brother.

Oliver regarded Leo gravely, his eyes narrowed slightly. "Is your last name Masterson, too?"

Leo straightened up with a chuckle and held his hand out to Oliver. "Yes, it is."

Oliver squared his shoulders, stepped forward, and pumped Leo's hand. "Hello, Mr. Masterson."

"He said call him Leo!" Lottie's words, although indignant, lacked some of their usual vivacity.

Leo leaned on his crutch, still smiling. "He can call me what he wants."

Oliver's face, which had darkened, relaxed. "Mr. Masterson," he said quietly.

Joan's heart twinged. Oliver so clearly wanted to do what was right and be strong. Maybe having Leo here would help him. She leaned over to touch Leo's arm. "He calls me Mrs. Masterson," she said reassuringly.

The corners of Leo's eyes crinkled just the tiniest bit. "He's a very polite lad." After hopping back to his chair, he scooped Sophie onto his lap and gestured to the other chairs around the table. "Won't you both join us?"

Joan gave them an encouraging smile and stood up. "Would either of you care for tea?"

"Yes, please." Lottie wiggled onto her chair, her whole body bouncing as she nodded her head.

Oliver nodded once.

"Two teas coming up." Joan kept her voice calm but put a smile into it as she ran more water in the kettle.

"What happened to your leg, sir?" Oliver asked suddenly.

Joan whirled around to stare at Leo, whose shoulders had tensed up. Her husband was quiet for a minute. She edged around to see his face just as he spoke.

"I ran so hard chasing after the Germans that it fell off." Pain lingered in Leo's eyes, but a grin hovered at the corner of his mouth.

Sophie and Lottie both gasped, and Oliver frowned in puzzlement, then bent down to peer at Leo's leg under the table.

"What about your other leg?" Lottie asked. Concern puckered her lips and forehead as she stared at Leo.

Leo paused again. "I guess they decided to send me back so I could keep the other one safe."

A grin tugged at Oliver's lips. "My dad's a pilot. He doesn't have to worry about losing his legs."

Joan sucked in her breath. The careless comment could upset Leo. It wouldn't have upset him before, easygoing man that he was, but who knew what would set him off now?

Pain flashed through Leo's eyes again, but he leaned an elbow on the table and bent toward Oliver. "I wanted to be a pilot, too, but they told me I'd be of better use chasing the Germans on foot." In spite of the pain on his face, his tone was that of an excited young man—the kind of man he'd been before the war.

Everyone had wanted to be pilots.

Joan slid her arms around Leo and kissed his cheek, overwhelmed with grief and gratitude. In spite of the continuous reminder of his missing leg, her husband hadn't let his emotions get the better of him. In fact, he was putting Oliver's and Lottie's emotions before his own.

As Leo turned his head to nuzzle her cheek, she realized that they had both sacrificed something for these children that weren't even their own. She'd sacrificed what she had believed might be her only chance to spend time with her husband in order to comfort the children, and now Leo was sacrificing his comfort to keep their minds off the loss of their mother.

And although it didn't seem like such a big sacrifice now, yesterday when she'd been holding Lottie on her lap and listening for the lorry, it had been excruciating.

Later, after she'd spread preserves atop one of the cake layers and sandwiched them together, and everyone had a piece, Joan glanced out the window.

The sky was still dark with rain clouds, and rain still splashed onto the window. But now, the sun shone from somewhere beyond the house and turned all the raindrops into liquid pearls that shimmered as they fell.

A burst of static from the radio snatched her attention. The legato flute from Grieg's "Morning Mood" began to float from the radio.

Her light had broken forth like the morning, and healing was coming. It would come to Oliver and Lottie, even though it might not be as speedy as they might like.

This was what the Lord had called Joan to: to comfort Oliver and Lottie, care for Sophie, and be there for Leo. Although He'd also called her to the WLA, He'd called her to motherhood first.

And if He had called her, He would abide with her and help her fulfill her calling to the best of her ability.

That knowledge was worth more than an extra ration of chocolate and sweets.

Joan smiled as she bit into a piece of the beautiful, pink cake.

Epilogue

August 1941

The late-afternoon light stretched the shadow of Joan and her bicycle as she pedaled down the road. She tilted her head up to the sky, drinking in the last rays of the sun before the evening's chill began to seep through the air. Her neck and shoulders twinged, and she rolled them to gain a little relief from the tension that had gathered there all day. It was no wonder farmers were always so stooped and hunched in old age.

Even Farmer Gould, barely into his fifties, was beginning to walk like an older man. He'd started the day with his usual cheery "Hullo, Joan!" as he lowered himself into the potato field, but after lunch, he had needed Tilly's hand to get up.

"I'm sorry, girls," he said, sweat beading on his red face. "I'm done in. I hate for you to be out here while I'm resting my bones inside."

Tilly had shushed him, sliding one tanned arm around him. "You've done this your whole life! You deserve to take it easy every once in a while!"

That had pacified Farmer Gould a bit, and he'd stumped off to have his wife fix him a cup of tea.

Joan smiled in spite of the weariness that made the pedals on her bicycle hard to push. But soon, the inviting green of the gate greeted her, and she slid off the bicycle to enter the yard.

After depositing the bicycle in its normal place in the garden shed, she trudged over to the house. Her spine popped as she bent down to unlace her boots, slide them off, and leave them on the doorstep.

When she pushed open the door, the clinking sounds of silverware on dishes made her pause. Moving silently on her sock feet, the only sound was the swishing of her corduroy breeches as she peeked into the kitchen, a smile spreading across her face.

Leo sat at the head of the table, facing the empty spot where she normally sat, with Sophie's high chair pulled close to him. Oliver and Lottie took the two sides of the table, and they were all busily eating.

Eating what? She still had to warm up the leftovers. Unless Leo had done that already?

She slid into the doorway just as Leo turned to put part of a potato on Sophie's plate. His eyes caught Joan's, and he brightened the way he had when he'd seen her at their first school dance together.

"Look who it is!" He threw his arms wide. His eyes shone and crinkled at the corners, and his smile stretched all the way to his molars. After his return in May, his smiles barely went past his crooked left canine tooth, and sometimes his smiles weren't real. But more and more often, his true, old smile appeared.

"Mummy!"

"Joan!"

Sophie and Lottie exclaimed at the same time, Lottie almost tripping over herself in her haste to rise. She flung herself into Joan's arms.

A rush of joy flooded through Joan as she gathered the girl up and kissed her forehead. "Oh, you're getting big!" she chuckled, quickly swinging Lottie back onto her chair. Joan bent down to kiss Sophie, avoiding the bit of potato stuck to the side of her mouth.

Sticking out her hand across the table to Oliver, Joan waited until he set his fork down and reached across to shake her hand. Over the summer, his face had widened and his shoulders had broadened a bit.

"Hello, Joan," he said evenly. The tiniest hint of a smile glimmered.

There was that rush of pleasure she felt whenever he called her by her first name instead of the old "Mrs. Masterson."

"Hello, Oliver." Joan gave him a smile and moved around Sophie's high chair to get to Leo, who was bracing one hand on the table. "Don't get up," she said quickly, bending down to smooth his hair back and kiss him.

Leo tilted his face up toward her and snaked one hand around her waist. Joan heard Lottie giggling, and pulled away to see the girl covering her mouth to hide her laughter, sharing a conspiratorial glance with her brother. Oliver's nose had scrunched up, and boyish disgust marred his normally solemn features.

"I think someone doesn't like us kissing." Joan leaned into Leo and raised an eyebrow at Oliver, who wrinkled his nose farther.

Leo followed her gaze and chuckled. "Sorry, Oliver. I can't help it after she's been gone all day." He nudged Joan. "I've got a plate on the stove for you."

Joan patted Leo's shoulder and retrieved her plate from the stove, then took her seat at the other end of the table. "I didn't expect to find you eating already." She picked up her fork and glanced down at her plate. A pile of beans nestled next to half a potato, and a puddle of broth surrounded a sliver of roast.

"I *told* Leo we should wait for you." Lottie adjusted the red bow in her hair and pressed her lips together primly.

Joan tried to hide a smile as she shredded a bit of roast with her fork. Leo hadn't turned it to rubber, at least. Oliver snorted at the same time Leo put a hand to his mouth to stifle his laughter.

"You don't tell grown-ups what to do!" Oliver whispered across the table.

Leo nodded and pursed his lips, which did nothing to disguise the humor still lingering in his eyes. "I did ask her opinion. Maybe I ought to have listened." He scraped the last bit of potato from his plate and looked up, suddenly pleading. "But it gave me something to do."

Joan nodded back at him as the flavor of the beef broth and potato mixed in her mouth. Since his return, Leo had become more industrious than he'd ever been before the war began. Whether the paint needed retouching or bushes in the garden needed trimming, he was doing it or having Lottie and Oliver help him do it.

And the house looked the better for it. The new, shiny, red paint on the front door proclaimed victory as loudly as Joan's lipstick, and the overgrown corners of the garden bloomed with fresh greenery and flowers.

After swallowing, Joan flashed Leo a smile. "I know. I'm glad you did."

Lottie gasped suddenly and pushed away from the table. Her chair skidded backward across the floor and rocked on its back legs as she darted out of the room.

Joan felt her eyebrows furrow, and she glanced at Leo, mouthing *"What?"* at him as Lottie's steps pounded across the hallway and into the parlor.

He cut his eyes at Oliver and muttered, "Letter."

Joan choked on a bit of potato. She thumped her chest and swallowed hard, following Leo's glance to Oliver, who stared across the table as if he couldn't hear or see them.

Lottie flew back into the room and thrust the letter at Joan, almost jabbing her eye with it.

Joan drew back and grabbed the letter before it could actually poke her. "I take it it's ... good news?"

"Read it!" Lottie settled back onto her chair but wiggled excitedly. "We've already read it, but we want you to read it!"

"All right, dear. Give me a moment." Joan wiped her fingers on her napkin before opening the letter.

> *Dear Mrs. Masterson,*
>
> *I hope this letter finds you and the children well. I've been considering the best thing for Oliver and Lottie as the school year approaches, as I know you have. The bombings have slacked off a bit, but all the posters are urging parents not to bring their children back to the city yet. I think it is in the children's best interest if they stay with you a while longer. That is, of course, if you're willing to keep them and if that's what they want. I've had no word from their father. No news is good news, they say, so I pray for the best.*
>
> *Yours,*
> *Clara Jernigan*

Joan looked up from the letter to meet Lottie's hopeful gaze. The girl, now back on her seat, folded her hands on the table but unclasped them a second later to grab Joan's hand.

"Please say we can stay! Please!"

Well, that was easy. Joan glanced at Oliver, who picked at his potato and kept his gaze on his plate.

Leo cleared his throat.

Joan looked up to meet his searching gaze as he pulled Sophie out of her chair and onto his lap.

"I think they should stay." Leo's voice held a note of finality, and the earlier humor in his eyes flitted away, chased by the shadows he still hadn't told her about.

Joan nodded. "I would like them both to stay."

Lottie squealed in delight, and Joan squeezed her hand.

"Stay!" Sophie banged her hands on the table. One hand caught the edge of Leo's plate and tilted it up like a seesaw. The harsh *clank* it made when it smacked back against the table made Joan jump.

Oliver's fork clattered onto his plate, and Lottie gasped. Leo sucked in his breath, his shoulders going rigid.

Sophie's face started to turn pink. "Too tight!" Her voice trembled, and her lip poked out.

Horror washed the color out of Leo's face. He scooted back on his chair and readjusted his arms around Sophie. "Sorry. I'm sorry, Sophie. I didn't mean to." He exhaled shakily and kissed the top of her head, blinking hard.

Joan exhaled with him, her heart crumpling as the kitchen light reflected on the tears in her husband's eyes. He'd been doing so well. It'd been nearly a week since he'd last been so startled by a loud noise.

Sophie turned her face up to Leo. "I love you, Daddy." All traces of her earlier discomfort faded, including the pink in her face.

Joan cleared her throat. "Oliver, would you like to stay?"

Oliver picked up his fork again, but he paused, his knuckles turning white around the handle of the utensil. "What if ... what if my dad comes back to London?"

Leo leaned forward and rested a hand on Oliver's shoulder. "Mrs. Jernigan will tell him straight away where you are, and they'll send word to us. And do you know what?"

"What?" Oliver locked eyes with Leo. The boy's grip on the fork loosened, and as Joan watched, he leaned into Leo's touch.

Leo scooted his chair closer as if he was about to tell Oliver a secret. "I think your dad would want you and your sister to be where it's safest."

Oliver gnawed on his lip, nodding slowly, then set his fork down. "All right. We'll stay."

Lottie squealed again. "Oh good! Joan, we get to stay with you!" She flung herself from her chair into Joan's arms.

Joan had just enough time to drop her fork before she was enveloped in Lottie's embrace. "Yes, Lottie. Yes, dear." Her throat closed up. She would get to keep her children for a while longer.

Not children by blood but by choice.

"I love you, Joan." Lottie's voice, muffled by Joan's shoulder, sent a surge of happiness through Joan.

A tear slid down her cheek as she rocked Lottie back and forth on her lap. "I love you, too, Lottie."

A Note from Bailey Gaines

I loved getting to research and write about England for this anthology. During my time in college, I had the opportunity to study at Oxford University. It's not in Surrey, but while I was there, I was able to walk around various parts of the country, including Oxford itself, Bath, and even Wales. With its fields, stone walls, narrow country lanes, and abundance of sheep, England was so different than anything in Georgia that I was captivated by it (even more than I had been previously).

In 2021-2022, I wrote and revised a novella retelling of Alfred Noyes's "The Highwayman." Although the original poem is not specifically set in Surrey, it was inspired by Surrey's Bagshot Heath. While writing that retelling, I got to research the roads of Surrey along with highwayman lore, the aftermath of the Battle of Culloden, and the Jacobite Uprising.

It's been a pleasure to visit Surrey again, this time in an era a little closer to mine. I didn't know about blancmange powder until I was researching rations and cake recipes, but now my list of recipes to make includes a blancmange pudding. I've also become fascinated with the Women's Land Army and want my own pair of tan corduroy breeches. Maybe that will be my next sewing project!

Thank you for reading. If you'd like to find out more about my writing and me, check out my Instagram @baileygainesauthor!

Her Heart's
Home

a novella by Grace A. Johnson

Dedication

To those with wandering hearts and restless souls.
Grace will lead you home.

Chapter One

County Surrey, England
Spring 1921

I'd fought tooth and nail for this old house, with its patched roof and peeling shutters, ever since Father left it four years past. To leave it now, to leave not only what crumpled and creaked but what was warm and welcoming, what ignited long-ago memories and stirred a sense of *home*, after all we had been through together, this house and I, seemed to my sentimental heart like leaving a body at the graveyard.

And in some small way, I supposed I was. For I had never gotten to bury Papa, lost amid so many other broken and lifeless bodies in Belgium, but here rested his soul, his heart, his booming laugh, heavy footfalls, and always-working hands. And here I departed from what remained of my dearest papa, the only parent I'd ever known, and finally laid his soul to rest.

Even as my foolish heart cried out against it—and I say "foolish" because, in truth, there was no longer anything I could do to avoid the inevitable—I took up my suitcase and valise and trudged out the door … down the brick pathway lined with dandelions and daisies … into the yard that was a wee bit overgrown but not so much that it didn't still look as lovely as ever. As lovely as I'd always worked to keep it, once alongside my mother's nearly blind gardener, but most recently, by my lonesome since we could no longer afford to keep Mr. Halloway on.

Poor Mr. Halloway. I hoped he had something to occupy those gnarled, old hands now that he lived with his children.

If only you *had children to move in with, Meredith.*

But if I had married Peter Griffith all those years ago and bore his young ones, I wouldn't need to move in with anyone, as it were.

Regret only begat bitterness, my father would say, and he was right. It was of no use rehashing the past, which was already, well, past. I could only march on and make for myself a new home somewhere.

I recoiled at the thought of a *new* home, a different house, even as I craved one. *Lord, prepare the way before me and soften my heart to receive whatever You have in store.*

Benji, my only remaining servant, who wore the hats of butler, maid, and footman, came up with my trunk and hefted the last of my belongings—what hadn't been sold months ago, auctioned off yesterday, or left for the bank—into the back of the cab I'd hired. "How are you holdin' up, Miss Tate?" he asked, a softness in his eyes that tinted my own with moisture, despite my efforts to constrain it.

"As best as I can, I suppose, Benji. The worst of it's that, after all we did, all the positions terminated and furniture sold and funds raised, I still must leave. *We* must leave, leave it all behind—what remains of it anyway—and start anew. How am I to start anew as a penniless spinster, Benji? Where am I to go? I've known only this life of comfort and provision for all my thirty-six years, and with that life gone, I feel ... so ..." I sighed, the tears now clinging to my lashes as my mind groped for words amidst all my fears and worries.

"Helpless?" Benji offered, guiding me into the cab and pressing a handkerchief against my palm as he did so.

"Yes, thank you. And ... purposeless, I think. As if all I've known was but a waste. As if my whole life up to this point was a waste. Now that I'm free, so to speak, to make my own way, I realize how much time I spent simply minding the house when, perhaps, I could have done something more. If anything, something that would have prepared me for this."

Benji nodded along for a moment, but then he speared me with a bit of a glare. "Now, Miss Tate, you've never been without purpose. You took care of your father, you provided jobs for folks like me, you housed all those soldiers during the war, and you did what God wanted you to do in that season of your life. It's time to move on to the next one, from winter to spring, ma'am. And just because winter may have seemed dormant and lifeless doesn't mean there wasn't a lot of important preparation goin' on."

His words struck me, and for a moment, I simply stared at him in wonder—and gratitude, for he very much was right, and I certainly had needed to hear that. "Why … thank you, Benji." I patted his hand and returned his handkerchief. "When did you become so wise?"

His cheeks pinked the slightest bit, and he cast his eyes down. "Well, I reckon I learned from a right wise woman, Miss Tate. Thank you for everything," he said, with his boyish toothy grin, "and just know you've been like a mum to me these years, and I'll never forget you."

Tears streamed down anew at the young man's kindness, and I enveloped him in a hug. "It has been my utmost pleasure to know you, Benji, and I'm honored by your words. I shall never forget you either, my boy. May God go with you on this next leg of your journey."

With our parting words, the cabbie snapped the reins, and we were off, rattling down the winding country roads into the heart of spring.

Deepdene House and Gardens, once the pride of Dorking and the Duke of Norfolk, now a hotel. I leaned out of the cab window to spy, peeking through the trees, the beautiful white-gray stone, Palladian-style manor with its many archways and shining windows. Only glimpses now, but as we wound through the majestic gardens, the flowering bushes and stately trees gave way to a full view of the glamorous house.

To think that within mere days, I went from a derelict Georgian cottage to a duke's manor that was as enchanting now as it had been two hundred years ago.

A part of me wished I could afford to stay here as a guest, that I was more than just an answer to their advertisement for kitchen help ... and the other part of me shrank away from the prospect, even from the house, as my mind was overwhelmed by the manor—and the new life it symbolized.

Thy will be done, Father. The prayer echoed throughout the caverns of my soul, as it had every day these last two years—no, since the war first started. The routine I thrived on had shattered the day that England—and, subsequently, my father—had joined the war, and ever since, my control had faded into helpless pleas unto God.

I'd thought, when Peter had slipped through my fingers, that I trusted Him, that I was willing to go wherever He led, but the past years were a testament to my failings and my desire for command over my life. And now ... now I feared I was almost too resigned to let fate have its way.

"Not fate, Meredith," I whispered to myself, letting the words permeate the confines of the carriage. "Providence." And Providence was holy, right, pure. Providence would lead me to a future of hope ... a future with, I prayed, a home.

The cab fairly clattered to a halt before the entrance of Deepdene, and I lurched forward, grasping the first steady thing my hand touched ... only to feel the door give way as I unwittingly shoved the latch down. With all my weight against the door, I tumbled headfirst, my calfskin heels caught on the step and my arms flailing as I sought a handhold ... anything.

Anything to keep me from landing directly in the muddy puddle, soiling not only my best dress but also my reputation.

There was nothing.

Mud soared through the air and splattered every inch of my body as my head, shoulders, and bosom hit the puddle and my stomach and legs hit the hard ground. At that point, I was fortunate that only *one* shoe flew off and landed in a nearby puddle and that my other foot wasn't twisted. And that none save the cabbie had witnessed my utter lack of composure.

Well, except for the man now racing toward me, riding crop cast to the ground and boots splashing through the mud.

Oh, for pity's sake.

Before I could scramble to my knees and reach for my missing shoe, the man was at my side, taking me gently by the elbow and lifting me onto my feet. Then he snatched up my shoe and shook off what water and sludge he could, then knelt, glancing up at me to ask my permission.

Mutely, with my face awash with heat, I nodded.

He made quick work of refastening my shoe, but I took full advantage of what limited time I had to *try* and regain the slightest bit of grace and decorum I had left. I fished a handkerchief from my reticule and blotted a fraction of the moisture out of my blouse—or perhaps I was simply smearing more mud in. No matter. I just tucked the kerchief into my collar and wore it as a napkin over the greater portion of the stain. At least then I—and the gentleman at my feet— wouldn't be forced to look at it. The hotel staff was another matter entirely.

As he rose, I brushed matted strands of hair away from my face … only to remember how dirty it was as well. The gentleman merely quirked a brow—since he was thankfully kind enough not to outright laugh at me, as the cabbie was doing behind his hand—and retrieved his own kerchief, then dabbed my chin and beneath my eyes.

"Are you hurt, miss?" His voice was low and bore the smallest hint of a Hertfordshire accent, his touch gentle as he scrubbed at my nose and cheeks.

His *miss* warmed me, when I was so used to being mistaken for a *madam* due to my mature age and drab clothes—or so an old friend had described me. I straightened my skirt and lifted my shoulders back. "Only my pride. I appreciate the help, sir."

"Of course." He tucked his kerchief against my dirty gloved hand and tipped his head. "May I escort you inside?"

And have him realize he had so graciously assisted a potential employee rather than a future guest? "I think not, sir. I wouldn't want to take you from your ride." I gestured to the horse, now munching on grass, and the crop on the ground.

"No matter—"

"No matter indeed. Thank you," I clipped, ducking my head and brushing past him. I hated to be so brusque—'twas not my way—but neither was being humiliated when there was something I could do to prevent it.

Fortunately, a porter soon darted out of the hotel to fetch my bags, and I marched alongside him, mucky head held high, into the Deepdene.

As I chanced one last glance at the silver-haired gentleman, acid churned in my stomach. All of a sudden, what I had wished would be my future I now prayed would soon become a blot on my past.

Chapter Two

Two weeks. I had two weeks to prove my merit as a kitchen maid, or I would be politely discharged and left, once again, to my own devices.

When I'd mentioned to the hotel clerk at the front desk that I had come in response to their advertisement for help, he had been gracious enough to permit me to clean up and change into one of my spare dresses in the women's lavatory downstairs before I met with the hotelier for our interview. Though the hotelier had been skeptical about hiring me at first, it was clear he was grateful that someone had answered his advertisement, and though I had no work experience, my three decades of housekeeping and cooking alongside my house staff had appealed to him—enough to give me a two-week trial period, that was. Whereas something permanent was preferable, the hotel offered living quarters in the form of the refurbished servants' floor downstairs, and none of the other jobs I had looked into could claim that. Unless I met the hotelier's standards, I could at least raise enough money working these two weeks to pay for a room and search for a better, securer job.

A war waged within me, my tinge of embarrassment from earlier today having festered into a boil of distress and anxiety that conflicted my desire for stability and purpose. Was this a sign from God, a delayed answer to my prayer for guidance, that I was meant to be elsewhere? Or was it, rather, opposition from the devil, trying to distract me from my destiny?

I would find out in two weeks, and instead of giving in to my nerves, I would do my absolute best as an employee of Deepdene House and, furthermore, as a servant of the Most High God. If my best wasn't good enough, well, that was up to God and the hotel manager to decide. In the meantime, I'd continue praying that the Lord would lead me where I was supposed to go ... even if I feared where that may be.

Taking up the bags the porter had left in the doorway, I left the hotelier's office and made my way to the live-in staff's quarters. I would not officially begin work until first thing tomorrow morning, and the hotelier had already taken me on a brief tour of the spacious manor as he peppered me with questions, which left me with the remainder of the day to explore the house and gardens and get to know my fellow staff members.

I began with the latter, trekking down to the kitchen and slipping quietly into the shadows to watch the chef chop, stir, and sauté, and the maids clean, sweep, and prepare. All but one of the staff were entirely focused on their tasks, and this singular maid lifted her mousy brown head and gave me a timid wave. Dodging a broom and a pile of crumbs, I came up beside the girl and offered her a hand in chopping carrots.

"Are you the newest addition, ma'am?" she asked in a gentle, lilting voice, shifting to allow me to stand with her at the worktable.

"Hired on about an hour ago, yes. Are you new here as well?"

"I'm the hotelier's niece, actually, so I was one of the first employees." She brushed a strand of hair out of her eyes and paused, glancing about the kitchen before settling her gaze back on me. "Name's Amelie. And you ...?"

"Meredith. Meredith Tate. You'll have to show me the ropes, Amelie, since I'm sure you know this place best."

"It'd be an honor, ma'am!"

And with that, we made quick work of chopping the carrots, celery, and onions for the chef's soup, chattering quietly all the while. When we finished, Amelie fairly shooed me from the kitchen and promised to take me on a tour once dinner preparations were complete. I found myself deposited from the servant's doorway into a vibrant garden, immaculately trimmed shrubbery flanking the rustic, cobbled pathway that gave way into a a rainbow of pastel geraniums, fragrant verbena, lively petunias, large, flowering rhododendron, and stunning coleus.

A breeze came in, carrying luscious aromas, velveteen petals, and silken leaves on its wings and pulling me down the path into the garden's arms. I meandered through this corner of the sprawling garden, which seemed so secluded, magnolia trees shading this portion like the towering hills around us. Sunlight and wind danced, their sparkles blinding me to all else but the bright wonder of this place.

To think, such an estate, such a beautiful jewel, now reduced to service and paying customers who came and went with little regard for the palatial experience they were granted. No more early mornings with the master or soirees with family and friends or hallowed visits from diplomats and artists.

Perhaps Deepdene, if walls of stone and gardens of flora could harbor emotion, felt as displaced as me.

The thought drove me to a startling halt, one my feet were not prepared for, and I tripped for the second time today, the garden spiraling around me as I reached … reached … through the air for a handhold. A tree branch. A flower pot. Anything …

Something firm yet warm gripped me by the waist and drew me upright. My hands locked on a thick, muscular arm around my midsection, and I took in a quavering breath.

And then I realized, the very same gentleman from this morning had rescued me once again.

I quickly wrested away from his hold and spun around, waves of hair falling from my pins and into my face. "Why do you always find me in my most precarious, shameful situations?"

What appeared eerily like a smirk creased the man's face for but a moment, then vanished as he cleared his throat and stepped back. "I'm afraid what would be more shameful is if you arrived to dinner this evening with a knot the size of the Rock of Gibraltar on your forehead."

I wasn't quite certain if he was serious or meant it in jest, for the granite in his eyes and the smile that had flickered a second ago both led me astray, and I struggled to reply until he stuck out a hand in a black leather glove.

"The name's Trevor Seaton." He spoke so curtly that I *was* certain he didn't enjoy introducing himself, or else regretted prolonging his interaction with me.

I gingerly shook his hand, his firm grip cracking my knuckles. "Oh, I-I'm—"

"Meredith!"

Amelie's cheerful voice rang out through the garden as she darted down the path toward us, rescuing me from my painfully awkward interaction with Mr. Seaton whilst at the same time, making it considerably *more* awkward.

I inwardly grimaced.

As if bound by an unspoken law never to acknowledge or address the guests, Amelie ignored Mr. Seaton almost entirely, tugging me by the hand farther down the path and away from the now-frowning gentleman with a knot in his brow. A glance over my shoulder in his direction informed me he was continuing on his merry way, Oxfords gliding gracefully across the stones, even for a man of his stature and bearing.

Lord, if it be Thy will, let me never see him again and further embarrass myself. And cure me of this wretched clumsiness.

I could not recall ever being so maladroit, as I was accustomed to my home and the quiet farmland surrounding it ... but there had been moments when Peter first came calling and when we took in those five soldiers that my nerves had gotten the better of me and I had knocked over a vase or dropped a pan. Goodness, I hoped that wouldn't persist. I couldn't bear another incident, lest I was terminated even before my trial period was up.

Fortunately, though my cheeks still burned for another five minutes, Amelie quickly took my mind off my two tumbles as she prattled on with practiced ease about the gardens, the estate, the mausoleum, the temple, the previous owner, the last esteemed guest, and the driver's new baby. She toured me through every nook and cranny—even one particularly sequestered cranny a young couple were *enjoying*—before the sky grew dim and the sun shot beams of fuchsia and lavender across the horizon. We made our way back into the kitchen just in time to wash the evening dishes and prepare for my first night in the Deepdene House hotel.

I surveyed the women's quarters, with its sparse furnishings and musty aroma that reminded me of my final years at home, when moths fluttered about my all but empty attic and dust began to settle over my shut-off upstairs rooms. Perhaps I was better suited to being a staff member after all, especially considering my simple upbringing and my parents' nonexistent connections. Today had more than proven that graceful movements, respectful conversation, and genteel behavior were not my strong suits.

With my mother's Bible—one of my few remaining belongings—in hand, I whispered my nightly prayers, including a new addition for grace and strength, and lay down on my cot with a wandering heart and restless mind.

Chapter Three

Dawn broke later than I remembered, for it felt like I had been up all night rather than only three hours by the time the sun crested the horizon and dusted the gardens in gold. The kitchen staff had been afforded a moment of rest as the bread rose and the upstairs staff cleaned, so Amelie and I took tea over yesterday's leftover scones with Mrs. Beech, the old cook who'd stayed on as the chef's assistant after the change to hotel, and young Master Eugene, the stable boy who was apparently found more often in the kitchen than in the stable.

I stifled a yawn as I rolled my shoulders, tight from kneading bread dough for the last hour or so. I'd not baked so much since the war ended and the group of soldiers recovering in my house had returned home.

At least here I wasn't forced to make polite conversation with striking, silver-haired gentlemen whilst covered in mud.

"Meredith?"

Amelie brushed my knuckles with her calloused fingertips, and I jerked my head up, nearly dislodging my cap and curls. "Hmm?"

"You seem a bit lost in thought, ma'am. Thinkin' about that handsome gentleman who arrested you in the courtyard yesterday?"

My eyes widened and brows jumped at her accurate assumption. "He didn't *arrest* me, Amelie dear. Just … caught me. When I tripped."

A bit of the dickens twinkled in Amelie's eyes as she said, "But you don't deny it."

"Deny what?" I took the last sip of my now-tepid tea.

"That you find Captain Seaton handsome."

Out went the tea.

Mrs. Beech handed me her kerchief, and I made quick work of dabbing up my Earl Grey and cleaning my shirtwaist before folding the handkerchief in clean, crisp lines, effectively avoiding the subject for all of thirty seconds before Amelie repeated herself.

Or perhaps that was my own mind asking me the question, begging for insight into why I felt so strongly about Mr.—no, *Captain* Seaton always coming to my rescue.

I almost glanced around now, half expecting to find him offering his kerchief as well, or offering to launder my blouse, or *something*. Speaking of his kerchief, I was yet in possession of it and now required to encounter him again to return it to him.

Rats.

"I think he's a right 'ansum bloke meself," Mrs. Beech remarked as she stood and gathered our teacups and Eugene's mug of milk.

I wasn't getting out of this one easily, was I?

"He's not hard on the eyes, no, but to be honest, I hadn't much time to notice, as I've been preoccupied each time I've met him."

Amelie and Mrs. Beech exchanged a look, one just like my cook and lady's maid had given each other regularly when Peter Griffith came calling.

No, Meredith, you're not going to relive those wretched months. You're not going to make the same mistake and fall for a man only to lose him to the military because you waited too long to commit.

Because if what happened with Peter were any hint, that was what would happen if I let myself think about Captain Seaton. I'd fall like a schoolgirl for the first boy who gave her a second thought, but I would never make my feelings known … and then duty would claim him, and my affection would prove to be nothing more than shallow—but nonetheless heartbreaking—infatuation.

And then he'd come back with a lovely young bride from France, whilst I remained a lonely spinster.

The thought plagued my mind for the remainder of the morning as I swept, dusted, and prepared lemonade, petit fours, and cucumber sandwiches for a picnic several of the guests were to take this afternoon. I'd thought years ago, when the war raged and Papa had joined up, that I had overcome my discontent. I'd thought that serving soldiers on leave, offering my home as a hospital for the wounded, and aiding the war effort had been enough to give me purpose. I'd thought, foolishly, childishly, that I would always have my papa with me.

I was wrong, for here I was now, four years later, no Papa, no home, no purpose. Just this hollow, aching feeling and this girlish dream for a home of my own, a husband to love, children to raise.

I took up the large picnic basket, bedecked in ribbons and lace and bearing the sweets and treats, with napkins spilling from its top, and emerged from the humid kitchen. The Deepdene—the heart of the manor and not the underbelly, where the servants and staff worked and lived—greeted me in all its finery and beauty, the priceless artifacts, breathtaking artwork, and ornate designs inviting both wonder and envy.

If only Lady Halsworth were so welcoming.

The snobbish noblewoman, who'd arrived, the day before I did, with her adolescent daughter, no husband in sight (gossip in the kitchen was that she was newly divorced), did not even condescend to look at me as, with the snap of her fingers, she directed me through the foyer-turned-lobby and a series of hallways, then out onto a balcony as if I were *her* servant. The afternoon sun behind us cast shadows on the members of Lady Halsworth's party, encapsulating her flaxen-haired daughter in shades of copper and rose and burnishing the stately gentleman by the stairway like a bronze statue.

A stone settled in the pit of my stomach as the aforementioned gentleman turned, the sunlight flickering across his face and revealing the gilt glitters in his hazel eyes. Something barely perceptible rippled across his features, and at the glance he swept over me, the stone seemed to gain an extra ten pounds.

There goes my façade of being a highborn lady.

Before Captain Seaton could speak, I unceremoniously shoved the overflowing picnic basket in Lady Halsworth's hands, gave a stiff curtsy, and darted back into the manor.

Oh, Papa, why did you have to leave? Things were so much simpler, far less awkward, when it was just you and me at home.

And perhaps that was the problem. If I continued pining for home, I'd never learn how to thrive outside it.

"Telephone for you, Captain."

Trevor Seaton pivoted on the garden path to find one of clerks behind him, the man's outstretched hand bearing a small card. The welcome interruption led him away from the garrulous Lady Halsworth, her demure daughter, and Mr. Fothergill, who'd spoken not two words through the duration of their outing.

Not Trevor's usual set, to be sure. Years of sailing and war had ruined him for genteel company—although he wasn't complaining.

"A Mr. O'Rourke, sir," the clerk continued as he walked with Trevor to the front desk and one of the five telephones in the Deepdene.

Trevor nodded his thanks and reached for the receiver, cradling it against his ear as he leaned into the transmitter. "Mr. O'Rourke, good to hear back from you so soon."

The estate agent chuckled. "I know you're anxious to hear about Ackford Hall, Captain, and I'm pleased to tell you that the previous owner has moved and the hall is officially going on the market. However, since you've expressed your interest, I wanted to give you the chance to lay claim to the property first."

"I appreciate it, sir. Would we be able to schedule a day to tour the property sometime this week?"

"Absolutely. How's Saturday afternoon? I think I can convince my wife to let me out of the house for a couple hours." The jovial man laughed again, and the infectious joy lent a curl to Trevor's own mouth.

"Saturday's fine. I look forward to it."

They exchanged good-byes, and Trevor returned the phone to its cradle. Lord willing, he would have a house within the next two weeks. All that was left was a wife.

Miss Meredith's winsome face flashed in his mind's eye: tendrils of warm strawberry-blonde hair winding 'round her cheeks, a generous dusting of pink across her nose, her eyes as boundless and untamed as the sea. Perhaps he had been too long without the company of a woman—but no. Lady Halsworth, even with her "striking" and "decadent" good looks (her words, not Trevor's), did not taunt his mind and heart as Meredith did.

At least Lady Halsworth did not run and hide at the sight of him, not that such was enough to persuaded him in her favor or *dis*suade him from properly meeting Miss Meredith. Assuming she *was* a miss and not happily wed with an abundance of young ones.

Just my luck, eh?

Were his mother still here, she'd promptly scold him for spending thirty-eight years at sea, leaving him bemoaning his lack of experience with females now that he had finally decided to settle down at age fifty.

A scolding he thoroughly deserved, but it was far too late now, wasn't it?

As rude as it may have been, Trevor took his telephone call as an excuse to avoid returning to the picnic and meandered down one of the various hallways in the Deepdene. The manor was alive with movement and chatter at this hour: staff bustling down corridors, guests promenading through the galleries or dining in one of the many alcoves that afforded an envious view of the gardens, doors creaking and footsteps thudding and the deck beneath him roiling.

He blinked.

The floor, solid marble and cream colored and very much unmoving, shone up at him as shafts of sunlight sailed across the surface.

He wasn't at sea anymore. Not at war anymore. Not drifting anymore.

Trevor blinked once again to be sure and then continued on his way, hoping for a glimpse of Miss Meredith, wherever she'd run off to. And while he wandered and sought the elusive siren who had already so captivated him, he prayed.

Dinnertime arrived with a clang and the sizzle of butter in the sauté pan, and much more quickly than I'd hoped, for my time hiding and sulking and praying (if one could call the garbled words swimming in my mind *prayers*) had been cut short.

I clung to my broom like a lifeline, loathe to release it and accept the duty of serving the guests their drinks. Shouldn't there be footmen or a butler or *someone* other than I to do this? But no. Until the Deepdene found its footing and a full staff, I was forced to assume the extra responsibility.

Meredith, you ought to be ashamed of yourself. I did not shirk responsibility or cower in the scullery. I was a grown woman—though a quiet and sheltered one—and I had been raised to face my problems head-on.

Resolved, I squared my shoulders, returned the broom to the closet, and took the fresh towel Amelie offered me. Wine bottle in hand, I marched into the candlelit dining hall, where the aroma of cream of watercress soup and fresh artisan bread wafted through the room. The two girls who served the first course backed away from the table and disappeared from sight.

Then I stepped up.

If Captain Seaton had not deduced by now that his damsel in distress was a kitchen maid, he'd discover the truth soon enough.

I bowed my head and kept my eyes trained on the bottle in my hand and the glass beneath the flow of wine as I made my way down the table—past Lady Halsworth (I knew her by her shrill laugh) and Mr. Fothergill, whose portly stomach I was forced to reach over, and an array of other guests—before I met with the last empty glass.

"We meet again."

The low rumble jolted through me, and my hand slipped, the glass tumbled, and none other than Captain Seaton ended up with a bright-red stain on his dinner suit.

Chapter Four

Trevor began soaking up what liquid he could with his napkin as he watched Miss Meredith reel. The woman looked the perfect combination of indignant and mortified, and with her nostrils flaring and face aflame, she squared her jaw, rolled her shoulders back 'til she stood aright, and proceeded to rub at the stain on his suit jacket.

Trevor didn't know whether to be amused or equally as mortified for being the cause of her spill.

Slowly, so as not to shock her again, he cuffed her wrist and removed the towel from her white-fingered grip. "I apologize for startling you, miss. Allow me." He managed to thoroughly stain both the towel and his napkin, and once everything in his lap was blood-soaked—*no, Trevor,* wine-*soaked*—he folded the cloths and laid them aside.

"I-I …" Her throat jerked. "No, I apologize. Would you like to change?" The wine bottle now sat on the table, and her empty fingers flexed as though she intended to undo his buttons and remove his jacket.

And for the briefest of moments, he nearly let her, his pulse pounding in his ears like the staccato thumps of boots on the deck above, his teeth clenching to prepare himself for the onslaught of pain …

But no.

He was not in the surgeon's quarters below being mended from the nigh-fatal blow that had cost him his mind … and eventually his position.

He was at dinner.

And everyone around him was stifling laughter.

His gaze flicked up to the guests surrounding the table before him, and he flashed them a silencing glare, one that had worked on far too many insubordinate officers in the past. Then he, too, rolled his shoulders and met Miss Meredith's probing stare. "Nay, thank you. I'll be fine," he said, keeping his voice a near whisper and inquiring calmly if she were all right as well.

Her features relaxed, the lines 'round her eyes fading as she murmured, "Thank you for your kindness," ducked her head, and departed as quickly as she'd arrived.

The moment the clock struck midnight was the first I was able to take a breath all evening. Rather than turning in to bed like Amelie, Mrs. Beech, and the other staff members, I stuffed my arms into my raggedy, old overcoat and slunk outside, my shoulders as slumped as they'd been at dinner. It wasn't until I was well out of sight and earshot of those near the house, enveloped in the dark of night, that I let myself relax. Breathe. Close my eyes and let the worries roll off of me like sea billows against the rocky shore.

The last couple days—yes, it had been only two, although it felt like a dozen—since my home had been lost to me had been almost as overwhelming as those long days and weeks during the war. They shouldn't have been, no. This ... this should have been easy. Relieving. Exciting.

Instead ... I felt suffocated, pinned down by tons of water, drowning. Surviving one day at a time had been simple, natural even, when one knew where they would lay their head to rest, where their food would come from in the morning, what they would do when night fell and they were alone.

But here, despite its grandeur and the assurance of a small paycheck at the end of the week, I felt like I was struggling to live in the middle of the ocean.

"Oh, God." My knees aching and buckling beneath me, I collapsed onto a stone bench and held myself up with my hands splayed behind me. "Oh, God, what have I done? I don't want to work here forever—You know that. You know h-how selfish I am, how many worthless dreams I have, and how petty I am that I sit here complaining that I have a job and a place to sleep when a-all I want is a home. A husband. Children. I want to wake up in the morning to the sound of the rooster crowing, to walk into my own kitchen and bake whatever I know my family will enjoy. I want to— oh, Lord. You know what I want. But is it too much to ask?"

I babbled on, my prayers coming in the form of tears, tirades, and what thanks my plaintive heart could manage. Yet, even when all I offered up to God was pleading and complaining and unfinished sentences and pointless questions, He took all my words up in His hands and sorted through them, one by one. And when I finished, when I sat in silence but for a frog croaking and a cricket chirping, I felt infinitely more at rest. Not quite at peace, although I prayed for it as well, but rest. I could at least be content in knowing that God heard me, He understood, and He would give me the strength to bear His response, whatever it was.

For a long moment—perhaps a second, perhaps an hour—I soaked up the quiet and reveled in God's creation surrounding me. To think, whether I were here, at my old home, or a million miles away, if I lifted my eyes unto the sky, my gaze would be met with the same glistening stars, the same lustrous moon. "I'll always have the moon, won't I? Thank You for the moon, Lord, and for all the many and wonderful blessings You've given me. Forgive me for taking them for granted."

"He will."

I almost looked back at the moon, expecting to see the Man in the Moon's winking face. Rather, common sense won out, and I cast a furtive glance about me, searching for the intruder. *Lord, please, let them have only just come upon me and not have witnessed my entire prayer.*

The intruder shifted out of the shroud of darkness and into a shaft of moonglow, the pale gleam illuminating the silver hair of Captain Seaton and giving his eyes a roguish gleam.

Why was I not surprised? Perhaps because this strange man appeared like a specter haunting me at every turn.

As if in response to my unspoken remark, he came toward me, floating over the promenade of shadows and light with silent footsteps in a way that made him seem disembodied. His voice, too, carried through the night like an echo when he said, "'Tis the same moon that followed me across the oceans. I thought as a child, why have a light burn when the world sleeps? But then, out upon the sea, at war, the moon was the truest blessing. So many things I took for granted when I was young—and time was foremost."

I hummed in agreement, still too startled to verbalize whole words, especially in the face of his confession.

The captain remained silent for a while yet, then, with the rustle of his clothing, he sat across from me on the rim of a flower pot. "I apologize for interrupting your prayers, miss. I admit I've wanted to seek you out since yesterday."

"I, um, yes." *What kind of a reply is that, Meredith?* Had he not sat there, I would have smashed my palm against my face. Then again, had he not sat there, I wouldn't be in this predicament to begin with. "*I* apologize for my behavior every time you've encountered me. I … I have no excuse, really."

"You need none, nor an apology." He thrust his hand out all of a sudden. "We've never been formally introduced. I'm Trevor Seaton."

I likely stared at his hand a moment too long, but when he didn't retract it, I gingerly gripped it, and he shook mine heartily. The slick ridges and grooves of deep scars distracted me, but I resisted the urge to investigate the scarring I felt. "M-Meredith. Meredith Tate."

"A pleasure to finally meet you, Miss Tate." His hand fell back to resting on his knee—or, no, gripping it. Tightly.

"Do your knees give you fits, Captain?"

"Call me Trevor. And you could say so. I was injured during the war."

Keep your thoughts to yourself, Meredith! "Oh my, I'm sorry." As if that were any less pathetic than inquiring about a near-stranger's joints.

"Don't be. Didn't stop me from becoming captain." He gave a rueful chuckle.

"So … are you still in the navy?"

"No, I was discharged, but not on account of my knee. 'Tis age that makes this old wound act up."

"Oh." Curiosity, morbid curiosity, burned within me, but I bit my tongue to keep from asking what *had* rendered him discharged. *No wonder things didn't work out with Peter, if this is how you converse with men.*

"Are you from here?"

The question gave me a momentary jolt out of my thoughts but not enough to keep me from replying "no," as if he'd meant the Deepdene. "That is, I'm from just outside Dorking. A small farm in the country. I ..." *Have nothing left to say that won't stir up my regret.* "Are you?"

"No, no. I was born in Hertfordshire, but as we never had a family home, I've drifted since the war. And I mean the Great War this time."

It truly wasn't the least bit funny, but the way his eyes twinkled in the pallid light inspired a laugh. Which lasted only a moment before his words sank in. *Without a home.* Yet for all his life, unlike me, who'd at least known the blessing of a home and land for thirty-six years.

"Is it hard to drift? Do you ever think you'll settle somewhere?"

The hand on his knee relaxed as he heaved a sigh that answered my first question. Then the twinkle faded, and his gaze bored into me, unyielding but so full of unspoken words. "Yes. Once I find the right woman to settle with."

Chapter Five

My third day working at the Deepdene went by with relative ease. Amelie was still "teaching me the ropes"—although there was little left to learn regarding the routine of cooking, cleaning, and serving after I had cooked, cleaned, and served far more during the war. But I humored her, for it was obvious she relished her bit of authority.

I was yet in the process of getting to know all of the staff members, and at this rate, I doubted I could meet them all, much less remember their names, when I was only now growing accustomed to the kitchen personnel. Fortunately, I had spent today cloistered away in the kitchen, which allowed me to get to know several people better as I talked with Mrs. Beech about her grandchildren and Eugene about his pet chick and Chef Fraise about his life in France before the war—and it also allowed me to avoid any embarrassing mishaps in front of the guests.

No more spilling or tripping or falling or stumbling over my words or feet. Here, with the steady hum of work and gentle companionship, my nerves were not in bunches and my thoughts in jumbles.

Well, they weren't … until Amelie returned from serving tea with a note in hand, my name written in a firm, masculine slant upon the paper.

Amelie's eyes glowed with mischief as she bounced on her toes, waiting for me to open and read the note.

I took my precious time, torturing both her and myself, as I unfolded the paper and focused on the words rather than the sensation of my throat constricting.

Just as I thought.

Captain Seaton was inviting me to rendezvous with him in the garden tonight.

All right, so those weren't his exact words, but they may as well have been for the amount of trepidation that filled me. The captain *appeared* to be a considerate and honorable man, a bit old-fashioned—which was something I could surely appreciate—but who was to say it wasn't a façade? Why else would a hotel guest of good standing send a note to a staff member downstairs unless he desired a less-than-savory encounter with her?

Oh, Meredith. I could hear Amelie's scoffing voice, the same tone she took with me during our lessons. *It isn't the 1900s anymore. The world of men and women isn't what it was—prim and proper, with a specific structure—when Peter would come calling.*

Who was to say Captain Seaton's intentions weren't pure, if not entirely platonic? He could simply be interested in speaking with someone from the area.

Right?

After I had gripped the note 'til it crumbled, Amelie snatched it from my grasp and scanned the words in under a second.

"Mer-ee-dith!" She shrieked my name unlike I'd ever heard it. "You must accept!"

"Are you sure, Amelie? I-I don't know."

"Pish posh! Why, who knows what this could mean." She waggled her eyebrows, flapping the note in my direction.

I snatched the missive right back and stuffed it into my uniform's pocket. "That's exactly what I'm afraid of."

Like the naïve girl she was, Amelie simply giggled. "Oh, just think! A mysterious, handsome guest falling in love with the shy but lovely maid. It's like a real-life romance novel!"

I resisted the urge to clamp a hand over her mouth and opted for hissing, "Lower your voice, Amelie Causey-Jones. If rumors start spreading of a 'romance,' I'm sacked."

That quieted her. She pursed her lips, bobbed her head, and slipped back to her station.

I almost regretted speaking so harshly to her, in the voice I'd reserved for only my father's impertinent dog that always dug up Mr. Halloway's roses. But the truth was, I couldn't risk losing this job so soon …

Or losing my heart to a near-stranger.

Throughout the rest of the day, I tried valiantly to strengthen my resolve to turn down Captain Seaton's invitation and head straight to bed after my shift, but once everyone else had retired for the night and I hung up my apron, my resolve crumpled. I was too on-edge to sleep—which was, no doubt, due to the anxiety his note had brought me—and yet, too exhausted to stay awake and read.

My own traitorous feet led me through the old servants' entrance out into the moon's wan glow, and within moments, my gaze was met with the figure of Captain Seaton, the light casting a shadow of his broad shoulders and long legs across the pathway.

I stalled in the obscurity provided by the entrance's overhang, my thoughts surging ahead of me. *Am I certain of this?*

Why wouldn't I be? This is, after all, what you've been longing for since Peter left eighteen years ago.

And yet, all the same, it was what I had feared ever since I'd let Peter go when I was sixteen years old.

Meredith, what if this is God giving you a second chance?

Despite my better judgment, that thought spurred me on. I stepped into the jasmine-scented air and the gleaming starlight, my footsteps hushed as I approached the captain.

I would not go seeking romance or giving my heart away as I did as a foolish girl, but would accept the simple companionship of a walk with a stranger—provided Captain Seaton's intentions truly were that innocent.

His words of last night echoed within my mind: *"Yes. Once I find the right woman to settle with."*

Time would only tell when he found the woman and who she was. Until then, I was determined to enjoy this one conversation with no expectations toward the future.

Captain Seaton met me in the midst of trailing vines and arching branches, offering his arm, though his hand remained in his trousers pocket.

I slid my hand into the crook of his elbow, noting the tenseness and quake beneath my fingers. When he released a heavy sigh, the trembling faded and his muscles relaxed. He turned to me, the dark of night hiding any traces of stress or frustration that might have resided in his expression.

"Thank you for coming, Miss Tate."

The phrase was so common and his voice was so gruff, but something in the way his lips tipped up and his free hand came to cover mine revealed more meaning behind the words.

"Of course. Thank you for inviting me, Captain Seaton." *Aha! Finally a sentence that wasn't unintelligible blather!* The satisfaction of not embarrassing myself yet again gave me a small boost of confidence, which I proceeded to utterly destroy when I said, "I'm sure you were growing tired of Lady Halsworth's exhilarating conversation."

In hindsight, I suppose I had intended to make a joke and ferret out the reason why he'd invited me, but instead, I felt like a dog for insulting Lady Halsworth and plain stupid for saying anything more.

I shrank back, flexing my fingers nervously. *Oh, how can I clear this up?*

Before I could summon some modicum of sensible dialogue, the captain laughed softly into the night. "I'm that obvious, eh?"

Stunned, I merely laughed with him.

This was going to be a long night.

Much to my surprise, the night ended far too soon. Captain Seaton's wristwatch read eleven o'clock by the time we circled back toward the servants' entrance. Though our walk was drawing to a close, I was loath to end our conversation. Within two hours, I'd uncovered the story of Captain Seaton's family—his mother and baby sister who died of scarlet fever in 1883 and his father who died in the Boer War—and his early years in the navy as a boy of twelve. Though they were unpleasant subjects, he approached them calmly, with the grace of someone who had borne the weight of death for years.

I doubted I would ever reach that state, for it was torturous to even mention my parents' deaths, though my mother had died not long after my birth and my father had been gone for three years now, having died just a year into his service. Perhaps because I had never actually opened up to anyone about them to begin with.

For the last thirty minutes or so, we had traded anecdotes about our childish dreams—his of being a jockey, mine of being a ballerina—until we returned to the topic that united us last night: settling down.

"Captain—"

"Please, Miss Tate, call me Trevor."

Well. Trevor *certainly wastes no time in dispensing with formalities.* For a brief moment, Amelie's claim that romance was brewing flashed in my mind. Why else would one stay up 'til nearly midnight talking about everything and nothing with someone they had just met?

"Trevor, what, uh, what drew you to Surrey? Of all the places in England?"

His brow knit as he released a long breath. "Well, I grew up in a small village, so the countryside is part of me, as much as the sea … but I remember how difficult it was to live so far out, so sequestered from the rest of the world. My mother and sister died because of it, because times were tough and help was miles away. But Surrey's different; it's close to London, with lively communities. And it still retains a sense of simplicity. I like that."

The way his eyes widened and his fingers flicked as he spoke betrayed him—he more than just "liked it." He had already fallen in love with Surrey and its simple but vibrant charms. I understood, and I couldn't imagine myself living anywhere else.

Even if that meant working in a fledgling manor-turned-hotel just to stay near home.

"And what about you? Why haven't you left, joined one of the Russian ballet troupes?"

Though he kept a straight face, I couldn't suppress a laugh. "Beyond a tremendous lack of talent, I just can't see myself living anywhere else but here. Surrey is … *home.*"

Trevor merely smiled.

Then, after a moment, when our feet had stilled beneath the entrance's awning, he whispered, "May I call you Meredith?"

My sleepy heart beat a bit faster. "Yes."

"May I meet with you again tomorrow night?"

My heart, now fully awake, shot up to my throat. Was I certain of this? There was no denying that Trevor Seaton was the perfect gentleman, with the traditional values and attitudes lost on many of this next generation ... but was I willing to let him become part of my chaotic, unbalanced life? Whatever *kind* of part that was?

I wasn't sure.

But I told him yes.

Chapter Six

The last week had come and gone with the speed of an automobile, and with every passing day, I had grown closer and closer to Trevor … and more and more ill at ease.

Thanks be to God, my clumsiness had abated as I learned the day-to-day routine of the Deepdene, but rather than embrace the monotony as I had at home, I was consumed by discontent. Lady Halsworth had made herself a nuisance beyond my wildest nightmares, Mr. Fothergill's quiet masquerade had been disregarded when a boisterous Sir Stallard began engaging him in every political discourse imaginable, and the hotelier seemed so displeased with my work that I doubted I'd last beyond my original two weeks.

And try as I might to be disappointed at that prospect, I wasn't. I wanted to be free of this. I wanted a future.

A future with Trevor?

Unbidden, his face, with its weathered lines and light scars and fathomless hazel eyes, flashed in my mind's eye—and just as quickly as his likeness appeared, I banished it with a frown. *A future with a man* like *Trevor.*

Despite my resolve, his admission that he'd been discharged haunted me. Unlike every other man, from Peter Griffith and my father to my uncle and my butler, Trevor couldn't leave me. At least, not for the military.

Whether anything came of Trevor Seaton's interest or not, these past few days in his company had been … wonderful. A taste of liberty the likes of which I had never known. Like a knight in shining armor, he'd rescued me from the brunt of Lady Halsworth's condescension and whisked me away from the stress of my duties each night for a walk amongst the scintillating stars and checkered snake's head blossoms. Our time together was quiet but no longer in an awkward manner. Rather, we simply enjoyed the peace and the companionship. I had a feeling that Trevor had spent most of his life amidst noise and hustle, blood and battles, rage and despair—and, no doubt, the silent, soothing peace was a more welcome reprieve than anything.

Much as it would be for me today.

I rolled my shoulders, then pressed my fingertips to my temple in a vain attempt to assuage the horrid ache echoing through my skull. The morning had begun on a high note—Lady Halsworth slept 'til noon, and breakfast and luncheon had been prepared and cleaned up after with relative ease. Then the hotelier, Mr. Dreyfus, appeared just as I was sweeping shards of a broken dish (which he wrongly assumed I had broken) to inform the kitchen that Lady Halsworth had insisted upon hosting a "formal" dinner party, complete with dancing.

Suffice to say that a disaster of a cake, tongue-twisting punch, and royal mess later, the entire staff was exhausted. As much as I longed to retire and sleep for as long as I plausibly could whilst still retaining my job, I knew I would never be able to rest until I had taken a breath, rid myself of this awful headache, and prayed.

And seen Trevor.

Not that I'd dare admit that aloud—especially not to Amelie, who had enlisted Mrs. Beech in pestering and teasing me to no end about my friendship with Captain Seaton. Or, as they claimed, my burgeoning, secret romance with him.

No, there were no butterflies or moony eyes involved in this relationship, not even if I found Trevor's gruff exterior and rare half smiles and gentle grip appealing.

Especially not then.

If nothing else, I had a friend. A "kindred spirit," so they said, in this lonely, drifting captain. He, too, had chosen duty over love and marriage, and spent every day from age twelve onward at sea, until the war ended and he was released. Oh, I was ever so grateful that I had not spent these last twenty-four years since *I* was twelve waging war at sea … but I had no doubt he was just as grateful that his prospects for a home and marriage were vastly more improved than mine. A middle-aged man of strong stature and stronger character would have no shortage of potential wives, but a spinster at the ripe old age of thirty-six?

I sighed to myself as I had every day the blasted thought entered my mind since I had surpassed twenty-five and my childhood friend Persephone Tierney, pregnant with her fourth child at the time, declared that "all hope was lost" for her "dear friend."

"Dear friend" indeed.

But as Amelie had mentioned whilst thumbing through one of Miss Lucretia Halsworth's new magazines, we were entering a new, "vogue" era. Thanks to the suffragists, women thirty or older could vote if they owned land, and because of the war, women already wore pants and had joined the workforce. They lived *and* loved whomever they wanted. The concept of a spinster was becoming a thing of the past, Amelie claimed.

Yet she was only a child at seventeen, with a beau in one of the boys at her church. She was a fine one to talk, if you asked me. And though she may enjoy the benefits of the twentieth century, some of us were still stuck in the past, living out the rest of our lives spinning yarn and crocheting baby blankets for the friends who snubbed us.

My sigh became a rueful chuckle as I donned my shawl and was swallowed into the night. These melancholic thoughts, this downward spiral of depression, was exactly why I relished Trevor's and my walks through the garden. Here, gathered under the wings of night, I was nestled in the arm of a world untouched by time, unspoiled by society and disappointment.

And truth be known, when I spun down the cobblestone pathway and Trevor's rumbling laugh echoed in the distance, even *I* felt untouched by time, like a schoolgirl walking home with the finest boy in her class. Like the world was at my fingertips, and if I reached, I could lay hold of all my dreams and unfurl them like a sail, watch them catch the wind and carry me far.

No more lonely, aimless drifting. No more painful, impatient waiting. No more silence from God. No more disappointment from men.

Just the serenade of starlight and the dance of darkness.

"Enjoying the crisp air, Meredith?" Trevor rounded a shrub and offered me his elbow.

I took in a breath, savoring the scent of gardenia and datura, as I threaded my arm around his. "Indeed, Captain."

We glided across the cobblestones and wove around the trees 'til we neared the hidden glade obscured by cherry trees and wisteria vines. This little alcove, though doubtless discovered by others in the past, was relatively unknown in the present day, so upon our finding of the thick, lush grass flanked by overgrown boxwood beyond the carefully curated flowers and shrubs, we claimed it as our own.

I disentangled my arm from Trevor's and did another girlish twirl, nearly colliding with a tree. From the corner of my eye, I glimpsed him flex his fingers and massage his knee, a telltale sign his twenty-year-old injury was flaring up on him again. If only there were something I could do to ease his pain, but alas. I had no medicine, no block of ice, no soft pillow, so I simply plopped down on the grass and urged him to sit beside me.

Once he sat and rested his leg, I lay back, sinking into the luscious grass and soaking in its cool sweetness. My eyes slid closed, and time seemed to slow, the sound of Trevor's deep breathing and the whisper of the wind fading away ...

"Meredith."

I looked up and found the sky looming above me, a million stars calling my name. No, wait; that was Trevor. Rolling onto my side, I propped myself up on an elbow and gazed at the quiet captain. The slits of moonlight that beamed through the trees gave his expression a hollow, shadowed appearance, wrinkles overpowering the curve of his brow, line of his nose, dip of his chin, curl of his mouth.

He murmured my name again, softly but serious, and I answered with a hum. It wasn't until then that I realized how close he was, how his focus was steady on my mouth, how the air between us had grown warm.

"May I court you?"

I blinked. Had I misheard? It sounded like he asked if he could kiss—I mean, *court* me.

I ...

I didn't know what to say.

My heart became an orchestra within my chest, thumping to the tempo of the Presto movement of "Summer" in Vivaldi's *The Four Seasons*, and the warm spring air began to stifle me.

Isn't this what you want, Meredith? A husband? Or at least a man interested enough in you to offer to court you?

Why, yes. Yes, it was exactly what I wanted. Almost everything I wanted.

And yet ...

My chin quivered, and I longed to look anywhere but at his patient expression and him. Something was wrong. Something was so terribly wrong, and it was within *me*, but I had no way of knowing what *it* was or how to fix it, and so I felt as awfully out of control as if it were something outside of me, outside of my power.

O God, what's wrong? What is the matter with me?

Blinking back the sharp sting of tears, I sat upright, mustering my last remaining shred of courage, and gave Trevor the most honest answer I could: "I don't know."

Chapter Seven

I had cried myself to sleep last night, muffling my sobs with my pillow and praying no one heard. This morning, on my first day off, which was supposed to be restful and rejuvenating, I dearly paid the price for wallowing in self-pity with a splitting headache that rivaled the one I'd had when I tried Papa's scotch for the first—and last—time.

My red-rimmed eyes burned, the cool spring breeze whipping hair into my face and making my sore eyes sting all the more. For the first time in the entirety of my life, I was making the two-mile walk down to my little village chapel all by myself. Most of the remainder of the staff attended St. Martin's in Dorking, but I'd always come to the ages-old barn that was the village chapel of ease since before my mother had died. With the pleasant company of my father or Benji or *anyone*, really, this trek through shady trees and dusty dirt roads had been refreshing and enjoyable.

But today?

I dreaded arriving at church. I dreaded staying at the hotel. I dreaded walking.

And yet, I kept walking, step by step by muddy step.

Trevor had asked to court me, and what had I said? I replayed my silly, stupid response over in my head for the twelve hundredth time. *I don't know, I don't know, I don't know.* And the truth was, I didn't. I didn't know why Trevor, while I treasured his newfound friendship, frightened me. I didn't know what his plans were or even what *mine* were. I didn't know what I wanted anymore.

Oh, Papa, why did you leave me?

I forced back another stream of tears as I egressed from the road through the woods, the quaint chapel coming into view. The path merged into a smooth paved road that adjoined the chapel's enchanting courtyard. I pushed aside the wrought iron gate that was always unlatched and descended the weathered, old steps to the door, then slipped inside and onto a back pew.

Services were only held here on the second and fourth Sundays of each month, since most villagers could afford to make the longer trip to the parish church now, but it was always open for prayer. As luck (or Providence, perhaps) would have it, I was the only one taking advantage of the open doors today, for the chapel, small though it was, echoed with the rasp of my breathing, shallow from my walk, and the creak of the bench beneath me. The silence gave my mind an opportunity to shriek and wail and guffaw and ramble into utter nonsense ... until I opened my Bible and started praying.

The prayer I'd begun on that fateful night Trevor stumbled upon me poured out once again, but a thread of hope tangled with the knots of fear.

"Lord, I don't know, and that's quite the long and short of it. I wish I could hear You, see You, glimpse the writing on the wall—*anything!*—to assure me of the path You have for me. Am I simply to start walking and expect to figure it out, to feel some measure of peace come over me, along the way? Or should I know what to do and where to go ahead of time, to be confident as I carry on? I don't even know if I am *supposed* to know!

"I suppose, O God, in the end, I desire to please You above all. I do not want to be outside of Your will or to make a choice that will disappoint You. Show me ... Oh, show me, Lord! Show me the way to go. Do I accept Trevor's suit? Do I pursue a relationship with him? Do I take a leap of faith? Or do I continue working at the hotel until something else comes along, or perhaps even until I die?"

The questions persisted, growing more and more specific and intimate as I went on, 'til streams of tears poured down my face and my deepest fears were laid at the altar, before the feet of Jesus.

The fear of being rejected ...

The fear of missing what God had for me ...

The fear of hurting someone else ...

The fear of losing what little I had ...

The fear of being lost and aimless and searching and discontent forever ...

The fear of settling for what I did not truly desire …
The fear of desiring things God did not want me to desire …
And the fear of being alone again, no matter what I did.
All this, I mused as my thoughts trailed off and my tongue stilled, *because of a house.*

Trevor could not wait on Meredith for this task, even though his heart urged him to. No, she might never make up her mind, never accept him, never choose him once she knew what she'd be getting in him.

And so, his head won out against his heart's eye-rolling and scoffing, and Trevor bought Ackford Hall, with its dilapidated exterior and empty interior … and the sound of laughter in the walls and tearstains in the garden and love all around.

He never would have thought, during all those adventurous years at sea, that he'd be thanking God for overgrown gardens and chipped birdbaths and peeling shutters and faded paint. Then again, he never would have thought, during those first thirty-seven years in the navy, that he would endure the … incident … that rendered him discharged.

Now the image of him sitting back on a soft, leather chair and indulging in a newspaper while a child or two played at his feet and Meredith—

And Meredith.

Trevor's mouth crimped in a frown. He would complete that illustration later, when he had some idea where, if at all, Meredith fit into the picture.

Mr. O'Rourke, good man that he was, had sensed Trevor's anxiety to purchase the house before it was officially put on the market, and had brought the papers with him to St. Martin's for them to go over after service. Trevor now had them signed, sealed, and tucked beneath his arm—the deed to Ackford Hall and the bill of sale from the bank to him—as he strode into his room at Deepdene.

He tossed his suit coat onto his bed and locked the papers away in the bottom of his chest. In the back of his mind, doubts niggled— that Meredith would never want him, and no other woman besides. That even if Meredith *did* decide to court him after she learned the truth behind his discharge, behind *himself*, she would never want the house and all the work it needed.

That nothing, not even throwing away his old life as he had his jacket and settling into something entirely new, could save him.

His eyes drifted shut, blocking out the sight of his rumpled bed, so much akin to his bunk aboard the HMS *Mercy* in shade and form, and granting himself access to only one thought, one truth, above all the lies. *God, my God, I put my trust in You. You alone have the power to heal me.*

And heal him He would, in some way or another.

Chapter Eight

Peace came like a river, gentle and slow. I raised my head, and my neck popped as my eyes scoured the fore of the chapel: the cross mounted on the wall, the altar before the pulpit, the candelabras hedging both in. Light from the windows at my right floated in on a shimmering cloud of dust, illuminating the pews and alerting me to the time.

When I rose from my seat and peeked out the door, the sun at high noon confirmed that I'd been praying for more than two hours.

Yet that was all it took to uncouple all my burdens from my back and surrender them to God.

As I left the chapel and slipped into the shrouded forest for my return trip, I lifted my voice to sing the old, lovely hymns they had no doubt sung at St. Martin's, for the Lord duly deserved every note of praise. Though I had wandered, He had not left me. Though I had doubted, He remained faithful. Though I was uncertain, He was confident.

And He was in control.

I shivered against a fresh wave of goosebumps skittering over my arms, the refrains of "'Tis So Sweet to Trust in Jesus " on my lips and the words of Psalms 139:5 on my mind. I so longed to know every detail and be in control of every decision, but *God* was my vision and on Him I would meditate, not my future or my present or my past. Only God's faithfulness through it all.

'Tis indeed so sweet to trust in Jesus! To rest assured that His promises will be fulfilled and that He will go before me, behind me, and on all sides.

Thank You, Father God.

The walk back to the Deepdene seemed but only a few minutes, and when I returned, rather than groan at the sight of my temporary workplace, I savored its beauty and splendor. The sun, unusually bright today, arrayed the gardens in a sheen of golden glitter and set the manor agleam. From the back path I'd taken, I could see carriages and an automobile tucked away in the carriage house, proof that the guests had returned from church. However, not a soul was among the gardens, despite the gentle spring breeze and warm, effulgent sun.

Not a soul, that was, except for the one bent over, legs twisted and head bowed, by the water fountain.

The man was in obvious pain, and as I dashed closer, the shadows peeled back, and I could see the lines of Trevor's broad shoulders and hear his labored breath. He appeared as though he'd been in a fight, and yet there was not a mark on him. Only a thick layer of sweat on his forehead, matting his hair in place, dark crescents rimming his eyes, and reddened knuckles.

O Lord, what's happened?

"Trevor!" His name cracked on my lips, and tears and panic ignited within me. Why had he thrown himself over the fountain? Why did he look like he'd wrestled a demon? Why …

Why didn't he answer me when I called to him? Instead, he slumped onto his haunches, resting his head against the fountain's edge, and mumbled over and over again, "Mercy, have mercy."

I dropped down beside him, and when I cupped his jaw and pulled his face toward me, I knew. I had seen this before, after all.

And, just like in those days when wounded soldiers thrashed against their cots, clutched their missing limbs, and screamed bloody murder all throughout the night, there was nothing I could do.

I simply dragged his leaden arms away from the fountain and tugged his head down, tucking it against my breast and holding him close. He trembled violently beneath my grip, but I held fast, praying softly in his ear and rubbing circles on his back.

Minutes could have slogged by, or perhaps hours flew, before his panting became long, shuddering breaths; his shaking reduced to a small twitch in his neck; and he cried out softly to God, his words muffled against me. His hands stole around me, and he clutched me to him, fingers lost in the folds of my dress. The tighter he held me, though I could've sworn he popped my back, the calmer he grew, 'til at last he lifted his head, his rough jaw brushing against my shoulder.

His eyes were bruised and glazed-over until they met mine, and as he blinked, they cleared. "O God, thank You for Meredith."

A smile threatened to appear. *Thank God indeed.*

His hand raised, and his thumb gently traced the curve of my cheek, meeting with a tear I'd not realized had fallen. "I don't deserve you," he whispered, his voice thick with anguish.

"No, I don't deserve *you*, Trevor. I'm a selfish woman who doesn't know her own self, yet you would have me—"

"No."

The hard answer physically drew me back. No ... what? No, he wouldn't have me? No, I wasn't selfish?

"You deserve someone, Meredith, who won't come to you broken and dead inside, but who could give you life." Then his hand fell, and he clenched it into a fist. "See? This ... this is why I was discharged. Not because of a physical wound but a mental one. I-I couldn't perform my duties any longer without breaking down a-and weeping. I couldn't sleep without being awoken by terrors. My mind's broken. My spirit's dead. How could you say yes to a man like that?"

Chapter Nine

The look in Trevor's eyes will haunt me for the remainder of my days—fear, regret, anger, disappointment, bitterness, and agony swirling like a dark and dangerous whirlpool. To think, every morning he awoke and every night he fell asleep lost in the same whirlpool. This ... this was his life.

The thought made me shudder, and when I did, Trevor drew back, casting those lost eyes down as though I were disgusted by him.

But he was wrong. Oh so wrong.

"I understand, Meredith. And I respect your decision. You ... you needn't feel sorry for me. I—"

Before the fool man could get swept away deeper in his tirade, I seized his face and kissed him, hopefully hard enough to silence his self-pity and help him *truly* understand how I felt.

Perhaps I was too hard.

When his firm mouth didn't move beneath mine and his body became stone, I tipped my head back and whispered against him, "Trevor Seaton, I am not ashamed of you. I *want* you. You, and every broken piece that comes with you. Nothing else. No one else." My hand slid to the nape of his neck, my fingers tangling themselves in his hair, and I leaned in once again to press a softer kiss to the corner of his mouth. "I've spent my entire life praying for a future, for a man who loves me and whom I love in return, and I'm willing to fight every demon that plagues you for that. So don't you dare feel unloved or unworthy. You are *beyond* worthy of my love and my life, for Christ has already given His for you." I kissed him again, this time behind his ear, lowering my voice to a murmur. "My answer is yes, Trevor. Yes, you may court me."

At last, I fell silent and rested my face against his, turning all the jumbled words in my mind into prayers.

This man was an answer to twenty years of prayers. He was the man God had been keeping me for, turning aside the Peter Griffiths and rearranging my life to bring me to Trevor. I had not realized it until those hours spent at church this morning, but it was clear now. I couldn't let him go.

Lord only knew what might be in store for us, through a courtship at a hotel to … well, whatever it was He had planned. Whether it be a quiet life in the country with a few children or a life spent battling the war in Trevor's mind, God would go before us and prepare the way. And He would carry us through.

Something rough but gentle caressed my face, calloused fingers stroking my cheek and playing with wisps of hair. Trevor tilted my chin and met my eyes, his at long last lucid and sparkling with hope. "Thank you," he said, his voice husky and warm. Then he kissed me, his touch soft but hungry, exploring yet anchoring. Unknown and unlike anything I'd ever experienced … yet *home*.

"So …" Amelie's cheery voice drew the word out in a singsong. "How are you and the captain?" She waggled her eyebrows as she handed me another dish to dry.

I had senselessly thought that our courtship had been unbeknownst to the guests and staff alike, as we met under the cover of night, when the manor shook with snores and was silent with slumber. Obviously not, for Amelie knew *everything*. Even what was not meant to be known.

As for whether or not I could trust her with the knowledge that a staff member was courting a guest, I was still unsure.

If only I could play dumb.

"We're fine," I lilted back, eliciting a giggle from her and hopefully, just hopefully, avoiding too many questions.

The truth was, though, Trevor and I were more than fine. These past two weeks had been, for lack of a better word, magical. There were no flowers and chocolates or romantic dinners and dancing, as Amelie had with her boyfriend. Rather, we had long talks about our deepest hopes and fears, faith and politics, his experiences during the navy and mine at home, and our families. To Amelie, boring conversation would be the dullest courtship imaginable, but to me, it was exhilarating. Sharing my heart with someone who not only cared but understood and shared his in return … exploring a love like a gentle tide that swept me into a life I'd only ever dreamed of … and growing through prayer, discussing the Word together, and, yes, even working through Trevor's breakdowns. What more could I ask for?

To think, after all this time, God had been preserving us for each other—the hard navy captain and the country lass—and fostering within our hearts a singular desire: to create a home that honored God. And soon, that desire would be realized. Trevor had yet to propose or provide a time-line for when he would, but he had spoken of the home he was having repaired and promised to show me on my next day off. Truth be told, he was still nervous about moving forward, and I didn't blame him, for we had only known each other three weeks, but I sensed that once he had my approval of the house he had purchased, most of that nervousness would dissipate.

At least, I knew most of *my* anxiety would. I so yearned to be gone from the Deepdene, not because my experiences here had been unpleasant but because leaving would mean being with Trevor and starting our new life, no longer lost in this limbo between maid and married.

And tomorrow was the day.

Another wet dish was shoved into my hands, and I blinked out of my thoughts to find Amelie snickering. "Oh, just 'fine'? The expression on your face looks more like 'madly in love' to me!" She clapped her hands and bounced on her toes.

I speared her with the glare my father used to give me whenever I persisted in asking for something he'd already said no to. "The expression on *your* face looks like 'guilty of snooping' to me."

She sighed and let her cheeky grin simmer out, although her eyes still bubbled with mischief. "Why, I haven't snooped the teeniest bit. If I had, I'd know if he's kissed you yet."

Oh, now she had gone too far.

Biting back a smile, I flicked my dish towel at her arm, and she jumped back with a shriek—though I doubted it hurt. She quickly recovered and retaliated with a splash of dishwater at my face, which *I* jumped at and wiped off with my towel.

Her smirk returned in full force, and she poised herself to splash me again. "Tell me all the details, or the uniform gets it."

Technically, my apron would take the brunt of the water, but I still conceded, lest we end up making a mess and disturbing the rest of the kitchen staff with our childish antics. "Very well, I'll tell you, but let's get back to the dishes, hmm?" With a hand on her shoulder, I turned her to the sink.

"Yes, Mummy." She dunked her hands in the water and began scrubbing at the plates and saucers from breakfast.

As we resumed our process of washing and drying and stacking, I related to Amelie what details I could without divulging everything or hinting at Trevor's struggles. Perhaps discussing it with her could take my mind off of how slowly this day dragged by and how far away tomorrow felt.

When I had left my father's house, I brought only what remained in my possession—my mother's Bible, a few knickknacks in the false bottom of my trunk, and several faded and outdated dresses. The newest, nicest dress I'd owned had been purchased before the war, so one could imagine what I was left with by now. A dress that was frayed at the hem and stained with dirt at the sleeve cuffs. One that was so faded it was an unbecoming pallid yellow. Another that was so old it could hang in a museum.

Wearing these ugly things or my uniform to cook, clean, and walk under the cover of night was one thing. Wearing them on a day outing with my beau was another.

A fit of womanly displeasure, something I'd had no cause to feel these last few years, seized me, and I stuffed all the dresses back in my trunk and locked it shut.

As the lid thudded and the locks snapped, another heavy sound echoed behind me, and I turned to see one of the upstairs maids entering the sleeping quarters. She was perhaps a few years my junior, her hair luminous and skin clear, though the definition of her facial features and figure bespoke age and maturity. I recognized her but could not remember her name.

"Meredith, right?"

Apparently, she was much more proficient with names than I was.

"Yes. I apologize, I'm wretched at recalling names."

"I'm Sadie." She dipped her head a measure. "Were you dressing? I'm sorry if I interrupted."

"Oh, well. I *was*, but suffice to say, I haven't a thing to wear." I gave a rueful chuckle, though I inwardly cringed at how girlish that sounded. "You know how it is."

Sadie laughed, walking over to her cot and the large wooden chest beside it. "Indeed I do." She opened the trunk and withdrew a lovely, moss-green dress that had to be brand-new. The hemline was higher than any dress I'd ever worn, falling several inches above Sadie's ankles when she held it up, and the neckline was in a flattering *v* shape. "We look about the same size," she said, thrusting the dress toward me. "Here, try this on, and if it fits, you must wear it! I think this shade would complement you perfectly."

Oh. *Oh.* My mind stalled like the engine of an automobile, even as my hands reached to accept the dress. Once I held it, its soft fabric flowing through my fingers like water. "Why, I … I couldn't, Sadie! This dress is positively gorgeous."

"Exactly! I'd rather you be able to enjoy it than it sit and deteriorate in my trunk until it's years out of style. So, please, try it on and wear it." She shooed me behind the dressing screen with the wave of her hands.

As I slipped into the dress and smoothed its fitted material over my hips, my displeasure and frustration faded away. Once again,

God had my back—even in the small things, like a nice dress. *Oh, why do I ever doubt You, Lord?*

Trevor paced back and forth across the portico, waves of nervous energy tossing inside him. These last two weeks had felt like two *years* as he awaited the completion of the repairs on Ackford Hall and, subsequently, the day he could take Meredith to see it. Although he was impatient and a bit annoyed, he couldn't fully begrudge the feeling of anticipation, for he had never been so consumed by excitement in his life. Life at sea had been thrilling and adventurous, but not like this. Not in a way that brought him pure joy and, besides the aforementioned nervousness, *peace.*

It was all he could do to keep his mind focused on praying that Meredith would love Ackford Hall as much as he did, and when he heard light footfalls behind him, he welcomed the interruption, pivoting on his heel to see who approached.

Halting, the tumult within him immediately dying down, as he took in the sight before him.

Meredith had shed her apron, her cap, her oversized, patched coat, and stood before him in total radiance, like the morning sun setting the ocean ablaze. Her green dress hugged her curves and deepened the shimmers of red and gold in her strawberry-blonde hair, which had been curled and piled onto the top of her head, a few ringlets framing her face. She needed no further adornment, her natural beauty already as bright as the sunrise and just as beloved after a long night of darkness.

What did I do to deserve such a magnificent young woman?

After staring at her with his mouth agape like a dumb donkey for a good few minutes, Trevor surged forward, took her chin by his thumb and forefinger, and tasted her rosebud lips. She melted into his arms and returned his kiss with the pure passion he had come to crave, her fingers finding their rightful place in his hair.

At the sound of an automobile engine rattling just below them, she pulled away, her face charmingly pink, and he reluctantly turned to take her arm and lead her down the steps. He helped her into the automobile, and they were off.

As they rounded the corner and crossed onto the main road, Meredith sidled up next to him, her hip against his and her hemline grazing his trousers. "So," she began, a sprightly twinkle in her eyes and mischief in her voice, "aren't you going to tell me where we're going?" She beamed up at him and batted her eyelashes like an adorable but harmless little minx.

"Haven't I? We're going to see my house." He patted her knee and gave her a mischievous smile of his own.

She scoffed, and for the next ten minutes, she attempted to weasel their destination out of him, even going so far as to employ a few lethal kisses. For what it was worth, had she kept her focus on the roads they traveled, she doubtlessly would have deduced the location of the house, as she had previously lived in this area—but he wasn't about to turn down having her attention all to himself.

Just as the road curved into a rocky driveway and the trees around them gave way to trimmed shrubbery, Trevor leaned in and whispered in her ear, "I'll tell you," then captured her mouth with his.

The automobile shuddered to a halt, and I forced myself to pull away from Trevor. Of course that devious man had promised to tell me where we were headed only for us to arrive there a moment later—not that I would complain about his chosen method of distraction. Breathless, I detangled myself from his arms and, in my signature style, nearly fell over my own limbs as I scrambled to debark from the automobile. For once, I did *not* land on my face on the muddy road …

But I did fall to my knees when I caught sight of the house.

Chapter Ten

The morning sunlight made the brick path glisten like wine, set the dewy grass to sparkling like diamonds, and illuminated the fresh paint that covered the exterior walls and window shutters like a gorgeous new gown.

I could not believe my eyes. I ran my fingers through the lawn I'd collected beetles from as a child, and I still could not believe it. Rising from my knees, I traced the lines of the wooden picket fence I had painted alongside Sergeant McCrary and Lieutenant Payton, and I still could not believe it. Crossing the pathway, I caressed the petals of Mr. Halloway's prized roses, and I still could not believe it.

I was *home*.

O God, You brought me home.

My hands began to tremble as I pressed my palms to my eyes, damming the river of tears that rushed down my face. After all my struggles, all my grief, all my doubt, God had brought me home. This entire time, He had been orchestrating everything to restore my childhood home and lead me back to it.

Now, instead of it wasting away under the management of a penniless owner, it was flourishing. The scraggly weeds and lackluster plants had been replaced with vivacious flowers and fresh soil; all signs of death and decay had vanished, and in their place was the beauty of new life.

The heavy thumps of Trevor's boots sounded behind me, and a moment later, a firm but gentle hand came to rest on my shoulder. "Meredith." His voice was a low murmur brimming with concern. "What's wrong?"

I turned into him, then wrapped my arms around his waist and buried my head against his chest. Words eluded me, for there were none that could adequately express all the gratitude and love within my heart—and even if there were, I could not voice them through the sobs that pushed forth.

Rather than ask again, Trevor merely held me tighter, and for what felt like hours, we stood enveloped in each other's embrace on the path to *our* home.

One Year Later

I trimmed back the stems of the flower I'd just brought in from garden and plucked off a few leaves, then arranged the primroses and forget-me-nots with the ferns in my mother's crystal vase and set it on the breakfast table. The sunlight streaming in from the bay window caught in the vase and scattered rainbows among the flowers and across the table.

After turning back to the window, I retrieved the loaf of bread I'd left to cool and cut a few slices for breakfast, along with some cheese and the berries we'd picked last night. As I began setting the plates on the table, a soft crooning entered my earshot, and before I could look over my shoulder, a strong arm snaked around my waist.

"How's my favorite girl?" my husband whispered into my ear, peppering kisses across my jawline.

A sigh escaped my mouth and became a moan as his lips met the hollow of my throat. "She's hungry." I stepped toward the table. "For breakfast."

He chuckled, and the crooning began again. I turned to see the bundle of joyful gurgling tucked into his papa's other arm. "And how are my favorite boys?" I traced the curve of little George Tate Seaton's cheek, savoring the feel of my son's smooth skin.

"Happy to see Mummy," Trevor said as he shifted Georgie against his chest and pulled out my chair.

I sat and accepted Georgie from him, cradling the precious two-month-old as his papa took the seat beside us. He held my hand and let his son curl his tiny fingers around his thumb. Then Trevor blessed the food God had provided ... the home He'd preserved for us ... and the family He had so graciously prepared for us to create, even before the foundation of the earth.

I didn't deserve any of this, and for years I doubted I would ever have it—and yet, my Heavenly Father, in His immense love and grace, had led my restless heart to a home more marvelous than I could've ever imagined.

A Note from Grace A. Johnson

I didn't realize until I was halfway through with this story that it isn't Meredith's—it's mine. I'm in a stage of transition, like so many people, where I have dreams but no plans. Aspirations but no resources. Hope but no substance.

Maybe you're in the same stage. If so, I pray you learn the same lesson Meredith and I have learned: faith is the substance of things hoped for. When we put our faith in God and surrender our dreams to Him, He will give us something to hold on to, and He will lead our wandering hearts somewhere more wonderful than we could ever imagine.

A special thanks goes to Saraina and Issabelle, my lovely alpha readers who gave me faith in this story, and Kellyn, who never gave up on me through many missed deadlines and dumb questions.

All the glory to God our Father.

The Tussie-
Mussie

a novella by Katja H. Labonté

Chapter One

*"What you do in this world is a matter of no consequence. ... The
question is, what can you make people believe that you have done."*
A Study in Scarlet by Sir Arthur Conan Doyle

Spring 1903

As all England debated the depth of her sin, Miss Caitrìona Roylett
was headed for Surrey on the early morning train, accompanied only
by her chaperone.

It would have been difficult for her companions of last Saturday
to recognise her now. Then she had been the merry, young Miss
Roylett, promenading on Lord Saxford's arm in her embroidered,
ivory-cream silk—the dress that was the talk of every woman in
town and the obvious envy of her rival. That straight-backed, clear-
toned, confident Miss Roylett so lauded last week could hardly be
compared to the low-voiced, shrinking woman she was now, hidden
beneath a dull black outfit and thick veil.

For Caitrìona was returning home in a spirit of shame and self-
hatred that her worst enemies could not have wished stronger. Ugly
whispers threaded their way around her soul, squeezing ever tighter
like the deadly pythons they were.

She is only a merchant's daughter, you know.

*Rather a pretty face, but of course no money—not at all the
marriageable type.*

*Oh, her looks have been greatly overestimated. She is quite
plain, I assure you.*

Caitrìona stifled a sigh. It was raining, and the world outside seemed as heartsick as she. What future could there be for a woman despised and rejected?

"It really is *most* unbelievable," a female voice emphasized suddenly.

Caitrìona started and looked round. The train was nearly empty, and she quickly discovered the speaker. On the seat before her sat two young ladies, evidently twins, both absorbed in a paper and clad in deep mourning.

"It simply doesn't fit his character *at all*," the speaking twin continued. "He is evidently a very modest, bashful young man. That is not the character of the fellow who broke into Lady Hilda's."

Caitrìona perked up her ears at once. Of course these girls were talking of Duscan—little else was discussed in London just now. And their most cordial opinion gladdened her. It was so very evident that Duscan was not the type to burglarize—but Scotland Yard was not interested in her protests concerning her brother's personality.

"True," responded the other girl. "I am not certain about Miss Roylett, however. In fact, I am inclined to suspect *her* far more than Mr. Roylett. She seems much more of the calculating type—witness her strategic entry into society—and she is evidently excellent in social occurrences—she adapted surprisingly well for a woman of her background. She seems a rather cool, not to say cold-blooded, person."

"Yes ... and she seems somewhat ... *searching*," said the first twin, slowly, her eyes wandering to the window. "As though she were on a quest for something and would not rest until she found it ..."

Caitrìona shrank back involuntarily. The second girl's keen words did not trouble her; she had heard it all before, in the last week. But the first twin—she had read a part of Caitrìona that was buried scrupulously beneath the surface.

For Caitrìona *was* on a quest.

A quest for the perfect man.

She had no intention of wasting her whole life away in her little Surrey village. She wanted a worthwhile life, championing causes and making ripples in the world. To do this, she must enter society and climb the ranks, and thus she must marry well.

But there was a nobler side to her goal. Her family *needed* the money. Duscan's education and allowance was paid by his godfather, the late Colonel Edward Duscan; but Amy, Lucy, Caitrìona, and their mother existed on the diminutive income derived from the investments their father had made before his death. Although Caitrìona would never have breathed word of it to a living soul, she was forced to acknowledge they were not as well off as even Mr. Nowan, the yeomen whose large farm sprawled near the Royletts' cottage. Irrational as it might be, it was a constant source of fear to Caitrìona that something should end their income, forcing her mother to the poorhouse and her sisters to the factories. At least *one* of them, as in the case of the immortal March sisters, *must* marry well. Amy was too young and Lucy too sickly; therefore, Caitrìona accepted the burden she had placed on herself and spent years scheming for ways to find a good match.

Here was a splendid example of the cold-blooded calculation she was accused of.

"Are you all right, Cat dear?"

A gentle hand patted her shoulder. Caitrìona summoned up a wan smile. She had forgotten about Mrs. Beckham. Her dear friend and chaperone had endured a great deal of anxiety during the last week over Duscan, and Caitrìona had no intention of allowing her to fret over Caitrìona herself.

"Yes, of course," she said, striving to keep an even voice.

"Would it disturb you if I went up carriage?" Mrs. Beckham asked eagerly. "Mrs. Van Astelyne is here, and I should rather like to speak to her before she returns to America."

"Not at all, ma'am."

"Thank you, dear. I shall leave you to your rest. Do let me know if you are in need of anything."

Caitrìona contented herself with a smile and a nod as Mrs. Beckham rustled away. How much Caitrìona owed that good friend! She had never expected the chance to enter society, let alone London society; and the Beckhams' offer to take her up for the Season at their own expense, furnishing her with an entire wardrobe, had been such stuff as wild dreams were made of. Mother, ever reluctant to borrow, had not approved, but Caitrìona had accepted. During the next month, the celebrated phrase *the end justifies the means* became her buckler to deflect all arrows of conscience. The Beckhams were well-off and able to afford it; she would pay them back every cent as soon as she were married, and always remain their firmest friend …

Yet notwithstanding the soothing promises she made to herself, her

London enjoyment had never lacked a sting of discomfort over her borrowed plumes, unlike the famed jackdaw.

Sighing, Caitrìona brushed a hand over her gored, black skirt. After months of elegant clothing, it was galling to return to the severe dresses and hats of a decade past. To be sure, the Beckhams had made it clear she was to keep the wardrobe they had provided her with, but she'd insisted she would not wear those clothes before Mother. In her heart, though, Caitrìona knew the truth. She did not wish to wear those dresses because they reminded her of the debt she owed the Beckhams.

The debt she now had no method of repaying.

She had been so near the goal. Lord Saxford was remarkably taken in by her and very attentive in spite of the obvious jealousy of the other women—notably Lady Amelia Harlow, who had been Caitrìona's manifest rival since the two girls had first met last November. What was most vexing was the knowledge that Lord Saxford had been on the very brink of proposing and was only held back by unforeseen interruptions. Caitrìona had been pleased with her conquest. He was a pleasant man, already interested in her family's plight, and she would receive no difficulties from him in her projects both for her family and, later, in taking up various public causes.

But Lord Saxford had most certainly heard of the scandal by now, and despite Caitrìona's slight hopes, he had not rushed over to hear the story from her own lips or declare his undying affection. She had an uncomfortable sensation of having wasted her time and attention on a worthless … *fellow*. He did not count as a *man* any longer for her. A *man* would have given her a chance to explain, asked for the truth, helped to conclusively prove Duscan's and Caitrìona's innocence.

But he had failed her. And now she was leaving London on this miserable April morning, several weeks before the end of the Season, in ignominy.

Another ugly python of a whisper wrapped around her, hissing insidiously in her mind. *One of those silly girls who believe they are handsome enough to need only appear once to score a brilliant match, of course. A little fool, that's what she is, if you ask me.*

Lady Amelia's mother had spoken those words, and they stung all the more deep because of how true they seemed. Yes, Caitrìona was, after all, a little fool. And probably a *very* plain one in the bargain.

Caitrìona closed her eyes, willing the tears to remain unshed.

Measured footsteps came up the train, and a gentleman's calm, incisive voice spoke at her shoulder. "Excuse me, miss."

Caitrìona shook the tears from her cheeks quickly, and cautiously raised her head towards the stranger. Please God, the veil would muffle her features enough to preserve her anonymity …

"Miss?"

The gentleman standing in the aisle at her side was young, and clad in a Norfolk jacket and knickerbockers. His mouth was firm and his chin determined, but the kindness in his eyes was prepossessing.

He caught her gaze and smiled. "I beg your pardon for disturbing you, but I wonder if you might be able to help me. You are heading to Surrey, I presume? I am bound for a village near Guildford myself. May I be so bold as to ask, miss, if you are *from* Surrey and know anything about that locality?"

"I—no, I am afraid not …" This young man did not seem the type to pack up and head for the country for a week's shooting without preparation. What motive could he possibly have in asking her this? Irrational fear suddenly spiked in her heart. Did he suspect who she was? Was he trying to ascertain her identity? *O Lord, let me not be discovered* … She searched his face, but his expression remained ingenuous.

"My sisters elected to come down themselves, and we have decided to stop together; but the village I had in mind would not be quite suitable for ladies—the only inn is rather too rough; might we presume upon asking if you know of any other good inn thereabouts?"

Caitrìona drew in a sigh of relief. "I am afraid I am not familiar with Guildford and the surroundings. I have never been there. Nor am I well acquainted with any inns thereabouts."

"Thank you, miss. And I beg your pardon again for disturbing you." He doffed his hat and went up the carriage.

Caitrìona breathed a prayer of thanks and turned back to her window, only to discover the train was just pulling into the little country station that lay a few miles from her village. Far before she was ready.

God help me.

To face Mother and her sisters and go over with them the dreadful news that Duscan was imprisoned with that ridiculous charge of stealing Lady Garrett's tiara, and that Caitrìona herself was under suspicion and banned from society—well—for five minutes, as Mrs. Beckham's and Caitrìona's luggage was carted off the train, Caitrìona seriously considered whisking off to Brighton and starting a new life in a small room in the home of a respectable but down-in-the-world old widow, with a spirit lamp to cook eggs and bacon, and a simple job where she could find opportunity to do some heroic deed that restored her to public favour and freed her brother.

These lofty and implausible ideas were dashed by a clear, childish voice suddenly crying, "Cat—oh, Cat!" And the next moment, Amy hurtled herself against Caitrìona for a rapturous embrace.

"Oh, Cat, you're home! Where are your pretty dresses? Did you have a fine time? How were the ballrooms? Did you see the Queen? Or Mr. Sherlock Holmes?"

"Mr. Holmes lives in The Downs now," Caitrìona murmured, dazed by this flow of questions and unwilling to answer the first two.

But Amy was already rushing off again, not awaiting any response. "You'll be able to wear your pretty dresses again quite soon, Cat, for Mr. Stanhope is inviting everyone to a celebration. Miss Stanhope is betrothed!"

Dull pain throbbed in Caitrìona's temples. Miss Stanhope was a confirmed spinster with a small dowry and no societal experience, yet *she* had already made a match. Why had Caitrìona failed?

"How simply delightful!" Mrs. Beckham said as she took Amy's hand.

"Yes, and you are invited too, ma'am, and so is Mr. Beckham—where *is* he?"

Caitrìona was too weary to rebuke Amy's curiosity, but Mrs. Beckham only smiled. "He stayed in London, dear," she answered.

Caitrìona winced. The Beckhams had been so understanding throughout all this terrible week. When that first horrible rumour began, Mrs. Beckham had immediately offered to take her home, though it upset all their plans, and Mr. Beckham had supported the decision vigorously although it would cause him much inconvenience in his business. And when Caitrìona had found only a retreat to the country could save her from the misery London held for her, they had suggested the early-morning flight and would not hear of letting her run any risk of more malicious gossip by taking a later, more frequented train.

"Did you have a good trip?" Amy asked eagerly.

"That we did," Mrs. Beckham replied as they approached the carriage. The servant leaped down from the seat, then raised his cap with a welcoming grin.

"How do you do, Tom?" Mrs. Beckham greeted him. "And how are Nancy and the little ones?"

"Right as rain, mum, and glad t' be seeing ye again," the man replied heartily. He helped the two ladies into the carriage, then lifted Amy in and assisted the porter with the luggage. Amy, tucking herself between Mrs. Beckham and Caitrìona, chatted on. Mrs. Beckham attended closely to every word, but Caitrìona leaned back on her seat and closed her eyes. She had a terrible headache, and in spite of being home, she felt lonelier and more miserable than before.

Her London Season had been a spectacular disaster, and she had come home in all the glory of it, with her goals and dreams tumbling about her ears.

Chapter Two

"What use is [my life] to anyone?"
"The example of patient suffering is in itself the most precious of all
lessons to an impatient world."
The Adventure of the Veiled Lodger by Sir Arthur Conan Doyle

It was a grey, drizzly morning, and Ewart Alinac hated those mornings.

Groaning, he threw down his pen and stretched back on his chair, dropping his gaze from the window to his desk. A splendid coincidence. His eyes now rested on the flowing, flawless script of Lady Margaret Kissel ... his mother.

He had no need of reading the letter again. The cool words were branded in his memory.

> *Marguerite shall come up next winter and enter*
> *Madame Guenot's Seminary for Young Females. She*
> *must have proper training and preparation with a*
> *good governess this year. You have let her run wild*
> *and bothered yourself not at all concerning her*
> *education, but that is ended. She shall come out in the*
> *1908 season. Lord Anthony Harlow will be ready*
> *then, and the wedding date has been chosen.*

He knew his mother did not care for him—never had cared for him—but every fresh proof was like a living coal held to his heart. At any rate, he thought the pain must be *somewhat* equivalent, though he had never tried the experiment. But Lady Kissel's callousness towards Maggie now was a new source of agony.

Foppish Lord Anthony Harlow, whose fate had so summarily been decided, was a weak, amiable youth, fully controlled by his ambitious mother and avaricious friends. The alliance proposed by Lady Margaret Kissel and Lady Charlotte Harlow tended only to their own aggrandizement. A union between Lady Kissel's only daughter and Lady Harlow's only son would be a marriage of money and status that made a great impression at court and went far to usher the ladies to their ultimate goal: the coveted private friendship of Queen Alexandra.

Ewart scowled as he tossed his pen in the air. The thought of his little sister trapped in such a farce of a union made his blood boil. After his father's death, his mother had abandoned both Maggie and him, relocating to London, where she quickly found herself a new and much more desirable husband. For eleven years, Lady Kissel had fully ignored her children, having no intention of burdening herself with them; but now Maggie was old enough to be useful to her mother, and so the callous letter had been written and sent, ordering the girl prepared for the destiny placed upon her.

Ewart had no intention of letting Maggie be sacrificed any more than she had already been on the altar of her mother's ambition, let alone abandoning her into a loveless marriage at such a tender age— and yet what could he do? He could not hide her, nor take her away, nor forbid his mother from any action she might take. He could only try to support Maggie in her miserable new position and strive to keep her from becoming as the other silly, malicious women teeming in London society—and that in itself was a tremendous obstacle, for how could he possibly live in London?

Living in London.

For one delicious moment, Ewart dreamed of the possibility, forgetting even his sister's danger in the wonderful fancies he had built so long ago. London had always been the seat of his ambition—not for the sake of fame or fortune, but to mix with the populace, to rub shoulders with other men, to hear different opinions and study other perspectives, to grow and expand and *live*. The countryside was sweet and lovely and filled with delightful souls, but the metropolis—ah, *there* he would find the experience and knowledge he craved.

You will never do anything worthwhile, and certainly never enter society. No one will wish to know you. You will only find yourself despised.

The words, uttered with such calm indifference by his mother that brilliant autumn day long ago, had echoed through his mind for twenty years, and were still as mockingly painful now as they had been then to his eight-year-old self. They were the words that had pursued him day and night, prompting him to study under the old vicar instead of entering the boys' school nearby. They were the words that had kept him penned up within his own property, barring long, solitary rides over the countryside and his venture to the village church every Lord's Day.

They pounded in his brain at night and hung heavy over him in daylight as he watched the world from behind his windows. They had him shrinking passionately from contact with any save the old friends he knew and trusted. They were the words which moved him to write, write, write, pouring out his mind and soul on the white pages that accepted him and listened to him and would someday go throughout the world and move it as he could never do himself.

They were the words that chilled his fervour and paralysed him with inability whenever he tried anything.

Unmanly, his father had sneered when alive. *Timid*, the country boys chuckled. *Weird,* old wives whispered ominously. *A bit of a milksop*, gentlemen explained with polite succinctness to each other.

Likely enough, he was all of those things.

Ewart took up his pen again, then threw it down and rose. Writing was not easy today. It never was on rainy days. Which, as he lived in southern England and not in South America, was more often than not. Had the sun the delightful propensities it bore in the tropics, Ewart's manuscripts would be thrice as large and at least four times multiplied.

It was quite unfortunate he didn't live in some place such as, say, California. *There* life was more of a fight than an easy walk as it was here—at least, it *might* be, although in this year of grace 1903, it was probable that his romantic ideas of California were quite inaccurate. Well! Perhaps California had been improved into civilization now. But any other sunny, wild place would do, and—to return to his original thought—*there* he would be forced by sheer necessity to find motivation, discipline, courage. *Here* it was too easy to be a coward—although God Himself could bear witness to how Ewart's life was already anything but easy. To be sure, the whole village knew too … but only the Almighty saw the whole extent of Ewart's struggles.

That would be one disadvantage to London. As much as Ewart longed for the city, he was forced to admit that writing would be difficult to pursue in a place that never stood still. There would be too many living stories vying for his attention. Even now, the developing mystery of the football player and society belle duo that filled the papers distracted him dreadfully. There was so much fascination in those principal characters, Mr. and Miss Royal, or whatever their name was … how could he ignore the siren song of *that* dramatic tale?

Suddenly the study door flung open with a crash, and Maggie rushed into the room, her face alight with eagerness. "Ewart! May I go to the Morrisons'? Mam says there's new kittens, a tabby and a black, and I might have one if you agree. Please will you? I would so love another kitty!"

Ewart smiled at Maggie's pet name for their tenant's wife, but he shook his head. "You left the last three to me to manage. I simply can't care for *four* cats, Maggie."

"*I* didn't leave *them, they* left *me,*" retorted Maggie. "Oliver Cromwell has no interest in exploring. He only wants to sit about in the library, like you, and be an old mossy." She tossed a disdainful look towards the cat, a magnificent grey-blue puss with golden eyes particularly dignified and contemptuous, even for a cat. He rose slowly and turned his back on her with emphasis.

Ewart chuckled. "Well, I'll let Oliver Cromwell pass. But what about the others?"

"It's your own fault for naming them Christopher Columbus and Gustavus Adolphus. All Gustavus Adolphus does is fight with the other cats and go provoke them. And Christopher Columbus only wants to explore and run wild."

"But that is what you just complained Oliver Cromwell wouldn't do. Besides, if it *was* their names that caused this issue, Oliver Cromwell would fight too."

Maggie was not thus to be sidetracked. "And he will if you don't let him rule. But Christopher Columbus doesn't explore what *I* want to explore."

"And this kitten shall?"

Maggie stuck out her chin obstinately. "I'll call her Mary Kingsley."

Ewart laughed in spite of himself at the unexpected response. He had never guessed Maggie would remember his lecture last week on the famous explorer. She had seemed so uninterested.

"Very well, then, Mags, you may have a kitten—"

Maggie opened her mouth, but Ewart held up a warning finger.

"—*but* you must promise to care for it yourself. The day I catch anyone else doing so shall be the day I return it to the Morrisons'."

Maggie gave a shriek of triumph and fled, leaving Ewart grimacing over his perforated eardrum. He hurried after her and found her at the kitchen door, recounting her good fortune to Mother Morrison in breathless excitement.

Drawing near, Ewart smiled upon the short, homely woman, his eyes full of the love he'd never been able to give his mother. The Morrisons had always been good to him. With them, neither his lack of classical education, nor his clumsiness and timidity, nor his passion for literature and writing had ever been cast up to him, unlike within his blood family. The Morrisons' little farm, warm and happy, was his refuge on the many days where Father raged and Mother stormed. When Father had died and Mother had left, the Morrisons had been at hand night and day with advice and support, and Mother Morrison herself had been Maggie's nurse. To a lonely boy of sixteen, burdened with the sole guardianship of a newly born sister and with running the small estate generating his only income, they had been a Godsend.

"It's quite damp out, my dear," Mother Morrison said as Ewart approached. "Better throw on a cloak. Ah, Master Ewart! I haven't seen you in several days."

"Yes, I have been … occupied," Ewart offered distantly. *Counting raindrops, mostly…*

Mother Morrison's keen eyes sought his, and he dropped his gaze. She had a most uncanny way of reading his thoughts, and he was unwilling to burden her once more. He was a grown man, fully capable of bearing his own pain.

Maggie came rushing back, brown curls waving as they escaped her blue hood. "I am ready, Mam! Will the ducks be out, do you think?"

"Quite possibly, child. Take the basket. Now, let us be off."

Maggie flung open the door and sprang out into the rain, laughing with frank enjoyment. Mother Morrison stepped after her, then turned back. "Do not forget, my boy," she said gently, "you have a Father Who is not only able but eager to bear your burdens. And there are two old friends ever ready to help in any small way they can. The whole world is not against you."

She smiled—a smile of benediction and earnest love—and shut the door quietly, leaving Ewart alone.

Her words quivered in the air after her, and Ewart sighed. After a decade of walking with the Lord, how was it that he still failed to remember He was there? How did he still doubt the love and attention that was waiting for him when he approached the throne?

Forgive me, Father. My mind is running away with me again. Center it upon Thee.

Stepping closer to the window, he raised the curtain and peered out, watching the little girl and the old woman tripping hand in hand down the lane, basket swinging and heads turned sociably towards each other, smiling despite the rivulets that ran down their hoods. A boy appeared suddenly at the turn of the lane, nodding politely to the pair. They spoke for a moment and then set forth down the lane together.

Ewart eyed the boy with a feeling dangerously akin to jealousy. He envied the youngster his easy stride, his confident bearing, his bright smile, his ready response. Hadn't Ewart seen him about somewhere before? He seemed to remember that face. Perhaps it was the son of one of the outlying farmers.

Ewart dropped the curtain and turned away. Despite any rhetoric about his higher position, never had he been as confident as that country boy. As far back as Ewart could remember, he had been a silent child, round-shouldered from his efforts to hide, walking with the lightest of footfalls. No wonder the world despised him, in spite of all Mrs. Morrison could say. Everyone knew his failing and disdained him. Everyone, that was, except Maggie, who, in the twelve years that he'd spent raising her, had never discovered the elder brother she adored was a fool.

And the Father Who loved him notwithstanding his weakness … from Him, too, there was no contempt.

I thank Thee for Thy mercy.

The comforting reminder eased a little the burden his mother had just placed on him. He would have to pray long and hard to know what to do about the situation. He did not want to get Maggie a governess. Despite Lady Kissel's opinion, he taught his sister himself, and he did not wish to hand over her education to another, disinterested person. He had heard many tales concerning governesses, and by and large, they did not sound like an appealing class.

However, it was true that he could not teach Maggie comportment or etiquette. Perhaps he might find a young woman who would limit herself to teaching only that—a curtailment of her duties that would be very much appreciated by his slim pocketbook, because although the estate generated enough income for him to keep up the respectable lifestyle he'd always known, there was little left over.

Ha. That was only a dream—an idealistic dream unlikely to ever occur. What governess would agree to such terms? And furthermore, where was he to find *any* governess, let alone the respectable, friendly woman he desired Maggie to know?

Ewart groaned. *Lord, help me.*

Chapter Three

"It's every man's business to see justice done."
The Adventure of the Crooked Man by Sir Arthur Conan Doyle

Caitrìona awoke with a dull headache the morning following her ignominious return to the country. Rain pattered, irregular yet methodical, on the roof. Usually, it would have been calming and cosy; but now, it wore upon her nerves. She closed her eyes against the grey light filtering into the bedroom and wished she could slip away again to the realms of sleep, where blissful unconsciousness reigned.

"Will you have an egg for breakfast, Cat?"

Caitrìona stilled her breathing and froze in place.

"You aren't asleep, Caitrìona Roylett; I saw you wake a moment ago," continued the voice. Feet crossed the floor and came to stand by the bed.

Caitrìona attempted to breathe still softer. Perhaps Lucy would be deceived and leave her.

A sudden stream of water into her face broke her resolve, and she sat up, sputtering as she snatched blindly in Lucy's direction.

A peal of triumphant laughter followed as Lucy sprang away, singing, "Lie-abed, lie-abed, lie-abed!"

"I'm not a lie-abed!" Caitrìona fumed, even as she realized the argument was worthless. What was it about siblings that caused one to contest every possible point with them? She snapped her mouth shut and reached for a towel from the washstand by her bed. In spite of her moodiness, she was glad to see Lucy well enough to tease and play. The family had been very worried about her last winter, and she'd not picked up much over the summer before Caitrìona left. The letters Caitrìona had received since then had seemed rather positive, but she always supposed it was Mother's and Lucy's way of screening her from their worries "back home"—though she wondered privately how they thought she could ever stop fretting over them at all. Evidently, however, there had been some grounds for their good news.

Lucy glanced out of the window and shook her head. "Rather a grey morning to welcome you home, I'm afraid. *But* one never knows what a day may bring forth!"

Caitrìona frowned. The words that to Lucy were full of promise were to Caitrìona a dire warning. One never knew what a day may bring forth. Such as death, or monetary failure, or social disgrace. Anything might happen in this uncontrollable world, and frequently did, too. This was what made her so frantic to control what she could … and sometimes what she couldn't, though she was always last to admit this—and only to herself.

Caitrìona rose languidly and began to dress as Lucy made the bed. A simple, white blouse and blue skirt, both of which she had sewn herself last winter, comprised her outfit. She frowned at the wan girl and drab clothes in the mirror.

"Try your belt," Lucy suggested helpfully.

Caitrìona only nodded as she began brushing her hair. It was still as long, thick, and silky as it had ever been, and she felt slightly better as she coiled it round and round her head. When she had cinched the belt at her waist and adjusted the buckle just so, she pinned at her throat her brooch of the English rose and Scottish thistle entwined. Grandmother Roylett had left her native Scotland to marry Grandfather Roylett, and he had commissioned the brooch for their twenty-fifth anniversary. At her death, Grandmother had bequeathed it to Caitrìona, her namesake; so highly did Caitrìona prize it that she had left it at home, lest it be lost. It brought her a spark of joy now.

She eyed herself critically. She was becoming a little too plump for this style. And her chin, too, was certainly developing an extra fold. If only she had her earrings! The delicate, silver jewellery she'd worn in London had complemented her face nicely and would add the perfect touch to her simple costume. But the bijouterie had gone the way of all her past splendour.

"You look just lovely," said Lucy admiringly.

Caitríona winced. If only the girls had seen her as she'd appeared so often in London, in her signature yellow silk, with the embroidered neckline, the drooping sleeves fashioned in the shape of roses, and the ruffled train. How Lucy would have wondered at her elegant mess of curls—so different from her usual smooth rolls!—and how Amy would have exclaimed over her jewellery set, complete with the headband. Only rhinestones, but they would seem magnificent to her—as indeed they had to Caitríona herself. The outfit would be completed by a tussie-mussie of oak-geranium, heartsease, Austrian roses, and heliotrope from Lord Saxford—the tasteful message he sent every evening: *lady, deign to smile*; *think of me*; *you are all that's lovely*; and *devotion*. He was too cautious for any stronger expressions of his interest in her. But Caitríona always placed the tiny bouquet in her little cone-shaped posy holder and pinned it over her heart, knowing this declaration of love would encourage him more than anything she said aloud.

But there! Lord Saxford's avowed devotion had failed the test.

Amy and Lucy would never see Caitríona in that splendour, nor experience it themselves. And all because of ... Well, who was there to blame? She was innocent, and she had never conducted herself in a way that seemed remotely conducive to making the public believe she had a predilection for robbery. Poor Duscan had always been irreproachable; and there was no single person to blame for the whole affair, unless it was the Garrett butler and maid—but they had only spoken of what they had seen with their own eyes; *they* had never convicted Duscan. It was much more the fault of the flatfeet and Inspector MacKinnon ... but again, circumstantial evidence was more against Duscan than anyone else.

"Do come and have your breakfast," Lucy said, going downstairs.

Caitríona nodded and followed her sister, wishing the old, impotent wish that there were *some way* she could help Duscan and solve the case. But it was only in books that fearless, intelligent maidens ran about the city and interrogated witnesses and built elaborate theories to present to skeptical constables. This was reality, and she had no more hope of becoming the next Amelia Butterworth than of discovering a gold mine. True, there were female detectives—Mrs. Kate Warne had been active for the famed Pinkerton Detective Agency in America, and here at home, Miss Kate Easton had just become notorious. But there was no chance

Caitrìona could enter that profession, let alone master it in time to save Duscan—

To save Duscan.

Suppose they went so far as to *hang* him?

For one awful moment, Caitrìona seemed to disappear into a yawning black cavern of horror before her sense returned. No, theft was no longer a capital punishment. She had not the faintest idea what sentence Duscan would receive, but thank God, he was in no danger of death.

Weak with reaction, she stumbled over the last two stairs and staggered through the hallway, then collapsed onto a kitchen chair.

"Dear me, child!" Mother exclaimed, turning with her wet hands burrowing into the voluminous folds of her apron. "Are you ill?" She hurried over, her face tight with anxiety.

Caitrìona summoned up a smile she could only hope was not ghastly as she answered, "No, no, Mother; I'm quite well; I ... I merely stumbled on the stairs."

Mother did not seem satisfied. "You are dreadfully pale. Amy, fetch the cod liver oil!"

Caitrìona grimaced. After Father's death and Mother's dangerous sickness at the same time, and Lucy's ill health that plagued her from her birth, poor Mother had become something of a hypochondriac, and the medicine bottle was ever present.

"She must be well; she made a face," Amy said positively, running to Mother with the dreaded bottle in her hand.

"How could that possibly mean anything?" demanded Lucy.

"If we don't do what we normally would, Mother always says we are sick."

"But the inverse is not always true!"

"Girls, don't," said Mother, administering a large dose which Caitrìona swallowed meekly, shuddering her distaste as the liquid ran slowly down her throat. She rubbed her forehead, discovered it was wet with sweat, and wiped it discreetly. It was fortunate Mother had not tried to test her temperature.

"I'm all right, really," Caitrìona said with forced briskness, rising with the desperate hope that her legs would not fail her at this crucial moment. "It was only a stumble, and I am always pale."

Mother frowned, and Lucy raised a skeptical eyebrow.

"If there is anything at all wrong with me, the oil shall help," Caitrìona continued, whipping up a cheerful confidence she by no means felt. "Come, Amy, let us make breakfast."

"I already have," stated Amy. "We breakfasted quite an hour ago."

"Ah. Yes." This would not impress Mother and Lucy with the conviction that Caitrìona was well. "I forgot how long I lay abed. It is a very bad habit I have contracted over the Season—no one ever retires until four o'clock in the morning in London—no one in society, that is—and I was more fatigued than usual yesterday, what with that dreadful week and the journey. I shall make myself a slice of bread and cheese and be all ready to help with the housekeeping again."

She could still feel Mother's and Lucy's suspicious gazes on her back, but she moved calmly about the kitchen, cutting her bread and cheese and toasting it over the little fire as though she had not a care in the world.

"Cat," said Lucy, "we know about it all, you know."

Caitrìona flinched and hoped her face was sufficiently hidden. "Yes," she said with deceptive calm.

"You needn't try to shield us."

"No."

"Don't, then."

Something in Caitrìona crumbled at her sister's solid words of common sense—a sort of wall she had built up against her family, a wall formed of her own unspoken hope that somehow, *somehow*, they had been spared the disgrace and fear she combatted.

"I can't," she said, and her voice trembled.

"My poor, dear girl," Mother breathed, and the next moment, Caitrìona was in her arms and the tears she'd held at bay for days gushed out soundlessly.

"They won't hurt him, will they?" Amy asked in a small voice.

"I don't know, child," Mother whispered. "It's all in the Good Lord's hands."

Amy buried her face against Lucy's chest. Caitrìona moaned and hid her own eyes against her mother's shoulder. She could not bear to see her sister's distress.

Even Amy knows.

That hurt worst of all, for Amy was the baby, whom they'd all so carefully sheltered for many long years. This, more than perhaps anything, intensified Caitrìona's impression of failure. At ten years, she'd struggled through her father's death and the sharp illness that prostrated her mother. Lucy, then six, was already an invalid, and Amy only a newborn babe and very weak. Already the family poverty had stared Caitrìona in the face as she attempted to care for her siblings alone and as Duscan, a splendid, healthy boy of eight, dreamed hopelessly of school.

Since then, much had changed. Amy had grown into a fine, strong little girl, and Lucy, though still very sickly, was in no especial danger. Mother, too, had become somewhat healthy, thanks to Caitrìona shouldering most of her load and sparing her all she could; and Duscan had flourished at Eton. Although still poor, the Royletts were no longer living from hand to mouth. Caitrìona had been fiercely proud of what she had accomplished and how far they had come, and she was determined her little sister would never know the turmoil she'd faced herself at the same age.

But she had learned oh-so-bitterly this week how little she was in control, and it was being demonstrated to her again now. *Poor Amy.* No child deserved to wrestle with the knowledge that her adored elder brother was accused of theft by one of the most prestigious families of the land, while her eldest sister was ostracized forever by the same uncommitted crime.

"We must talk it over," Mother said softly as Cat's weeping subsided. "Talk settles many emotions, and perhaps we can hit upon a way to help our poor, dear boy. And we must *pray*. 'The effectual fervent prayer of a righteous man availeth much,' James says. If the prayer of faith can heal the sick, it can deliver the innocent."

Caitrìona composed herself and wiped her eyes. It was all very well to pray, but one must *act*. And there was no way sweet Mother and innocent Amy could aid Duscan. Lucy was sensible and shrewd in a quiet, practical way, but she would be no use in this situation. It was Caitrìona who must find the solution and wipe this ignominy from the family name. If she caught the thief herself, her popularity would overshadow her disgrace and she would once again rise high enough in public favour to find a suitable match ...

Pipe dream. That was simply a pipe dream.

She allowed herself to be seated in one of the rockers, and as Mother and the girls put together a hearty breakfast for her, she sought seriously for a solution. Her last week in London had been spent in disbelief. She had pleaded for Duscan's release, she had waited for his innocence to be proclaimed, she had recalled *What Katy Did at School* and applied Katy's brave motto "live it down!" Nothing had succeeded. It was now time to fight back. Yet how could one simple woman possibly hope to solve a case that baffled Scotland Yard itself?

Despair filtered into her heart even as she strove to batten the hatches against the rising tide of hopelessness. Her eyes roved the room aimlessly but suddenly fastened on the newspaper Mother had left neatly folded on the table. Bold black words assailed her sight: "VINCENT WOODTHORN TRIUMPHS AGAIN."

In that moment, a fully-fledged plan flew into Caitrìona's brain, and she clutched it rapturously.

She must hire Mr. Woodthorn to vindicate Duscan.

It was a simple plan yet difficult. She was unsure of the fee Mr. Woodthorn requested. It could be quite high, considering his fame. She was certain she'd heard a rumour that he had worked for very humble clients and been found willing to accept little or no remuneration, following the habits of Mr. Sherlock Holmes. She could only hope the case would interest Mr. Woodthorn enough to make him willing to accept a little now and await the full payment upon her marriage. Not even for Duscan could she swallow her pride enough to beg gratis service. But for his sake, she would find work and *earn* enough for a small remittance.

Caitrìona Louise Roylott would not sit by and watch her dreams and ambitions be shattered without standing and waging a vigorous fight in their defence. She must care for her family. She must marry well. She must return to society. This was only a small setback—and one which, in fact, could be of much use. She was championing the cause of justice.

Yes, everything would work out well in the end.

It *must*.

Chapter Four

"Our highest assurance of the goodness of Providence seems to me to rest in the flowers. ... [T]his rose is an extra. ... It is only goodness which gives extras, and so I say again that we have much to hope from the flowers."
The Adventure of the Naval Treaty by Sir Arthur Conan Doyle

Ewart had passed a miserable week. The process of finding a suitable governess hung over him like the proverbial sword of Damocles. Venturing out to find and interview *young ladies*, of all creatures, was terrible to think of. He had put off the task but found himself unable to think of anything else, and so any form of distraction had proved utterly worthless. To finish with proper torment, Sir Robert and Lady Anne Fairfax had seen fit to invite him to the function they had thrown in honour of their niece's coming out. Ewart was fairly certain Lady Anne had invited him out of an unwanted, pitying desire to introduce him to the new belles, and Sir Robert had likely agreed with the hope of a game of billiards, there being few gentlemen about to afford him any other—and better— competitors.

Ewart would have given a flat refusal, but Mother Morrison got wind of the affair through Maggie and roundly ordered him to go. "'Twill be good for your constitution," she declared. "You'll grow old and mouldy away here by yourself. Besides, perhaps the lady can aid you in your search for a governess."

The idea was appetizing, and it was thanks to it that, despite an onslaught of anxiety and the thought of the whispers and stares that grated upon him, he now stood against the wall of the Fairfax parlour, avoiding all eyes and hoping unhappily that Lady Anne would be content to have him as a wallflower. He could bear to be a spectator, but to ask him to mingle and chat—no, he would only make an even greater fool of himself.

"Mr. Alinac! Have you a partner?"

Ewart stifled a sigh as the very source of his nervousness bore down upon him, resplendent in the latest fashions. "No, my lady," he answered truthfully. "But I am quite content, I assure you."

"Oh nonsense, you must have a partner," the lady said, glancing around for the first victim she could lay eyes upon.

"You are too kind, my lady," Ewart murmured deprecatingly.

"What do you seek, Anne?"

Ewart groaned in spirit at the voice. *Lord, rescue me ...* Resignedly, he turned to face Lady Hilda Garrett, who approached, fanning herself vigorously. She, too, was dressed in the height of fashion and looked most uncomfortable. It seemed dancing was too strenuous a task for her avoirdupois.

"Mr. Alinac, here, has no partner, Hilda," Lady Fairfax explained. "Have you seen any disengaged girls?"

"Why yes, there's Marianne Rosencroff just over there."

Ewart stifled another groan. "Really, ma'am, I'd rather not."

The ladies signalled Miss Rosencroff over without any pretence of subtlety.

"Don't be shy, my dear boy. And she's a lovely girl, I assure you. She'll draw you out quite properly." Lady Hilda patted his back heartily.

Ewart winced. He had no desire to be drawn out quite properly by anyone, least of all Miss Marianne Rosencroff. "I—I'd rather be alone," he blurted.

The ladies turned slowly towards him, eyes wide with astonishment. Lady Hilda's mouth hung quite agape. Too late, he realized that the room was unusually still. His declaration had been overheard by every guest, and all eyes were fixed upon him.

Miss Rosencroff tossed him a withering gaze of offended scorn and flounced away.

Ewart flushed redder than Lady Fairfax's tussie-mussie of hothouse roses. He did not try to salvage the situation; he bolted straight through the side door conveniently yawning behind him and onto the grounds.

Why, Father?

He felt like a child again as he posed the question. *I trust Thy wisdom, and I know all things turn to good and so forth ... but why must I be so publicly shamed?*

Hot with frustrated humiliation, he wandered away from the manor. The evening was fine and still young, and its quiet coolness soothed his frazzled nerves. He strolled through the garden, enjoying the fragrance of the night flowers.

After all, it was true he would far rather be here than in the crowded ballroom.

I thank Thee, Father. I thank Thee for proving once more that Thou know'st better than I.

Rounding the bend of a flowerbed, his eyes on the starry sky overhead, he stumbled over something on the path and only just saved himself from pitching headfirst into the rose bushes. A decidedly feminine exclamation of dismay completed his discomfiture.

"I—I beg your pardon." Ewart recovered his poise with difficulty. "I hope I didn't hurt you?"

"No, not at all," the young woman answered nervously, scrabbling for something near his feet. He backed up a few steps, settling his vest. There was the sound of a match striking, then a small flame flickered to life. The next moment, warm candlelight streamed from the lantern in the woman's hand. By its radiance, Ewart and the young lady examined each other gravely.

She was a small, plump woman with dark-brown hair swept up in the usual, graceful coiffure. Her round face was pale and rather stern in its state of repose, but her grey-blue eyes were mild. Her white dress was severely plain but somehow still dainty, and in her hand was the basket he'd crushed, overflowing with roses. She was not, according to societal rules, *beautiful*, but she was refreshingly feminine and simple.

Then she smiled, and her atmosphere morphed entirely. Large dimples dented her cheeks; her eyes sparkled; vivacity and expression shone all about her.

"I didn't expect anyone to come out here just now, during the dance," she said lightly. "Sir Robert gave me permission to cut roses for my sister's birthday—we haven't any—and I had no time to come fetch them earlier, but I thought I should be no bother now."

"I beg your pardon." Ewart was most uncomfortable. "I suppose it is not the thing at all for a lone guest to roam about the grounds in this fashion, but, you see, I am not used to functions …"

The woman laughed, a cheery sound of hearty, honest joie de vivre. "Evidently, or you would not call this little frolic a *function*! You must not be a regular in the London Season."

Ewart strangled a wince. She meant no cruelty by her words, yet they stung somehow. "No, not at all."

"You must have found it quite stifling," she sympathized. "I do not wonder that you came out into the fresh air."

"You are used to these things?" Ewart was not aware of any other eligible young lady in the neighbourhood aside from those he had seen in the house, and he was quite unable to recollect her features. Besides, it was most puzzling how she seemed familiar with society yet was now in a garden picking roses rather than conversing with one foolish young buck or another … and had she said Sir Robert had *allowed* her to cut his roses because *her* family had none?

But he was not fated to learn more of the mystery that night. The woman's face closed off, a veil of distrust falling over her. Her voice was abrupt as she answered, "I used to be. Good night."

She moved off into the night, and he followed her bobbing lantern with his eyes, wondering if the direction she went off in was a clue. But she took the main road, which did not narrow down her possible destinations. How odd, too, that she was traipsing about the countryside at twilight alone! To be sure, there was no danger, but it was unusual.

Presently, Ewart put the matter from his mind, sauntering up and down the garden paths as he wondered what to do next. There was no sense in returning to the house; the ladies Fairfax and Garrett would only insist on finding him another partner. Perhaps he could find refuge in Sir Robert's billiard room, but he was in no mood for even a small, friendly game. His purposes in coming had been to placate Mother Morrison and to seek aid in finding a governess. He *had* come, which would have to satisfy Mother Morrison, and after seeing Lady Fairfax, he was by no means disposed to trust her taste in governesses. He would have to strike out on his own again.

No, not alone. *Father, I thank Thee that Thou art with me.*

Comforted by that reflection, Ewart went to the stables, where he found the hands most astonished at his sudden departure and his horse quite willing to go. He rode Ebony slowly homewards, pondering. As always, when he whipped himself up at last and faced his troubles, he was ready to give it his all.

Where could he possibly find a suitable governess? There were most likely agencies—he was sure he had read of some—but where? How could he find them? How would he carry out the interviews? Would they allow him to exercise his own discretion? Would such a clever, independent woman as a governess should be respect him? How could he truly find if she was quite worthy of being placed in charge of Maggie? And if she fit *his* idea of suitable, she would fall quite short of Lady Kissel's—how could he reconcile the two?

So many questions, and not a single satisfactory answer.

Help me, Father.

It was the very next morning that Maggie began talking of "Miss Cat."

At first, Ewart, with whom late hours did not agree, thought she spoke of her new kitty. Presently, however, as the fogs of sleeplessness dissipated, he began to realize that Miss Cat was undeniably not feline.

"Who is this Miss Cat?" he inquired when at last Maggie paused her chatter to scoff down her egg.

"Why, she's my new friend," Maggie answered simply.

"Yes, Mags, but what *kind* of friend?"

Maggie's expression said she considered him a raving lunatic. "My *best* friend, of course!"

"But who *is* she?" valiantly persisted Ewart. "Is she a little girl?"

"Oh, no, she's a woman! A very short one, though—I'm nearly as tall as she is. I'm tall, aren't I, Ewart?"

"Yes ... Is she a ... a farmer's daughter?"

Maggie frowned. "No, but I *believe* she is poor."

"Why?"

"She dresses very, very plainly, and she talks of helping with the chickens and the housework."

"Then she must be a country girl."

"But she speaks like a lady," insisted Maggie. "And she has been to London. In society. Like Mother."

Ewart flinched. A girl who associated with the likes of Lady Kissel was not a desirable companion for Maggie—despite Lady Kissel's own opinion.

"Mother wishes you to have a governess, Maggie."

The words were no sooner out of his mouth than Ewart would have gladly given a year of his life to recall them. Now was not the time to disclose that information, nor was this the fashion. What had possessed him?

Maggie's eyes widened. "But *why*? She doesn't care about us! Why should she want me to have a governess? Why can't you just keep teaching me? Governesses are so poky and stern! I don't want a governess, Ewart! And I don't want to study any more than I already am, either. I have enough classes as it is."

Ewart ignored her last sentence and dropped his gaze to his nervous hands, which tore his toasted bread into shreds. He could not argue with her. But now that he had spoken, he might as well tell her the whole truth. It was best for her to grow used to the idea.

"She has a ... a plan for you," he said slowly, trying to frame Lady Kissel's callous design in the kindest words possible. "She wants you to prepare for society. She has a—a young gentleman in mind—"

"No—*no!*"

That was not Maggie, that strangled cry. It was the voice of a trapped creature striving desperately to free itself. It pierced his heart as sharply as it did his ears.

"Ewart! You shall stop her, shan't you? You won't let me go—you won't let her take me—you won't let this happen!"

"How can I stop her?" Ewart whispered helplessly. "*She* is your mother. She is *my* mother. I am not your legal guardian, and you are not of age."

Maggie cried out again and fled.

Alone at the table, Ewart buried his face against his arms and fought the tears. *Father, why? Why must it be this way? Must it be so? Canst Thou not rescue us—rescue* her*? I do not know what to do—O God, show me how.*

No splendid plan came to him, despite his frantic prayers. Presently, he fetched Ebony from the stables and spent the morning roaming the countryside, alternating between thoughtful ambling and wild gallops. The day was cool and grey, fitting his mood well, and as he prayed and wondered, the soothing promises of his Lord eased the anxiety from his heart. He did not know how—he could not conceive how—the Lord would act, but he knew it would all work to the best. And in the meantime, the Lord would support them to the uttermost.

It was late afternoon when he returned home. He heard a laugh he recognised as he crossed the woods adjoining the house, and he smiled in relief. Maggie was playing in her secret dell by the creek. Ewart turned Ebony's head and cantered towards the sound. What a pleasant surprise that Maggie was already enjoying herself instead of floundering in despair …

But as he broke through the trees, he was still more surprised to find a small, white-clad figure standing on the bank by his sister.

And he was astonished most of all by the realization of who this new woman was.

Chapter Five

"... the chief proof of man's real greatness lies in his perception of his own smallness. It argues, you see, a power of comparison and of appreciation which is in itself a proof of nobility."
The Sign of the Four by Sir Arthur Conan Doyle

Caitrìona started as the black steed emerged through the trees into the dell. The place was secluded, and there was no reason for riders to wander through these woods. Who was it, and what were they seeking?

It was such an unexpected, lone rider who had broken upon her peace once before, ten years ago, announcing Father's death ...

Her heart caught in her throat. Had something happened to Lucy—to Mother—to Amy? Had Duscan ... had Duscan been ... *hurt?*

But this rider looked neither hurried nor worried. As he drew nearer, she recognized him—the curious gentleman from the Fairfax garden. His brown eyes were still filled with the wondering surprise they held last night.

Miss Maggie, however, was entirely at her ease.

"Ewart!" she exclaimed triumphantly, running to meet him in entire fearlessness of his vigorous mount. "Miss Cat knows *all* about society, and *she* shall teach me!"

Caitrìona gasped. *This* was the mysterious Mr. Ewart Alinac? She had, indeed, seen him about the village and at church; but it was always at a distance and with his face shadowed by his hat. She saw now that he was good-looking, of average height, and very gentlemanly, and he had an unconscious dignity and manliness about him that belied his doubtful reputation. Just now, his manner was quite puzzled, although he only raised his hat and swung from the saddle.

"I don't believe I've had the pleasure," he said courteously, offering his hand.

Caitrìona swallowed and straightened her shoulders. Now for a broadside of the shock and maliciousness she'd left behind in London.

She took his hand with her head held high. "I am Miss Roylett," she said distinctly. It would not be said that *she* was ashamed of her name or sailed under false colours!

But the startled, dismayed expression she expected did not follow. He only shook her hand briefly, smiling as he answered, "Ewart Alinac. I see you've met my sister."

"Miss Cat and I have had *such* a lovely time," interrupted Maggie, drawing close to Caitrìona and taking her hand.

Caitrìona risked another glance at the imperturbable gentleman. He seemed entirely unmindful of the effect her name should possess. Perhaps he was recluse enough to avoid or be unaware of the newspapers …

"Indeed? And how did you meet Miss … I beg your pardon, I have forgotten your name. I am strikingly bad at remembering names, I'm afraid."

"'Miss Cat' will do quite well," said Caitrìona impulsively. "Miss Roylett" was her London name, and it bore no pleasure for her now. "Cat" was her name here, among the family and friends she loved.

"Well then, and how did you meet this Miss Cat, Mags? Did you put a stop to her afternoon stroll and drag her to your little hideout to make her skip her tea?"

Maggie burst into laughter. "No, she was sitting here when I came yesterday morning! She told me about herself. I asked."

"I'll warrant you did," muttered Mr. Alinac with a grin of amused annoyance. "I don't suppose it occurred to you that she *might* have come here for privacy, just as you did!"

"She was glad to see me!" Maggie asseverated. "Didn't you say so, Miss Cat?"

"I did," Caitrìona admitted. She rubbed her forehead. If only she could invent a truthful excuse to escape the situation. Mr. Alinac's eyes were pleasant, but they were intense—the eyes books meant when they spoke of gazes that "searched out all the secrets of your existence."

"And she will teach me about London, Ewart," Maggie said confidently.

Caitrìona winced.

Mr. Alinac looked at her enquiringly.

"I did not *quite* say that," she demurred. "I said—"

"You *said* you know all about society! You said you could teach me how to act!"

"The key word there, Mags, is 'could,'" Mr. Alinac remarked. "We do not doubt Miss Cat's *ability*. We are contesting her *availability*."

Caitrìona swallowed a laugh. She already appreciated this young man's quiet wit.

Maggie threw her arms around Caitrìona and gazed at her beseechingly. "Oh, Miss Cat, won't you *please*? I don't *want* a *real* governess—I would *die* with one, I *know* I should!"

"I'm afraid you overrate your fragility," said her brother dryly. "Don't tease, Mags. And leave some italics for the rest of us."

"But *she* needs money, and *I* need a governess, and *she* can govern. Please, Ewart! Do say she may!"

Caitrìona could only guess how crimson her face had become. Mr. Alinac, however, preserved his aplomb.

"Are you quite sure, Mags? You were complaining earlier that you didn't want a new teacher or extra classes. You understand that if Miss Cat comes you shall have to be quite obedient and respectful and work *hard*?"

"I shall work much harder with Miss Cat than with Miss Anyone Else!"

Mr. Alinac surveyed Maggie, lips pursed. Then he looked frankly into Caitrìona's eyes. "Would you be interested in the position, miss?"

Caitrìona's face grew more heated. He clearly had no suspicion of her status, yet she was deeply ashamed of her position. Despite her decision to find employment, she struggled to resign herself now that the situation was actually before her. A *Roylett* working? What would Father have thought? What would Mother and the girls say? Her grandparents would surely turn in their graves. It was true that already they did work in and about their own cottage, but that was entirely a different thing than working outside of the home.

Domestic work had never been seen as ungenteel in their family. But never had any Roylett girl been obliged to work for her keep.

But what could she do? Money was a necessity she could not afford to despise—especially in order to carry out any plans she conceived for Duscan's release. And then, work as a governess was far more respectable a position than she had expected to find. After all, it was not disgraceful. Many proper ladies were governesses, and for one to marry an important man was not so *very* unheard-of.

"I would," Caitrìona answered Mr. Alinac solemnly. Her knees shook as she pronounced the words, but she pushed aside the fear. She was doing what she must. She was following her plan. It would all work out in the end.

Maggie squealed and threw herself into her brother's arms. Mr. Alinac's face softened, but he shook his head warningly. "Wait a moment, Maggie. We cannot simply rush ahead like this. I must interview Miss Cat."

"But I *like* her!" cried Maggie.

"Quite right and proper, Mags, but there are a few things to be consulted besides your predilection for her. 'Oh, what may man within him hide, though angel on the outward side?'" He offered Caitrìona a gallant, apologetic bow, and she smiled understandingly, pleased by his caution. It was very good of him to be careful of who had access to his sister and, even more so, one who would tend her mind and soul. Caitrìona's respect for the reclusive gentleman was rising rapidly.

"She's *not* a man," said Maggie.

Mr. Alinac and Caitrìona burst into laughter, exchanging a conspiratorial glance.

"You took that from a book," Maggie declared in disgust.

Mr. Alinac chuckled.

"Shakespeare," said Caitrìona with an unladylike grin.

"*Measure for Measure*, act III, scene I," confirmed Mr. Alinac. "You are familiar with the classics?"

"Yes, but that was not such an obscure quotation." His obvious gratification embarrassed her. She was not used to airing her knowledge of books. Her mother had been raised to abhor bluestockings, and she had instilled in her daughters the idea that it was not done in society to advertise your taste for reading. Certainly in London, Caitrìona had discovered that Lord Saxford and his circle were not friendly to women who "aspired above their natural sphere," as his mother graciously put it. She had a horror of the "modern woman" and the recent Gibson Girl ideal that had swept across North America and into Europe. Her son, of course, docilely adopted her opinions with all the absolute trust of a disciple.

"Miss Cat likes books too," Maggie said tolerantly.

Caitrìona giggled before she could stop herself.

Mr. Alinac smiled and waved a hand towards a fallen tree near them. "Won't you be seated, miss? Though I wish I had a better seat to offer you."

"This will be quite all right, I assure you. It's quite comfortable," Caitrìona assured him as she seated herself gingerly, lest the trunk choose this precise moment to shatter beneath her.

"She always sits there," Maggie added. "She told me so."

"*Always?*" Mr. Alinac repeated amusedly, raising quizzical eyebrows as he glanced from Caitrìona to Maggie.

Caitrìona flushed, laughing slightly. How *did* the child manage to make the moment more awkward with every word she spoke? "I must admit to trespassing frequently, sir, although I was not fully aware this was your land."

Mr. Alinac gave an undeniable smirk, but he only said, "Don't fret. We have no objection to sharing our woods with respectful borrowers. Which means, Mags, people who don't hack the bark off fine, full-grown trees ... I beg you indulge your disfiguring tendencies upon the bushes and weeds and refrain from damaging valuable woods."

Evidently, Maggie was used to her brother's loving sarcasm. She ignored his words but obeyed, swiping at the bushes with a heavy stick she'd picked up as she moved away.

"Don't leave the clearing, please," Mr. Alinac added politely as he perched on a tree stump near Caitrìona.

"Why? I always go through these woods. Nothing shall hurt me. And I won't hurt anything."

"I know, Mags, but I would appreciate if you could stay here with us for now," Mr. Alinac requested with firm kindness. "Now, Miss Cat, shall we commence our interview?"

Caitrìona smiled back at him, touched by his consideration of their reputations and applauding the style he took on with his sister. Here was indeed an unusual man, the most upright, gentle, *manly* one she'd ever come across—nothing like the London coxcombs who had so irritated her.

The interview that followed only heightened her approval. He was conscientious, thoughtful, and intelligent, unashamedly displaying the love he bore for his sister. He spoke of his mother, too, with respect and reserve, and carefully outlined Caitrìona's need to follow both Lady Kissel's and his own requirements. Knowing slightly that formidable lady, Caitrìona understood his predicament and promised him her best aid. He also broached the topic of remuneration—from which she shrank—with a mixture of delicacy and frankness she greatly appreciated, and the price he offered her was princely in her eyes, though he assured her it was quite average. At any rate, it would be enough as a deposit to satisfy Vincent Woodthorn.

At last, mutually pleased, they fell silent and watched Maggie, who lay with unusual quietness, studying an insect.

"Thank you," Mr. Alinac said gently, his eyes finding Caitrìona's again. "We were most disturbed about the need for a governess. I am forever in your debt for your kindness."

"As I am to you," Caitrìona murmured, wondering why he was so deeply grateful. It was not difficult to find good, respectable governesses. Was it her friendship with Maggie that he sought? Conviction niggled in the back of her mind. Should she ensure Mr. Alinac *really* knew who she was ...?

No. She had told him. He had not recognised the scandal associated with her name. She needed the position. Maggie would not be harmed by her in any way. So she silenced her conscience, although his next words did not tend to help her in her efforts.

"I never imagined I would find so suitable a lady, though I should, for I prayed night and day to be led to the right one. The Father truly answers far better than we deserve."

He was evidently devout. Caitrìona resisted the urge to squirm. His speech, so indicative of a deep connection with the Lord, put to shame her own fitful relationship. She was not a nominal Christian, like so many she knew; she had converted and earnestly desired to grow in the faith; but it was difficult—and particularly was it difficult to be still and allow the Lord to work ... something Mr. Alinac clearly found very easy. But she was glad to discover he was a true follower of Christ. She had never known any besides her father and brother, and she admired him all the more for it.

Nor did that admiration plummet in the following weeks. Caitrìona told her family of the arrangement—suppressing that bit of information concerning payment—and spent her days at the Alinac manor, arriving there soon after breakfast and leaving directly after supper. It had been decided that she should tutor Maggie in conjunction with Mr. Alinac, partly to constantly model and implement deportment but also because the shrewd young man knew his sister would be far more likely to apply herself when in the presence of a friend she admired so much. Caitrìona was quite pleased with the arrangement. Mr. Alinac was an excellent teacher, and Caitrìona enjoyed study. Particularly she appreciated the chance to learn much she had been too restless or indolent to learn in her own schooling under her father and, later, the old vicar.

Maggie herself was not the most patient of scholars; she had not in the least inherited the academic strain her brother carried, and she seemed serenely untroubled by ambition's stirring call. She appeared, moreover, far more inclined to move and speak than to sit and listen. During the first few weeks, she strained Caitrìona's forbearance to the full by her inattention, irritation, and indifference. But Mr. Alinac, after a reasonable—and much better—display of patience, informed her that if she continued to shirk, Caitrìona would be discharged, and they would find another, real governess.

This was the only threat Maggie needed, for she had become nearly inseparable from Caitrìona. Not for all her old, lamented liberty would she have severed their friendship, and she studied doggedly. Indeed, she grew interested in learning for its own sake and joined Caitrìona and Mr. Alinac in their enthusiastic research.

Together, they studied and sang, gambolled and conversed, ran and read. Day by day, Caitrìona became fonder of the adventurous, merry, stubborn little girl. She was amused by Maggie's bluntness, comforted by her fierce loyalty, charmed by her childlike wonder. She grew to understand the danger of Maggie's position in the hands of her unscrupulous mother, and matched Mr. Alinac himself in anxiety over the child. Unlike Mr. Alinac, however, Caitrìona's anxiety took the form of aggressive, improbable plans and endless worry.

As for Mr. Alinac, his character was most intriguing to her. With Maggie and her, and the delightful Morrisons they loved so dearly, he was quiet and reserved but spoke with fluidity and power. He was deliberate but quick to act in emergency, self-effacing but a splendid leader. When they came across any others, even the few servants of his own household, he suddenly became painfully shy, struggling to meet their eyes, doubly silent, evidently paralyzed. She could not divine why such a strong man should become so utterly undone. It contrasted sharply with his deep faith, in which he reminded her of the psalmist David—frankly admitting his fear yet placing his trust fully in his Father and praising Him all the while, despite uncertainty and pain.

Yes, she had become attached to this loving, simple pair of siblings, and it was more, now, than an opportunity to earn money. But in spite of her enjoyment of these long, full, happy days, Duscan was never far from her mind. She agonized often over his pain, cooped up in a narrow prison cell with all sorts of coarse or evil men, possibly mistreated by those about him. At night, she wept over him and swore a little more fiercely to free him. Every day she counted off as one less before she could approach the famous detective—her last hope and the only link between her goals and reality.

Chapter Six

"... to underestimate one's self is as much a departure from truth as to exaggerate one's own powers."
The Adventure of the Greek Interpreter by Sir Arthur Conan Doyle

Meantime, the weeks passed, and the fullness of spring advanced upon the land. Ewart was sure it was more beautiful this year than it had ever been before.

Ewart, Maggie, and Miss Cat studied out of doors as much as they possibly could. To all of them, there was something intoxicating and magical in the rebirth of the world. The scent of fresh earth and growing things invigorated them; the warm sunshine and whispering breeze brought a sense of calm; the neighbourly visits from the animal and insect kingdoms spiked interest and curiosity. It was a time of depth and richness, physically and mentally, which Ewart enjoyed to the full and forever looked back upon with wistful longing and pure happiness.

They explored the woods together, dissecting flora and fauna, watching everything from the beetles to the hawks. They lay hidden, spying upon deer; tracked bees to their hives; tamed and fed rabbits. After borrowing ponies from the Morrisons, they rode over the hills and discovered the beauty of springtime in Surrey and the everlasting charm of the wind. Beast and flower yielded their secrets to them, filling them with endless wonder at the marvels of the Creator and deepened respect for the world about them.

At home, they read masterpieces and acted plays, learned geography and studied grammar, tried new languages and explored science. The lessons in deportment took place in the parlour, and

Ewart learned as much as Maggie did from Miss Cat, who every day grew more of a conundrum.

She only spoke of her family with great reticence but evidenced the tenderest love when she did. She refused to elucidate upon her London experiences yet had obviously moved in the best of society. She never revealed the location of her home, but she clearly lived in the neighbourhood. She was reserved about her faith, yet whenever the conversations grew deep and personal, she revealed great devoutness and an eagerness to do right coupled with willingness to change based upon the words of the Holy Writ. She was proud and controlling but deeply sensitive of others and willing to sacrifice herself in both large and small ways for those about her. She was apt to be blindly loyal, but she was quick to see and admit mistakes and actively work to rectify them. She was clever, modest, feminine, and strong—very different from any other woman Ewart had ever known.

Maggie frankly adored her, and Miss Cat was wonderful with her at school or play. But Ewart preferred when Maggie frolicked with little bewhiskered Mary Kingsley (the kitten proved to have as much of an exploring turn of mind as her mistress) and left Miss Roylett and him free to trail after her and converse. Very variable were these discussions, sometimes amounting to friendly debates, as they spoke of man, the world, and the Almighty, exploring topics both serious and simple. They saw eye to eye in many things, and where their personalities gave different perspectives, they were both enriched and challenged. Indeed, they grew so familiar with one another that one afternoon, Ewart confessed his greatest struggles to her.

Maggie was sketching a pheasant on her nest, which she had neglected to do for a week; Miss Cat and Ewart supervised from nearby tree stumps and having just finished *A Tale of Two Cities*, enthusiastically discussed the great value of good writing.

"It is, in my mind, one of the noblest of all gifts," Miss Cat insisted. "There is something truly grand in the ability to string together ideas, emotions, and messages to reach and touch and change so many human souls, even ones who would normally be closed to the Scriptures."

"I have written several novels," Ewart admitted. "I suppose it is rather foolish of me, as an inexperienced *rustic*"—he laughed deprecatingly—"but I have often indulged in feeling that my words could revolutionize the world … if not for many, then even for a few. One soul is worth enough; if my words only change *his* world, I shall be satisfied."

There was silence for a moment, and Ewart dropped his eyes to the daisies nearby as anxiety flooded over him. Never before had he spoken of this to anyone. Miss Roylett was a sweet lady, but suppose she lost respect for him? Laughed? Told him he was prideful and stepping out of his place? Was frightened away?

But when he glanced up again, she was looking at him with a world of admiration in her expressive eyes. "How marvellous!" she exclaimed. "What have you written as of yet?"

"Oh, nothing marvellous," he replied dryly, reaching over to uproot a few daisies. "They are most likely not very good—"

"Why must you always say that?" she interrupted, almost angry now. "You are so—so *self-deprecating*. You run yourself down, always undercut yourself. You never give yourself any credit."

"Well, I … it's … it's true," Ewart said uncomfortably, groping for any evidence to bolster his argument. He had a sinking feeling, however, that truth was on her side this time. He sat up straighter, plucking the petals from the flowers he held.

Miss Roylett shook her head. "I greatly doubt your writing is as bad as you insist. I have seen your prose when we wrote papers together, and I know your character and mindset. I am positive you are an excellent author. But it is not only in this that you underestimate yourself. In your riding, your speaking, your leading … in all you do, every decision, every encounter … you act as though you do not trust yourself; you appear … *afraid* of the other person. You seem as if you believed the world hated and despised you."

"I do." Ewart tossed the daisy stalks away, goaded by her rebuke. "I am not an able man, and I admit I am cowardly enough to flee rather than endure the dislike of the world."

"But the world does not despise you, Ewart. *You* despise *yourself.*"

That declaration rocked Ewart more than any other had in his entire life, save for those cruel long-ago words of his mother's. For he recognised Miss Cat's statement as *true*.

The truth that had so often been gently mentioned to him but which he had never believed.

He had become so convinced of his own lack of value that he carried the burden forever and imagined it in the actions of those about him. But now Miss Cat's passionate words burned into his soul with the weight of conviction upon them.

The world does not despise you, Ewart. You despise yourself.

His expression must have spoken for him, for she stretched her hand out involuntarily, as if offering support to a reeling man.

"I am afraid you are right," he said unsteadily. His whole worldview lay shattered at his feet, waiting for him to piece it together anew.

"You are an able man," Miss Cat persisted. "You show it daily. You are an excellent leader, a wonderful brother, a splendid teacher. You are not a 'rustic,' as you call yourself. You run your estate better than many older, greater men. You have displayed a rare strength of character in your treatment of your father and mother. You are well educated and open to learning. You are the best man I have ever met, all of London notwithstanding."

He would have laughed and wondered at her compliments if she were not so terribly in earnest as to have completely forgotten herself. So he passed over her last sentence and replied, "But I *am* afraid, Cat, dreadfully afraid, and that is a great flaw. I'm afraid"— he laughed a little at the irony of the phrase—"that you are biased and do not see me the way the world does. When you see who I truly am, you will see what a despicable, useless fellow—"

"Perhaps fear *is* a flaw—I daresay it is in most cases," she interrupted, missing or forgiving their accidental familiarity. "It is true that we are called to 'be of good courage.' But it is equally true that the Lord does not despise our fear but as a good Father, lovingly desires to deliver us from it."

She spoke with intensity, and her words carried that ring of truth as they settled upon him, heavy with conviction yet filled with life-changing lightness.

"Regardless, what the *world* thinks of you hardly matters. Man judges constantly and, most frequently, without legitimate reason. It is not Farmer Gaines or Lady Fairfax or the King's opinion of you that decides your worth. 'I will praise Thee; for I am fearfully and wonderfully made: marvellous are Thy works; and that my soul knoweth right well.' Have you the presumption to claim you are *not* one of His works? Yet if you *are* one, then your worth is established as 'wonderful' and 'marvellous,' a far cry from 'despicable' or 'useless.' You know your Bible—far better than I know mine—and you are well aware of our smallness and wickedness and such—*but* the wonder of salvation is that *despite* who we are, the Almighty claims us as His and calls us 'marvellous.'"

Miss Cat paused for breath, and Ewart nodded slowly as he thoughtfully tore up grass. He had always known he was loved in spite of his shortcomings, but true love implied *treasuring*. A father strove to help his child overcome his flaws, but he also considered the child infinitely precious in spite of them. How greatly it would break his heart to hear the child considering himself "worthless"! What had the Father felt, seeing Ewart holding the life-sapping lies close to his heart and wounding himself daily while ignoring the truth spelled out so clearly for him within the Word?

"*Furthermore* ..." Miss Cat rallied her forces for a second lecture. "The Lord has good works prepared for you. I don't know the reference—"

"Ephesians, second chapter, I believe," Ewart injected.

"Voilà. Therefore, you cannot claim to be useless, since He has clearly a use *for* you. The trouble is, you cannot *carry out* those works because you are mired down by your belief in lies. I believe, myself, it is the Evil One himself who orchestrated this; he knows you could be a powerful force for the Lord, if only you are fearless and secure in Him."

Father, forgive me. How many years had he lost, cowering away? What could he have done for the kingdom of God—no, what could the Lord have done through him—had he believed and acted upon truth?

"*Furthermore*," continued Miss Cat, who seemed to never give up a debate until she had exhausted every argument she could think of, "it is not *you* who need be strong and brave—or rather, you need not be that of yourself—indeed, you *could not* be that of yourself. He says, 'fear thou not,' but He also tells you '*for I am with thee:* be not dismayed; for *I am* thy God: *I* will strengthen thee; yea, *I* will help thee; yea, *I* will uphold thee with the right hand of *My* righteousness.' If we lean upon *Him* and let *Him* be strength through us, *then*—well, as David or some such fellow said, 'the LORD is on my side; I will not fear: what can man do unto me?'"

"Miss Roylett," Ewart said with a wry smile, "I suspect you are a humbug!"

She started violently, and a flash of real fear crossed her face as she repositioned herself on the tree stump.

Astonished by the effect of his words, he followed them hastily with, "The idea of telling me you did not know your Bible!"

She relaxed perceptibly. "Oh, as to that." She sniffed and shrugged, playing with a bit of bark. "*Sunday school* verses I remember. I memorized more than any of my classmates."

"Somehow, that is no surprise to me," Ewart mumbled.

Miss Roylett laughed and flushed. She brushed her hands off and folded them in her lap, refusing to raise her eyes back to his.

Silence fell, broken only by the scratching of Maggie's pencil.

"Thank you," Ewart said gently.

"I hope I did not overstep my bounds or be unwomanly or some such thing," she murmured.

"I do not believe so, and I am very much in your debt for opening my eyes. No one else would speak to me as frankly as you did."

She smiled a little, but her face remained unusually sober.

"And now," he said, with an attempt at lightness, "you must tell me *your* greatest stumbling block and allow me to treat *you* to a sermon."

She laughed then, and Maggie came running to display her sketch, and the moment passed. But that evening, Ewart seated himself at his desk and covered a sheet of paper with the lies he had always believed of himself. Against them, he listed the verses that disproved his worthlessness and shame and fear. Then he placed the paper in his desk, where Maggie could not accidentally come across it, and with the loving Father Who treasured him despite every shortcoming and strengthened him to battle every flaw, Ewart began the task of building a new, better worldview.

Chapter Seven

"When once your point of view is changed, the very thing which was so damning becomes a clue to the truth."
The Problem of Thor Bridge by Sir Arthur Conan Doyle

It was early June, three months to the day since Caitrìona had been engaged by Mr. Alinac, when the bombshell came. It was Thursday morning, and she arrived at the manor to find Maggie cutting out paper dolls and Mr. Alinac frowning over the newspaper. Both were too invested to do more than murmur a greeting.

What could claim Mr. Alinac's attention so deeply? He was generally the most polite of men. Caitrìona removed her hat and placed it on a side table, then came to peer over his shoulder at the paper. The bold headline assailed her at once.

BERKSHIRE BANDIT DISCOVERED
Our readers are certainly aware of the brewing scandal concerning Miss Caitrìona Roylett and her brother, Duscan Roylett. Only a brief recapitulation is necessary. For several hours before the disappearance of Lady Hilda Garrett's priceless tiara, the butler saw a man clad in a brown trench coat loitering about the grounds. Little attention was paid to him. Around midday, a maid entered the lady's boudoir in time to see a brown trench coat disappear through the window. She gave the alarm promptly. Two hours later, Duscan Roylett was found at a Berkshire train station, headed for Eton. Not only

was he clad in the trench coat seen by the servants but he also matched perfectly the description given by both the butler and the maid. He insisted on his innocence, and nothing was found in his pockets, but a station official informed Inspector MacKinnon that he had seen another young man brush against Roylett and a package be exchanged. Unfortunately, he had not seen enough of the second man to describe him, except that he wore the same style of trench coat.

It was instantly supposed that Miss Roylett would be a party to the crime, for she had been one of the most frequent guests at Lady Garrett's balls. Upon questioning, Mr. Roylett indignantly vindicated his sister, and Inspector MacKinnon admits there is no real proof of her involvement. Mr. Vincent Woodthorn, former pupil of England's greatest detective and his successor with the older man's retreat to The Downs in this year of grace 1903, and who has since had the greatest achievements, claims there is no conceivable reason for Miss Roylett to be involved in this. However, there are many witnesses who assert Miss Roylett had been devoured with covetousness for the tiara, and her family being of straitened circumstances, it is considered Roylett may have stolen the tiara for her either to keep secretly or to sell and purchase another. At the very least, she certainly could have furnished her brother with a plan of the house, while he himself had never been invited there. Scotland Yard is still working tirelessly on the case, and new developments have occurred.

Despite the focus on Mr. Roylett, our readers have certainly not forgotten the infamous Berkshire Bandit, who terrorized Berkshire and London with his habit of relieving train passengers of money, jewellery, and such trifles, as well as his numerous midnight robberies of rare, expensive jewellery or décor, from which the noblest homes have not been exempt. In the course of his brilliant investigation, Inspector MacKinnon has just discovered that Duscan Roylett and the Berkshire Bandit are one and the same. Mr.

Roylett goes to court this Saturday, and English law will at last be satisfied. It is not known, at present, what sentence the accused may receive, although it may come so far as the rope; regardless, England may congratulate herself on the capture of this unmitigated scoundrel and breathe freely once more.

Caitrìona was surrounded in a horrible mist—her knees shook—her heart seemed to have stopped entirely—she was only aware of those awful words: *the rope.* Her brother, the little brother who had been her constant companion as a child, was to be *hanged.*

"Oh, God have mercy!"

The choking cry vibrated through the room as Caitrìona wrestled with the supreme agony of utter helplessness in the face of a loved one's imminent destruction.

In the midst of her pain, she suddenly encountered the eyes of Mr. Alinac—wide with distress and betrayal.

"*You* are Caitrìona Roylett," he whispered.

His accusing words, quiet as they were, could not be borne. Caitrìona turned and fled.

She could not be seen like this. She could not bear sympathy or attempts at comforting. She stumbled through the woods towards her own secret place, where she crouched for hours, weeping, questioning, begging in utter grief.

Ewart did not pursue her. Maggie did not appear. Mercifully, she was left entirely alone until, at long last, she regained her composure. With quietness came some comfort. Duscan would not hang; the newspaper was only trying to raise the stakes, keeping tension high so readers would want to purchase their morning papers. But the idea of his lifelong imprisonment was still heartbreaking and torturous.

At last, around noon, she roused herself slightly. She was still lethargic and bore every trace of tears, but if she went home, perhaps she could slip in and bathe her eyes before anyone found her.

She could not return to the Alinac manor. There was no question that Ewart would discharge her promptly. Most likely, he would come tomorrow to pay her what he owed. She shuddered at the thought.

"I hope I never see him again," she whispered, hiding her face in her hands. She could not bear to see him angry and disappointed.

Too late, she realized that she had grown very fond of Ewart Alinac—nay, if she were quite honest, she *loved* him. In spite of her mercenary plans, deep in her heart had nestled a timid, little dream about the man she hoped to find—a man full of the love of God and the strength to do the right thing, who balanced out her flaws—a man she could spend her every day with, who drew her ever closer to the Lord and made her smile constantly—someone she could trust with all her heart.

She had never really believed she would find him. And now she had lost him. Thanks to her constant choices to follow her own wisdom rather than going to the Lord for His.

With these thoughts as her companions, Caitríona was ready for another round of tears by the time she reached home—tears over herself instead of Duscan this time. But as she went up to their pump to wet her handkerchief, Lucy came flying out of the house.

"Oh, Cat!" she gasped. "Amy is in hysterics, Mother has fainted, and I don't know what to do!"

Caitríona dropped her handkerchief and ran to the kitchen. It took some time to revive Mother, and when she came to, she lost herself in a wild grief that did nothing to help calm Amy. At last, Caitríona dispatched Lucy to fetch Mrs. Nowan from the neighbouring farm. The bustling housewife was an excellent nurse, and Caitríona left Mother in her care while Lucy and she soothed Amy. Eventually, the little girl sobbed herself into a deep sleep, leaving her sisters to collapse, exhausted, on the parlour chairs.

"Oh, Cat," whispered Lucy, "what will we do?"

"I don't know what we *will* do," said Caitríona firmly, "but I know what we are doing *now*. I am going to London, and you are staying here with Mrs. Nowan to watch over Mother and Amy."

"To London!"

"Yes."

"*Why?*"

"You will know when I return, if I am successful." Caitríona bit her lip. Was it cruel to leave them wallowing in their horrified grief? But there would be plenty of time to comfort them later on, if—as was most likely—she failed in her errand.

For Caitríona had decided that now was the moment to approach Vincent Woodthorn. She could not afford to wait. She could only throw herself upon his pity, promise coming payment, and hope he would take the case from interest in it, as it was rumoured Mr. Holmes himself had done.

Lucy said no more. She helped Caitrìona prepare, counted out the railroad fare from the household purse, and watched her off without a question.

Caitrìona herself was in a sort of blur. Only one thing was clear: she must get to Vincent Woodthorn. She moved like an automaton, walking to the station, buying her ticket, boarding the train. She was not aware of passing time or countryside. Continually, she repeated her story, smoothing and shortening it, moulding it into a crisp, clear, businesslike petition. Mr. Woodthorn was not likely to be interested in tearful ladies with grievous tales.

She reached London safely, hailed a hansom cab, and was driven to 221B Baker Street, where she rang and was greeted by a sweet, sickly girl.

"Mr. Woodthorn, please," said Caitrìona faintly. Then she was led to the small sitting room, where a tall young man rose politely at her entrance.

Caitrìona needed only one look before she realized. "*You* are the gentleman from the train carriage who asked me about hunting in Guildford!"

Mr. Woodthorn smiled a trifle mischievously. "I must admit so. You see, I had my own thoughts on the Roylett case, and when I recognised you in the train, I could not bear to let such a glorious, investigative chance slip through my fingers."

"He did not tell us until after that the illustrious Miss Roylett *herself* was there," complained another girl, materializing in the doorway. A glance between the two young women, and Caitrìona recognised them as the twins from the train.

"My sisters, Helene and Cathryn," Mr. Woodthorn introduced them with a sweep of his hand. "They frequently help on my cases. Now, Miss Roylett, if you have caught your breath, might you tell me why you have come?"

His face was impassive, but his eyes were free of judgment and tinged with the slightest bit of encouragement. The two girls, sitting down on either side of him, were similarly calm and considerate. Nor did they change after Caitrìona had poured out her story.

When at last, inwardly shaken but outwardly unmoved, she ended, Mr. Woodthorn leaned back on his chair and steepled his fingers in what was perhaps an unconscious imitation of his mentor.

"When I first read your case, Miss Roylett, I was greatly struck by it. I have no objection to telling you that I am by no means of the popular opinion about it. I have not investigated the case myself, but I have picked up all the ready information that I could. The case against your brother rests entirely upon circumstantial evidence. Now, as Mr. Sherlock Holmes once remarked, 'Circumstantial evidence is a very tricky thing. ... It may seem to point very straight to one thing, but if you shift your own point of view a little, you may find it pointing in an equally uncompromising manner to something entirely different.' The basis of Mr. Roylett's charge is he owns a trench coat similar to the tiara thief's *and* identical to that of the so-called Berkshire Bandit. In confidence, I may tell you it is rather a rare trench coat in that it was hand-crafted by a private seamstress from Lady Harlow's household."

"I beg your pardon?" Caitrìona exclaimed in utter astonishment.

"Yes, rather unusual, is it not? Especially considering your brother has no ties to the Harlow household, let alone their very German seamstress. We know, of course, the Berkshire Bandit has this identical trench coat; Inspector MacKinnon discovered this when he so nearly caught the felon last spring. Besides the coat, however, several items reported stolen by the Berkshire Bandit were discovered among your brother's possessions at Eton and in a strongbox he had secretly consigned to a friend in Reading. And finally"—his voice grew grave—"the tiara *has* been found ... there."

Caitrìona had all she could do to repress a groan. "But how can it? I *know* Duscan was not to blame—"

"He admitted to buying a small strongbox and placing it in the care of a friend of his, Mr. J.W. Jones, who happens to be a banker and who left it in his private safe in his office. But Roylett insisted it held only a very valuable watch from his godfather, which he had placed there the day the tiara was discovered stolen."

"I remember that," Caitrìona interrupted eagerly. "I travelled with him that afternoon. It was I who convinced him to have the watch secured away on account of the Bandit. He had packaged it up and carried it in his pocket. We bought the strongbox later in Reading."

"That is precisely the story he told. Now, the watch has also been found—in the possession of a Mr. Horace Willard, who was discovered in a Devonshire hotel, gravely ill, the night of the arrest. Your brother declaims all knowledge of the gentleman."

"But Duscan had it in his *inside pocket*," persisted Caitrìona. "It could *not* be in Mr. Willard's hands!"

"You would be surprised at the cunning of that type of man, Miss Roylett. Mr. Duscan cannot recall exactly, but he believes he removed his coat for a few moments in the station's café. At any rate, he remembers finding his package on the floor and slipping it back into his pocket. Now, you are quite right in that if the watch was, as you and your brother can affirm, in his pocket, there is no conceivable way it could have travelled to Devonshire and appeared in Mr. Willard's bag. Therefore, the obvious conclusion is that the watch was not in your brother's pocket long; he was misled by a similar package, deliberately planted, which held the tiara. Now, his original package contained not only his watch but also—forgive me for spoiling the surprise—jewellery he had purchased for you and your sisters."

Caitrìona caught her breath. Dear Duscan! He must have saved his allowance for several months to afford this. How like him!

"As a result," Mr. Woodthorn continued, "the package containing the tiara and Mr. Roylett's package were similar in size, shape, and weight. And of course brown paper wrapping is easily found. Therefore Mr. Roylett *did* have the tiara on him, and he subsequently deposited it in the strongbox in all innocence. He was then at the station heading back to Eton when he was apprehended. And so the questions remain, *by whom* was the tiara stolen and *why?* Your brother insists he has no enemies, and neither did his father or godfather. What about *you*, Miss Roylett?" He pierced her with his shrewd eyes. "As you are somewhat involved in this, it is reasonable to wonder if, perhaps, *you* were targeted more than he."

The accusation was startling, but it could be quite true and showed the detective's acumen. But Caitrìona could not recollect any person she had insulted or even incommoded enough to warrant this gesture of revenge—beyond Lady Amelia Harlow, but this crime did not bear the earmarks of that weak, spiteful woman. She shook her head and closed her eyes against a sudden rush of tears. If all this rested on her, Duscan was lost.

"I in no way view the case as hopeless," Mr. Woodthorn added more gently. "I cannot promise miracles, and I frankly admit this case is very dark. But I do pledge you my best effort."

Caitrìona could not answer. She struggled to compose herself. Her last resort was failing her. *O God, why? I asked for help ... I begged for help ... Where art Thou? Why hast Thou abandoned us?*

The Woodthorns were silent, respecting her grief. Through her pain, Caitrìona registered a firm knock on the door and Mr. Woodthorn's going to answer ...

Then a voice spoke—a voice she had not realized how greatly she loved until that moment.

"Good evening. Mr. Woodthorn, I presume? I have come to hire you to investigate the Roylett case."

Caitrìona sprang to her feet, fearing to hope yet eager to believe this wonderful, unbelievable moment could happen.

"You are too late, I am afraid," said Mr. Woodthorn whimsically as he led Mr. Alinac into the sitting room.

"Too late! Man, don't say he has already been *tried*!"

"Not at all, my dear fellow; that is a great deal too rapid for English justice. I only mean to say that I have already been hired, and by a young lady most interested in the case."

Mr. Alinac blinked, then his eyes, still troubled but clear of the angry fear she had seen before, met Caitrìona's. "Miss Roylett," he said unsteadily. "I did not think to meet you here."

Caitrìona rose, their audience forgotten. "You came."

"Of course I came. Your brother deserves the best aid. I am your friend, Ca—Miss Roylett. I could not leave you to face this alone."

"I thought you must despise me."

"I should have thought you would think better of me than that, Miss Cat," he reproached her.

"I thought—you are not—very trusting—I thought—"

"Yes, I know. But it was a misunderstanding on either side. It was not your fault. Maggie was too distraught for me to go after you at once, but when I could get away and went to your home, your sister told me you had gone. She did not say where. I could only think of one way to help you, and so here I am. I hope you are not offended by my meddling."

Offended! How could she possibly be offended? He had been splendid. To think of his abruptly braving the world, London, *and* a famous stranger—for *her*!

"No," she said. "I am not offended."

Chapter Eight

"... life is infinitely stranger than anything which the mind of man could invent. We would not dare to conceive the things which are really mere commonplaces of existence."
A Case of Identity by Sir Arthur Conan Doyle

Duscan Roylett's trial was set for Saturday. It was now Friday evening. Alone in his study, Ewart tried not to pace. Maggie's room was underneath, and she would be alarmed by his anxiety. He went to the window and looked out into the night. *O Lord, have mercy, and guide Woodthorn to the truth. Save Roylett and his family.* He had repeated those words endlessly since his journey to Baker Street, but they did not feel vain. He would continue to whisper them until the Lord saw fit to answer or permanently refuse.

Sighing, Ewart crossed to his desk and sat down. He pushed away his current manuscript—he could not write tonight—and drew forwards the book he was reading. Perhaps *The Tenant of Wildfell Hall* would sweep him away for a time. At the least, he would be facing the problems of others instead of his own.

"Telegram, sir," announced the butler at the open door.

"What does he say?" Ewart exclaimed, leaping to his feet.

The butler scanned the paper, but Ewart was already there, nearly snatching the telegram to read the printed words himself.

Have succeeded. Come promptly with
Miss R.
V.W.

Ewart hastily consulted his watch. It was past nine o'clock. He would retire now and make an early start tomorrow morning. But first, he must somehow inform Miss Cat and find a chaperone.

"Can we send a man to the Royletts' home, Barnesley?"

"Yes, sir."

"Good. Then give him this telegram to deliver, please. Ah, wait, just let me note the time we will be leaving. When does the early train leave for London?"

"I believe it is six, sir."

"Excellent. I trust your memory, Barnesley. Have this delivered to Miss Ca—Miss Roylett, then. It is of the utmost importance that she receive it. Thank you. And now, can you suggest a chaperone to come with us to London tomorrow?"

The butler seemed nonplussed for a moment, then offered, "Was she not accompanied by the Beckhams in London, sir?"

"Splendid, Barnesley, splendid! You are positively scintillating. Where is my notepaper?" After scrabbling for a clean sheet, Ewart hastily wrote the message without any of his usual overconsideration of words and passed it to Barnesley. "To be delivered as well, if you please, and just as important."

"Very good. Anything else, sir?"

"No thank you; I am going to retire. But if you could lay out my clothes for tomorrow, I would be very grateful."

"Certainly. Have a good night, sir."

"Thank you, and you as well, Barnesley."

Contrary to the butler's wish, however, Ewart passed a restless night. He rose before dawn, went to his study to immerse himself in the Word, and prayed the long hours away. Time spent at his Father's feet dissipated his anxiety, and when, eventually, he drew up before the Beckhams' in the carriage, he was able to smile and chat quite cheerfully.

Miss Cat, however, was in a state of pitiable worry when Ewart and Mrs. Beckham met her at the Royletts' cottage. She remained withdrawn through the entire trip, and Ewart had to almost pilot her around the station, to a hansom cab, and up the staircase to the Woodthorns' flat.

Mr. Woodthorn received them graciously into his sitting room, where two other young men were waiting.

"I have with me here Inspector Stanley Hopkins, who represents Scotland Yard," Mr. Woodthorn said, indicating the exceedingly alert man beside him. "We have a plan to propose, Miss Roylett. We could, of course, reveal our facts to Scotland Yard and have the malefactors arrested; however, there are high chances they will escape justice if we follow that course. Our second option is to let the trial proceed. I ventured to call a friend of mine, a lawyer who does his own investigations and has several cases to his credit; you might have heard of him—Cyril Barker."

There was a collective gasp as the famous young man across the room bowed.

"He would be quite willing to take on the case, and between us, we are all certain we would clear your brother and see justice done. The question rests on you, Miss Roylett."

Miss Cat swallowed hard, and despite her best efforts, her face displayed the battle in her soul. The others waited patiently until at last she answered in a trembling voice, "I—I think your plan is good, sir."

Mr. Woodthorn had been watching her keenly; now he permitted himself a satisfied smile. "Excellent. Let me explain to you what I have discovered." Leaning back on his chair and steepling his fingers à la Sherlock Holmes, he began.

"I started with the angle that Mr. Roylett was innocent, in which case it was evident that he had become a scapegoat. What was *not* clear was whether this was deliberate or an unlucky accident. Evidently, the trench coat was the starting point of the whole investigation, being the sole link between Duscan Roylett, the tiara thief, *and* the Berkshire Bandit. I loafed about the Harlow house, and thanks to the stableman's gossip, I learned that Lady Charlotte Harlow was seeking an assistant. My sister Cathryn—quite fluent in German—applied, and I accompanied her to the interview. The seamstress was a voluble woman, and we discovered fairly easily that in the whole of her service for the Harlows, she had only sewn *two* trench coats. One had been taken to Eton by Lord Anthony Harlow; the other had been given with great secrecy to Lady Margaret Kissel."

Ewart started violently at his mother's name. How could she be mixed up with this sordid business? Vague worry began to surround him. Surely ... surely Mother had done nothing *wrong* ...

"Asked how she thought young Roylett had gotten ahold of her coat, the seamstress observed that Lord Anthony must have given it away—which is indeed what happened. Both coats were identical, except that Lord Anthony's had his initials worked in the collar. I followed the thread of the other coat, and after some difficulty, I ascertained—never mind how—from Lady Kissel's maid that for several years, a gentleman had called upon her weekly, and they had long and most secret conversations. The gentleman, the maid added, had recently become quite irritable. He visited two days before the tiara was stolen, and the maid, lingering in the hall as Lady Kissel saw him out, distinctly heard him say, 'This is the last time,' to which the lady had agreed. Upon asking the maid for a description of the gentleman, I received a very accurate one which I recognized immediately as the unique features of one Perry MacNoughton, a Scotland Yard detective. Discreet inquiries proved Perry MacNoughton is an avid gambler and deeply in debt. He also owed £5000 to Colonel Merritt Alinac, Lady Kissel's first husband."

Ewart started again. This item of news was entirely unknown to him, and he did not like it. It did not bode well for his as yet indecipherable fears.

"I will not incriminate myself in the presence of the official police"—here Mr. Woodthorn's face lightened with a mischievous smile, and Inspector Hopkins shook his head in amused censor— "but I managed to examine Mr. MacNoughton's home and came across the missing trench coat matching the one Duscan Roylett so unfortunately wore. In this house, I also located several items stolen by the Berkshire Bandit. I now had a pretty clear thread running between Lady Kissel, Mr. MacNoughton, and the Berkshire Bandit, but I could not see why Roylett had become embroiled in this. Therefore I visited Lord Anthony Harlow, an affable, if very vacuous, youth; from him, I found that when they were fourteen and fifteen respectively, Duscan Roylett thrashed Anthony Harlow for speaking ill to a village girl. Lord Anthony himself told of the incident with great, good humour and evident respect for Roylett, but he admitted his mother and her friends hated Roylett madly for his act of retribution. Despite this, Lady Harlow had given Lord Anthony a trench coat with specific instructions to give it to Roylett, which he had done, assuming it was a peace offering.

"I then tackled the Horace Willard angle. Hopkins, here, supplied me with all the information I desired. Willard is a gambling pal of MacNoughton's, and the two men were sighted in confidential communication the evening of a Berkshire Bandit theft—not once, nor twice, but a score of times, and most notably, the day before the tiara theft. Willard was also spotted at the Reading station, hanging about Roylett. Two of the porters can vouch for that. He was likely the man who brushed against Roylett and pretended to receive a package from him, but of this I have no concrete proof.

"I waited until Lady Kissel left her house, following which Hopkins and I explored her boudoir, where we discovered a safe containing the greater portion of the jewellery, artefacts, etc., the Berkshire Bandit had stolen. During our search, MacNoughton arrived, nearly surprising us, and close on his heels, the lady herself returned, having spotted him from her carriage. A royal battle ensued, and my suspicions were proved correct. Lady Kissel, whose funds are rapidly draining due to her own profligacy and her husband's, blackmailed MacNoughton into working for her in exchange for freedom from his debts. She prepared for the theft of an unnamed lady's valuable Indian jewellery by terrorizing the country with MacNoughton as the Bandit; needing a scapegoat, she had pleased Lady Harlow by setting up Roylett. The appearance of Lady Garrett's tiara changed her plans, and she insisted MacNoughton steal it. He was reluctant, contending he had paid his debts and more, but at last agreed on condition that it would be the last job. He laid his plans and recruited Willard, who had been an accomplice before. Willard, however, as he trailed Roylett, heard of the packaged watch and resolved to double-cross MacNoughton to his own advantage. He packaged the tiara similarly to the watch and jewellery and effected the change, planning to recover the tiara later and flee the country. His unexpected illness silenced him for a time, but now all three villains are at each other's throats because of the complications they presently face."

The quiet voice stilled, and not a sound was heard.

Ewart sat with his face shaded by his hand. The horror and relief within him was almost too great. How glad he was that Miss Roylett's family would soon be free, once Duscan's trial proved their innocence ... but his mother! What would Maggie do? And what would the world think of Ewart now? His position was already precarious ...

Dazed with grief, plunged into a mixture of prayer and pondering, he followed the others mechanically from the room to a hansom cab and then into the courthouse. At last, when he had fully comprehended the situation, he set it aside to work through later and roused himself, only to find the trial going very badly. Roylett, on the verge of a severe prison sentence, was pale but composed, Miss Roylett was very agitated, and Mr. Barker was calling Vincent Woodthorn to the stand.

"Mr. Woodthorn, you were hired to investigate the case by Mr. Roylett's family, were you not?"

Gloom appeared on the faces of the judge, jury, and prosecutor. The public stirred appreciatively.

"I was," Vincent Woodthorn answered.

"Will you tell the court what you discovered?"

Ewart sneaked a glance towards the Ladies Harlow and Kissel, who were away towards the back, and MacNoughton, whose appearance was entirely due to Stanley Hopkins, beside whom he sat. The three villains seemed serenely undisturbed, but as Mr. Woodthorn repeated his story amid the greatest silence and attention, their composures failed them. Lady Harlow grew red with suppressed anger; Lady Kissel remained still, but her eyes—Ewart could not look at them; and great drops of sweat slowly rolled down MacNoughton's deathly-white face.

Against all odds, Duscan Roylett was being proven innocent.

The Lord had answered. Justice had prevailed.

Epilogue

"It will be cold and bitter, ... and a good many of us may wither before its blast. But it's God's own wind none the less, and a cleaner, better, stronger land will lie in the sunshine when the storm has cleared."
His Last Bow by Sir Arthur Conan Doyle

The trial of Duscan Roylett was soon hailed as "the trial of the century." Calling upon a host of eyewitnesses to confirm Mr. Woodthorn's testimony, Mr. Barker had succeeded in destroying the flimsy circumstantial case built against Duscan Roylett. The onslaught of evidence was too much for anyone to stand against, and Duscan had been completely exonerated. He was now back at Eton, striving to escape his newfound popularity.

Caitrìona had collapsed almost immediately after the trial. She was utterly drained by all she'd endured, and her physical prostration led to despondency. Her great goals had been accomplished: Duscan was free, and their name was wiped of blemish; but in her weakened state, it was far too easy to fall into the lies of worthlessness. She had failed her family: it was Mr. Alinac who really hired Mr. Woodthorn, for he had insisted on paying. She had lost Mr. Alinac—Ewart—the man she loved—through her deceit. She had no hope of making a brilliant match for her family's sake or her own grand plans to change the world. She had neglected the Lord entirely. She was a wicked, useless girl ...

The doctor prescribed complete peace and quiet, and everyone carried out his orders with the utmost strictness. Caitrìona had not been sorry to rest, despite the guilt over her shirking. Everything wearied her. Emotion was too much to bear, yet when she was alone at nights, she could only lie and weep. During the day, she could scarcely keep together the slightly cheerful façade she assumed. The weeks dragged by, each more miserable than the last, until she believed that if this continued, she should go mad or die—the usual conclusion of unhappy young folks, she supposed, but it felt quite real to her.

Maggie and Mr. Alinac visited her daily. Maggie always brought her new puppy, named Sir Walter Raleigh by her long-suffering brother. Despite his best attempts, Mr. Alinac was not proof against his sister's pleas for "something that *wasn't* a kitten!" He, for his part, always brought flowers and books, chatted cheerfully, and did not ask Caitrìona's participation in the conversation. But every day he gently enquired how she was and if she would like a listening ear. His persistent kindness wore through her pride and shame, and at last Caitrìona found herself sobbing out her story—how she had come face-to-face with her own insufficiency and was terrified of losing her grasp of life.

"Does it not frighten you, how unpredictable life is?" she asked him. "Don't you wish to plan good things and keep the evil away?"

"Oh, my dear Miss Cat," he said softly, "I trust my Father. He is good, and He will only allow what is best for me to happen. I am willing to surrender everything to Him, because I trust He will always give me better than my plans could ever yield."

Caitrìona Roylett's plans had always been her strength and her purpose. She was struck anew by this young man's simple faith that allowed him to hold his sister's and his lives so loosely, allowing the Father to dispose of them as He pleased. Could she surrender her plans and accept those of her Lord? Could she believe *His* plan would make her far happier than what she thought she needed?

She had her own idea of what composed a worthwhile purpose in life. But now she had watched this young man for months as he quietly cared for his tenants and raised his sister, writing "living epistles" as he invested so deeply in the lives and future of those around him—and how worthwhile a pursuit *that* was!

Yes, the Lord could grant her the dreams of her heart. Or He could grant her far better. She would wait on Him. He would provide for her family—He would give her life purpose—all in His time.

It was a daily decision to believe, surrender, and wait. It was not—it would never be easy ... but it was worthwhile.

Slowly, Caitrìona built up her strength. She spent her days in the garden, reading, praying, worshipping the Lord, and conversing with Ewart Alinac when he came. It was there that she sat one fine summer morning when Maggie appeared.

"I have something for you, Miss Cat! Guess!"

"A kitten?"

Maggie rolled her eyes. "No, Ewart made me give Mary Kingsley's all away. He says four cats is enough for any man. Try again. *I* don't think you shall ever guess."

"Encouraging, very," retorted Caitrìona. She thought hard for a moment. "Mother—?"

Maggie did not wait for the conclusion of the sentence. She laughed triumphantly. "From Ewart!" she crowed as she dropped something in Caitrìona's lap. Then she fled.

It was a tiny posy holder—and it held a tussie-mussie. Moss rosebud—*confession of love*. Forget-me-not—*true love*. Austrian rose—*you are all that's lovely*. Pansy—*think of me*.

There was no mistaking the message. Ewart Alinac was not the man to use flowers without knowing exactly what they meant.

Tears misted Caitrìona's eyes. A few months ago, she would have rejected the young gentleman with something very like scorn. He was not extremely wealthy nor very highborn nor unusually handsome. He was simple, quiet, spiritual—yet that was more than enough, now. He was not what she had planned for, but he was infinitely better than she had dreamed of. She had thought she'd lost him—but now he was declaring himself hers.

O Lord, Thou are indeed good.

Smiling, Caitrìona pinned the tussie-mussie to her bodice. A step sounded on the garden path before her, and she looked up to see Ewart.

"I have received permission from your mother to court you," he said simply.

"I knew you would," Caitrìona whispered.

He smiled and seated himself on the bench that stood near her own.

"I'm in great debt to your brother," he added in a light tone. "If he hadn't been arrested and charged, I should have remained completely unaware of your existence."

"If he hadn't been arrested, I wonder how much longer it would have taken me to change," Caitrìona mused.

"And I," added Ewart. "It's been a hard, bitter time for us all, but the Lord knew what He was about when He allowed it. I'm a better, stronger man now than I would have been otherwise."

Caitríona nodded. They had far to go yet. With the imprisonment of his mother and the sudden apoplectic death of his stepfather, he had stepped into a far greater position as head of a much more extensive household, and he was still adjusting to life in the world, not to mention life as a leader. She, for her part, still battled often with the desire for a more public role in life and the struggle of yielding her own plans in favour of the Lord's will. Yes, they had much to learn, but the Lord had brought them far, and He would take them still farther.

Her gaze fell to the knot of flowers over her heart. They seemed to represent the story of their love. His battle with self-doubt. Her journey into surrender. Brought together in a sweet-smelling, eye-catching cluster of blossoms—neither large nor expensive yet still pleasant and useful.

A tussie-mussie of love and trust, unfolding day by day into greater beauty and spreading greater joy until at last the Master took the blossoms to Himself and left the scent to linger among those left behind, blessing still and inspiring with its aroma new blooms for His everlasting bouquet.

A Note from Katja H. Labonté

This story would not exist without Bethany C. Willcox, my very own "Watson." When she invited me to help brainstorm her short story "Everything," for the *Everything* story collection (published by Rebekah A. Morris), we suddenly found ourselves creating Sherlock Holmes fan fiction … and Vincent Woodthorn was born. I loved him and his sisters so much that when I started writing "The Tussie-Mussie," I asked her for permission to include Vincent, and she graciously agreed. Bethany, thank you so much for your encouragement and excitement over this project, and for being the Watson to my Lestrade over the years.

And to any Sherlock fans out there, I hope you'll enjoy discovering the easter eggs I slipped in from the canon as much as I enjoyed putting them in.

Many thanks to Ryana Lynn, without whom the mystery would be quite incomplete; to Erika, who brainstormed so many plot holes with me; to Rachel, Kelly, and Andrea for your much-needed corrections and sweet encouragement; and to Mary, who believed in me when I didn't believe in myself.

To the entire Springtime in Surrey team, thanks for your love, support, and patience over this journey. You were the best anthology team a girl could ask for!

And thank You, Lord, for everything You taught me through "The Tussie-Mussie." May You use it to encourage and bless others as much as it did me.

Finally, thank you, reader, for joining me in exploring Caitrìona and Ewart's story. If you want to read more of my books, check out my freebies at littleblossomsforjesus.wordpress.com!

The Odd Duck Society

a novella by Rachel Leitch

Dedication

To all the women who have made up my own Odd Duck Society.

Chapter One

Monday

It was a good day for ducks. Not so much for the more unusual creature referred to as Jessamy Aubertine.

Rain dribbled off my windswept purple umbrella and onto the shoulder of my cardigan. I knew I should have questioned my "Here Comes the Sun" T-shirt beneath it. The damp air frizzled my springy, ginger curls even more than usual as I huddled under the tea shop's awning.

I hadn't visited this little Box Hill village in ages. The letters in the tea shop window may have long faded, but the chalkboard advertising the special hadn't. The ever-important neon Free Internet sign in the window wore thin its attempt to keep up.

Time had forgotten this corner, and I rather liked it.

I shifted my phone—and the hold music—to my other ear. This was the worst *Pride and Prejudice* soundtrack cover I'd ever heard, and I'd certainly stumbled across more than my fair share.

The chipped clock on the church green reminded me that I'd held for twenty minutes, waiting in the rain for a buyer that couldn't bother to show up.

Why in the rain? Because Box Hill loved Una Aubertine. And any news scrap must be phoned back to her, especially if it involved her daughter.

I caught my reflection in the window. Chai-colored eyes studied me back and strawberry-seed freckles dotted my milk-swirl skin. I'd rounded out quite a bit over the past semester, allowing myself to blossom in my natural shape for the first time.

I tugged my cardigan forward. Mum had enough to worry about without adding me.

Darcy, the university secretary, answered at last, her voice as tinny as the orchestra from before. "Hello?"

"Hello. This is Jessamy, um, Jessamy Aubertine." Suddenly, I trembled all over, even though I'd had plenty of time to rehearse. "I'm calling to find out how to change my program."

The silence humidified. "Right. Did you consult your tutor?"

"Yes, uh, yes I did. Wednesday, I think." I'd put it off as long as possible before spring holiday. "She agreed this was my best course."

"Which program will you switch to?"

"I can't, I don't want to switch just yet. I'll wait until the end of the semester." I took a deep breath of drizzle. "And I'll be switching universities."

"Oh." The sound pooled displeasure like the puddle in my trainer. Darcy likely didn't hear that message often. This university was a final stop for those who made it in.

I softened my voice and stepped away from a teen girl carrying a messenger bag and a fistful of posters. "Look, Darcy. I never chose international business management. Dad did." Scraped every penny he could and sold renovation projects he loved to get me there, forgetting to ever ask me if I *wanted* to be there.

"My professor caught me writing stories during lectures three times last week, *after* I'd skipped the essay he assigned. So he suggested I talk to my tutor. The university I'm switching to is much smaller, but I can study literature and writing, like I want to."

It was more than just a "want to." I couldn't go a day without stories and couldn't imagine one either. It was my calm, a place away from all the demands of everyday life. A place just the right size for me.

"You don't have to explain it to me, darling."

Exactly. But the lady I *did* need to explain it to had no idea I was making this call.

Mum would hug my shoulders and cheer without condemnation. But disappointment would linger in her eyes, and whispers would fly after she thought I'd turned out my light.

Mum wasn't unkind. She was just *so* good. Too good.

Everything I wasn't.

"Now let me see here." The phone crackled like leftover autumn leaves.

Spring holiday was supposed to be relaxing. A week to myself at the old Box Hill cottage, my childhood home. Dropping by Beatrix's bookstore every other day to see what Jane Austen editions she had in. Dancing alone to Beatles records. Riding my bike all over the grounds for hours, like when I was ten.

"Are you still there?"

I didn't bother forcing a smile. "Yes."

"We should have the paperwork sent your way by the end of next week. Does that work?"

No. I'd have to talk to Mum before those papers appeared at our London house. "Yes. Um, can I ask one more thing? Could you not let on to Mum about this call?" I'd purposely called on Mum's lunch break.

"Of course, darling," Darcy warbled.

I didn't at all feel assured, but I thanked her and hung up. Next, I checked my texts to be sure the buyer hadn't canceled. Nothing.

The puddle had sopped into both trainers. All I wanted was to watch the rain speckle the cherry blossoms through the window with a good period drama on the telly and an empty leather journal on my lap.

My gaze fell on the stained-glass windows across the street. Providence—that old-fashioned word intended to nudge God a touch nearer—must be giggling at me.

Loud laughter erupted across the street. London laughter, not Surrey laughter. A gaggle of university students breezed out of the gift shop that mainly entertained tourists.

Truly? I'd come to Box Hill to *avoid* running into them at every turn.

The business students who always studied and always spoke up during lectures. The students who were put together and ready for a photo shoot even in a rainstorm. The students who never wanted to grab tea or dally at the library.

I snapped my umbrella shut and ducked inside the tea shop. Dried lavender stalks rustled on the peeling purple door of the very place I was trying to sell.

The scent of rich black tea and left-behind blossoms washed over me. "The Muses" was hand-painted in scrolling letters over a chalkboard menu.

I knew every swirl by heart, because I'd been there when Mum painted it, when Dad stenciled the menu, when he still looked up at her like she was a queen.

When it was still ours.

Dad had owned it for years, always scheming to make something wonderful of it, as he had for every run-down thing he came across—including the Box Hill newcomer that he married. Mum had cast the vision for a tea shop and helped him renovate it. But after so many years, that vision had shriveled, so he'd left the shop to Mum. A gift, he'd called it.

Mum had cherished it as such for four years, despite Dad's lack of intentions. But even she had called it too much. Someone else would need to take ownership and turn a profit, or it would be sold.

Enter Jessamy Aubertine.

Bookshelves filled with worn secondhand books from Beatrix's lined the walls. Glass windows, now dotted with droplets, engaged the empty spaces.

Only two people haunted the tables.

A teen girl, maybe sixth form, slung one leg over the arm of a stained wing chair. She sported wavy, brown hair trimmed at her ears; large, wire-framed glasses; an unremarkable form; and a Peter Parker T-shirt. The worn clearance-sticker notebook on her lap teetered as she pressed a cell phone to her ear, speaking faster in Spanish than I could in English. She waved at the girl who was stapling a poster to the bulletin board.

From the cherry-wood table by the windows, an older Black lady watched the world pass. She glanced at me as if she'd been waiting for me, but then quickly looked away. Papers and books and old, yellow notepads covered in precise cursive were arranged across the entire surface. Her tight, silver coils reminded me of my professor, but her shade of lipstick reminded me of forties' movies. She wore a floral dress—simple, slender, but still classy.

The poster girl slipped past me and out the door.

"They went ahead and had the meeting without me?" the lady murmured, louder than she'd likely intended.

"Can I get you anything?"

The Asian barista's peppy voice startled me. Instead of the one-size-doesn't-fit-all uniform, she wore a splotched hand-embroidered apron, which complemented her generous figure beautifully. She secured her black messy bun with two wooden stirrers covered in hand-written Japanese symbols.

"Oh. Sorry. I'm good, thanks," I mumbled.

The girl with the glasses left her armchair and moved to the counter, bobbing her head to the record player. The barista slid a cup towards her in exchange for three pound notes. I caught a hint of peppermint.

"Thanks, Imogen." The girl sipped her tea and smiled at me—wry yet sympathetic. "Did you get ditched too? Seems this is the place for it."

The lady behind me chuckled and scribbled more notes.

I smiled awkwardly. As soon as the girl with glasses returned to her seat, I slipped out the door into the rain and set off for home as quickly as possible.

Chapter Two

Tuesday

I'd lost track of time riding my bike around the old gardens, just like when I was ten. I shook my curls out of my face and pedaled around the corner of the stone cottage toward the postbox.

A lone cut pink rose lazed beneath the postbox. Odd. Didn't think we grew those. If I saw our gardener, Allifair, I'd ask her.

I opened the off-kilter postbox, as I did every day simply because. It was always empty. All our old neighbors sent post to our London house.

White caught my eye.

I squinted into the box.

A letter.

Perhaps someone else's post had found its way into our box.

I set the letter in my bicycle's basket before riding back to the cottage. The envelope read "Jessamy Aubertine" in an old script. It hadn't come here by mistake.

After leaning my bike against the cherry tree's trunk, I sank onto a bench beneath the leafy branches. The letter's seal was in the shape of a rose, and when I slit the missive open, pink rose petals tumbled onto my lap. The same elegant handwriting looped across the page.

> *It is a truth universally acknowledged, that a young lady in possession of her own self, must be in want of a friend.*
>
> *However little known the feelings or views of such a lady may be on her first returning to an old*

neighborhood, this truth is so well fixed in the minds of the surrounding families, that rather than making her one of their own, they seem to avoid her at all costs.

I have come to Surrey to write and revise, not to socialize, and yet, I cannot put you—someone I have never met—from my mind.

Have you heard that Laureates is let at last? I hadn't until just this morning. Cassandra has been here, and she told me all about it, seeing as I am the last to know. Perhaps this will be my last day writing in this hall.

Do you not want to know who has taken it? I want to tell you, so I hope you have no objection.

Cassandra says that Laureates is taken by no one at all. A young man from the north of England came down in a chaise and four to see the place on Monday and was so much delighted with it that he agreed with Mr. Morris immediately; the young man is to take possession, and Laureates is to be opened to the public as an inn by the end of next week.

And I thought Morris and I were friends. Off goes my secret writing haven, as he well knows.

Everyone thinks it is a fine thing, that it will attract more eligible men for our girls and, therefore, be to the immense benefit of all of Box Hill, if not the entirety of Surrey.

How can they be so tiresome? They must know that I was thinking of possessing the place. I must admit, it was part of my design in settling here. Now it is very likely that it will become a great amusement and so full of people that I must find another writing haunt at once.

Nevertheless, I've gotten used to the idea. As I did so, I thought I might write a letter to whomever may occupy my writing corner next.

I frowned. The prose seemed old-fashioned. But how would someone so long ago have known I would come along next? It must have been written by someone from my own time, or at the very least, forwarded by one. I read on:

> *Perhaps that will be still better, for you, I am sure, are as clever as any of them. You certainly have your share of beauty, but you don't pretend to be anything extraordinary now, and I believe that's why it is so striking. In such cases, a woman has not often either trait to think of, so I like that you defy such expectations.*
>
> *You must indeed go back to Laureates and see who you find there. I'm sure it is more than you engage for, but consider my earlier words. Perhaps a want of companionship isn't for a lack of worthy people but simply a lack of sight. I'm throwing in a good word for you.*
>
> *You may not think you're half so handsome as Emma, nor half as good-humored as Lydia. You may not have ever gotten the preference from anyone. You may think you're silly and ignorant, too much like other girls or not enough like them, but you have something more than any of the rest.*
>
> *I hope you might believe that and live to see many such companions come into the neighborhood.*
>
> *Jane Austen*

I stared at the weathered paper, soft as the rose petals, and rubbed the waxy residue of the seal off my fingers.

I wasn't an expert by any means, but on all counts I could imagine, it looked authentic. Could this letter have truly been written that long ago, in the early eighteen hundreds? Could it really have been written by *Jane Austen*? An author I'd adored since I first discovered her in secondary school? The author whose novels I'd collected countless editions of?

Had she written this letter to *me*?

And who had thought to forward it to me?

Would the building she mentioned even exist anymore? After all, that had been hundreds of years ago. Box Hill preserved many historic buildings, though.

How on earth had this letter found its way to me? I ran my finger over the words gently, so I didn't smudge the ink.

What could it hurt to follow the directions? Who knew what I might find? I needed a little adventure, truth be told—even if it led to an empty lot.

I left my bike under the tree and marched out of the garden, letter in hand, into the sunshine and cherry blossoms without snagging my cardigan.

Once again, I stood before the peeling purple door of The Muses. With the rustle of dried lavender, my tremendous adventure seemed more like a lark sprang on a newcomer.

Dad had told me that the shop was a renovated historic building. Never told me much more.

Jane Austen's beloved Laureates had been renovated into The Muses.

Even Jane thought it great fun to hark back my failures.

I sighed and pushed open the door. Might as well get a chai for my trouble.

But two women stood from the cherry-wood table by the window: the Black lady who had sat there the last time and the sixth-form girl with the rapid Spanish and Peter Parker T-shirt.

Both of them held weathered letters.

Both of them approached me.

Wishing I'd worn a cardigan, I fussed with the hem of my T-shirt instead.

The older woman presented a slender hand, very primly, very cordially. "I'm Honora Welbeck. We have you to thank for this pleasant surprise." Her voice was dark, rich, and sweet.

"No." I gave my letter instead of my hand. "See? I got one, too. I'm as confused as you are."

Honora frowned. "But the letter said we'd find like-minded companions waiting here.

The girl with the glasses nodded, affirming that hers said the same.

"Naturally, I assumed it meant the author."

"I'm afraid not," I said.

The girl crossed the room and slipped three pound notes across the counter. "While we're already here, we might as well get a cuppa and figure it out, *sí*?"

Honora glanced at the clock. "I suppose so." She quirked an eyebrow, as if asking my opinion.

She *was* asking my opinion, I realized. "Sounds lovely."

Farewell, relaxing holiday in Box Hill.

Honora gestured to the line, which consisted of the sixth-form girl in front of us. "After you."

I shifted ahead of her and reached for my oversized tote bag.

It wasn't there.

Had I been in such a hurry to find Laureates that I left my bag at home? I had to have at least grabbed my wallet. Or my phone. I patted my pockets. Nothing.

My face bloomed warm as I stepped out of line.

"It's all right, darling, I'm in no rush." Honora scrolled through emails on her phone.

I'd hoped to not have to explain my blunder. "No, I, uh, left my purse at home. I'll go save our table."

Honora pulled three pristine pound notes from her purse. "I always bring extra."

Of course she did. She reminded me a bit too much of Mum.

Still, the notes felt cinnamon-warm as she pressed them into my hand. And no matter how perfect and prepared she was, it was nice to have somebody looking out for me.

We each received our cuppas and returned to the cherry-wood table. My hips spilled over the seat, so I finally settled with my ankles crossed and my fingers still worrying my hem.

"I'm Lula Carrington." The girl offered her hand, nearly upsetting her mint tea.

I accepted, since she'd gone to all the trouble of endangering her cup. "Jessamy Aubertine."

"What a beautiful name." Honora slipped onto the seat across from me.

"J.A." Lula wiped up some dribbles with a wrinkled napkin. "So Jane Austen wrote your letter, *sí*?"

"How did you know that?" I clenched my hands around my chai.

"All our letters are from authors that share our initials. Mine came from Lewis Carroll. Honora's came from H. G. Wells. Lucky guess." Lula took a long slurp.

Honora seemed a bit miffed at Lula's intrusion but handled it with the decorum of a Regency matriarch. "Not only did they come from authors who share our initials, but they're all authors who spent time here in Surrey. Have you always lived in Surrey?"

I hurried to finish my swallow, but sputtered instead. "Most of my childhood. London now, but I decided to spend spring holiday here." I coughed again.

Lula offered her napkin.

"I couldn't imagine living anywhere else." Honora gestured to the blossoms that tiptoed over the window glass, fluttering in the spring breeze. "What are you studying?"

I should have said "international business management," what I'd told everyone for months. But, for the first time, I confessed, "English literature and professional writing."

"No way!"

I steadied Lula's drink.

"Thanks, *amiga*. I write, too!" Lula relocated her cup to a somewhat safer place. "Urban fantasy. What do you write?"

"Historical fiction." How easily the words came when someone else cared and drew them out. Perhaps all those thoughts had been carefully bottled away for such a moment.

"I'm something of a writer myself," Honora spoke up.

Lula crisscrossed her legs, bumping the table. "What do *you* write?"

I tilted my head.

"Literary fiction." Of course Honora had such a distinguished answer.

I chuckled. "What are the odds? Three writers who have never met before being called together at a tea shop by mysterious letters from famous authors?"

Lula snorted. "Maybe they knew that was the only way to get us out of our caves."

My hands quivered on my teacup as I braved the lead on the next question. "Have any of you been published yet?"

Both ladies shook their heads.

Relief blossomed in my chest. For once, I wasn't the only one. "Me neither."

Lula tugged a large, army-green backpack onto her lap. "I found this the other day." She unzipped it, sending three papers and a bag of pretzels to an untimely end on the floor.

"Just to clarify, you found the backpack or that plethora of papers?" Honora quipped.

Lula rolled her eyes and lifted the poster. "This. I found it on the bulletin board."

I smoothed the wrinkles. It looked like the posters the other girl was putting up when I was last here.

Aspiring authors!
Bring your most worthy tales to Surrey's Just Ducky
Festival, the weekend of April 15. This year's theme
is "The Ugly Duckling," so begin penning your most
beautiful retellings now. Winner takes home eight
hundred pounds, highest prize ever awarded at the
festival. Accepting only short stories, no entries over
7,500 words.

Honora laughed, slapping her knee in her first show of anything less than decorum. "Well, I should know. I designed it, wrote it, and suggested the idea. I'm on the committee for the festival. Some might call that Providence."

"I would," Lula declared.

I smoothed the poster again instead of my hem.

Could I truly do this? A winning short story would improve my standing in my new program. And eight hundred pounds would help me get to a new university in the first place.

Providence hadn't looked out for me lately, but maybe He changed His mind.

"Keep the poster," Lula offered. "I wrote down all the details."

"If it's in that bag, darling, you'll never see it again," Honora murmured into her black tea.

"Thanks." I folded the paper and tucked it in my pocket, missing my purse even more.

"Shall we figure out these letters, then?" Honora perched tiny reading glasses on her upturned nose.

Each of us passed our letters to the next lady—mine to Lula, Lula's to Honora, and Honora's to me.

Honora's letter read:

The Writer (for so it will be convenient to speak of her) was expounding a matter to us. Her dark eyes shone and twinkled, and her face was flushed and animated. And she put it to us in this way—marking the points with a lean forefinger—as we sat and lazily admired her earnestness.

She controverted one or two ideas that were almost universally accepted, but never meant to ask us to accept anything without reasonable grounds for it. And all with a slight accession of cheerfulness, such that anyone, from schoolgirls to city management, would knit their brows and lapse into an introspective state.

"Yes, I think I see it now," they all said after some time, brightening in a quite transitory manner, their lips moving as one who repeats mystic words.

As to what those mystic words were ... I suppose that is for you, the Writer, to decide. I found many such words at the establishment known as Laureates. What I did not find so much of were such things as we call real or universally accepted.

What I found is that perhaps I preferred those flighty and fanciful things, those mystic words, to the things one might explain to their colleagues. More than mere fanciful things, I preferred the companions I found there. Follow this letter and you may discover the same.

To the Writer who uses this corner next, I wonder at what your decision may be.

H. G. Wells

Lula's letter read:

You get very tired of sitting by everyone else on the bank and of having nothing to do: once or twice, you peep into the books other people are reading, but they have no pictures or conversations in them, and what is the use of such books?

So you consider a great many things in your own heart, when suddenly something runs by, as life tends to do.

There is nothing so very remarkable in that, nor do you think it so very much out of the way. But it is. It is very much out of the way, for other people. When you think it over afterward, it occurs to you that you ought to have wondered at this, but at the time, it all seemed quite natural.

You start to your feet, for it flashes across your mind that you had never before seen something like this, and burning with curiosity, you run across the field after it and, fortunately, are just in time to see it pop down a large rabbit hole under the hedge.

You go down after it, never once considering how in the world you are to get out again. You look about you even as you're falling, and you wonder what's going to happen next.

People like you always seem to find Wonderland—as well as this corner of Laureates. I suppose the best I can suggest to you is to keep falling. I rather prefer it to crawling back out of the rabbit hole anyhow.

Whether or not you do crawl back out of the rabbit hole, I would advise having some companions to assist you. Perhaps Laureates could be of service?

Lewis Carroll

"I'm on the historical society." Goodness, was there any Surrey society that Honora *wasn't* on? "This shop was built in a historic building that had served as a pub and restaurant since the eighteen hundreds."

Lula gazed around as if seeing it for the first time, but I simply nodded.

Honora seemed surprised by my knowledge. "And all three authors were known to spend time in Surrey, if not Box Hill itself. Perhaps it inspired them."

That was why Dad had called this shop The Muses. *"The perfect name for a historic authors' haunt."*

But if I shared that tidbit, they'd wonder how I knew. And if they knew I owned The Muses, we'd wind up discussing my failure at running the shop.

Or selling it, as the case may be.

"Even *if* the authors wrote these," I countered, hating my doubts, "how did they get to us? Someone had to have sent them, but why? And why pick us?"

"Maybe they were meant to find us?" Lula clearly found the randomness of this quite cozy. "Since Honora brought up Providence."

"I believe they were," Honora declared. "But I can't deny wanting to know the reasoning behind it all."

"Is there anyone either of you know who might have done this?" I asked.

They both pondered for a long moment, then shook their heads.

"You?" Lula returned.

"No. No one." I answered too quickly compared to them.

Honora laid her empty tea cup just so on her saucer. "Perhaps we'll never know."

"Maybe we're not meant to." Lula clanked her stirring spoon.

I found that an oddly comforting thought. That something good had happened simply because Someone had meant it to be.

But as with all somethings good, it ended.

"I would love to stay and continue our wonderful chat, but I have a festival committee meeting." Honora's smile made it clear that she took great pride in her work. "However it came to be, it was wonderful to meet you two."

"Likewise." I reached for my purse before realizing once again I hadn't brought it. "I'm sorry I interrupted both your days for nothing."

"Interruptions are never nothing." Lula slung her backpack over her shoulder. "I love interruptions."

"I believe *that*." Honora rolled her dark eyes toward me. "Besides, it's not as if you wrote the letters, Jessamy. Even if it were an interruption, you wouldn't have caused it."

"What if we met again?" Lula hopped from one foot to the other as if she'd eaten a sugar cube.

"Well, I'm sure we'll see each other around, especially with the festival," said Honora.

"No, no, no. Like, what if we met here again? Just to talk. Maybe write." Lula gasped and clapped her hands. "Like a society."

I didn't say anything. Much to my surprise, only a teeny part of me screamed, "Absolutely not; you don't even know these people." A large part of me didn't want to disappoint Lula. An even larger part thought it seemed a grand idea, the adventure I'd been looking for.

The companionship Jane Austen had wished me to find.

"That sounds lovely. What a capital idea." Honora checked her planner, though I believed she'd already determined her answer. "I'm afraid I couldn't participate very often, though. I have quite a few committee meetings and friendly luncheons on a weekly basis."

Lula wilted. "You know, you're right, good point. I've got loads of homework. I don't know why I suggested that."

"I love suggestions," I said gently.

Lula gave me a grateful smile. "See you lot at the festival, then?"

I shrugged. "Sure." More likely, I'd be packing my bags or riding a train back to London by next Saturday, but I didn't want to disappoint her any further.

"Of course." Honora bade us good day and set off at a brisk walk.

Lula checked the bulletin board once more before she gave an exuberant wave and jogged the other direction.

I must confess, I stayed at the shop a while after both ladies left, savoring the something wonderful.

But when I finally did move towards the door, the barista—I believed her name was Imogen, a more recent hire—said, "Have a good night."

"You too," I returned for the first time. And I truly meant it.

Chapter Three

Wednesday

I woke up to "I Want to Hold Your Hand" blasting from my phone on the other side of the room. Rather than answer the call right away, I slipped my hand under my pillow. The letter was still there, safe and sound.

I stumbled out of bed and over to the phone, then snagged it on the last ring. "Hello?"

"Jessamy? Did you just wake up?"

Was it that obvious? Mum had likely been up for hours. Eaten yogurt and seized the day. Had I fallen short already? *Good gracious, stop being so defensive.* "Yes, Mum. It's spring holiday." I forced a laugh.

"Good morning, then." Her voice was cheerful, no hint of the censure I so easily imagined.

I parted the lacy curtains and peered out over the carefully tended garden and, beyond them, the open, rolling fields. The cottage sat on the outskirts of the village, just close enough to glimpse the countryside. "Good morning."

"Enjoying your stay?"

"It's been good." I didn't share all the details. Didn't want to bore her. "How are things there?"

I side-eyed the mirror. Mum had always been slim, a trait she shared with my sisters. She never mentioned my burgeoning waistline, but her lips pinched to the left sometimes when she thought I couldn't see.

"Oh, the usual. Leonie quarreled with Beth, but I expect they'll make up by week's end. Beth's stressed, that's all."

"They always sort it out, none the worse for wear." My sisters had always been close.

I popped into the family room to start a Beatles record. "How's Dad been?"

"He's got a new building. Takes up most of his time; we don't see him much. He's got a case of the blues, but he'll shake out of them."

"Hmm." He'd had "the blues" for months now, and Mum and I were at a loss at how to help. His schemes didn't bring in much, never had, so Mum picked up overtime at the university.

I set two slices of bread to toast on the stove, then set to work fixing an egg and a sausage patty. "How's work?"

"Busy. We'll blink, and the year will be over in a mountain of paperwork."

Mum chattered on. I supplied all the right words in all the right places. Dug under the surface when she didn't want to answer, read what she didn't say, and lightened the mood when it dimmed.

Because that's what she needed.

This is the perfect time to tell her about the university switch.

No. She had more than enough on her plate. She didn't need this, too. Besides, she'd been so proud when I chose international business management. After all, she excelled at crunching numbers and taking the lead.

When else would I tell her, though?

Mum's breathy laugh coaxed me back. "Would you just listen to me? All this time I've been complaining, and I didn't even ask about you."

"I'm fine. I don't mind."

"How did the meeting go at The Muses on Monday?"

I blew a curl off my forehead, but it flopped back. "A bit unexpected, but good."

"How so?" Mum somehow saw through me without even seeing me.

I flipped the toast onto a chipped plate. Drat. I'd burnt one side. I layered the egg, cheese, and sausage and topped it with the other slice of crispy bread. "Well, the buyer didn't show."

"Pardon?"

I bit into my sandwich.

"Who sets up a meeting to buy a place and then doesn't show?"

"Don't know. We're rescheduling it, though." And by *we*, I meant *me*. Yesterday evening, I'd sent texts, poked around Facebook, and even broke down and left a voice mail.

The buyer hadn't answered.

None of the Aubertines had the money nor the time to keep The Muses. Most of us had no desire to either. The one who did was at university, completely broke and helpless.

But if I sold The Muses, I could pay for university next year.

I scooted a leather journal and a copy of *Emma* off one of the barstools so I could sit at the kitchen island. Lula's poster fluttered to the floor.

Highest prize ever awarded at the Festival.

Eight hundred pounds would help pay for university too. And perhaps with that, The Muses wouldn't have to go.

"Jessamy, it means so much that I can rely on you," Mum said.

"So you've said." I hoped she heard my grin.

"I mean it."

How many times had I heard that? How many times had I answered the same way? Mum was always so sincere, and she always made me feel warm inside.

Even as I knew, no matter how well she intended, she hadn't room for the real Jessamy and her problems.

I told her I loved her, but said nothing about university at all.

I'd been fighting a stubborn plot point for hours.

First off, the Internet had no information on lavender merchants' paychecks in 1812. So I'd ridden my bike to the library. I didn't find the answer there either; however, I *had* discovered a good deal of fascinating information on films filmed in Surrey, which bloomed a new idea entirely unrelated to this one.

Admittedly, a stack of historical novels distracted me. I'd begun with a new release the librarian recommended, and then I'd browsed the whole section and found all the novels I'd passed so many rosy hours with. I couldn't just leave them there, so I curled up in a puddle of sunshine and read the afternoon away.

The only thing that would have improved it was a cup of chai.

And perhaps actually writing. But how dare I suggest such a thing.

As I returned my books to the shelves, I spotted Lula on the floor, surrounded by towers of fantasy novels, each book nine centimeters thick.

I scurried past before she noticed me.

I hated myself for not saying "hello." But more than that, I hated the thought of bothering her like I did Mum and everyone else.

Besides, Lula said she had homework. *Remember?*

My shoulder collided with someone's arm. Embarrassment pooled. I glanced over my shoulder to make sure Lula hadn't seen. "I'm so sorry! I wasn't paying attention."

The poster girl blinked hard and straightened her messenger bag. Her hair was halfway between straight and curly, her skin was apple-blossom white, and she dressed like she'd attended a prestigious university in the seventies.

Except for a Spider-Man pin on her bag's strap. Although, they had Spider-Man in the seventies, didn't they?

Lula would have known.

The girl's eyes disappeared when she smiled, but I wasn't sure if she meant it for me or something else. She bolted for the bulletin board, and I left before I could bother anyone further.

I popped in my earbuds and cycled back toward home to the beat of "All You Need Is Love." *Easy for them to say.*

I could research to my heart's content, but it wouldn't make my writing flow again. It was the pair of friends, my two main characters. They had no spark, and the plot bored me to tears. Not a favorable sign. I'd tried every trick I'd ever read, but nothing worked.

I pedaled through the park. A group of men and women strolled along the cracked pavement, all wearing yellow and clutching legal pads.

Someone behind me speed-walked toward the group, so I swerved off the pavement to let her pass. She carried three legal pads and talked louder than the rest, duck-shaped earrings swinging.

She sounded like Honora.

I paused my music and pedaled slower. Perhaps I liked drama more than I cared to admit.

One of the ladies in the group shared a desperate glance with her companion, then stepped over to Honora.

"This is the third meeting you've scheduled without me." Honora tilted her head, demanding an answer.

The woman brushed her arm and said something in a soft voice.

Honora softened her voice, too, but not enough. "Not help with the festival? I've served for five years."

"Exactly."

"But you need my help."

"We also need new blood, someone who can see things from a new perspective."

I didn't have it in me to keep listening. I pressed Play and rode on, but my heart squeezed.

Chapter Four

Thursday

The family of Aubertine had long been settled in Box Hill. Their estate was large, and their livelihood was The Muses, in the center of their village, where, for many generations, they had lived and loved and worked in so respectable a manner as to engage the general good opinion of their surrounding acquaintance.

The most recent keeper of The Muses, though Jessamy would never own that she was, was a single lady, who had lived for twenty years and had a constant companion in this establishment, and only in this establishment.

But her parents' falling out, which happened five years before, produced a great alteration in her home; for to supply the loss, her father abandoned The Muses entirely, and her mother displaced it for far more pertinent worries.

So it happened that The Muses invited and received into its govern the young lady. In the peace and calm of the shop, the young lady's days were comfortably spent, and her attachment to it—and, admittedly, its customers—increased. The constant attention of the villagers to her wishes, which proceeded not merely from interest but from goodness of heart, gave her every degree of solid comfort, and the cheerfulness added a relish to her existence.

Yet to her, therefore, the succession of The Muses was surprisingly ever so much more important as to her sisters or parents.

But the bills were read and, like almost all other bills, gave more disappointment than pleasure. It was not unjust nor so ungrateful, but the diminished patronage left The Muses on such terms as destroyed half the value. Both the father and the mother had wished for it not to be so, for their own, most private reasons. Jessamy had wished it not to be so for the sincere good of the shop.

But to them all, it was left no power of providing for the shop.

Jane Austen

I set the weathered paper on the bench beside me. I'd come straight from the mailbox to the garden when this new letter appeared in the post. I'd opened it right away, only to find none of the encouragement of the last note.

Clearly, this letter was written by someone who knew me, or at least, knew of me. Did that mean the first one was, too?

The envelope was still full. I pulled out a clear copy of the advertisement I had posted online seeking a buyer for The Muses.

I dropped the dried rose petals, shoved the letter in my pocket, and jogged out of the garden.

If Honora and Lula received letters that said the same …

Jane Austen—if she had indeed written the first letter—had been inconsolable over the loss of her writing haunt. I imagined vividly Honora and Lula being that same kind of upset with me.

What if they knew I was selling The Muses?

I arrived at The Muses puffing for breath despite my recent cycling excursions. But I didn't slow down. I couldn't. I swung the door open savagely.

No one waited at the cherry-wood table by the window. Was that a relief or a source of immense anxiety? Anxiety it was. I swiped my hair out of my face.

"I haven't seen them yet, love." Imogen's brow furrowed, something her round face didn't seem suited for. "Is there anything I can help you with?"

I shook my head too quickly and nearly tripped on my way to the table. I chose a window seat and watched the pavements, knees pulled to my chest.

Ten minutes *tick-tocked* past. Maybe neither of them was coming. Maybe they hadn't gotten letters this time.

Or maybe they had, and they weren't interested in seeing me.

"Let It Be" warbled from the record player. Grandmum's favorite song. Few songs calmed me quite like that one.

But not today.

At last, Lula whipped around the street corner. Her face lit up when she spotted me through the glass.

Guilt stabbed. Would she feel the same after we sorted this out?

She burst in, handed money to Imogen, and selected a seat next to me. "Best to figure this out with warm sustenance, I think. No sign of Honora?"

I shook my head, everything in me trembling.

"That's all right. We can wait a few minutes." She took a long breath and laid her hand over top of mine. "Don't worry about it. Or any of this. I'm not mad."

I blinked fast and swallowed hard. "I'd better get some tea."

Honora arrived shortly after, strolling along as if perfectly on time for a meeting. She ordered her cuppa, then took the seat across from me.

None of us spoke for an eternal moment. We wouldn't sort anything out this way. Someone had to say *something*.

"Looks like Lula got her wish." I forced a chuckle.

Honora frowned.

"For us to meet again."

Honora laughed then, but it didn't make me feel better.

I licked my lips. "Compare letters, shall we?"

We all spread our weathered sheets on the table, then passed them to the right.

Lula's read:

Curiouser and curiouser! For I am so much surprised that for the moment, I quite forget how to speak good English.

I wonder where you will go to get away from the worries of home and school and work now, dear? I'm sure The Muses shan't be able to have you! It shall be a great deal too far off to trouble itself about you: you must manage the best way you can. I wish I could say I knew that time should be kind to the old place.

We can look at the sad state of affairs, but to clear them up is more hopeless than ever. And I'll admit, I thought of no more than sitting down and beginning to cry again. But I knew I would be ashamed of myself, to go on crying in this way and not trying to better this situation.

Dear, dear! How strange everything is today! And yesterday, things went on just as usual. I wonder if we've been changed in the night? Let me think: was I the same when I got up this morning? I almost think I can remember feeling a little different. But if I'm not the same, the next question is, who in the world am I without The Muses? Ah, that's the great puzzle!

Lewis Carroll

Honora's read:

All sorts of interesting characters came here, whether early in February or late in September, through a biting wind or a driving snow, over the down or from the railway station. They carry all sorts of bags; their coats hide every inch of them. Their burdens have piled themselves against their shoulders. Some of them stagger into The Muses more dead inside than alive and fling their bags down.

And one of them, with that much introduction, took up govern of the shop.

> *The staff made her a cup of tea and left her there while they checked the counter. A guest in the wintertime was an unheard-of piece of luck, let alone a guest who was no haggler, and she was resolved to show herself worthy of a turn of good fortune. Although the fire was burning up briskly, one of the staff was surprised to see that her visitor still wore her hat and coat, standing with her back to the staff and staring out of the window at the falling snow. Her gloved hands were clasped behind her, and she seemed to be lost in thought.*
> *"Can I help you, miss?" Staff said.*
> *"No," she said without turning.*
> *Staff was not sure she had heard Guest and was about to repeat her question.*
> *Guest turned her head and looked over her shoulder. "I'm not sure anything can help us now."*
> *"In a bit, times will be better," Staff insisted.*
> *Guest made no answer and turned her face away from her again.*
>
> H. G. Wells

I hung my head when my own letter lay before me again.

Lula crossed her arms. "So this is an artsy way of someone telling us you own The Muses, you've fallen on hard times, and you've got to sell it. Do I have the gist of it?"

I nodded, because I wasn't sure my voice would work.

"By all appearances." Honora folded her letter precisely. "I'm not sure why this writer felt the need to tell Honora and me this. It's none of our business. We've met each other once."

But I should have known better. I should have said something.

"Clearly, these weren't written by the original authors." Honora tapped one red fingernail on her paper. "Rather, in the style of."

Who else have I disappointed by selling The Muses?

"But the first ones might have been. Written by the original authors, I mean." Lula crammed her letter into her backpack. "Do you think they were?"

This is all my fault.

"I'm sorry," I blurted out.

Both Honora and Lula swiveled and stared at me.

I wrapped my hands around my cuppa, the warmth infusing my palms as I forced the next words out. "This—The Muses, I mean—was my parents' dream. A tea shop in the favorite writing haunt of Surrey's most classic authors."

"Quite the dream." Lula slurped her tea and earned another frown from Honora.

"Put simply, there hasn't been any dreaming happening in a while. None of my siblings or relatives want to take care of the shop."

"Why?" Lula tilted her head.

"I … I don't … I suppose they all think it another of Dad's schemes."

"What about *you*?" Honora asked softly, laying one dark hand over mine. "What do you want?"

"I want to, I'd love to, but I'm at university in London, switching universities actually, and all my money is going toward that."

"How did you get put in charge of selling the shop, then?" Lula snagged a cinnamon stick from the center plate and spun it around her knuckles.

I shook my head, letting my curls hide my face. "Mum's got more than enough on her plate. She needs me."

Honora didn't look away. It felt like she was reading my mind, understanding the things I would never tell her and responding in kind. Lula, in her own spacey sort of way, was doing the same.

"Have you made any progress?" Honora scooted her saucer to the side.

"I was supposed to meet with a potential buyer on Monday. They seemed interested over email, but then no one showed for the meeting. I'm trying to contact them, but they won't take my messages." My hands clenched uselessly around my chai.

Realization dawned in her eyes. "What happens if you can't find a buyer?"

I pinched the corner of my lips, like Mum, to keep too much from escaping. "Close down, I suppose."

Honora's eyes never wavered from my face, while Lula stared at the table and nodded slowly.

"I'm sorry," I repeated, but it didn't help.

Lula wagged her finger. "Oh no. No apologies. It's not your fault. Hard times come for everyone." She sat stiller than I'd ever seen her, as if waiting for her idea to bloom. "What if I had some money I could give?"

I shook my head. "No. It's not your responsibility."

"But what if I really wanted to? Look, I have a small job after school, plus some quid headed my way soon. I could chip in, this once, so The Muses can get back on its feet."

"I certainly could do the same." Honora reached into her bag, as if searching for her checkbook.

"I don't have the money in hand, but I should by the end of spring holiday," Lula said.

"Likewise." Honora gave up the checkbook search. I would have thought her bag was compartmentalized, but this proved one might never know a person.

Their outpouring of kindness flooded over me, washing out my misgivings. "If you really have your heart set on it, who am I to stop you?"

Lula pumped her fist.

"I'm working on some plans of my own." It wasn't exactly true—after all, I planned to use the contest prize money to pay for university—but they'd been so kind, I didn't want to seem completely useless. I fussed with my blouse's hem. "Don't feel like you're obligated to donate."

"We want to," Lula insisted.

"Perhaps we could meet tomorrow." Honora whipped a pocket planner out of her purse. "Work through solutions to increase income at the shop and dig it out of debt."

"Oh, so we're meeting again?" Lula smirked and pointed the cinnamon stick at Honora.

Honora's smile was tight, but her eyes betrayed much more mirth. "I believe that will be the best course for us to discuss further options, yes."

The weight in my chest lifted just a smidge.

"You know"—Lula tipped back her chair—"if we keep meeting, that would make us a society."

"Only one way to find out." Honora drummed her hands on the table. "Put it to a vote."

Lula raised her hand.

"That's not how it works! Put your hand down." Honora grabbed Lula's hand and lowered it. "I'll announce what we're putting to the vote, and then we'll give a show of hands."

"I think Jessamy should announce the vote. After all, it's her shop."

Honora glanced my way. "Yes, most satisfactory. What say you, Miss Aubertine?"

They truly wanted *me*. "Sure." I sipped my chai, then cleared my throat. "All in favor of forming a society with our members three, raise your hand."

Both ladies shot their hands in the air, brown meeting black. Lula's hand collided with Honora's, and the cinnamon stick skittered two tables away. I shouted, "Aye!" loud enough that Imogen peered at us from behind the counter.

I felt silly, and it felt good.

"All opposed?"

A teapot burbled.

"The teapot doesn't count. Ergo, the vote goes to forming a society."

"And ..." Lula drew the word out. "If we're a society, then we need an official name."

"Something that speaks to why we're all together."

Of course, Honora suggested first. She'd likely picked out five names after our last meeting, just in case. "Something with *The Muses* in the name?" She frowned. "But The Muses isn't really the reason we're together, is it?"

"It certainly helped." Lula shrugged.

"But it didn't bring us together." Honora struck it off her yellow legal pad.

"Something with *tea* in the name?" I suggested. A simple, safe answer more based on the cup in front of me than any quick thinking on my part.

"That helped, too," Lula said.

"Box Hill Tea Society." I grabbed a napkin and started scribbling ideas down until Honora and I raced against each other.

Honora suggested, "Fine Tea Connoisseurs Society."

"How do you spell 'connoisseurs'?" I asked.

"All right, so we're not doing that." Lula retrieved the stick. "Federation of Certified Tea Delightfuls."

"Federation? This is a society!" I disagreed.

Honora leveled a glance at Lula. "Federation of 'put that cinnamon stick down or so help me.'"

After sitting back down, Lula stuck the cinnamon stick behind her ear. "What about something to do with the letters or the authors?"

"Mysterious Authors Society."

"Society of Authors of Yesteryear."

"Mysterious Letters Society."

"Putting mysterious in front of everything doesn't make it a name," Honora pointed out.

Lula stared at the ceiling. "It makes it sound like a movie."

I abandoned my napkin, propped my chin on my hand, and focused on the bulletin board instead.

Aspiring authors! Bring your most worthy tales to Surrey's Just Ducky Festival. This year's theme is "The Ugly Duckling" ...

I had the perfect name.

Yet I hesitated. What if Honora and Lula thought it was stupid?

A new thought budded, one I could never recall having before but that made an immense amount of sense.

What if I never said it and wished I had?

"The Odd Duck Society."

Lula and Honora both fell silent and thoughtful.

Oh dear. I needed to hurry and explain so they didn't think it was childish. "You know, with the ducks and how much Surrey celebrates them. And as for the 'odd' part, I ..." I swallowed hard. "I feel like *that's* what brought us together. That, and Providence."

For a long moment, I wished I hadn't spoken up at all.

Honora packed her legal pad away with a smile.

Lula applauded. "It's perfect! Odd Duck Society it is!"

I grinned as if maybe I would never stop.

Honora consulted her calendar. "If we meet tomorrow, we can gather before the festival and before the end of spring holiday."

"Sounds good. Same time?" Lula said.

"Same time, same place," I said.

"Next meeting's agenda is solutions for The Muses." Honora made a note on a different legal pad.

"And finding the author of the letters." Lula polished off her last sip.

"We should bring something we wrote." I'd always wanted to share my story with someone, and it seemed natural to ask them. One well-received idea paved the way for others.

Honora made another note. "I'd better run. I have a festival committee meeting to get to."

My heart squeezed a little, like it had in the park. If only she didn't think she had to keep up appearances for us. But then, hadn't I been doing the same thing? "Good luck."

She sobered. "I'll need it." Then the lines of her ebony face stiffened again, and she swept out the door.

"I'm getting a treat to go." Lula swung her backpack over her shoulder.

"Me, too."

As we waited at the to-go counter, the poster girl arrived once more. She held up the poster and hooked her thumb at the board.

Imogen stretched on her tiptoes to see past the machines, then smiled and nodded. "Those posters have been vanishing as fast as we get them in."

Lula waved at the girl.

The poster girl returned the gesture, nearly dropping the stapler she pulled out of her messenger bag.

Lula leaned over to me. "That's Florence. She's my next-door neighbor."

"Oh. I see."

"She doesn't talk much and does things a little differently, but she's super friendly. We've gone to the same school and seen every new movie that caught our fancy together for years." A touch of sadness infused Lula's voice.

I tilted my head, a silent "why?"

Lula softened her voice. "She's switching schools after break. I completely understand why she made the decision; it makes sense and fits her needs better. But we won't see each other except for school holidays. Her family will have to live in east London during the school year."

Florence waved at us both as she slipped back out the door.

Lula traced her finger over a ringed stain on the counter. "She's been having a hard time with it. Part of why she hasn't been talking as much."

"Can you go visit her, maybe? Throughout the school year?"

Lula shook her head before I finished. "I don't have the quid for that. But I shouldn't complain. We've got plenty of holidays. We'll make the most of it." She swirled her tea in the to-go cup. "Just not how I thought my last year of sixth form would go."

"I'm sorry." I'd never had many friends in sixth form, but the ones I had, I still missed even now in university. Couldn't imagine my last year without them.

Or, quite frankly, this year without the Odd Duck Society.

Chapter Five

Friday

Mum called as I finally made up my mind, pushing my leather journal in my tote bag for the third time this morning. I dove into my tote and rescued my phone. Vibrations tingled through my palm in time with the song.

The antique cuckoo clock—one of Mum's car boot sale finds—scolded me. I needed to leave now if I would be on time for the Odd Duck Society's first official meeting.

I had to answer Mum, though. She might need something.

Maybe she could leave a voice mail. After all, Mum had told me a million times that I didn't have to snatch up the phone every single time she called. I'd call her back, or she'd call me back.

I silenced my phone and surrendered it to the depths of my bag. Not answering didn't feel good in the least.

I grabbed a cardigan and set off. A few clouds scuttled across the sun, making me glad for the extra layer. But it was that leather journal in my bag that snagged my thoughts once more. It held a story that I hoped might send me off to a new university.

I'd typed the story up, also, and printed two copies, one for Lula and one for Honora.

Guilt twisted my stomach. I shouldn't have told Lula and Honora that I was putting the contest money toward The Muses.

Or maybe I *should* put the money toward The Muses. I could scrimp money here and there to get myself to university. Beg a few relatives, if necessary.

But I needed to make my own way this time. Needed to show them that Jessamy Aubertine could do this, that it wasn't an insipid dream of someone who'd read too many Jane Austen novels.

The Muses would have to wait. Lula and Honora would understand.

Of course, there wouldn't be much to understand if I didn't tell them. They didn't need the extra trouble any more than Mum did, I was sure.

I could handle this on my own.

Honora already sat at our usual table when I got there, and Lula skidded in about five minutes after I'd gotten my tea. She fidgeted more than usual, if that were even possible, jostling her leg in time with "Hey Jude" on the record player.

Honora pulled out her yellow legal pad, last-minute for her. "I have some bad news on The Muses front."

My stomach flipped. Had she found out I wasn't using the contest money for The Muses?

That was silly. But why was it the first worry I jumped to?

"I'm afraid I will be unable to put the money toward The Muses that I thought I would. A more immediate need has sprung up." Honora flipped to a clean page. Her words seemed a trifle rehearsed, but I was more relieved I wasn't the only one.

"Me neither," I said, then glanced over to Lula as I realized she had said it at the same time. Worry—or perhaps guilt, if I were truthful—pricked my chest. "So *none* of us can donate?"

Honora clicked her pen and dropped it on the table. "It would appear so."

Lula stared at her lap, bronze hands tapping an uneven beat as the record ended.

Frustration surged through me, but I tried to channel some of Honora's graciousness. "It'll be alright. This isn't your responsibility anyway. It still means a lot that you both wanted to help."

That prick inside sharpened. Why on earth should I tell them now? Neither one of them could donate. They'd never have to know.

But this seemed like one of those feelings I shouldn't ignore. Not that I was proficient in recognizing those.

I cleared my throat. "Truthfully …" Such a hard thing to say. "I *will* have money I could use." My face flamed. "I was going to put it toward switching universities instead."

"Darling, there's nothing wrong with that," Honora reassured.

I swallowed my sip of tea hard. "But it *was* wrong to say I would use it for the shop when I never planned to. It was dishonest." I didn't like that word. Didn't like that it was true about *me*. It had been so small, it hadn't seemed dishonest at the time.

Lula's hands stilled. She wouldn't raise her gaze from the table. "Then I haven't been honest either. I have the money, too, but I'm saving it so I can visit Florence in London later this year."

I wrapped one arm around her shoulders. "Oh, Lula. That's fine. You're not obligated to donate your money. Thanks for telling us."

Honora let out a long sigh and picked up her pen again. "You both had to confess, didn't you? Well, here's mine. I donated my money to the festival instead."

Lula shrugged, raising her gaze for the first time. "Makes sense for a committee member."

Honora pressed her lips together. "Yes, I suppose it does."

I pressed my lips together, too, to hold certain words back.

"Seems our Odd Duck Society failed already." Lula curled up on her chair, her voice tiny.

Was that it, then? We were just going to call it a failure?

No. Not this time. I raised my teacup. "A toast. Or rather, a pact."

Lula lifted her cup, but Honora only lifted her brows.

"A pledge that we, the members of the Odd Duck Society, will always be honest with each other. No lies."

Lula *clinked* her teacup against mine. "Hear, hear!" She looked over the rim of her cup at Honora.

Honora slowly lifted her teacup. "Cheers."

I lowered my cup and took a sip, knowing full well one of us was still lying and doing it very well.

"Now, about these stories. Because I, for one, have been waiting for this bit. Let's get on with it." Lula pulled several sheets of paper out of her backpack. "Should we just trade them around the table like the letters?"

"Perfect." Honora sounded a trifle relieved at the topic change.

I tugged my photocopies from my bag, hands trembling only a bit. *What if no one likes it? What if they think my story is dumb? What if they don't think I can write something good enough to win?*

Lula passed her story to me and I to Honora, who handed hers to Lula.

I released my breath and picked up the first dog-eared page. At least I'd have something to take my mind off my worries while the others read.

But I read no farther than the heading.

The Blood Feather: An Ugly Duckling Retelling by Lula Carrington

I raised my head. Honora and Lula stared at me with the same wash of uncertainty, holding up the stories they were reading.

A Hardship of Solitude: An Ugly Duckling Retelling by Honora Welbeck

Wild Swan: An Ugly Duckling Retelling by Jessamy Aubertine

We slowly handed each other our copies back.

Lula recovered her tongue first but even then, only in part. "Did we ... Did we all ... ?"

Honora pinched the bridge of her nose. "It would appear so."

I hadn't even thought that we might all have decided to compete for the same prize. My stomach sank with a second realization. "If I may ask, where were you both planning to get the money you needed?"

Their eyes answered the question.

"So ... " My fingers worried the edge of my blouse. "None of us have the money for any of the things we wanted. And only one of us can win the money."

Lula propped her chin on her hand. "This is a mess."

I stared into my tea and stirred, thinking hard. Lula wanted to visit Florence. Honora wanted to support the festival. And I wanted to get started at my new university.

I could get money from somewhere else if I put my mind to it. I'd wanted to show Lula and Honora–alright, and Mum too–that I could do this on my own. But I could ask for help. I was mostly certain it wouldn't kill me. I had enough writing credits; I didn't need to add the festival to get into university.

Besides, what if it allowed Lula or Honora to win?

I set my spoon down. "If I pull out of the competition—"

Lula exploded out of her seat, tipping her chair over.

Imogen glanced over the register but after spotting Lula, went on with her business.

"Absolutely not! You and your story are as important as us and ours. I mean, *Wild Swan*? That is a gorgeous title. You deserve to enter, too."

"Lula's right." Honora crossed her arms, still managing to look ladylike. "Besides, I'm sure Lula will agree, we want to win fair and square. I wouldn't feel right winning the money and knowing it might have been because you backed out. Everyone gets to do their best. Another Odd Duck Society pact." She raised her teacup and her eyebrows at me.

Lula *clinked* hers against Honora's, then took a long sip.

"We'll all enter our best work and let the chips fall where they may." I raised my teacup with a *clink*. "Leave it to Providence."

"And we'll all help each other write the best work we can." Lula traded her story back to me. "Starting now."

With less hesitation this time, I passed mine to Lula, who did the same to Honora.

"Shop closes in fifteen minutes," Imogen called from the counter.

"When'd they start closing so early?" Lula muttered, swiping my story off the table and tucking it into her backpack with more care than usual.

"Since we haven't the money to stay open later." I searched my tote bag to avoid having to meet their gazes.

"Fair."

"Oh dear. And we haven't even gotten to deciphering who the letters came from." Honora clicked her tongue.

"Or reading the stories," Lula added. "And don't we have to turn them in tomorrow?"

"That's tomorrow?" Honestly, I had so many dates and tasks scribbled in my planner, I'd stopped looking at it, because I couldn't stand the chaos.

Honora rubbed a finger over her full lips. I suddenly realized she wasn't wearing lipstick today. "How about this? We each make a list of anyone who could have possibly sent the letters. We meet first thing tomorrow to compare notes."

"And compare stories. We can each read the one we take with us. Then switch again tomorrow and read while we're here." Lula gave up trying to zip her backpack. "We can walk to the park to enter them in the contest together."

"If we're all still sure about the contest." I couldn't help but ask again. Maybe I still wasn't sure I could believe it—that they'd give up a better chance of winning to include me.

Fierce commitment crossed Honora's face. "And we are."

Lula nodded rapidly.

I tried to mirror Honora's commitment. "Me, too."

We each left to complete our assignments, leaving behind us the fading shop light and Imogen's soft "good night."

Chapter Six

Saturday

"I tell you, Jessamy, I'm a gardener, not a writer." *Snip, snip.* A few branches fell by Allifair Quazzle's shears. "Even if I had wanted to write you and your friends secret notes, which sounds like some jolly good fun, I wouldn't have the time nor the talent to." *Snip, snip.*

I stacked the branches and carried them to a neat pile at the corner of the garden. "You might be surprised."

"Who would take care of the cherry blossoms if I was off writing letters?" Allifair *snipped* her shears ferociously at the slightest hint of tousle on the lower branches of the tree before her. Her short, gray hair was streaked with pastel pink this time. Her Easter color, she called it. In a couple weeks, it'd be something new.

"You make a good point." I *had* seen Allifair here daily. That didn't exactly afford time for letter-writing.

I mentally crossed Allifair off my pitifully short list of suspects, then brushed the dirt from my jeans. "Thanks for putting up with all my questions."

"Anytime. Hope you find your writer, though. All around, sounds like a pleasant sort of mystery. Not at all like those ones I see on the telly."

A pleasant sort of mystery. I hadn't thought of it that way before, but I rather liked it. "Suppose it is." And if anyone knew anything about mysteries and true crime, it was Allifair. Hence why she'd made my list of suspects.

Of course, it also could have to do with the fact that I was desperate to have *any* insight that might help our society solve the mystery. What I had learned when I sat down to make my list last night was how few people I really, truly knew.

Except for Honora and Lula, that was.

"I'll tell you who I think it is." Allifair hopped off her step stool to reach a low-hanging branch. "I'd bet my best trowel it's one of those two ladies. Honora and Lula, right?"

I'd mentioned their names once, and she remembered. "The thought has crossed my mind."

"Not sure how you'd get that information out of them if it is, but I'm working on it." Allifair winked.

"Perhaps I ought to send you on the case."

"No. The cherry blossoms, remember?" The bush muffled Allifair's voice. "Have you texted your mum? Wouldn't put it past her either."

I wanted to give Allifair a simple yes but remembered the Odd Duck Society's pact yesterday. Seemed it would work outside of the society, too. "Thought about it. But I don't think she needs that right now, you know?"

"Maybe it's exactly what she needs."

"Hmm." I brushed my hand over the phone in my back pocket. No. I'd call her this evening. My stomach squirmed. "Got to run. I've got a meeting, but I should be back this afternoon. Help yourself if you need a snack or anything." I plucked a cherry blossom and tucked it into my hair. "Thanks for your hard work. The garden looks amazing."

"Exactly." Allifair crossed her muscular arms. "You go find your letter writer and leave the gardening to me."

I intended to do just that.

I hadn't been able to find my second copy of my story, so I'd printed another one. I pulled out Honora's story to return to her when I got there.

Honora's story followed a mayor's wife, who lived and worked among her people for years, yet no one ever truly knew her. It was far more literary and intelligent than most books I'd read in months—Honora wrote like that Regency matriarch that came over her face sometimes.

When I arrived at The Muses, Honora and Lula clustered outside the window with Imogen.

Odd. "What are you lot doing out here?" I adjusted the strap of my bag.

Honora and Lula both glanced to Imogen.

Imogen shrugged. She seemed strange without her stained apron, as if it were who she was and not just a uniform in a locked shop. "I tried calling. Power's out. Had to close the shop for the day."

I covered my face with my hand. "I am so sorry. I'll call."

Imogen squinted her almond-shaped eyes. She knew full well that I could call as many times as I wanted, but I wouldn't get anywhere without money. But she thanked me anyway.

Heat crept over my face as I turned back to Honora and Lula. "I'm so sorry, I ..."

"Don't worry." Honora rubbed my shoulder. "We'll find another spot to meet today. It will be all right."

Imogen raised her hand. "I don't know about you, ladies, but I'm going to the park. God's given us a lovely day, and I'm going to enjoy it."

I shook her hand, which seemed a strangely formal thing to do, but a hug wouldn't have been quite right either. "Thank you, Imogen, for all your help."

"Anytime. I love this place, too."

"Good thing it's got you looking out for it." I was doing a poor job.

Imogen waved, then strolled across the street into the rest of her day.

I searched my bag, finally locating my phone at the very bottom. I'd missed another call from Mum. I'd call her this afternoon and try not to think about how I should have called her yesterday. "Do you mind if I phone the power company?"

"Go ahead," Lula urged.

"It might be a while." I cringed.

"Lula and I can wait for you at the bookshop on the corner." Honora pointed to Beatrix's. "I don't think I've ever been. Have you?"

Lula shook her head.

"That borders on a crime." I shooed them with my hand. "I'll finish this up as quickly as possible and meet you there."

I waited until Honora and Lula entered the book shop before I dialed and ran through the cycle of automated messages and hold music, only to discover that the power bill was indeed more than we could pay.

I blew out my breath and turned toward the window so no one walking past would see the frustrated tears sprouting.

Maybe I should call Mum. She might have some connections or ideas I hadn't thought of.

She'd already been trying to call me yesterday, though. What if something else was going on with Leonie, Beth, Dad, or anyone else?

I could take care of one measly power bill. I *had* to.

The fizzled Free Internet sign taunted me.

Until an idea popped in my own mind.

I navigated through my apps until I had canceled our internet payment for the month and applied the money to the power bill. I had a feeling our patrons would prefer to have electricity over free internet, at least for a day or two.

I unlocked the door and slipped inside to remove the sign.

A quick fix.

Hopefully, a temporary one.

I hurried around the corner. Honora, Lula, and I browsed the bookstore until Beatrix went on her lunch break. Luckily, she let us store our purchases there, so we didn't have to carry the bulky bags with us. Since, of course, we had each bought a couple books. Were we supposed to simply walk into a bookstore and not buy anything?

We found a bench just outside, where we settled to finish each other's stories. I really enjoyed Lula's story, that of a girl hunting for spare parts to repair the robot her best friend left her. I didn't usually read fantasy—I preferred to stick with a solid historical or, even better, a classic. But the story was as whimsical and flighty as Lula, in all the best ways.

My own story was about a prestigious fashion designer's daughter, who decided on a lark to take a road trip across Europe with her best friend. The chemistry I'd struggled so hard to create between the two must have finally worked, because Lula praised my story, "Even though there were no explosions, the characters were so vivid and interesting!" and Honora added, "Your character conflict is exceptional; I couldn't help but care about them."

I stored their words away deep inside, deeper than they could ever suspect. And I passed on my own praise for their work.

I wondered if the Odd Duck Society had anything to do with the chemistry suddenly working.

Of course, it wasn't all praise. While we all acknowledged that we had done our very best for the contest, we all had suggestions on how to do even better in the future. Lula would do well to take a breath from the action to deepen her characters, Honora might think about curbing her vocabulary, and I could do without many of the lengthy monologues that were such fun to write.

But for now, all was well. And with those kind words, I had faith all would become even better.

I stretched and let out a long sigh—the good kind of sigh, the kind I hadn't felt in a while. "Where to now, ladies?"

"Imogen had the right idea about the park," Lula suggested. "We need to go turn in our stories anyway."

Honora set a brisk pace. "Have you thought of any suspects? Who could our mysterious letter author be?"

Come to think of it, Honora had brought that up frequently the last few days. And I already knew she'd kept her lack of festival involvement from us. Stood to reason she might keep quiet that she'd written the letters.

I'd have to ask Allifair the detective.

For now, I shook my head. "I doubt anyone in my family would have started this. I asked my gardener about it, and she said no. The only other one I thought of was Beatrix. But you pointed out you'd never visited her shop until today."

Honora added the names to her yellow legal pad. I sneaked a peek. She'd marked three columns *Jessamy, Lula,* and *Honora.* She added the suspects I mentioned in my column.

"You probably have the most potential suspects, Honora." Lula peered over Honora's shoulder.

Honora clasped her legal pad close to her chest. "I wrote down each member of every committee I'm on. I'm hoping to pay some visits this afternoon. But I highly doubt any one of them went to such elaborate measures. Lula, what about you?"

"I asked my family last night. Both my parents said no, and my brother, Joey, said it sounded like a telenovela pilot." Lula cleared her throat and tucked her hair behind her ear. "I did, however, think of one other person."

"Go on then," Honora urged, channeling a bit of Lula's excitement.

"Florence."

"Who's Florence?" Honora asked.

Lula explained to her, but the pieces all clicked together for me. Florence had been at The Muses putting up posters each time we were there. Moreover, she'd been all over the village—an easy way to learn post addresses.

"If we're taking that tactic, then what about Imogen? She's been there each time we met, too." Honora added her to the notepad.

"Less likely to have everyone's addresses, though." I was glad to have *something* to point out.

Honora squinted at the list of names. "I agree. I think Florence is our most likely option."

"Does Florence write?" I asked.

"Some," Lula offered. "She's pursuing filmmaking, so she writes scripts. But with Florence, who knows? I learn something new about her every day."

"I think it would be best if you were the one to speak with her about it, Lula," Honora said.

"And thank her," I added. "I, for one, would love to know why she brought us all together."

"Yes. I wasn't even aware your friend knew us," Honora said. "I didn't realize she was helping our committee, although, I may have met her once or twice "

My stomach twisted. I'd thought it was kinder to let Honora choose when to tell us, but the longer this charade lasted, the more I doubted. "About the committee …"

Honora's dark eyes widened.

"Good thing you're on the committee." Lula shielded her eyes with her papers. "Which booth?"

I counted four, all accepting items for the festival, ranging from pies to pickles to ponies. Volunteers and committee members in official yellow T-shirts swarmed the center of the park, dashing to and fro and loading items into the back of flatbed trucks.

"That one." Honora pointed, but her hand shook a bit. She buried it in the folds of her dress, then set off for the booth. Lula and I had to jog to keep up, falling in line behind Honora like ducklings following their mother.

The volunteer's eyes widened. She was the same woman who had confronted Honora. "Honora. What a lovely surprise."

Honora's stiff nod worried me, but that fled at the warmth of her voice. "It's good to see you, too." She slid her story across the table and accepted the entry form.

The volunteer scanned Honora's story. "*A Hardship of Solitude.* I'm excited to read this one. Your writing for the historical society was so well done."

"I enjoyed writing it." Honora bent to fill out her entry form. She tossed a smile over her shoulder to Lula and me.

We tossed it right back.

When Honora handed her completed entry form back, the volunteer whispered, "No hard feelings?"

Honora hesitated for a long moment, then sighed and shook her head. "I'd be more inclined to say you were right."

Lula offered me a quizzical look, but I pressed a finger to my lips.

The volunteer smiled softly. "Maybe we could get together for tea next week, then, after the festival? Just the two of us, to chat."

"That'd be lovely. Haven't had that chance for so long."

"We've both been busy."

Honora stepped away from the table. "I'll call you this afternoon, and we can settle a date."

The volunteer rolled her eyes good-naturedly. "So formal. Right then, let's get you signed up."

After we'd all filled out our entry forms, we parted ways— Honora to her committee members and Lula to Florence's house.

And me? Well, I didn't want to be totally useless, so I'd spend at least an hour thinking of other suspects before I settled in to watch *Pride and Prejudice*, since rain teased the horizon.

I found someone before I even reached home.

When I walked past The Muses, Florence was peering through the window at the empty tea shop, messenger bag at the ready. Her hands flew to the strap of her bag when she spotted my reflection.

I offered a tiny wave. "Shop closed for the day. Power went out."

She nodded quickly and spun on her heel.

I scrambled for my keys. "But I can let you in to drop off posters, if you like."

Florence rubbed her hands up and down the strap. Abruptly, she tugged some posters out of her bag and nodded.

I unlocked the door. She shifted her weight until I'd stepped in, then she slipped in behind me. She glanced at the darkened lights just once before beelining to the bulletin board.

I flicked the light switch. The lights flickered once, twice, then buzzed to life. Good.

Florence stapled five more posters to the board—for the festival this time, not the contest—counted them, then slid her thumbnail under an old staple clinging to a paper scrap.

"You don't have to do that," I said.

She pulled the staple out and cupped it in her palm. "I got it." Her voice was low and throaty. She ducked her head and started on the next staple.

"Thanks. I'm sure we have a staple remover somewhere." I stepped behind the counter—Imogen's domain—and surveyed the drawers. I really wanted to know more about Florence, but I didn't want to pester her either. Besides, we had already determined to let Lula talk to her about the letters. "You're Lula's friend Florence, right?"

"Yeah."

I pulled open a drawer and rustled through the odds and ends. Why were half these things even back here? "I'm Jessamy Aubertine. I'm—"

"I know." Florence peeked over the counter. "You're Lula's friend, too."

I hadn't dared to call Honora and Lula friends, even in my head. Florence's voice made it true. "I am."

Florence jammed her stapler back in her overfull bag, reminding me more than a bit of Lula. "I'm glad she has you, especially for when I switch schools."

Was that why Florence had written the letters? So Lula wouldn't be lonely when she left? A good motive. But weren't the ones with the best motives usually red herrings? If only I'd read more detective books. Maybe Beatrix had some Agatha Christie. Or I'd ask Allifair; she would know.

I expected Florence to slip out as quietly as she came, now that her work was finished. But instead, she plopped her messenger bag on the counter and opened the top drawer.

Maybe she wanted to chat as much as I did.

I spread the odds and ends from one drawer on the floor and sorted it into piles. "Lula said you're studying filmmaking."

She nodded, her hands still busy.

"What kind of films do you want to make?"

She tilted her head, not-quite-curls sliding over her shoulder. "Not sure yet."

"I was reading about films that filmed in Surrey. It's really fascinating."

Florence closed the drawer and started on the next one. "What's your favorite film?" She was trying to hold her excitement back, but it seeped out in her hands, her eyes, her tone. I wished she knew she didn't have to do that with me.

"*Pride and Prejudice.* The 2005 one."

"That's such a good one. I wrote two essays on it. Like, big essays."

"I'd love to read them."

"Ask my teacher, then." She laughed at her own joke. The sound was contagious. "That's why I'm switching schools. This new one has acting classes, animation, film, and screenwriting." She swung her legs over the edge of the counter, then kicked the drawers rhythmically. "I'm on the autism spectrum, so this school works better with my learning needs, too."

I replaced the items in the drawer and sat back on my heels. "That's great that you know your own needs and desires and are willing to work with them. I'm stuck in a year of international business management and trying to switch universities because I didn't."

She nodded slowly. A nod meant a lot of things with Florence, I thought.

I opened the next drawer. "Found it." I held up the staple remover.

She jabbed a thumb toward the bulletin board. "I got them all already."

"Oh."

She opened the top drawer. "It belongs in here."

"At least I've got organized drawers now." I handed her the tool, an idea dawning. "You know, I'd have to check with Lula and Honora, but I doubt either one of them would mind adding another member to our society."

Florence's face lit up even more than when she'd talked about films. "Lula's told me about it."

"We'd love to have you, if you can." I didn't want her to feel obligated if she wasn't comfortable.

"I think I'd enjoy coming." She ran her hands up and down the strap of her bag. "Well, I guess I'd better go."

"I'm glad we got to meet."

Florence turned back abruptly. "Me, too." Then she vanished out the door and around the corner.

Chapter Seven

Monday

I rode my bike down the lane to the postbox. Three envelopes nestled inside. Sadly, none of them were written on worn paper or sealed in the shape of a rose.

And none of them had been for a few days.

Had Lula talked to Florence? Was that why the letters had stopped? We needed to arrange another meeting.

I tossed the letters into the wildflower-strewn bicycle basket and pedaled back to the garden. Once there, I paged through the post.

A scam addressed to "current owners." Typical.

A letter from the festival committee. Did Lula and Honora get one of these? I'd have to text and ask them. Was this a good sign or a bad sign?

I was about to open it and find out when I spotted the envelope behind it.

A yellow manila envelope large enough to hold paperwork, with the university stamp on the outside. They'd sent the forms early.

It was forwarded by Mum.

"No, no, no!" I sprinted into the house, tossing the letters on the table. One promptly slid off in my wake.

I snatched my phone off the dresser in my room, dialed Mum's number, and paced.

She picked up before I'd had a chance to rehearse my explanation.

I gulped a breath. "Hi, Mum."

"Jessamy. I've been trying to call you for two days." She cleared her throat. "Did you get those papers from the university?"

"I was going to tell you about switching. But then there was Leonie and Beth and Dad and The Muses."

"Oh, Jessamy, you can *always* tell me. Anything you want, anytime you want."

I hung my head. "I'm sorry, Mum."

"You don't need to apologize. I only wish you had told me." Her voice was soft and earnest. "I could have helped you. You wouldn't have had to do it alone."

"You don't have time for that," I blurted out.

Silence crackled.

I covered my face with my hand. "I'm sorry. I didn't mean to say that."

"But did you mean *what* you said?" Mum always asked us girls that when we'd had a fight.

"Look, it's like this." I gripped the windowsill and stared out to the garden. "You have so much drama and stress you're mopping up every day. It's a lot to handle, too much, actually, but you do handle it, and you never complain." I tapped my fingers anxiously. "I can't add one more thing to that plate. You need a Jessamy who can take care of herself, who can help you take care of yourself, not one who changes programs on a whim." Tears blurred my reflection in the window. I was glad Mum couldn't see as I swiped them away. "There's not room for any more problems right now. And that's okay."

Still silence.

I dragged my toe across the carpet. "But I guess I *have* created another problem, haven't I?"

"Jessamy, you are not a problem. And I'm so sorry I made you feel that way." The hurt in her tone stabbed me.

I shook my head even though I knew she couldn't see. "I knew this would happen. I knew you would take it this way. It's not what I meant at all. You're not the problem here. You never have been."

I am.

Mum was everything good. And I ...

Every whisper I'd ever heard breezed through my head.

How have her grades been? Oh, that's unfortunate. Have you seen how much weight she's gained? What's she doing in her spare time? She's too flighty, that girl. And so strange.

I was always too much. Too little. And nothing in between.

"So why didn't you just tell me in the first place?" Only kindness infused her voice. Of course. She was trying to get to the bottom of everything, because, for some reason, she still wanted to help me.

"I'm too much, Mum. I laugh at weird times, I fly off on schemes just like Dad, I get bad grades, and I switch programs without telling anyone."

"We wouldn't want it any other way."

"You say that, but yes, you would. You do."

Another long pause. Maybe she'd hung up. I wouldn't blame her.

"I think"—she let out a little sigh—"we both need to take a step away from the situation. We each need time to sort out our own thoughts. Maybe we can talk again when you get home on Saturday."

I cringed. "I actually have plans on Saturday. I'm staying another week to participate in the Just Ducky Festival. I cleared it with the university."

"Oh." She drew out the sound. "I see. Well, whenever you get home, then. No worries. I love you, baby."

"Love you too, Mum."

I flopped backward on my bed, rumpling the bedspread. How had I managed to make such a mess? None of the scenarios I'd played out in my head even approached this disaster.

I dragged myself into the family room and dropped my phone on the table. This would be a good day to crash on the couch and watch *Pride and Prejudice.*

But I didn't want to stay home alone and watch films. I wanted the Odd Duck Society.

I could always text Lula and Honora.

No. What if I bothered them?

But what if I wasn't bothering them at all, and I spent the afternoon alone because I was afraid?

I stood slowly, like thick mud dragged each footstep. I found my phone next to the unopened festival envelope.

Did I dare open it? If it was good news, I could certainly use it now. If it wasn't …

I returned to the sofa, set my phone aside, and tore the envelope open slowly.

Miss Aubertine,
We, the Box Hill Just Ducky Festival Committee, regret to inform you that your story "Wild Swan" has been disqualified from our retelling contest. It was unfortunately one of two identical stories that were submitted under two different author names. Both entries have been disqualified pending investigation. A questionnaire has been included with this letter. Your answers would be greatly appreciated and speed the investigation.
Sincerely,
The Box Hill Just Ducky Festival Committee

What? I let the twelve signatures flutter to the floor and ran my hands through my unruly curls. This wasn't fair. I hadn't cheated. Who had copied my story? Angry, red tears pooled.

My phone buzzed. I rescued it from the depths of the couch cushions, beginning to wish I could lose it forever.

Imogen's name flashed on my screen.

Water's not running. Close again?

All the things hit me at once, and I let my phone *clunk* to the floor. I'd failed every task I'd set out upon. I'd failed everything and *everyone*.

So much for Providence.

I turned the film on, wrapped myself in an afghan, and cried.

Hello. This is Honora. Imogen's been trying to reach you about the shop, so I offered to try. Text me when you have the chance?

[Missed phone call from Honora Welbeck.]

Hey, this is Lula. You okay?

What's up?

We're worried.

The texts finally pulled me off the sofa and dragged me into the cloudy afternoon. I rubbed my loose sleeves across my eyes, hoping the puffiness would ease by the time I got to The Muses.

I pulled my cardigan tighter. If they hadn't already given up and left by the time I got there, that was.

My stomach flipped as I drew nearer. I didn't want to. Didn't want to face yet another person and tell them I messed up. I wanted to go home.

Honora, Lula, and Imogen were still clustered outside the shop. Was that dread or relief that slogged through me?

There weren't enough words in my head. I didn't even have enough energy to rehearse.

"Hey." Lula wrapped one arm around my shoulders. "Are you okay? We were worried."

I almost lost it all over again but bit my tongue. "I don't have any money to pay the water company, so until further notice, The Muses is closed."

Honora stepped closer. "Are you sure?"

"No! I'm not sure about anything. But I can't get any buyer to take the place, money's not appearing out of thin air, and I can't keep doing this anymore."

"It's okay. We'll figure this out." Lula rocked back and forth on her heels as if preparing to solve all my problems for me in one swoop.

If only.

"There's nothing to figure out." I stared at the awning speckled by a few faint drops of rain.

Lula stilled. "Then we'll figure that out, too."

"I'll call the rest of the staff and let them know." Imogen pulled her phone from her pocket.

"I don't even have money to pay for your time off." I rubbed my temples.

Imogen placed her hands on either of my shoulders. "We'll be okay." She pulled away and popped into Beatrix's to make her calls.

Rain splotched the sidewalk, but neither Honora nor Lula budged.

"You're getting all wet." My throat hurt. "We should go home."

"Can we go inside?" Lula's voice was tiny once more. "One last time?"

I shrugged and unlocked the door. I thought about staying outside, but when Honora glanced back, I followed her into the drafty shop anyway, wrapping my cardigan tighter.

Lula crossed her arms. "So, uh, I saw Florence off to London this morning."

Honora consulted her planner. She had Florence's departure in her planner? "She's not supposed to leave until the end of the month."

"I know." Lula sank onto her seat at our usual table. "Something changed with the apartment, and they needed to move in right away."

I sat next to her. "I'm so sorry. That must be so hard for you."

Lula swiped under her nose.

I sniffed and propped my chin on my hands. "My story was disqualified."

Honora slammed her hands down on the table. "What on earth? Why?"

"Someone else sent in an identical one. It's pending investigation."

"I'll speak to the committee." Honora laid her hand over mine. "Assure them yours isn't the fake."

"No. You won't. Because you can't." Slowly, I raised my eyes.

She let go of my hand and crumpled into her seat. "You're right."

Lula frowned.

"I broke the pact. I haven't been on the committee for a week. They asked me to step down. They didn't need me. Not many people do." Honora traced a saucer stain on the table. "I suppose that's why I've needed you two so much."

I rubbed under my eyes.

"We *all* need each other. God meant it that way, I think." Lula grabbed a stirrer from the table dispenser and drummed it against the edge. "Come on. One more pact. Even if The Muses goes, we won't go with it."

"Hear, hear." Honora raised an imaginary teacup.

I did the same but said nothing.

Lula tipped back her chair, staring up at the ceiling. "Do you think the letters will keep coming without The Muses?"

"Only time and Providence will tell." Honora shrugged one shoulder.

I wanted to ask if Lula had talked to Florence, but didn't much care to talk. Wasn't sure if I wanted to listen either.

Luckily, Honora asked the question for me.

"Didn't get the chance before she had to catch her train." Lula folded her arms and rested her chin on them.

Honora broke through the gloom, standing and raising her hand. "A toast to H. G. Wells."

I raised my head.

"Whoever he indeed may be, his reason has made my situation more reasonable, and, more importantly, his learning has made me more teachable."

"To Lewis Carroll." Lula stood next. "I have enough nonsense, but I needed the way to Wonderland shown to me again. Or at least to remind me that I already knew."

They didn't look to me, didn't force me to say anything. They simply held their imaginary teacups steady. Honora slipped her hand into my free one as Lula took hers.

And that made the words come anyway.

"To Jane Austen. For both being a companion and showing me companions."

"To The Muses," Honora declared. "May we pass many happy hours here once more. May your doors open again and your light burn long."

"And to the Odd Duck Society." Lula raised her teacup high above her head.

I released Honora's hand first and trudged to the door. I wanted to escape, but I also wanted to soak in every last detail about The Muses and the Odd Duck Society, just in case.

No matter what I did, I'd always regret something about today.

No rustle followed us when we closed the door. The bunch of lavender, dried and brown on the sidewalk, crunched beneath my trainer.

Nothing was as it ought to be.

Lula gathered up the withered bundle and divided it into three, handing us each a few stalks. "Still sweet."

I crammed mine in my tote bag.

Lula gave a tiny frown.

I rolled the edge of my cardigan. "I'm sorry." *For being weird and grumpy. For losing The Muses.*

For Jessamy Aubertine and everything else.

"Don't apologize, dear." Honora cradled her lavender.

"Maybe you two can come over for dinner tomorrow. My mom might make tamales." Lula rubbed a lavender leaf.

"Sounds lovely. I'll be there."

I hugged my arms. "Yeah, sounds nice."

We stood in awkward silence for several moments. I left first. Didn't speak, didn't wave. Just walked away.

The wind *whisked* the lavender out of my bag.

Chapter Eight

Wednesday

I didn't go for tamales the next day.

Honora and Lula checked. I was under the weather, and they ought to go on without me.

The next two times—a study date at the library, then tea at Honora's—I was packing for the trip back to London.

I lied. I wasn't doing anything. In fact, I had quite the impressive list of things I hadn't done.

I hadn't returned the festival questionnaire. I hadn't returned the lovely voice mail Mum had left. I hadn't filled out the university transfer papers. I hadn't even changed out of my pajamas.

Knock, knock, knock.

I waited, hoping whoever it was would go away.

But Allifair didn't wait for an invitation, the same as I didn't turn down the fifth *Downton Abbey* episode of the day.

The pink in Allifair's hair had changed to a sky blue. "Morning, Jessamy. Haven't seen you about lately. Didn't know if you'd seen the lavender patch yet; it's coming in all lush and thick."

"Thanks for telling me. I'll walk down this afternoon."

We both knew I wouldn't, but we both pretended otherwise.

"Ever find that mysterious letter writer?"

I blew out my breath and faked a smile. "I don't think I ever will."

"Oh, I wouldn't be too certain." Allifair winked.

I tilted my head and frowned. A wink from Allifair could mean any number of things.

She handed me an envelope with a rose-shaped seal. "Brought your post in for you." With that, she saw herself out to resume her gardening.

Part of me wanted to toss the letter on the table with the rest. But of all the things I could ignore, I couldn't let go of this.

I foraged a butter knife from the kitchen and slid it under the seal. I needed a good, old-fashioned letter opener.

Jessamy Aubertine, handsome, clever, and rich in the ways that truly matter, with a comfortable companionship and happy disposition, seemed to unite some of the best blessings of existence, and had lived twenty years in the world, despite all determined to distress her.

She was the eldest of the three daughters of a most indulgent, if distant, father. In consequence of circumstances beyond her control, she had been mistress of a small business called The Muses from a very early period. Her mother worked hard, so hard that Jessamy sometimes felt she had only an indistinct remembrance of her. The place of companionship had recently only been supplied by two excellent women.

Between them, it was more the intimacy of sisters.

The real evils, indeed, of Jessamy's situation were the power of having rather too much to weigh her down and a disposition to think a little too lowly of herself; these were the disadvantages which threatened alloy to her many enjoyments.

Sorrow came—not a gentle sorrow. The shop was gone, she didn't wish to face her friends, and she was left to dine alone, with no prospect of even a letter to cheer a long evening. She had, then, only to sit and think of what she had lost.

But there was still every promise of happiness for her. She was a girl of unexceptionable character and pleasant manners, and there was some satisfaction in considering with what self-denying, generous friendship she held with those two excellent women.

It could be sure, they recalled her past kindness

and affection—how she had taught and laughed with them, how she had devoted all her powers only to help them, how she had nursed them through their various troubles. A large debt of gratitude was owing here.

She had been a friend and companion such as few possessed: intelligent, well-informed, useful, gentle, knowing all the ways of her companions, interested in all their concerns, and peculiarly fascinated with each individual, in every pleasure, every scheme of hers—one to whom anyone could speak every thought as it arose, and who had such an affection for her as could never find fault.

That is Jessamy Aubertine.

Jane Austen

I held the paper so my sneaky tears didn't splotch it.

The letter writer was still out there. And right now, it didn't matter so much that I knew who they were than that they knew who I was and that they still cared about and believed in me.

Like Lula and Honora.

I wiped my eyes and huffed a shaky breath.

Lula and Honora never stopped caring about or believing in me.

Neither did Mum, no matter how little we had in common. Dad, Leonie, and Beth, in their own imperfect ways. Allifair and Beatrix and Florence.

God.

I didn't have to be all the things I thought I should. They'd care about me just because I was Jessamy Aubertine and all that name meant.

Knowing someone believed in me made me want to do the best I could. Not to impress them but to be the greatest me I could be.

I laid the letter amidst the scattered rose petals on the coffee table. I stepped into the kitchen and rummaged through the drawers until I found a yellow legal pad and a pen, which reminded me of Honora.

I made a list of all the little things I needed to do before I returned to London. A small gesture, but it made the chaos seem a few steps closer to calm.

The doorbell rang. Was Allifair back? My face was all red and blotchy, but strangely, when I passed the mirror, it made me smile.

The last people I could have expected waited on the step— although I should have expected them.

Lula and Honora. The Odd Duck Society.

"Hey." My voice cracked.

"Hey," Lula returned, but it meant a lot more than that one simple syllable.

"How are you doing?" Honora asked politely.

I smiled. "Right now, I'm doing good." I stepped aside. "Do you want to come in? It's a bit of a mess."

"Sounds lovely," said Honora.

A little shame bubbled up as they stepped past the unopened letters and wrinkled blankets.

Lula gasped loudly. "Is that *Downton Abbey*?"

"*You* like *Downton Abbey*?" I raised an eyebrow.

"Who wouldn't?" Lula crash-landed on the love seat, then grabbed one of the throw pillows.

I settled on the couch next to Honora. "I'm sorry I ignored you both. Guess I had some things to figure out after all."

Honora abandoned her perfectly crossed ankles to turn more comfortably toward me. "And have you puzzled it out?"

"Getting there. Thank God I have both of you."

"I do every day," Honora said.

"Me, too," added Lula.

I tapped the coffee table. "I got another letter this morning."

"Really?" Lula's voice was a tad too high.

Honora pressed her lips together. "How interesting."

I hesitated. "Hang on. You two didn't get letters?"

"It would appear not."

So I'd received a letter from my author, but Honora and Lula had not.

Lula glanced at Honora and mimicked her face.

I crossed my arms. "Remember, we promised no lies. Did you two write this letter?"

"Yes," Honora admitted. "And thank goodness you found out, or I do believe Lula would have exploded."

"We wanted to do something encouraging, but we also didn't want to shove you if you weren't ready." Lula sent a throw pillow tumbling.

"You did perfectly. I wouldn't have opened that door had it not been for this letter." A sneaking suspicion crept over me. Like Allifair had said, her best bet. "So did one or both of you write the other letters, too?"

"Heavens, no," Honora declared. "As I said, we were as surprised as you."

Lula shook her head, waves bouncing furiously.

"Did you ever ask Florence?" I leaned forward. "I'm dying to know."

"I did, not long after The Muses closed." She hugged a second throw pillow tighter. "She said no. But she had more information that might help us. In fact, she thought what she had to say was so important, she ought to come and tell you herself." Lula cupped her hands around her mouth, although she didn't really need to. "Florence!"

Two minutes passed before Florence actually arrived. "Sorry. I missed my cue, didn't I? Your house is so old and amazing. I took some video, if that's all right."

My mouth fell open. "Of course it's all right, but what are you doing here? Aren't you still unpacking in London?"

"I have important information on your little case. Can't stay in London for that. Friends look out for friends and all that." She perched on the hearth. "Right. Where were we? Letters? I didn't write the letters, but ..." She drew the word out as if she'd misplaced a train of thought. "I *did* deliver the letters."

"Because you knew post addresses from delivering the posters," I said.

Lula tapped her foot. "Keep going, Flo."

"I got the letters directly from the writer. She claimed she didn't write them, but I know better, because the handwriting on the letter matched a note I saw in the tea shop."

A note in the tea shop? Directly from the writer?

Like the *clatter* of a teaspoon on a saucer, the truth fell into place.

"Imogen," I said. "It was Imogen."

"How do you know?" Lula lost the last pillow to the floor. "Florence hadn't even told *me* this part yet."

"Like you pointed out, Florence and Imogen were the only ones always there when we were at The Muses. Imogen wrote the letters, which explains why Florence saw the handwriting on a note at the shop. Florence was dropping off posters anyway, so it was the perfect cover."

"But why?" Honora wondered. "What was her motive to bring us all together?"

Florence shrugged. "You'll have to ask her."

We stood in unison.

"Do you know where we would be most likely to find her, Florence?"

Florence had already turned her camera back on and was wandering the room. "Easy. The park."

True to Florence's word, we finally found Imogen on a bench far away from the festival preparations and very near the duck pond. A plastic baggie of instant oats sat next to her, and a true crime podcast whispered from her phone's speaker.

She scribbled notes wildly in a leather journal but closed it when she noticed all three of us approaching. Understanding dawned as she silenced her podcast.

I squeezed onto the seat next to her. "*You* sent those beautiful letters."

Imogen nodded, looking ashamed, though I couldn't fathom why.

Lula sat cross-legged on the grass. "Your writing is amazing. You have no idea how much we needed those letters."

"Thank you." She ducked her head.

Honora leaned against the arm of the bench.

"What made you decide to bring the three of us together?" I finally asked the question that had spun round my mind for the past week.

Imogen traced her bare toes over the grass. "Because I wanted to meet you so badly." She laughed. "That sounds really weird, doesn't it? Let me try to explain. I moved here a couple months back. While I came by a job quickly, connections weren't quite so easy. I'd see the three of you at The Muses, and you lot seemed so interesting, but I never managed to strike up a conversation beyond your tea orders. Of course, I knew Jessamy, but only from business, nothing more."

"Why on earth didn't you join us, then, after you sent the letters?" Honora laid a hand on Imogen's shoulder.

Imogen covered her face with her hands. "It's embarrassing! I chickened out. I kept thinking I'd do it the next time and the next, but then it got too weird and awkward to even think about."

I hugged her. "Imogen, you are always welcome in the Odd Duck Society."

"You might not think so once I finish," she mumbled against my shoulder, then pulled back and looked me straight in the eye. "I stole your story for the festival."

I didn't pull back, even though confusion clashed with disappointment in my chest. "What?"

"I heard you discuss pulling out of the contest, but after that, I had to refill a carafe. I'd hoped to enter the contest, too, to save The Muses. But none of my stories would come. So I figured since you weren't entering, I might as well use your story."

"How did you even find it?"

"One of the copies fell out of Lula's backpack on the way out."

Lula's eyes widened. "I must have put two in my backpack instead of one!"

Imogen squished the bag of instant oats. "I only realized my mistake when I got the disqualification letter. I just got back from clearing it up with the judges. They said your story is eligible for the contest again. No matter how it had ended, it was wrong, and I'm sorry."

"You were honest about it." Lula twisted a blade of grass. "That's a point in my book."

"Moreover, you made it right," Honora added.

I smiled and nudged her shoulder. "Sounds like you're complying with the pact."

Imogen beamed. She scooped a handful of instant oats out of the baggie and offered some to each of us.

Together, we fed the ducks.

Chapter Nine

Friday

Hey, Mum. Know this week has been rough. Entered a story in the festival retelling contest this weekend. I'd love for you to come, if you can.

Maybe we could talk, too.

Chapter Ten

"Festival food is amazing; why can't we have it all the time?" Lula bit into her churro.

I snagged a piece of the cinnamony treat. "Then it wouldn't be festival food."

"Fair." She swatted at me good-naturedly.

I licked the dusting of sugar from my fingers and scanned the crowd, for something to do.

All right, more than just something to do. We'd been at the festival all day with no sign of Mum. What if she was upset about our phone call the other day? Maybe she didn't want to discuss it anymore.

Or maybe she did. Maybe she simply had to work or had too much going on at home. It didn't mean she had deliberately chosen not to come or that she didn't want to talk to me.

Goodness, Jessamy. It's not all about you.

"It's ten minutes past when they said they'd announce the winner." Honora paced and stared at her watch. "Aren't you at all nervous?"

Lula handed her a piece of churro.

Honora popped it in her mouth.

A few more festival-goers gave up waiting and moved on to the next attraction. That was my cue to scan the crowd once more.

But this time, I found a familiar face.

Mum.

Hesitation stuttered in my chest. Should I move first? Or wait for her to be the first?

We both moved at the same time. She waved and tripped through the crowd as I took a few tiny steps forward. "Mum, you're here—"

She wrapped me in a hug. For once, I didn't explain, didn't worry—I just was.

"I want to say one thing, and we'll lay the matter to rest," she whispered in my ear. "There is always room for you, Jessamy Aubertine."

I squeezed my eyes closed. It didn't keep the tears from escaping, but it wasn't meant to. "There's room for both of us."

"Love you."

I held on tight. "Love you, too."

Mum stepped back and wiped her eyes with a long sigh—the good kind.

Lula offered her a piece of churro.

Mum chuckled and accepted. "Now," she spoke around the bite, "what title am I listening for so I can cheer?"

Honora grabbed my sleeve. "She's coming!"

The committee member approached the microphone. "Many apologies for the delay. To clarify, we hold rubber duck races, so we would not advise bringing a captured wild duck."

Everyone chuckled except Honora.

"At long last, I am here to announce the winner of our Just Ducky retelling contest."

Honora grabbed one of my hands. Lula claimed the other, while Mum clasped my shoulder.

Please, God, call my name. If it can't be me, can it at least be Honora or Lula instead?

A volunteer handed the speaker an envelope. Carefully, painstakingly, she slit the top.

Honora grumbled. "Just open it."

As if she had heard Honora, she unfolded the slip of paper. "Our winner is …"

Please …

"*A Hardship of Solitude* by Honora Welbeck!"

A tiny drop of disappointment plopped in my chest, but it dried up quickly. We all exploded into cheers, jumping and hugging Honora—even Mum, who didn't know her yet.

The attention seemed to startle the perfectly poised Honora. We pushed her toward the podium until she finally recovered herself and ascended the steps.

The speaker handed her the second envelope the volunteer passed to her. "As promised, eight hundred pounds. Congratulations on your magnificent work."

Honora spun abruptly, took the steps two at a time, and crossed to me.

"Get back up there! This is your moment!" I pushed her back toward the stage.

She pressed the envelope into my hands. "This is for The Muses."

I shook my head. "It's yours. You do as you please."

"This *is* what I please. With it, I have a confession to make as well."

I crossed my arms. "Another?"

Honora smiled. "I'm your buyer."

Lula dropped her churro partway to her mouth.

"What? But I have you phone number. It didn't match."

"I used my home phone for calls on The Muses."

"Why didn't you answer my messages, then?" I swatted her arm gently. "Or tell me, all those times we met at The Muses?"

"At first, I didn't know you were the owner. Truthfully, I never had the money to buy it anyway, I only wanted to hold on to my favorite writing haunt, not unlike your Jane Austen. By the time I realized, I feared you and Lula would back out of the competition so I could win and save The Muses. I wanted to win fair and square."

I hugged her. "And you did. Now go enjoy it."

Mum wrapped her arm around my shoulders as the speaker announced, "Now for your enjoyment, Honora will read her winning story, *A Hardship of Solitude.*"

Epilogue

One Month Later

"Here Comes the Sun" filled the shop from the record player in the corner. I strolled into The Muses, ordered my usual with a reassuring smile for Imogen, and squeezed into my seat between Lula and Honora. We'd had to switch to a larger table over the past few weeks. "Goodness, Allifair. You left your bluebells?"

"I've got fifteen minutes, and that's all." Allifair crossed her soil-speckled arms. Who would have known she wrote stories based on true crimes?

"Florence is on!" Lula set her phone at the empty place next to her.

Florence waved from the video box on the screen, film posters filling the background.

I *rang* my spoon against my teacup. "We've gathered for a very important occasion today—important enough that I thought we all needed to be here and that Allifair's bluebells could languish for fifteen minutes."

Everyone chuckled.

I turned to the counter. "We're initiating another member as we voted on last week."

Lula led the cheers as Imogen slipped out from behind the counter.

I stood and laid a hand on Imogen's shoulder. "Meet Imogen."

Imogen selected a place at the table, between Florence and Allifair.

"She writes crime novels, so she and Allifair ought to get along well. As we've already seen, Imogen is brave, honest, and creative. A perfect fit. Or misfit, since we're all odd ducks here. All odd ducks in the care of Providence, which seems a pretty good place to be."

Everyone applauded.

I raised my teacup. "And now, a pact."

Honora, Lula, Florence, Allifair, and Imogen all raised theirs alongside mine.

A Note from Rachel Leitch

I have so many people to thank and not nearly enough space. Here goes. Meet my real-life Odd Duck Society! A toast—

To Momma: You have been my biggest supporter even before I decided to write. You always remind me my stories will go where God wants them to go. And they have.

To my siblings: Rebekah, Lydia, Julia, Noah, and Jonah. Thanks for putting up with me and celebrating with me even though writing's not your thing.

To my critique partners: Emily, thanks for reading an early draft and giving your unique perspective on it! You helped shape it into the story we're holding in our hands right now. Lulu, thank you for always cheering me on, no matter how much you had going on.

To my friends: Rachel, thanks for always listening to how the story was going. (Did you find the plethora?) Hope, thanks for sticking with me for so long and being such a strong friend. I can remember some of the early stories I sent your way, and I cringe.

To my mentors: Amy and Rebekah, you have a million things to do, and still you show up for me and make sure I know I matter. Thank you for taking time to see me.

To my church library: Thank you for supporting and nurturing a love of stories in me since I was a child and for cheering with me when I published my own.

To the Young Writer's Workshop: I absolutely would not be here today if it hadn't been for all the teaching you've shared with me, as well as the fellowship, friendship, and encouragement.

To Linda Taylor and Taylor University's Professional Writers' Conference: You were the first writers' event I attended, and I still look forward to going every year. It always makes me smile to walk in and spot people who are excited to see me, even after all this time. Thanks for reassuring this anxious writer and sending me on my way.

To the fellow authors and team at Wild Blue Wonder Press: You made my first true publication experience an incredible one. Thank you for your patience with me and for coaching me through the process.

And to you, the reader: You saw all the stories out there, and you picked this one. That's an honor that I don't take lightly. Thanks for giving me your time, your imagination, and perhaps, a bit of your heart.

This story is very different from everything else I've ever written. I never would have expected that this would be where I would wind up. Don't be afraid to do the different. Sometimes it's what you need the most. If I want you to take one thing with you, it's that you matter. You have something to say, you are beautiful, and you are loved.

If you want to keep up with my writing adventures, please subscribe to my newsletter at https://racheljleitch.com (where you'll receive a free short story about a magical violin) and follow me on Instagram @racheljleitchauthor.

P.S. Yes, Jane Austen, H. G. Wells, and Lewis Carroll really did have connections to Surrey, England.

Fear Not Tomorrows

a novella by Erika Mathews

Dedication

To my Eternal King, with Whom I can fearlessly trust every one of my tomorrows.

Chapter One:
The Old English
Parsonage

From an old English parsonage down by the sea
There came in the twilight a message to me;
Its quaint Saxon legend, deeply engraven,
Hath, as it seems to me, teaching from heaven.
And on through the hours the quiet words ring
Like a low inspiration: "DO THE NEXT THING."
Adapted from "Doe Ye Nexte Thynge" by Emily Elizabeth Steele Elliott

An anticipated tomorrow is the most delightful thing in existence. For one, nothing could hurry on the mundane-work worries of today like a tomorrow that promised a revel in restful beauty and unalloyed companionship with the very star of one's existence. For another, anticipation was half of enjoyment itself.

And that very same anticipation just now proved to light Margaret Enfield's humdrum, parsonage existence aflame with the most ardent joy that lent romance to duty, charm to chores, and a steady, unfailing hope amid the difficulties and challenges of existence as the eldest daughter and caretaker of many small, clamoring siblings.

"Tomorrow!" The single word captured delight itself. "Do hurry with the potatoes, Polly. I'd like to finish the dishes before the boys get back from Mrs. Wheaton's."

"What's tomorrow?" her fifteen-year-old sister asked, haphazardly swiping the peeler across yet another potato, no signs of increased speed visible. "Is Lester coming to help you with supper instead of me?"

"No." Margaret flew to the bedroom for a dry towel from the freshly-washed pile on the bed, then whisked back to the sink to lift the dripping kettle. "No—that is, I suppose in a way, he'll be helping with a meal. But no. Lunch! He's taking me to the lake for a picnic! Why, we haven't been to the lake for—I don't know how long. And I've never been there with just Lester." She emphasized the last phrase with a vigorous swipe of the cloth to the pot.

"You've never been engaged before." Another potato tumbled into the half-filled bowl.

Margaret righted the pot, the outside now dry, and filled the inside with water. After setting it on the old woodstove, she hesitated only a second before dumping the bowl of potatoes into the kettle, then snatched up another potato from the unpeeled pile and set to work with a knife of her own. "I'm so glad we get a bit of time tomorrow. It has been *so* busy these past months. What with the planting and the plowing and the children and the meals and the spring cleaning, I feel like I've scarcely had a moment to breathe!"

"Not to mention *wedding planning*." If the heavy accentuation of Polly's words could be missed, her raised eyebrow and conscious side-glance certainly couldn't be.

"There *is* that," Margaret admitted. "Everything needs to be done at once, it seems to me. Just when one rush is over, the next begins. Oh, Polly, are you *sure* that you will be able to take over enough of the work here? Even if I'm only next door, it's not like *living* here. And June isn't so far away ..."

"Nonsense. You're getting married, and there's nothing more to be said. We'll manage just fine, see if we don't." Polly's nod sent a tiny shower of peelings spinning toward the floor, and at once, Margaret dove to scoop them up.

"I'm not so sure ..." Margaret sighed, the first hint of pensiveness creeping into her voice and manner. "But Mama is adamant—"

"And Lester, of *course*, has nothing to do with it," teased Polly, jabbing the peeler in her sister's direction. "Mama is adamant. Haven't you seen how much she's improved the last month or two? Things must be looking up if she's sending you out with Lester on a day when all the children will be at home."

"True." The sparkle jumped back to Margaret's eyes. "You can eat leftover potatoes while I'm gone, at least. And it's not like I'm marrying a man with a handful of children of his own already for me to take care of, or someone who will carry me off to the other side of London. I can run over whenever I please. And I'm sure I shall, when my own small housekeeping is done and Lester is busy with his timber."

"But the wedding itself?" Polly's peeler stilled again as her eyes landed somewhere out the window.

Margaret, too, drew her eyes out the open kitchen window. Whiffs of wet earth, new growth, fresh grass, tiny flowers ... Surrey was coming back to life after the winter of frigid blasts and grayness, and springtime, in all its glory, promised to burst into full bloom before many days had passed. And then would come the warm breezes of early summer and the June roses ... a whole arbor of them for Lester and her to stand together underneath as they said the covenant vows that would join them as one for life ... uniting her forever with her very best friend in all this world, the Lester she'd grown up with, the one who knew her quirks and flaws and loved her anyway with all his heart. The one she'd shared childhood hideouts with. The one who'd been there with oceans of comfort when her father had passed on to the fullness of glory that he'd preached about weekly at the little church next door. The one she'd laughed with, cried with, and ministered with. And the one with whom she shared a hundred little secret jokes and phrases and habits all their own.

What could be better?

Ah, only that day of June roses and covenant vows being followed by a lifetime of married bliss with that same best friend, living together with him alone—no siblings bursting in and interrupting every sentence they spoke to each other, no constant noise and chatter, no hindrances to unfettered *time* together—and then, perhaps, one day raising their own children together, just him and her.

How could it be that the dream of a lifetime was so close to coming true?

"The wedding?" Polly's insistent question cut into Margaret's reverie. "Where will it be? And what shall you have to eat? And of what material shall your dress be?"

"In the rose garden, I hope. I don't know what we shall eat—whatever's on hand, I suppose. Or what we can procure without any great outlay of funds. Plenty of time for all those details later. As for now, I intend to do my best to make tomorrow's picnic the *best* there ever was!"

"I'm sure you shall." Polly's murmur faded into the distance as Margaret scurried into the bedroom for yet another clean towel.

"We're back!" The announcement preceded the banging of the door as the boys—Elias, Levi, and Archie, ages eleven, nine, and seven, respectively—trooped in with an empty basket and growling stomachs. As the door slammed behind them, the little girls, Joyce and Rosina, stumbled from the bedroom where they'd been napping.

"We went to Mrs. Wheaton's!" Archie announced. "We brought her cookies. And … other things."

"She was happy to see us," Levi added. "I think she must get pretty lonely in that house all by herself."

"Why doesn't she get a husband, then?" Joyce piped up.

"She *had* a husband." Polly shushed Joyce and tied on Rosina's bib. "I don't think she wants another one right now."

"But she *might*. She loves seeing people. At least she always loves seeing us," Joyce insisted.

"Remember when we made cookies at *her* house?" Levi piped up, kicking his shoes across the kitchen. "I think she liked that better than the cookies we bring her from our house."

"She used to write letters to me." Elias pulled back a chair and then reached for a potato. "She'd give me one every time I went over there, just for fun. And she always has the best stories. Even if she *is* stuck in bed."

"I remember the first weekly supper basket we brought to her." Margaret placed forks on the table and turned to grasp the water pitcher. "I was shy. But she was friendly, even if she didn't quite know what to say to us. That was the first time she told me apple fritters were her favorite, because her daddy used to make them for her on her birthday every October."

A moment of silence spread around the table as each child took his or her place. Memories of their own late father hovered in Margaret's heart. He hadn't ever made her apple fritters, but she'd never forget the annual birthday picnic he'd always shared with her. Recollections of sunshine, happiness, racing across flowery meadows, treats she only tasted once a year, and her father's broad hand clasping her tiny one as he thanked God for their meal and for his daughter mingled in her soul. Picnics and happiness went together.

All the more reason she couldn't wait for the morrow's picnic with Lester—the only one whose presence gave her as strong of a sense of loving security as her father's presence had.

She carried a plate to Mama, then sat down to her own potatoes before the evening chores began. The table was cleared and scrubbed, the dishes washed, the children's toys and books and miscellaneous odds and ends replaced in their proper locations, the floor swept, the tea kettle refilled, the wash folded and put away, the children's nightgowns put on, their teeth brushed, and each child tucked into bed. At last, Margaret sighed contentedly in the quiet parsonage. It was in order, just as it should be—just as it had been every evening in the years when Grandpa Enfield had lived and preached there, and before that, when his father had done the same.

Silently, Margaret retired to the bedroom she shared with Polly. Once there, she laid out her outfit for tomorrow and made what various and sundry preparations she saw fit before stretching out on her own bed with a heart of anticipation for the rising of the sun.

"Tomorrow" dawned as brightly as Margaret's spirits. She flew, as was her wont, through the morning's work. Not even the grumpiness or self-will of some of her younger siblings could dampen her mood. Mama joined them for breakfast, seeming more herself than she had since autumn.

The sun seemed to creep through the sky whenever Margaret paused to look, but the flurry of cramming an entire day's worth of work into just one morning ensured that she did not find many occasions upon which to note the position of the sun. As it approached its zenith, a cheerfully whistled tune floated through the open window and alighted upon Margaret's eager ears. At last! Her heart bounded as she snatched up her handbag and flung open the door to greet Lester Vincent with her countenance reflecting the joy of her heart. Of course, the children swarmed after her, but for once, she scarcely heeded them except to wave good-bye as her other hand slipped into Lester's, and they strolled down the lane.

Once their steps turned the corner and sight and sound of the parsonage had faded into the distance, Margaret drew a deep sigh of contentment. How freeing it was to be able to go off without responsibilities for a few hours. How secure to feel the pressure of a strong hand over hers, mutely reassuring her that for once, someone else could care for her instead of her always caring for everyone else. And above all, how restful to gaze up into that loving face and know that he was hers, and he was here. Forever.

Under the majestic beech, Margaret leaned back on the blanket Lester spread out for her, soaking it all in. How often she'd played under this very tree as a child, both with and without Lester. How many happy days had been spent splashing in the lake that lapped softly on the rocky sand before her. Above all, how fondly she recollected the memory of Lester's gently sliding onto her finger the intricately engraved gold band encircling it. He'd nearly dropped it in nervousness and excitement, and how adorable it had been to watch him swoop to deftly catch it before it actually fell.

The afternoon passed in a blur—partly on shore and partly in his old rowboat. They chatted pleasantly about anything and everything, savoring the rare moments where sunshine merged with friendship, love, and precious time.

Margaret's fingers trailed in the azure-hued lake water as she leaned over the side of the rowboat, and Lester dipped an oar in. Her eyes fluttered closed for a moment as she breathed in the sweet, spring-scented air. New life lingered there, and hope. Promise. Her gaze rested on Lester's face and then the shore beyond. The picnic basket, tiny on the blanket, nestled under the beech tree. Hints of iridescent green bathed the branches in a gauzy film—a mute pledge of the full bloom of the summer to come.

"Lester." Margaret broke a comfortable silence of several minutes. "Sometimes I wonder how I'll get everything done in time for our wedding."

"Why, is there *that* much extra to be tended to, my beloved?" Lester's tone perfectly blended teasing and tenderness.

"The list is endless," Margaret sighed. "For a day, I might perhaps feel like I'm caught up on the work, but then the next day, I'm a week behind again. I do one thing only to have it undone a moment afterwards. The daily chores never stop long enough for me to have time for the duties that stay done a bit longer."

"'One thing at a time, all things in succession.' Isn't that how it goes?"

"If by *it* you mean that book we shoved into the crack in our attic-fort wall, then *yes*, I do remember. I definitely don't think 'all things in succession' meant shoving *all* Grandpapa's books into that fort wall." She grinned as she recalled the circumstances directly following the first time Grandpapa had quoted that maxim to Lester and her—so misunderstood by them as children and so literally followed in the unfortunate task of repairing their fort.

"At least I did it one at a time ..."

"And you *certainly* enjoyed putting them all back on the shelf one at a time, too." Margaret's eyes twinkled at him.

"Of course I did, since I had *you* to help me." Lester emphasized his words with a raised eyebrow. "But truly, one thing at a time. That's all you *can* do. Do the next thing—the thing in front of you."

"I suppose that's always the answer. I just like to see progress, to see the bigger picture. Or at least to have *something* to look forward to beyond the duties."

"That is why you are marrying me, beloved." Lester winked.

"Of course, I—"

Distant shouting wafted across the water, jolting Margaret's thoughts to a crashing halt.

"Is that Oswald?" Lester's voice was anything but pleased. "What's he going on about? I thought we warned your brothers *not* to disturb our picnic."

"Polly told Elias, Levi, and Archie, but Oswald was in town. I didn't expect him to finish work so soon—perhaps something is the matter!" An unnamed fear rose in Margaret's heart. Mama? Was she worse? Was caring for the children too much for her? Oh, why had Margaret left her with all that? Margaret drew a deep breath, her fingers tightening around the side of the boat in an effort to calm herself as Lester bent the oars toward the shore. No use fretting over the unknown yet.

"A letter for Lester!" Oswald's shouts were discernible now. "It says 'Urgent'!"

Chapter Two:
Many a Fear

Many a questioning, many a fear,
Many a doubt, hath its quieting here.

Lester leaped from the boat almost before it ground against the sandy shore. After hauling it farther up the bank, he stretched out a hand to Margaret and pulled her onto land before whirling to grasp the envelope Oswald held. "Beloved, pardon me. Would you mind?"

"By all means, read." Margaret motioned to the letter, then stepped forward to the beech for the double purpose of giving him a bit of privacy and rearranging the picnic basket.

Lester's eyes traveled quickly up and down the paper, and Margaret laid the spoons straight for the third time as she impatiently watched.

When at last Lester folded the missive and reinserted it into the envelope, she dropped all pretense and went to him, gazing straight into his eyes.

Still, he did not immediately speak. He seemed to be measuring his words, selecting them carefully so as to disturb her the least amount possible.

Margaret rubbed her thumbs over her fists.

When he finally spoke, his voice radiated soothing calm. "Sidney has fallen ill. As he is currently unable to care for either Emily or his business, his mother-in-law has asked me to come."

"So severely ill? With what?" Margaret pressed her hands together, her heart aflutter at the as yet unknown dangers surrounding Lester's twin brother and six-year-old niece.

"Consumption, they think. It doesn't sound like he is in too much danger—at least not yet—but they are taking all precautions." Lester's tones were calm, but his demeanor betrayed how much he felt the gravity of the situation. "Emily is all right. Her grandparents took her the moment the illness struck. They've managed so far, Mrs. Williams says, though Mr. Williams's lameness has hampered his ability to help care for her."

Margaret nodded, suppressing the strong longing that surged within at the thought of Lester's traveling so far from her just now. She closed her eyes an instant. Nothing would be as she thought. Perhaps the wedding must be postponed. The bright spring day seemed to suddenly dim to dullest grey—a portent of the season ahead.

But she mustered up her most cheerful voice to answer Lester. The separation would be as difficult for him as for her, no doubt, and she could at least paint these last moments with memories of joyful acceptance instead of disappointed wailing. "Of course you must help him," she said with as much energy and blithesomeness as she could manage. "We couldn't have him languishing all alone. And dear little Emily, how lonely she must be without her father close by! As her father's twin, you must surely be a halfway decent replacement in an emergency."

Lester's mouth quirked in the ghost of a smile. "Ah, that's my Margaret, always making the best of a bad situation."

"Why, you know it yourself," she replied. "And just think! You'll have them straightened out before we can lament your departure much, and by the time you are back, well! We shan't have much longer to wait before our wedding day arrives at last. I shall be sure to keep myself quite occupied while you are away—with planning and preparations, besides the housework and the children as usual. I'm so glad you've nearly completed our home—that ought to be ready. And I'll write so often you shan't have a chance to miss me."

"Was that a dare?" Lester teased, even though his demeanor remained serious and hints of sadness crinkled in the corners of his eyes.

"Only if you choose to take it so." Margaret swallowed. How much longer could she keep up this levity when her heart wanted to burst? She missed him already. How endlessly—and emptily—the weeks seemed to stretch out in front of her now! There would be nothing to look forward to—nothing certain, for who knew how soon Lester would be able to return?

"I am thankful my own business is in such good order. We just finished the last of that big timber sale, and the men should be able to run the day-to-day operations just fine without me, for the present." Lester turned and gazed into her eyes, and she blinked to avoid the overflow of tears.

He's leaving. I won't see him ... She drank in the sight of him, staring as if to indelibly imprint every detail of his appearance upon her memory. *This is so sudden!* "How *will* I go on without you?" she whispered, the words breaking past her will to keep them inside.

"The same as always, beloved. 'One thing at a time, all things in succession.' Like our Savior Himself, I say to you, 'My peace I give unto you,' only I ought to say, '*His* peace I give unto you.'"

She swallowed. "I *will* miss you."

"And I will miss you."

"I wish you didn't have to go." Again, her statement was a mere breath.

"So do I." He paused, perhaps swallowing his own threatening tears. "But I must. This is my next 'one thing,' it seems. Or rather, more specifically, my next 'one thing' is answering Mrs. Williams. I shall telegraph her this afternoon."

Margaret did not reply. *He* was the one leaving; of course he had many new tasks to undertake and questions to occupy his mind. He'd be seeing new sights and living in a new place. *Everything* would be fresh and new to him—and yes, he'd miss her, but he would have so many other things to distract him from loneliness.

She, on the other hand ... Life seemed to stretch drearily before her. Chores. Children. Cooking. Cleaning. Cares. And no Lester to liven it up, to give her something to look forward to on evenings or weekends when the work was finished.

Perhaps he'd be able to return sooner than they thought. She grasped the idea like a steadying rope on a rocky cliff about to crumble about her.

In spite of the cheerful face she'd put on, she'd be missing him every moment.

"'One thing at a time,'" she whispered. "I-I'm afraid of these tomorrows."

"Because you are not there yet. When you get to tomorrow, you will find that He is already there." Lester's voice couldn't have been more earnest.

"He is already there," she repeated.

"'Perfect love casteth out fear,' beloved. I love you more than you could ever imagine, and He loves you even more than that. Don't forget that, no matter what happens. No matter what tomorrow might bring."

"I shan't," Margaret murmured. "And I love you just the same."

The next few days passed in a blur. Lester popped in and out every moment he could, but travel preparations in his business and personal life prevented many spare minutes from falling to his lot. Margaret carried out her work with a weight dragging at her heart, seeming to sense the impending parting afresh at every turn. Who'd cheer her up when homelife seemed unbearable? Who would provide a new perspective when everyone around her was as stuck fast in the trials of living in the old Enfield parsonage as she was? Had she even realized how much she'd leaned on him and looked forward to the small, regular interactions? Had she been spoiled by having him next door?

Could there be *any* hope about a springtime tomorrow when it only promised the departure and absence of the one she loved best in the world?

Chapter Three:
Child of the King

Moment by moment, let down from heaven,
Time, opportunity, guidance, are given.
Fear not tomorrows, child of the King;
Trust them with Jesus: DO THE NEXT THING.

The train steamed north, carrying Lester Vincent away with it, and the little parsonage to the south felt more desolate than ever. Despite her determinations to be cheerful and to do her duty, Margaret felt her spirits flagging. One moment, she resolved to be calm, serene, and collected, do the one thing in front of her, and trust Lester to God; the next moment, she found herself simply aching, yearning, missing him, unable to move past the tremendous hole in her heart that was his absence.

To be sure, she wouldn't wish him back—she certainly didn't want Sidney or his child to suffer worse in health, mind, or finances. But if only Lester could be in more than one place at a time! Or if only Margaret herself could have seen her way clear to marry him on the spot and accompany him!

But that was the one thing she simply could not do. There was Mama to think of, and the children. The temperatures dipped again and the winds howled as a late blizzard dashed snow against every window, sending the promise of spring scurrying back to its holes in the dark corners of the woods even as it sent Mama groaning back to her bed.

"I'll be better once warmer weather comes," Mama insisted, when Margaret's worry lines must have etched themselves more deeply across her face than usual.

As the days stretched before Margaret, each one seeming longer than the last, she resolved, "I *will* do my duty, regardless of the cost." Everything this springtime crawled painfully slowly, especially each stitch of the long seam of the sheet she mended. Her gaze snagged on the snowflakes whirling against the window. So much for picnics and rowboats and dreams of roses and happiness. Everything was buried under a mountain of gray-whiteness. No hints of a brighter or warmer season could be seen, and Margaret felt keenly the heaviness of the outer world reflected in her heart.

Evening fell early, and Margaret lit the lamps as the soup boiled, and the children squabbled over a book, then a game. Rosina spilled her water, and Archie slipped on it and bumped his arm. Levi yelled about something, and the other girls begged Margaret to let them help with supper … She felt like her head was about to explode. No doubt Mama felt even worse.

Why Margaret? Her soul yearned to fly away to some other existence, to a place where she felt less stuck. On the one hand, she'd never leave her family when they needed her. On the other hand, there were definitely days when she felt she couldn't stand another moment of this life. She *knew* God loved her and had His best for her, but it was *so* difficult to feel it.

Oswald flung the door open, far too much of a whirlwind of snow blowing in with him before he finally got the door securely latched. Margaret bit her tongue. *"One thing at a time."* Do the next thing. So many things loomed on her to-do list, but giving Oswald a hard time when he was probably doing his best wasn't one of them. So instead, she grasped a ladle to set on the table along with the stack of bowls.

Her forbearance was rewarded the next moment by Oswald's announcement. "Stopped for the post. A letter for you."

Margaret dropped the ladle onto the table and flew for the missive Oswald tossed toward her. "Thank you! Supper's ready!" It only took a quick glance at the address to confirm that it was Lester's.

As the children swarmed the table with the usual commotion and Polly ladled a bowl to carry to Mama's room, Margaret slipped to the rocker by the fireplace, breaking the seal of the envelope even before she was seated. Hope and fear both alight, she unfolded the paper and scanned the lines it contained.

Indeed, love and cheer radiated from the page. Lester missed her. Sidney was stable, though not yet recovering. Yet one section stood out sharply to Margaret's gaze.

Business complications have proved much more serious than we first imagined. Straightening things out and catching up on what has fallen behind with his illness completely fills my days. I don't want to dishearten you, but I also do not wish to give you false hope. I expect to remain here for many weeks— perhaps months. There are so many unknowns—both in the business and with his condition.

While I may be here longer than we both wish, beloved, remember: you and I are children of the King, and this is His commission for me and for you in this time. He gives the time to do what He calls us to do, and He is the Light for our feet when we cannot see the path ahead. As His child, we follow our King willingly whithersoever He goes. I know you might be fretting over the long, dreary tomorrows of this spring that looks so different from what we thought, but fear not. Fret not. Rest as the beloved child of the King, which you are.

Over and over, Margaret read those lines, the supper hubbub fading away. *That* was what she'd been forgetting. She wasn't stuck here; God had placed her here specifically for this time. God wasn't surprised by Sidney's illness or Lester's absence.

God was the King. She was His beloved child.

She could rest in that.

But even as her soul grasped at that truth, her heart sank under fresh waves of disappointment. Lester wouldn't be back soon. Maybe not even by their wedding date. Could she face an unknown amount of time without him—without the hope of the life with him that she knew God had called her to?

But not now.

Why would God give her the confidence that He wanted her to marry Lester this spring and then pull it aside indefinitely? Did

God's will conflict with itself? Why would He seem to tell her one thing but do another?

She didn't have time to sort it out just now. She had to get the children through supper.

Back in the kitchen, she located and tied a bib around Rosina, made the boys sit down without pushing each other off the bench, fetched a rag to clean the endless spills that seemed to multiply faster than any soup reached hungry mouths, picked up Rosina's spoon time and again, refilled the boys' bowls, then refilled the girls' bowls halfway, somehow managing to tuck a bite or two into her own mouth in between everything.

By the time she'd wiped up the last drop of soup from the table and swept the final breadcrumb from the floor, exhaustion hung upon her disappointment. Every moment, she missed Lester.

There wouldn't be any roses at her wedding at this rate.

She dropped into bed and woke aching and still tired. The wash she hadn't found time to do yet this week piled up in the bedrooms. She couldn't remember when the last time she scrubbed the floors was. The curtains hung limply over the smudged windows. With all the cold weather recently, spring cleaning had been interrupted so many times that even the tasks she had completed would probably have to be redone once it was finally warm enough. The provisions in the pantry were dwindling, and she'd have to take inventory. Perhaps Oswald would help restock. Polly would do her best, of course, and the little ones aided in what small ways they could, but nothing eased the mental strain of possessing the lion's share of the responsibilities of a large household. It would be midsummer before Margaret caught up with everything just around the house.

Perhaps it was good Lester wasn't here to divide her time and attention even more. She could at least throw herself into her work to distract her mind. It sounded like Lester was doing the same—if nothing else, they could be lonely and busy together.

"'One thing at a time,'" she told herself as she pulled on her shoes. It didn't seem to help the disgruntled feeling in her heart, however.

Nor did the sounds coming from the kitchen—sounds of conflict, of chaos.

Neither did a peek out the grimy window. Would all this snow *ever* melt? Was the fullness spring a lifetime away?

If she were truly a child of the King, what kind of a kingdom was this?

Chapter Four:
Do It With Prayer

Do it immediately, do it with prayer;
Do it reliantly, casting all care;
Do it with reverence, tracing His hand
Who hath placed it before thee with earnest command.

Green grass peeked through the mud-splattered snow at last, and Margaret's spirits lifted a bit as she trudged through task after task. Lester might be gone, but at least he was well. At least he was helping his brother and niece. At least he'd be able to return to her. And at least they *did* have a wedding to look forward to sometime after that. She'd marry him when he returned, whether it were this summer, next winter, or ten years hence.

"Are there any cookies left from last night, Polly?" she asked, surprising even herself with the cheerfulness masking the heaviness of her soul.

"A few, unless Elias ate them before breakfast," Polly answered, pausing in her methodical washing of the morning dishes to regard the corner cupboard with a long, critical stare, as if she could see through it to ascertain the state of the cookie jar.

"I think I will take a few to Mrs. Wheaton, along with one of these loaves of bread." Margaret wrapped the loaf as she spoke and tucked it into the market basket.

"Can I come, Margaret? Please? I want go to Mrs. Wheaton's with you," little Joyce pleaded, bouncing on one foot around Margaret.

"Me too! I want to come!" Rosina echoed.

"Where are you going?" Archie burst through the front door without warning, scattering mud droplets in every direction. "Can I go?"

Margaret drew a deep breath, her cheerfulness seriously threatened by the chaos. "Perhaps some of you can. Archie, you need to do your sums. You know you're supposed to finish that before going outside. Rosina, you need to nap." She'd really prefer to go alone, but there were the children to think of. "I'm taking a basket to Mrs. Wheaton, picking up a few supplies in town, and stopping at the post office." She *had* to check, even though there had been no letter from Lester this week.

The enthusiastic clamor magnified its volume, and Margaret whisked into her room to freshen up, Joyce at her heels. All was hurry and flurry until at last Margaret was out the door and walking to town, Joyce and Levi dancing around her.

There was a strange sort of balm in handing a stocked basket to Mrs. Wheaton and seeing the smile lines on her face light up. Somehow, the joy in the widow's gratitude sent a ray of gladness to Margaret's lonely heart. After all, Margaret's *own* lonely heart wasn't the only one in the world, and if the pang she carried could lighten the load of another, perhaps this long spring wouldn't be worthless.

The post office, though unusually busy for this hour, stood last in her errands, and with both hope and fear warring within, Margaret requested the mail for the Enfield household. She snatched the envelope with her name on it, her trepidation hardly lessening, for the address certainly was not in Lester's hand.

"Hold this," she instructed, taking and then handing Levi an envelope for Mama and moving a few steps away to tear open hers at once.

> *Dear Miss Enfield,*
> *I regret to inform you that Lester Vincent has fallen ill with the same malady that Sidney suffers with. Furthermore, Sidney's little daughter,*

Emily Vincent, has also shown signs of the illness today. Lester requested that I write to you, since he is unable to do so himself, and to say that he is doing as well as could be expected and not to fret. He only wishes you to understand the cause of his silence and assure you that he is thinking of you even as he lies abed. Though he misses you, he also begged me to tell you specifically not to come to him, since he is well taken care of and wishes, above all else, not to expose you or your mother to this illness. He also sends this message: "Remember His omnipotent hand Who placed this before us. You and I are still both safe in His care."

He is currently with Mr. Williams and me, and, with hired help and doctors, we are giving all three of them the best care we can. Thanks to his purse, his care is indeed some of the best we can access.

I remain yours very sincerely,
Leticia A. Williams

The paper fluttered to the ground even as a great, black cloud of despair seemed to settle over Margaret. Lester, ill! Oh, why could she not be with him? Why must he be there and she here? Now he could not possibly do Sidney, his business, or his daughter the least bit of good, and yet her separation from him remained!

Numbly, she scooped up the letter and staggered homeward, her siblings following. What if the consumption killed him? What if he became as incapacitated as Sidney? Would he lose his timber company? Would she need to care for him as an invalid all her life as she now cared for her mother? She'd so looked forward to a time when she'd be able to lean on the arm of another instead of everyone constantly depending on her for everything.

And now, it seemed it was not to be. A wild prayer rose within her—a desperate cry for Lester and health and healing and strength and his speedy return ... Oh, she knew not what she prayed! She felt her prayers must be very selfish, but she couldn't help it. She had to petition or die.

Heal him. Heal him. Heal him. The plea echoed in her mind. She couldn't stop it if she tried. Her wishes for him built within her with such force that they must be expressed.

In the midst of the never-ending litany came the words of the letter—words straight from Lester's mouth: *Remember His omnipotent hand Who placed this before us. You and I are still both safe in His care.*

If God were omnipotent, why hadn't He stopped this from happening? Why hadn't Lester stayed here? Why hadn't he remained well? Why hadn't they already married before this happened? Why, why, why? The power of God had stopped none of this from happening.

She kicked a pebble, and, as it flew into the ditch and disappeared, she watched it with a sort of grim satisfaction. Above all, *why* couldn't she seem to wait patiently? Why couldn't she *trust* the power of God to watch over Lester? She knew that God loved Lester more than she did ... but somehow, she couldn't seem to quite bring herself to actually believe that He would keep her beloved safe. Oh, for a sense of control! Oh, to be able to protect Lester from anything and everything bad that might happen to him!

But that wasn't possible, and all that was left to her was this ominous piece of paper and the ache in her heart.

A drop of rain splashed on her shoe-top and rolled into the dust beneath. A second quickly followed, then more splattered upon her coat. "Run for the house, children," she called to Joyce and Levi. The parsonage loomed in the distance, hardly visible in the early-evening darkness preceding a storm, but the children quickly sped towards it and disappeared inside.

Margaret followed more slowly. The gray fog crept over her, without and within, the slimy cold seeping into her very bones like the hopelessness that begged permanent lodging there. The spring that ought to have been dancing with joy and beauty and life in the midst of wedding plans now wept with her.

Still, the litany pulsed in her head. *Protect him. Heal him. Keep him safe.* Each phrase pounded ceaselessly, keeping time with the light rain now dashing down.

These past few weeks, she'd been trying to distract herself from Lester's absence. She'd thrown herself into work and busyness. While that wasn't wrong, it wasn't enough. It hadn't helped. Something was missing, and there was no locking the situation away in the cellar and pretending it didn't exist now. It was not enough to do "one thing at a time" and "all things in succession" ... God had called her to Lester's side in this life, and if that couldn't be in person at this moment, it must be spiritually.

All of a sudden, lightning flashed, a thunderclap sounded overhead, and the gentle rain became a torrential downpour. Margaret pulled her hat farther over her face and quickened her steps. Even if her heart was crying and she didn't want to go into the house, she didn't need an entirely soaked outfit—or a head cold—to deal with on top of everything else.

Before she could approach, a flash seemed to blind her almost at the same instant as thunder deafened her. At once, she froze, unable to take a single step. Surely that flash had been right at the house. The children were all in there—except Oswald, still working in town—and Mama! What if the house burned down? What if they were injured?

An impulse to sprint to the house and see if everything was all right washed over her, but nearly simultaneously, the thought that had been suspended in her mind when the storm unleashed returned, hovering with a certainty that stilled her steps.

If I can't be there in person at this moment, I must be there spiritually. Through prayer.

She wanted to rush physically to everyone's aid—Lester's, her family's, everyone's. She wanted to protect everyone, to save everyone, to be in control and mitigate any and all evils.

But God was calling her to be there with Lester spiritually. To pray. To leave it in His hands. To trust Him.

She couldn't control anything herself anyway. What happened had happened, and what would happen would happen. There was little or nothing she could do about it.

But God could. And she could join Him in that work through prayer.

All this flashed through her head in mere seconds, and the next, her heart was pouring out through her chattering teeth. *God, protect them. God, heal him. God, move in a mighty way for Your glory.*

Short sentences, some of them hardly coherent, spilled out even as her steps sped faster and faster toward the porch.

Everyone was all right. She saw that in a glance, though every face radiated various levels of terror. "What happened?" she gasped.

"I think lightning struck a tree in the backyard or somewhere." Polly's tones shook, and her fingers twisted more tightly around Rosina.

Margaret peered out the window, but between the growing darkness and the sheets of rain, she couldn't see any damage. "The trees I can see look fine," she said. "You're certain it wasn't the house? There was no shock, no damage?"

Polly shook her head. "Just the bright flash and the huge crash. It seemed like the house shook. It was so loud. But that was all."

Margaret inched along the walls, inspecting every corner for any signs of damage or fire. At last, she exhaled a deep sigh of relief. "I think we're all right."

She slumped onto a chair, her energy suddenly leaving her body. Utter exhaustion washed over her. She'd definitely need the strength of her Heavenly Father just to do the next simple task tonight.

Chapter Five:
Leave All
Resultings

Stayed on Omnipotence, safe 'neath His wing,
Leave all resultings: DO THE NEXT THING.

Why did Mama always seem the worst during stormy weather?

Everything went worse during stormy weather, Margaret was sure. The mud on the floors doubled and tripled. Everyone argued more. No one played outside much, meaning messes kept pace with the mud. Margaret's head felt fuzzy, as though stuffed with wool. Still, the days after the lightning strike remained gloomy and stormy for a week or more without even a glimpse of the sun.

She just wanted summer to come. She just wanted Lester well and home again. She just wanted her happy family life back.

Little news came from Lester these days, and Margaret couldn't help but feel impatient. She knew he must be too ill to write, and no news, in this case, meant the bad news of his continued malady.

But at least he wasn't worse.

The thought began as a tiny seed in the corner of her mind that grew steadily larger as she sat by her bedroom window one morning. Lately, she'd had no appetite for reading her Bible, but she knew avoiding the Word of God wasn't going to make anything better.

Just like avoiding breakfast wasn't strengthening her to face the day ... She shoved that thought aside and fixed her wandering mind back on the words of the page in front of her.

In every thing give thanks.

Everything?

She flipped pages backward. Not this right now. Give her a comforting Psalm or something.

Let every thing that hath breath praise the LORD.

She threw her head back. Clearly, it was no use. God was speaking to her, and she was trying to ignore His instruction.

She drew in a deep breath and reread the verse again. *Let every thing that hath breath praise the LORD.*

Praising. Giving thanks.

But HOW? her mind screamed. Lester was sick. She *couldn't* praise his illness. She couldn't praise Mama's invalid condition. She couldn't praise the tasks that piled around her, higher than anything she could accomplish.

She threw herself across the bed, burying her face back against her pillow as the stresses and woes of a lifetime she'd been stuffing deeply within her soul swarmed to the surface and rushed over her, overwhelming her in waves of sorrow. Maybe she needed to go back to sleep.

The ache in her heart throbbed deeper and deeper.

She couldn't praise the way Papa had died so awfully and left them so suddenly.

She couldn't praise the little sister that lay under one of the tiny stones in the churchyard, gone before she'd even taken a breath.

She couldn't praise her grief and loneliness.

This wasn't right. It wasn't what God had created. It wasn't the way He'd designed it to be.

There was nothing to praise here.

Besides, giving thanks wouldn't devour her sorrow. It couldn't take away her grief.

But I can.

The whisper spoke in her spirit, and she involuntarily stilled in the presence of her King.

He could. *You can.*

Wasn't there a Psalm about God inhabiting the praises of His people?

This grief and loneliness weren't what God created ... but He *had* created her heart to praise Him, and praise Him she must. Circumstances didn't change what she was designed for. *"Christ in you, the hope of glory,"* she quoted to herself. The Hope of glory. Surely there was Hope of glory somewhere in the midst of these sorrows.

There was something she could praise—the Hope of glory living within her.

And that Hope of glory could and would devour her sorrow.

But only as she acknowledged and received Him through thanksgiving.

Pushing the pillow aside, she scooted across the bed, back toward the window. The morning sun peeked above the clouds, shining golden rays across the grass that glittered with a thousand dewdrops.

Thank You, God, for Lester.

She paused.

Thank You for his illness.

That had been hard enough. She didn't want to go on, but after a moment, she continued.

Thank You for Mama and her condition. Now Margaret bit her lip. *Thank You for the children and all the tasks they create.*

She swallowed hard. She simply couldn't go on, but already, she felt the presence of God seeping into her heart through the thanks beginning to well up in her. Even though it was so faint she could scarcely grasp it, she allowed herself to embrace the tiniest sliver of peace—a trust that He *was* holding her no matter what.

A bell sounded. Mama needed her. Margaret spun quickly out of bed, dressed, and hastened to answer. After supplying Mama's needs, she lingered a moment in the doorway. She hated to burden her mother further—Mama already directed the household as best she could from bed—and yet the need to speak compelled her. "Mama? How do you bear everything?" she asked hesitantly. "All the losses, all the sorrows, all the disappointments, all the ... Your life going—like this." Margaret gestured vaguely, hoping Mama understood what she was trying to ask.

"Because it's all I *can* do," Mama's weak voice answered, more calm emanating from the tones than Margaret would have expected.

"What do you mean?" Margaret asked.

"I mean, I could worry myself sicker over all the things I can't do and don't have, or I can lie here and make the best of where I *am* at right now."

"But—isn't that hard? Painful?"

"Of course," Mama whispered. "Painfully hard, one might say. Depressingly hard? Can drive one to distraction. But what can I do? 'Fret not.' That's about all I have control of here. My response."

My response. Margaret pondered this as she scurried through breakfast, cleanup, and making sure the children were dressed and on task. That accomplished, she immediately decided to bake more cookies—and perhaps more bread, too, while she was at it. It certainly needed to be done, and it wouldn't do for her to have a spare moment for repining just now.

The baking dishes must be washed, then dried, then put away. Rosina's dress must be changed—again. The boys must be settled to the arithmetic—again and again—and the difficult sums explained. The wash must be folded and put away. The vegetables must be chopped for dinner. The crumbs must be swept from the floor. The tasks never ended, and Margaret tackled one and then another with a sense akin to relief that her hands could keep busy enough to prevent her brain from going places she'd rather it avoid.

Even in the midst of the busyness, Margaret found time to return to Mrs. Wheaton's with another basket of goodies. Before today, Margaret hadn't wanted to speak of her own difficulties—it seemed like complaining surely could do no good when she was meant to bear it—but after that little chat with Mama, she found herself pouring out a bit of her troubles to the kind, friendly ear that listened so sympathetically and yet so cheerfully—not at all what Margaret expected.

"Why yes, dear," Mrs. Wheaton replied, as Margaret fell shyly silent, wondering if she'd said too much. "It's so always in life. Things don't come 'round just as we'd expect or wish them to. And living with the praise of the Lord Almighty in our hearts just makes things brighter somehow. It doesn't take the troubles away—oh no, not a bit of it—but it makes them easier to bear. There's a reason He's said once and again, 'In every thing give thanks' and 'I will praise Him as long as I have breath.' You've got breath, I've got breath, so we've got a reason to praise still."

"I've been trying to keep busy, to do the next thing that is to be done," Margaret replied hesitantly, "but somehow it didn't swallow the sorrow, though it did help."

"Ah, if your heart is sticking fast to yesterday's grief, that won't solve your problems," Mrs. Wheaton answered, rocking back and forth as her hand ran up and down the armrest in a curious fashion. "You can keep busy with the next thing all you want with a complaining heart. But it won't help. Let Him do the next thing in you, and you make sure you receive it with that praise."

"Have you found it so?" Margaret inquired, not quite liking to ask Mrs. Wheaton about her own troubled life. "I mean, you don't seem in the happiest of circumstances … and …"

"I have found it so." Mrs. Wheaton's eyes shone straight at Margaret now. "Even in the darkest valley, God has been my help. And singing through the darkness not only helps me to survive but to see Him. Why, when George passed on to glory, I thought I should never be able to go on, but God's Word was a lamp for my feet, and the neighbor boy stepped in every evening and did George's chores without even asking 'til I thought it must be an angel in the form of a lanky youth. And then dear, old Grandma Duncan visited nearly every day, even though she could scarcely limp sometimes, and if her ministrations weren't heavenly, I don't know what was. And the little things: a basket of lunch left on my step or an envelope with just the right amount to pay a bill—when I walked in the spirit of praise, I saw the hand of my Lord just everywhere."

Margaret's eyes were nearly teary now. *Could* she trust her Heavenly Father like that? And would He *not* prove Himself faithful even through every trial, big or small? If He cared for precious Mrs. Wheaton in her loneliness and sorrow, would He not care for Margaret? And if Mrs. Wheaton could trust Him with the loss of everything and everyone close to her, could not Margaret trust Him for this little separation, this concerning illness, the burden of daily work that seemed not so very black and daunting in the light of the deep sorrows of the widow before her?

But Mrs. Wheaton still lived alone. She still faced the loneliness. The care of God hadn't taken away or altered her circumstances.

And the yearning fear still nagged Margaret's heart: Perhaps God wouldn't give Lester back to her. Perhaps all her hopes and dreams were indeed nothing. Perhaps a weary life of solitude and hardship would be her lot.

Springtime in Surrey

And yet the whisper echoed in her heart: *would she trust Him anyway?* Could she leave all results to Him and live in full trust no matter what? With Job, could she say, "Though He slay me, yet will I trust in Him"?

She wanted to. She dared to say it—even as it rent her heart.

I praise you, O my God, even if you slay me. Or him. No matter what the results may be.

392

Chapter Six:
Ever Serener

Looking to Jesus, ever serener,
Working or suffering, be thy demeanor!

After that, the days seemed to warm more quickly, the flowers seemed to bloom more profusely, and springtime really seemed to overtake Surrey at last. Margaret, rocking gently on the old swing in the oak before the children were awake, let half a smile blossom briefly on her face before she gently flipped the page of the Bible on her lap.

The story of Asa had called to her today, and she perused the account deliberately—something rather new to her, for she generally felt unsettled and wished to hurry off to the next urgent task.

But when they in their trouble did turn unto the LORD God of Israel, and sought Him, He was found of them.

"'When they in their trouble …'" she repeated in a whisper. What time she'd wasted this spring not turning to the Lord God immediately with her troubles! He could have been found of her so much sooner!

And in those times there was no peace to him that went out, nor to him that came in, but great vexations were upon all the inhabitants of the countries.

No peace. She'd certainly felt that. Even now, her restless mind wandered to reckon up the number of days it had been since she'd heard from Lester …

But no. She wouldn't let herself be stuck in the "great vexations." Or, rather, she'd need to deliberately set her mind upon God and ask *Him* to not let her be stuck here.

Be ye strong therefore, and let not your hands be weak: for your work shall be rewarded.

She repeated the verse three, then four times over. *Be ye strong therefore ...* Her mind continued the rhythmic echo even when her lips had ceased their silent movement. *Let not your hands be weak ... your work shall be rewarded ... shall be rewarded ...*

With God, she could get through this spring. She'd keep up hope regarding Lester. Worries and cares only contributed to her weakness.

She didn't forget to intercede on behalf of her beloved and his health before she finally rose from the swing.

A thrush sang cheerily above her as she strode back to the house to prepare breakfast for the children.

Be ye strong therefore ... The words sang themselves together in Margaret's head, the birdcalls providing a melodious backdrop. *Let not your hands be weak ...*

Inside, the children had tried making their own porridge, with disastrous results if one were to judge by the state of the floor and their clothing. Margaret inhaled a deep breath and closed her eyes. *Be strong,* she told herself. *You're a child of the King. Nothing can ruffle you.*

"Here, Joyce, let me help you stir in the meal. And, Levi, do take care with the milk. That's all we have today. Could you get a rag for the spills?" Speaking evenly wasn't as difficult as Margaret had feared it would be. "Archie, please set the bowls on the table, not on the floor. Rosina, do you want to get the spoons out? Put them right up here."

"Post for you, post for you!" Elias suddenly sang out, pausing his rummaging through the papers on the old corner desk to find and wave a letter toward Margaret. "It's not Lester, though," he announced after carefully examining the address. "Le—Leticia Williams?"

Margaret snatched the letter, almost too hastily. "Can I see?" Archie asked. "I want to see."

"No, I do!" Joyce paused mid-hum to shout.

"Please!" Margaret drew a deep breath and started over. "Let's just get breakfast on the table. I am going to read the letter myself. It may not be any of your concern." She thrust the envelope into her pocket and whirled back to the stove, dishing up bowls right and left and ushering children to the table.

Once food filled every young mouth, Margaret stepped aside, letter in her hand. She simply could not wait another moment.

The note was brief—only a few words from Sidney's mother-in-law to explain that things in the sickroom remained about the same and to assure her that both Lester and Emily were well taken care of. Sidney remained unable to return to work, but Lester's efforts on behalf of the business, prior to his getting ill, had stabilized it enough that it ought to remain afloat with little difficulty.

Margaret emitted a short sigh as her eyes landed on the final few words and involuntarily scanned the back for some extra little message, some hidden text. There was nothing. Oh, how she missed the tender, loving words that filled the letters from Lester's own hand! And how much she'd longed to hear he was improving, that he would return to her soon, that he'd personally sent some communication, however brief!

Why had her Lord and King even taken away this small mercy from her?

Fear not tomorrows. The gentle whisper spoke to her heart.

She clung inwardly to the words, not daring to let them go. It seemed as if it were the message she'd hoped to hear from her beloved … It was just the sort of thing he'd written in previous letters and whispered in previous conversations. Always something wise, something profound, something encouraging, something that directly addressed her life situation.

Fear not tomorrows.

Ah, that had been her greatest fear. The springtime that had once promised hope and beauty and light and joy had only offered fears, worries, sorrows, struggles, loneliness, unending labor, and hope deferred. Once, tomorrow was anticipated bliss. Now, tomorrow was a dreaded burden.

But God said, "Fear not"—for Margaret knew the voice of her King. How often His Word repeated those two little words!

And how often could she seem to do nothing but ignore them.

She drew a deep breath, then lifted her father's Bible from the top of the corner bookshelf. Reverently, she brushed away the dust and smoothed the cover, then she opened it, her eyes filling with tears. Had anyone opened this Book since Papa had passed to glory?

Each page flip brought fresh moisture to her eyes. Papa had *loved* this Book. He'd marked it—oh, how he'd marked it! Every page boasted margin scribbles—this and that he'd noted, words God must have spoken to him through various verses and passages. Underlines ran liberally across the pages, sometimes veering upwards or downwards or abruptly transforming into a circle around a particular word.

Margaret blinked and found herself staring at a quartet of verses in Deuteronomy 20, bordered in red ink:

> *When thou goest out to battle against thine enemies, and seest horses, and chariots, and a people more than thou, be not afraid of them: for the LORD thy God is with thee, Which brought thee up out of the land of Egypt. And it shall be, when ye are come nigh unto the battle, that the priest shall approach and speak unto the people, And shall say unto them, Hear, O Israel, ye approach this day unto battle against your enemies: let not your hearts faint, fear not, and do not tremble, neither be ye terrified because of them; For the LORD your God is He that goeth with you, to fight for you against your enemies, to save you.*

Margaret's gaze escaped to the window and then her eyes fell shut. Wasn't that just for her? Silently, the words reformed themselves into something like a prayer, only it was an encouragement for her: *When you go out to battle against your enemies, and see fear, and loneliness, and responsibilities more than you can handle, be not afraid of them: for the Lord your God is with you, Which brought you up out of the land of your slavery. And it shall be, when you are come near unto the battle, that Jesus your High Priest shall approach and speak unto your heart, and shall say unto you, Hear, O Margaret, you approach this day unto battle against your enemies: let not your heart faint, fear not, and do not tremble, neither be ye terrified because of them, for the Lord your God is He Who goes with you, to fight for you against your enemies, to save you.*

It was true. The God of Israel was the God of Margaret, and He would not forsake her. He loved her with a perfect love, and perfect love cast out all fear—even when Margaret couldn't feel it. Margaret didn't need to struggle with the giants of loneliness, fear, worry, discouragement, and frustration: that's what Jesus lived in her for.

As she received His life in her with thanksgiving, He fought for her. The battle was already won. She needed only to walk in doing the next thing He'd set before her—in perfect, full, complete trust— a trust that no earthly circumstance could ruffle.

This day, she'd battle her enemies—with Him.

She closed the Bible and set it in its place, gratefulness tugging at her heart for this sacred Word sent from both her earthly father and her Heavenly One. Resolutely, she marched back toward the kitchen. But just before entering, she hesitated. If she didn't take a moment now, who knew when another might come? She rapidly snatched a paper from the desk in the corner, reopened the Bible to the passage she'd just read, hastily copied it, added a few words of her own to the note, signed her name, and addressed it to Lester. Maybe he couldn't write to her, but she could write to him, and perhaps the Scripture might encourage him in the same way it had her.

That done, she opened the kitchen door and took her place at the table, determinedly pasting on a radiant face and doing her best to ignore the various stages of discontent or apathy on her siblings'.

"Now, now, this is a bright, new day for us to redeem the time and make the most of it," Margaret exclaimed vivaciously. "What would each of you like to do today, once schoolwork is finished?"

Clamor from all directions met her ears, and she did her best to listen to the ideas given by each child.

"Perhaps," Margaret suggested at last, when the hubbub had diminished enough for her to hear herself, "after your schoolwork and chores are completed, we could pack a little picnic and eat it beside the lake. After all, one could scarcely imagine a finer spring day."

Cheers arose, and despite the verbal, excited chaos, her suggestion seemed to be a wide success. Bowls were emptied and dishes cleared away in record time, and even the dreaded arithmetic seemed to fly by more quickly and agreeably than usual. To be sure, the exhaustion seeping into Margaret's eyes and muscles (once the picnic basket had been lugged underneath the lakeside beech tree) threatened to overtake most of her enjoyment, but there was something quite satisfying about the situation, on the whole.

After the food had been eaten—a loose term, certainly, for due to the excitement of the outdoor atmosphere, the little ones hadn't eaten half as much as they were accustomed to at home—she felt better, even with the mishaps of the event. The pitcher only upset three times, and just one sibling fell into the lake (and was promptly pulled out with no ill effects other than a few articles of wet clothing), so by the time the shadows lengthened across the grass, Margaret voted the picnic a decided success and lay down on the blanket under the beech to rest, keep an eye on the little girls, and ponder the doings of the day.

And above all, what was Lester doing just now? This picnic was nearly in an identical spot to the one Lester and she had enjoyed the day he'd received the letter that had called him away, and yet everything seemed so different. Most notably, she felt as though she were looking back upon a very young, naïve girl—a girl who had no idea what trials she was about to face, who had no clue that her beloved would be called away, a girl that couldn't have imagined such an illness overtaking her fiancé so rapidly.

But that had been her place in life at that time. She couldn't regret it—she certainly recalled that joyous day with fondness and thankfulness—but the very contrast between that day and this caused a myriad of somber, thoughtful reflections.

Indeed, that day felt better than this one. She wasn't so emotionally alone, for one thing. She had something to look forward to and someone beside her. She didn't have the burdens of uncertainty weighing on her.

And yet—if she could live it over, she wouldn't choose a different path. Not just for Sidney's sake or Emily's, but for her own.

She *was* a different person than she had been a few months earlier. Somehow, adversity had touched something deep within her that all the joy of her previous existence had not reached. When Papa had passed, she'd grieved, but mostly for Mama's sake. After Papa's suffering, the end had come more as a release than as a dreaded surprise. Margaret missed him—they all did, every day—but she'd been a child then.

But this—so unexpected and coming on the very cusp of her nuptials—had shaken her, and for a while, she hadn't known where to find a solid rock. But through the shaking, everything that could be shaken *had* been, and it was falling away from her, leaving only the things that could not be shaken: her identity as a child of the King, her trust in her Savior, the perfect love of her God, an urgency to live as a prayer warrior, and a serene calmness of unmoving faith no matter what.

No, she couldn't wish things differently. And deep within her heart, even deeper than the pulsing ache that missed Lester with every heartbeat, lay a fierce courage and a stronger love, intensified by the separation and made sweeter by the suffering.

And with this realization, she sat up with a smile. At last, for the first time, she could truly give thanks for this trial.

And for the first time in many weeks, the smile that rested on her countenance stemmed directly from her heart.

Chapter Seven: The Rest of His Calm

In His dear presence, the rest of His calm,
The light of His countenance be thy psalm;
Strong in His faithfulness, praise Him and sing;
Then, as He beckons thee, DO THE NEXT THING.

"A letter for you, Lester. Would you like me to read it to you, or do you think you can manage it yourself?"

"From Margaret?" Lester's eyes instantly snapped to Mrs. Williams's hand. He sighed. Of course he wanted to read it himself, but he wasn't sure his body would let him do even that much yet. "How long is it?" he asked.

"Not long." Mrs. Williams ran her eyes down it quickly. "There's a short note and a longer Bible passage."

"Let me read the note, please." Lester held out his hand for it. It took a moment for his eyes to focus. He really needed to figure out a way to write back to her himself, illness or no illness. Lying here messed with his mind. Helpless. Away from his beloved. Unable to assist either his brother or anyone else. And most of all, lonely. That was a side effect—too much time to think. To miss her.

a Wild Blue Wonder Press anthology

Dearest Lester,

My beloved, I am sure this separation must be a trial for us both. I have faced, as I am sure you have also, the enemies of fear, loneliness, discouragement, and uncertainty. Neither you nor I know what shall come. But He says to us, "Fear not tomorrows," and He gave me these words to arm me for the battle. I pray they equip you similarly. I love you with all my heart.

Your beloved,
Margaret

Lester blinked several times, then held out the letter to Mrs. Williams. "Read me the verses, please."

She reached for the Bible on the bureau. "What passage is it? You keep the letter; I'll read it from here."

"Deuteronomy 20:1-4." Lester examined the letter for a moment before clutching it and closing his eyes.

The soft rustle of pages sounded, then Mrs. Williams's soft voice read, "'When thou goest out to battle against thine enemies, and seest horses, and chariots, and a people more than thou, be not afraid of them: for the LORD thy God is with thee ...'"

This illness was certainly an enemy more than Lester could handle on his own. He *had* feared it—not for himself but for Margaret. As Mrs. Williams continued, Lester let the words wash over him. If Margaret was believing this, certainly he could also.

"'For the LORD your God is He that goeth with you, to fight for you against your enemies, to save you.'" Mrs. Williams paused a moment, then kept reading beyond the section written out in his letter in a softer tone. "'And the officers shall speak unto the people, saying, What man is there that hath built a new house, and hath not dedicated it? let him go and return to his house, lest he die in the battle, and another man dedicate it. And what man is he that hath planted a vineyard, and hath not yet eaten of it? let him also go and return unto his house, lest he die in the battle, and another man eat of it. And what man is there that hath betrothed a wife, and hath not taken her? let him go and return unto his house, lest he die in the battle, and another man take her. And the officers shall speak further unto the people, and they shall say, What man is there that is fearful and fainthearted? let him go and return unto his house, lest his brethren's heart faint as well as his heart.'"

Lester stilled. *That* was something he could relate to. He'd built a new house—and he hadn't dedicated it—whatever that meant in today's terminology. He hadn't planted a garden yet, but he'd prepared the ground. He'd planned to plant something this spring for Margaret and him to harvest this year, but he'd left before planting time, and at this rate, he wouldn't be back before far too late. He'd betrothed a wife, but he hadn't taken her. And above all, he'd been fearful and fainthearted these past few weeks—and he certainly didn't want to share that with his brother in the same way they'd apparently shared physical maladies.

He swallowed. He'd done all he could for Sidney. He'd saved Sidney's business, and it wouldn't need him any longer. Sidney himself, though still unable to work in any capacity, had recovered enough to not need close tending.

But Margaret. Lester's house. His postponed wedding. His garden. His bride-to-be.

They needed him.

The silence that had fallen when Mrs. Williams stopped reading stretched on.

Lester roused from his reverie and looked her straight in the eye. "When did the doctor say I could be moved?"

"The middle of next week, he thought, if things don't get worse. He said you could be walking, though he wouldn't have you resume any sort of work for several more weeks."

Lester calculated. That was so much later than he wished, but it would do. "Please book me a seat on the earliest train to Surrey that I can catch next week. I have unavoidable business to attend to."

"But ... the doctor said ..."

"Not work business, if that's your worry. Other business. It won't require physical exertion, so don't you fear."

Mrs. Williams nodded. "I hate to send you back in such a state—but I'll ask Mr. Williams. He'll do it. And we've grown quite used to keeping little Emily. She's no trouble to us now, so nothing to fear on that score. Go home to your fiancée."

Lester held her gaze. "Thank you, Mrs. Williams. For everything."

A train whistle echoed faintly across the hills as Margaret pulled the curtain shut, the bar of moonlight across the bed narrowing and then extinguishing altogether. She tiptoed to her pillow and climbed into bed, careful not to wake Polly.

Margaret's eyes shut immediately, the weariness of the day finally able to meet its remedy. She'd been looking forward to this moment. Ah, the comfort of settling onto a soft bed after a long day of hard work … She barely heard the train whistle once more in the distance. Sleep was good. Tomorrow … It would come quickly, and she would take whatever it brought. A verse from the Psalms echoed through her mind as she drifted off: *When I awake, I am still with Thee.*

A thrush's melodic note warbled through the predawn stillness. A second joined in a gentle chorus as the first hint of pink touched the wispy clouds. Margaret's eyes fluttered open, and the melody of the thrushes pierced her consciousness even as her body groaned for more sleep. Yet she rolled over, then slipped out of bed. After pulling on a few articles of clothing, she stepped outside. Often, she guarded her sleep jealously, taking all the extra she could, but some days, especially in the warmer seasons, she felt the pull to rise with the dawn. And outside, she could move about to her heart's content without fear of waking the little ones.

Her steps bent toward the lake—not to the picnic spot this time, but closer to the house, where a wooden dock successfully invited her to sit down and savor the quietness of the morning. Once settled, she drew in a deep breath of contentment and peace. What a beautiful morning. What a beautiful world. What a beautiful spring.

Perhaps one day, Lester and she would enjoy such spring sunrises together. The thought, instead of stinging with loneliness, settled sweetly upon her heart. In the presence of her King, she could delight in the present moment without worry about the future tomorrows.

Somewhere, a waterfowl *honked*. Very slowly, the darkness lightened to gray. Pink reflected off the still water now, only the tiniest ripples here and there creating motion over its glassy surface. Ethereal mist reflected rose-toned hues and lent extra softness to the radiance. The gentlest of breezes stirred, both warm and cool at the same time and stirringly refreshing. The whole world seemed to be holding its breath, waiting for the sun to burst over the horizon in its blaze of golden glory.

She pulled out a letter from her pocket—a letter she wanted to reread here and now, alone. It wasn't recent—it predated their separation—but she'd treasured it. The little bits of Lester's poetic heart that flowed through the lines warmed her soul, and the spiritual richness of the words themselves strengthened her heart.

The morning's rays of beaming light shine down for many hours,
And afternoon, with sunbeams bright, will long delight the flowers.
Black darkness of the inky night seems endless in its length.
Oft cloudy days obscure the sight of sunlight's quick'ning strength.
For many hours, we see the way of daytime, and of night—
But sunrise comes but once a day in radiant, pulsing light.

Our place is here; our time is now; we rest midst dusk and dawn.
We rise, we work, we live somehow; through life, we journey on.
We taste of sorrow and of pain; we struggle, fall, and rise;
We feel a loss; we earn a gain and handle cruel surprise.
We wonder, question, muse, and pray; the hour comes and fades—
But sunrise comes but once a day in stunning, subtle shades.

We know the hours of the day, the moments of the night—
But have we paused to gently say, "I saw the dawn's first light"?
Or rush we on through daily cares, our battles fight alone?
The moment of the dawn prepares the heart we call our own.
The Father's touch of love we may observe in dawn's still haze,
But sunrise comes but once a day in brilliant, blooming rays.

In the fields in still, pale morn with pink and purple haze
A fellowship with God is born as prayers and hymns we raise.
The beauty of the morning sun allows me Him to see,
That I with Him am joined as one. Each sunrise brings to me
His presence in a special way; like light, mercies diffuse—

But sunrise comes but once a day in thrilling, glorious hues.

He is like the dawn's pure light! He thrills the soul and heart!
So at the dawn, let us delight to watch the night depart.
His beauty is beyond compare, revealed through sunlit sod.
Take time His light and love to share; at sunrise, meet with God.
So let us rest and trust His way through dusk, morn, eve, and dawn.
Though sunrise comes but once a day, God's love goes on and on!

The richness of the tinted clouds intensified, and Margaret caught her breath. Had any spring sunrise ever been this glorious? More birds began to raise their harmonies in heartfelt praise to their Creator, and Margaret, feeling a bit humbled, followed their example.

Golden white shone on the undersides of the clouds nearest the horizon now, and the lake danced with little bits of reflected light and color. Every moment, the hues intensified until Margaret felt she simply could not stand it and the sun *must* blaze into view at any moment—and still the brightness increased.

And then one ray of sunlight broke above the horizon—then another—and suddenly the sun was coming up, breaking forth in all its splendor over the lake, spilling onto the new, green leaves of the trees, highlighting the dew on each blade of grass, and warming Margaret.

She simply watched, unable either to draw her eyes away or to gaze on the fullness of the sunrise. A smile blossomed. So, too, in glory and beauty, the Son of righteousness had arisen upon the darkness of her lonely heart and granted her the peace to live one day at a time in His presence, come what may.

Footsteps startled her from her reverie—startled her in quite a literal sense. Her heart leaped and pounded fiercely within her. She knew those steps!

She turned—and a sight more glorious than the sunrise greeted her.

Her beloved approached—perhaps more slowly than his stride had once been—and a grin overtook her smile. Her feet ached to fly across the distance, and she yielded to the impulse.

The next moment, she was at the side of the one she loved most in this world and gazing up into the face she'd longed to see for all these weeks.

What words can convey the joy with which they met, the bliss with which they conversed, and the delight in which they basked after the weeks of separation and uncertainty! Truly, Margaret and Lester themselves had none for the first several minutes after their reunion.

"How—how are you here?" Margaret gasped out at last, utterly overcome by the sudden joy and surprise. "And are you well? Truly well?"

"I am nearly well—well enough to come home. I came without warning because I could travel faster than the post, and I was vain enough to suppose my presence might be more agreeable than a mere letter."

"Your letters are a treasure, beloved—every last one of them—but I cannot think of a better way to begin this day than the sight of your face."

"Even after that gorgeous sunrise?" Lester pointed back toward the lake.

"Even after that gorgeous sunrise." Margaret couldn't stop smiling, and she definitely didn't take her eyes off of Lester's long enough to glance back toward the sky. She'd seen plenty of sunrises this spring already but not nearly enough of Lester. "Was there a train this early? Or did you run all the way?"

"I came on the last train last night," Lester replied. "I stayed at our house and came up here just as early as I dared. I always loved how the lakeshore is visible from the road if you know exactly where to look."

"Which you do, of course," Margaret half teased. "Oh, you don't know what a relief it is to see you! I had such a time not worrying or even just missing you ..."

"'But you were not afraid, for the Lord your God was with you, to fight for you and save you,'" Lester quoted softly, a tender smile on his countenance as his eyes piercingly yet tenderly rested on her face.

"That's right," Margaret replied. "Not at first, certainly. But oh! When you weren't here, I found that God was. I think it's easy to turn to you in my hardships first before God—but when you were gone, I couldn't. And now—oh, thank God for every hard tomorrow that brought me to this day!"

"About that." Lester quirked an eyebrow. "Are you particularly busy today? Because I intend to spend it with you. I missed nearly the entire Surrey springtime, and today is my last chance to enjoy it with you."

"I'd be disappointed if you didn't," Margaret returned, doubly grateful now that she'd taken the extra time to finish the work yesterday instead of leaving the house a mess.

"I don't know about you, but I have visions of picnics and wildflowers and finishing the rest of that row on the lake that was interrupted three months ago."

"Strange. I seem to have similar visions."

"But that's not all." Lester grasped her hand now, his seriousness showing through his delight. "I missed you while I was confined to my room. I was unable to work, unable to care for anyone—and it was a trial. I *want* to care for you. I want to be with you. And I want to let you care for me when I need it. Margaret Enfield, you told me by this very lake that you'd marry me … and now I want to ask: will you marry me—tomorrow?"

"*Tomorrow?*"

"I know it's sudden, and I know we won't have much time to prepare, but the date would not be much different from what we'd originally planned."

"We'd talked about marrying in early summer …" Margaret trailed off.

"Yes, and summer begins tomorrow," Lester reminded her. "This spring has taught me some valuable lessons. I don't regret them, but I'd like to learn the next ones alongside you."

"But what about the timber business? And the house?" Margaret's mind raced, weighing possibilities and popping up with a hundred little details that must be tended to in order to agree to what her beloved was suggesting. What about Mama and the children? But Mama had been up this week, apparently strengthened by the warmer weather. Polly could manage the little ones, the older boys were finished with school for the year, and Margaret would still be close by. The firm conviction settled upon her heart: *this was God's next thing for her.*

"The timber has been steady without me all spring—another month won't hurt anything. The house—it's ready enough, or can be within a day. It all has to be done anyway; why not today and tomorrow? And besides, I'm not strong enough to return to work yet, and I'd rather spend my time with my new wife than alone." Lester leaned toward her, earnestness dancing in his eyes. "What say you? Will you marry me tomorrow?"

"I think I can—I will—I'd love to!" Margaret burst out. After all, despite her initial shock, the timing seemed perfect. The boys could help move her things today, and Polly would be in her element preparing a special wedding dessert. The little girls would love picking wildflowers for the occasion, and the landscape had never looked lovelier. "Oh, Lester! I feared what tomorrow might bring so many times this spring, and now this! The best tomorrow I've ever imagined! No, better, for you're here, and you're well, and oh! Beginning tomorrow, we shan't ever have to say, 'Good night,' and shut the door upon one another anymore."

"It *does* seem too good to be true." Lester grinned. "That's the King's business, you know—taking what we feared and making it turn out to be far lovelier than anything we can imagine. And I know He'll continue that in us from now 'til eternity and forever. But we know that married life will contain its share of trials, after all, and we can accept whatever the tomorrows bring from the hand of God."

"And praise Him for them *together*," emphasized Margaret as their steps slowly swung up the lane, back to the cottage, where a myriad of pink, gold, blue, white, and purple blossoms raised their faces to the heavens and sang in their own, mute language the glory and praise of the One Who had formed for them this glorious tomorrow.

A Note from Erika Mathews

Fear Not Tomorrows found its inspiration in the poem "Doe Ye Nexte Thynge," credited to English author, editor, and hymnist Emily Elizabeth Steele Elliot. It was quoted in the 1890 book, *Christie's Next Things*, by Mrs. George A. (Minnie) Paull, as well as often repeated by missionary and speaker Elisabeth Elliot. In its publication in various sources over the years, some spellings have been modernized and a few words or phrases substituted or adapted. In my quotation of the poem in this book, I have chosen to use the updated spelling and wording of the poem for readability and clarity.

The concept of a hardworking yet overworked young lady struggling with "hope deferred" due to a fiancé called away by duty fit perfectly both with the theme of this poem and with the gorgeous setting of a springtime in Surrey. It draws from real-life experiences as well as literary inspiration from vintage authors such as E. D. E. N. Southworth, O. F. Walton, Margaret Sidney, and Martha Finley. A special thanks is extended to my fellow *Springtime in Surrey* authors for all their support during the writing and editing process!

My prayer for you, the reader, is that you walk away from this story encouraged, inspired, and challenged in your own walk with Jesus—whether through storms or sorrows. What is the "next thing" in front of you? How can you support those around you through prayer and trust? And in what areas of your life do you need to receive God's presence through praise and thanksgiving today? Whether monotonous or majestic, may His kingdom truly come and His will be done through you in your daily life as you do the next thing, trusting Him for every one of your tomorrows.

If you'd like to learn more about my historical fiction short stories, kingdom fiction novels, poetry, or Christian living books, subscribe to my newsletter at restinglife.com/signup. To connect on a more personal level, find me at instagram.com/erikamathewsauthor.

Courage to Stay

a novella by Kellyn Roth

Dedication

For Janelle
Thank you for pouring sunlight into my soul and dragging me back
to the light of hope.

Chapter One

County Surrey
Spring 1812

Rosalind startled to awareness as the carriage jarred its way over a rut. She met Matthias Emmet's brown eyes across the carriage. Of course, he'd been watching her—for what bride fell asleep on the day of her wedding when she could have been reacquainting herself to her new husband? Rosalind hoped Matthias would have the patience for her that he'd had throughout their childhood.

Only, Timothy had been there then, softening everything with his gentle voice and ways. She shook her head firmly and gripped the material of the simple, brown skirt she'd slipped into after the wedding, leaving behind the unfamiliar pastel, lace creation her uncle had ordered from a high-fashion modiste. The gown she'd worn on her wedding day had been so unlike anything she'd ever chosen to wear in her life.

However, it was better to think of the wedding gown than of anything more pressing. Her thoughts must not wander down that dreaded path, to Timothy and to James and to all that had been lost. It was far better to focus on the moment—for it was here that her life might take its first good turn—or it would be the worst turn of all.

No, she would not think that it was "supposed to be Timothy" sitting across from her, as had been intended since the earliest days of her youth. That thought was neither here nor there. Never mind that their parents had made the match when she was hardly out of leading strings, and Timothy and she—childhood friends who spent all their time together—had never seen a reason to protest. Never mind that she'd been eager, now that her parents and brother, James, were gone, to establish herself in her own household apart from her uncle. Never mind that Matthias seemed to tolerate her rather than truly like her, meaning their marriage could theoretically have a difficult beginning if he still didn't care for her.

Never mind that she'd secretly been infatuated with Matthias since she was fourteen years old.

She took a moment to examine Matthias then. He was a tall, lanky man, much as he'd been when he'd left for war. His curling brown hair and soft, chocolate-colored eyes, reminding her vaguely of a horse's in their depth—and she meant that as a compliment— were reminiscent of Timothy's, but there was something else to Matthias. Despite being very like his older brother, he was handsomer somehow, in a way that was difficult to place a finger on.

It was hard for Rosalind not to compare her own looks to him. She knew that beauty was to be found in the heart, but she failed in every way to conform to the current standards. There was little to her figure—were she taller, she would've been James's twin in appearance as well as by birth—and her hair failed to be exactly blonde or brunette. Her eyes were also an in-between sort of color, and her face held nothing interesting to remark upon.

Maybe that was why Matthias had never cared for her. Did he even realize she was a woman now, not the scrappy tomboy who'd followed at his heels through the surrounding forests and meadows, clingier than a burr? Surely there was little to remind him of her recently-attained adulthood.

"Did you sleep well?" Matthias's deep, even voice recalled her to the present, as her wayward thoughts were not likely to arrive back to reality on their own. "We are near to Willard Place now."

She pressed her lips together, unsure if she should speak, but pressed forward. "I'm sorry I fell asleep, M-Matthias." Restless nights had plagued her since the first day her betrothal to Matthias had been announced, and she might never sleep well again at this rate.

"That's fine." As always, his lack of response—at least, in any true way—started another round of silence between them.

Lord, how am I supposed to become this man's wife? He barely acknowledges that I exist. This cannot be Your plan for the rest of my life!

She knew that this was not simply her mind playing tricks on her. She had known Matthias a long time, and she knew this was not his normal manner of behaving. Oh, like as not, he'd matured somewhat, but the simple passage of years could not have taken the twinkle from his eye. What had happened to the cheerful, happy young man she'd known—always in trouble, never one to turn down an opportunity for a good romp, and pleasant even if they hadn't been the best of friends. He'd been more her brother, James's, friend than hers. Of the three boys, only Timothy had treated Rosalind with serious kindness. James had accepted that she would follow him around the countryside regardless of his preferences, and Matthias had adjusted to that fact, too, in time. Timothy had always valued her company.

The war had changed everything. It had taken Timothy and James from her and transformed Matthias into a man she didn't know. Yet her uncle had insisted that none of the arrangements between the families could end, and Rosalind was his means to the Emmets' properties, especially Willard Place.

She wished her mother were here. The late Mrs. Daniels had never failed to tell her romantic love story with her husband. Despite his being, by all accounts, below her in status and wealth, she had chosen to marry him—and the union had yielded many happy years. Rosalind felt that her own marriage could not fail to thrive with her mother's excellent advice—but that was impossible to obtain. The Lord would have to provide her all the necessary guidance ... and though she ought to believe in her heart that that would be more than sufficient, doubts swarmed.

God, don't let my marriage be a failure. I know 'tis not a love match, but surely he will come to love me in time.

The carriage turned up the long drive toward the familiar estate, and Rosalind preemptively straightened her skirts, ready to disengage from the vehicle at a moment's notice. She had no wish to be trapped in this small space with Matthias any longer. Though presumably the evening would be far worse.

He, too, stiffened and shuffled, hands fisting the material of his black breeches. The carriage reached the house, and Matthias launched himself from the vehicle far too swiftly. It was as if he had no interest whatsoever in spending a moment more in her presence than was necessary.

Her throat tightened, but she wouldn't cry. She *wouldn't*. She was made of stronger stuff than that—and more than that, was too toughened by her late brother's teasing—and she would carry on. Maybe Matthias and she could be friends again—she hoped so.

If only she knew what had gone wrong in the first place.

Matthias paced back and forth in the study, the half-drunk glass of port in his hand sloshing about with every move.

What am I going to do?

He was married. Married—to Rosalind. *His* Rosalind, who he'd dreamed about for all those years despite his best attempts to do otherwise. They'd stood before God and man and promised lifelong devotion to each other.

And Matthias had no idea what to do with her now that he had her.

Oh, it had all been different before the war. With a wry smile, he paused in front of the fireplace, not lit as the warmth of the spring day had led to its being unnecessary, and tapped his foot restlessly. He couldn't sit still—the carriage ride had been torture. Sitting across from her, not knowing what to say or how to begin—knowing the truth of their situation better than she herself did.

He'd ruined her life. He'd ruined the life of the woman he loved.

He groaned and set the drink on the mantel. This allowed him to run his hands through his hair for the hundredth time since he'd entered his father's old office an hour ago.

Not a year ago, his father had been alive, and Matthias had stood next to his brother, Timothy, and bid good-bye to him. They were going off to fight Napoleon—a fine adventure for two young lads, they'd thought at the time. For Timothy, it had also been a chance to prove himself before he settled into the managing of Willard Place, true lord of the manor. Though Matthias had always done his best to assist his father in managing the tenants and properties associated with their significant wealth, he'd not been like Timothy. No,

Timothy had always been up before dawn, in this office with Father, eager and willing to do whatever it took to learn how to manage the estate.

Now Matthias's hands shook whenever he thought of those days, for he would never return to them again.

What was worse, Timothy had not returned at all.

He pressed his eyes tightly shut. He couldn't linger here much longer. First, his thoughts would overcome him if he did so. But second, he was due in his wife's bedchamber.

But how could he do that? He paced to the windows and looked out at the gathering gloom. What if the worst happened? What if ... what if he had an episode and *hurt* her? The glass of the window reflected his own face back to him. He couldn't let her see him like this, a trembling fool with crazed, red eyes, his face pale, and dark circles apparent above his cheeks. Oh, she would take one look at him and run off screaming.

He marched back to the mantel, picked up his glass, and finished the drink in a resolved gulp. He would do his duty by her, but he couldn't stay. What if his nightmares caused him to hurt her in a fit of confusion? He was not himself; he couldn't be trusted. He'd hate to hurt her in any way.

He remembered a scattering of quotes Timothy had shared from the few of Rosalind's letters that had reached them during the war. She had shared her desire for children—for a home of her own—and to be married ... to Timothy. Yet Matthias would've known that even without the benefit of hearing bits and pieces of those letters. He knew her; he had always known her, from the time they were children. Everything about her spoke of the high expectations she had for marriage. Expectations only a man of Timothy's caliber would be able to fulfill.

But Matthias? Oh, before it would've been a struggle, but now? It would be impossible. He could not.

Lord, help me. I'm going to hurt her. Another prayer. They'd grown less and less frequent over time, but he clung to the last scattered pieces of his faith with determination. Perhaps it was the only thing holding him together anymore.

Yet Matthias had no choice but to join her now. He must. After all, she was waiting for him, and he couldn't be so little of a man as not to manage—well, something.

One last, deep breath, and another half-harried prayer for guidance, and he disappeared up the stairs.

God help him, but he had no choice.

He walked through the dim hallways of the old house, his feet *creaking* up the familiar steps. This house had been such an empty one to return to after the war, but he had been grateful at the time. The emptiness suited him well—and the lack of family members and the distance of his bedchambers from the servants' quarters allowed him to be confident that his nightmares would not be discovered.

Everyone at the wedding had talked about how he would be relieved to not be alone in that big house once more. Did they know how many of his nightmares had included Rosalind in the last two weeks? How often he had feared for her, dreaded the life that must come?

Yet how could he stop the wedding? He knew she was owed the connection with his family. It would be paramount to jilting her, and he could not do that to Rosalind—his Rosalind.

I'm ruining her life. I might as well have taken my musket and shot her in the heart. I've crushed her. It's all my fault ...

His mind fluttered back to the days of their childhood. She'd always been right at the heels of her twin brother, Matthias's best friend. James was lost now, too—killed in the same attack when Timothy ...

He swallowed. He couldn't think about that now, or he'd never get through the night.

Matthias forced his thoughts back on Rosalind and the task at hand. Yes, she'd always been near to him—and at first, he'd found her both annoying and awkward, a gangly, little girl who never failed to get in the way. But she'd been tough, too, and he'd come to admire her resilience and strength, her ability to keep up with men, her honesty, and her plucky nature. Yet it hadn't been until a few years after that that he'd realized she was becoming a lady—and suddenly, his heart had been inexplicably drawn to the girl his brother would marry.

If only Timothy had married her. That would've been so much simpler. Matthias could've gone back to war and died with a guilt-free conscience, if nothing else. As it was, he would return to war in two months' time to leave her alone—possibly without even the comfort of a child to come.

He arrived at the door of her bedchamber. For one, two, or ten minutes, he stood, hands in fists by his side. Then he raised one fist and knocked.

Once, twice. Three times.

"Come in."

He swallowed. She had no reason not to believe that he wouldn't be as suave and interesting as Timothy had been. Perhaps she thought they could still make something of this marriage. If he could get in and out of this room unscathed, without causing suffering on her part, that would be enough, surely. He ought to grant her the possibility of a child—he knew she wanted children, had always spoken in her letters to Timothy of having a large, boisterous family. Matthias had to give her this—at least this.

Maybe a child will be enough to give her the comfort I cannot.

If she didn't conceive quickly, he didn't know what he would do. She was owed a child, but to suffer under his touch for long—when she did not love or admire him, when he was as hideous a creature as he was, and when he might at any moment cause her harm—was equally as cruel.

His mind screamed at him to turn and run, but he opened the door and walked in.

"Matthias." She sat at the dressing table of this room that had been closed off for so many years—the mistress's suite, that had not been occupied since his mother died bringing Matthias into the world. Another reason it'd have been better if he hadn't been born, but he brushed that thought aside. Rosalind wore some sort of lacy thing over what he presumed was her nightgown. It was far from shapeless and reminded him that there was some substance to the girl. She was easy to hide under whatever clothing she wore—she was still a straight, slight thing. Perhaps it was for the best she didn't possess more in terms of womanly curves—though that had never mattered to him before, and it didn't matter to him now.

He swallowed. It was not difficult to be attracted to her, but that hardly helped anything. He wanted her to be with someone she wanted, too. This just wasn't fair to her—she deserved ... *everything.* Everything in the world. She was the loveliest woman to exist, and to bind her to a monster like him? Though his appearance was not beastly, she would be far better off with a brave, physically scarred man than a creature like him, with a mind torn to shreds due to weakness of character.

"Matthias?" Here, she repeated his name with the tiniest arch of her light eyebrows, comparative to the lilt in her voice. "Your hands are shaking."

Grand. And now her voice was shaking—with amusement. She might as well laugh at him—he was hilarious, much as all comedy starts from a source of pain and pity. He shuddered. "I'm sorry."

"Don't be sorry. I'm glad I'm not the only one who's nervous." She gestured to the bed. "Will you sit down?"

Stiffly, not sure what else to do, he trudged across the room and perched gingerly on the edge of her bed. He oughtn't to be here, with a creature like *that*. She was too angelic—his very presence dirtied her. There she sat, with her sandy hair about her shoulders and her eyes—like fragments of sunshine working their way down in an old-growth forest—full of curiosity and not the repulsion she should rightfully feel.

"I say I am glad your hands shake." She held out one of her small, white hands; it barely shook. She nodded her head toward said hand as if her own scruples—and she was kind to not admit they were greater—were comparable to his entire lack of capability. "Look at mine, Matthias! Yet I'm sure many a couple has known each other less and got through more. We shall be all right, for God has turned many a weaker foundation into a strong marriage." She smiled brilliantly, and he attempted to smile back.

Hopefully it wouldn't come off as a grimace. He looked down at his hands, clasped on his lap.

"I know you do not love me." Her soft voice caused his eyes to quickly jerk up to her face. Now her lips were trembling slightly. Even his brave Rosalind was upset at his terrible treatment of her. As she had every right to be. He must do better—but how? "I understand. Neither of us were supposed to be married to the other. Yet … I think you may learn to love me. I believe I could easily learn to love you."

He shook his head. She didn't know him. How could she say that?

She laughed again, though it sounded pained. "You do not think you may learn to love me?"

"N-no." He gritted the word out. "I think I … I think I … I don't know that you could learn to love *me*." It would not do to reveal the truth to her. They were bound now; there was no escaping. If she knew him, she must ask him to leave—common decency would require that she did so. No woman would be seen in his presence if they truly knew him. Yet she must have the child she wanted—even if he was not a suitable father, she would make an excellent mother.

Here, she smiled again, soft and inviting. "I shall prove you wrong. My heart is much more easily persuaded than you think—I know I don't seem it, at times, but I am as emotional as any woman. I am sure I already like you—we have been such great, old friends, and friendship is a good beginning to any love, for it is perhaps the purest type. How is that?"

Dumbfounded, he nodded, even though he didn't believe a word of it. Soon, she would know the truth—for how long could he keep it hidden?

Perhaps he could cure himself? Before she ever found out, even. Yet two months of strength and determination had only rendered him worse for the wear. How could he change who he was? Was it even possible?

She rose then and approached him, and he leaned back as far as he could to avoid her touch when she reached for him. There was only so far he could lean without lying prone on the bed, and that would be unfortunate in its own way.

She frowned, her lips puckering. "I did not think myself so unattractive as to repel a man so greatly, in all honesty."

"It's not that. It's Timothy." His scrambling mind provided his brother's name. "You are ... you are *Timothy's*." That only accounted for a fraction of his thoughts in regard to her. What cruelty, to be married to the woman he loved but not able to possess her because of the memories of his brother—and of the war that killed him.

"Oh." Her face softened, and she sat next to him. He straightened up and made very, *very* sure not to allow their legs to brush together. "Yet if you know Timothy as I did, which I do not doubt you do, you know that he would want us both to be happy." She reached out and placed a hand on his leg.

He forced himself to remain still, though he wanted to jump up—away—anything to allow distance between them.

"I believe we could love each other. I know it is not a requirement in most marriages, but I believe it is a requirement in a *godly* marriage, which is what I want. At least—I believe you and Timothy shared the same faith."

He nodded tightly. Or they had, before … *everything*. Now the demons felt more present in his spirit than God did.

"We need a place to start, and this is our start." Her hand came up to his face. He didn't flinch this time, but it took an enormous amount of restraint. "Perhaps we could share a kiss?"

He didn't say anything, do anything. Her eyes fluttered from his to his lips, then she leaned in, and they were kissing.

A wise man might have drawn away. A wise man might have not allowed the strain of the day to break him until his self-restraint was gone, and he found himself kissing her back.

He knew then that he'd stay, even if it were a poor choice. Even if he risked everything because of it.

He would stay—at least until she slept tonight. Because what else could he do? He could not abandon this woman any more than he could stay there with her.

What was he going to do with the rest of his life?

Chapter Two

Why did he leave me?

Over and over, the next morning, Rosalind debated this one thought.

Oh, he had stayed as long as she supposed any man would. Yet she'd expected more of Matthias than just "any man." She'd expected more of him than to share his love so willingly, then abandon her when she most wanted his comfort and reassurance.

He knew, surely, that she was an innocent. She believed he was, too, to a degree, but he had been at war, amongst men of all types, and certainly, he knew more than she did. Yet he had left, too soon, without giving her the opportunity to understand fully what had passed between them.

Not that she didn't understand the essence of the encounter, but there were some things that needed clarified, in her opinion.

She acquainted herself with the staff, some of whom were familiar to her and some of whom were new. She tried to settle into the duties of running the household. Matthias had, as far as she knew, been in his study since the early hours of the morning. She doubted that he had slept at all—he seemed so upset by her presence.

A part of her wondered if it weren't due to the war. Her brother, James, had mentioned in his last few letters before he was killed that sometimes men came home from war different. He had feared he would and that she would be afraid of those changes in him. Yet Rosalind was made of sterner stuff—she could bear it if Matthias were different. She just could not bear that he refused to talk to her.

She ought not to make assumptions about her husband. Perhaps Matthias had business to attend to. After all, he had been away from this house for two weeks to finalize their betrothal and marriage. She was very much a new bride, and weren't new brides afforded a period that one might call a honeymoon, even if no bridal trip were included?

She wanted him to be at her side. She wanted him to show her around the house as if her childhood had not been spent wandering the halls with their brothers and him. She wanted him to be tender and caring and thoughtful—and reassure her somehow that what had felt like love *was* love and not some baser instinct.

She would cry if it had just been lust. She would. It wasn't fair, really, to make lust something so loving, if that's what it was. She prayed, again and again, that it was not, but there was no confirmation within her spirit. Perhaps she was too wound up to hear anything from the Lord at present—she was so puzzled, so preoccupied.

Several times, Rosalind approached his study door, only to be told by his valet that he was not seeing anyone. She decided that, once she had taken care of every distracting chore she could think of in terms of acquainting herself with the household, she would force her way in. Yet she had best let him lick his wounds—if that were indeed what a man did after allowing emotional vulnerability, a trait so often identified with the weaker sex, to show. She assumed he was pouting. She couldn't think of anything else.

If only her mother had lived past Rosalind's young childhood. Or even, though it would have been dreadful, if Matthias's mother were still alive and a member of the household. An older woman to confer with would've been a secondary blessing in her husband's absence.

She'd so much rather hear the words from his lips, in the broad daylight. Because he had said, "I love you," several times the night before, and she wasn't at all sure if he'd meant it. Was that just the proper form in such moments?

She had not said it back; she didn't feel that was the right moment to make the confession. Besides, how dreadful it would've been to confess her feelings for him only to realize in the morning that it had been nothing but desire that made him say those things.

Rosalind continued about her duties, obsessed with the idea that maybe, just maybe, for the first time in her life, she was beloved.

Even if her husband was plainly an idiot who had no idea how to properly do so in the daytime.

Matthias spent half of the next morning sitting in his office with his head in his hands, too tired to sleep and not daring to let himself drift off. After it had been confirmed that his wife—his poor, abused wife—had been repelled at the door of the office, he tiptoed out, swiftly changed into his riding outfit, and summoned his horse.

If he couldn't sort this out by himself, he'd go to someone who could.

The ride over to Grimsby Court was short but effective in clearing his thoughts enough that he felt he might be able to communicate some of his thoughts to his old friend, Graham Jones. Graham had been in Scotland until two days past, so Matthias had yet to see him since returning from France.

Matthias arrived at Grimsby Court in record time and handed his horse off to the servant. He half jogged up the steps, eager to meet his friend and hoping he would be available to speak shortly …

To be met in the foyer by not only Graham Jones but two other familiar faces: Tacitus Ward and Hugh Turner.

That changed things significantly. Matthias hadn't seen Tacitus or Hugh in longer than he'd seen Graham. Both of them lived in London, and though he'd seen them regularly throughout his school days, as they'd all attended together, they'd become more and more distant over the years, only joining Matthias and Graham in Surrey for the occasional hunting trip.

But why were they here now?

"Matthias." Hugh didn't exclaim the name as most friends would have, but there was a fondness to his tone, certainly.

"What-ho, old chap!" As always, Tacitus chose a rather ridiculous voice. "How fortuitous that you should be here today, of all days! It's fate! It's destiny! It's at least a stunning and unnecessarily perfect coincidence!"

What's fate? Yet Matthias's questions weren't answered, as Graham Jones and Mrs. Jones, with a pink-cheeked baby on her hip, emerged, and a round of greetings began again, followed by the introduction of Young Master Jones, a cheerful fellow with Graham's abundant red curls.

"Tacitus is right," Graham pronounced once everyone had settled down and Mrs. Jones had disappeared with her son to another room. "This is fortuitous, for I was about to send word to Willard Place requesting your presence."

Matthias's brow furrowed. Had he been? Graham must've learned from someone, though Matthias couldn't think through whom, of his marriage. So his secret was out—and they would know at once that Rosalind was meant to be Timothy's bride. They would know that he had ruined her life, and all because Timothy wasn't there.

All because it was Matthias's fault.

"Oh?" was all Matthias could muster. After all, if, before he'd gotten a chance to rationally explain his side of things, the secret was out, he would have to take a scolding from all three of his friends, and that was the last thing he needed just now. His shoulders slumped as he awaited the beginning of the rebuking.

Yet Graham's words held no anger. "Yes! We're going hunting for two weeks. I thought you might like to join us—and it's always better to issue such invites in person. You've been home long enough to sort out most of the estate problems, haven't you? I know you'll have been faithful to it." Graham grinned, his broad smile taking up the whole of his round face. He was the eldest of the group, and the *de facto* leader. They all respected him, and he, in turn, usually took time to learn everything about his friends and do his best to lead them accordingly.

Unfortunately, it appeared he knew nothing of Matthias's current situation. It would be unwise to go anywhere just now—even Graham would not have suggested it.

At least, that was what Matthias thought. He opened his mouth to say these words, but it occurred to him that perhaps his absence was exactly what Rosalind needed just now.

After all, shouldn't he give her the benefit of distance? Wouldn't time help her sort through some of the wounds he had caused, and come out stronger? He knew she was a brave woman and, more than that, deserving of being the mistress of Willard Place and the properties thereof.

If he just got out of her way and didn't force his attentions on her for a time, wouldn't she be grateful? She could do what she was meant to do—step into the role of mistress and manager—and not have to bother with the unnecessary luggage that was Lieutenant Matthias Emmet.

He cleared his throat. "You say you'll be gone two weeks?"

"Yes, and it'll be a grand adventure. Just like old times! Sleeping under the stars, cooking on an open fire, hunting to our hearts' content … Why, it'll be like being boys again." Tacitus clapped his hands together. "Huzzah!"

Graham smiled. "It's not something I have experienced in three or four years, as you know, but I thought one last hurrah would do us all some good. Tacitus has met a lovely lady in London who he hopes will be his bride, and we all know Hugh is ever busy with his business. I've a wife and child, and you—who knows what your next adventure will be, Matthias, but you always find the grandest. All the more reason to come along with us. You have stories, surely?"

Matthias swallowed. None that he could look another man in the eye and tell. "I suppose I do," he said nonetheless, because that was the expected answer.

Could he go on this hunting trip? Yes, he could. Never mind that the sound of gunfire sent him reeling into visions he could never shake. Never mind that the nightmares plagued him both day and night. Never mind that he had a brand-new bride at home that he was none too eager to tell his friends about.

He wasn't afraid, was he? No, he wasn't. He was no coward. He couldn't be. There was too much to prove in this life to allow cowardice to color his future actions—right?

"I'll go."

Chapter Three

Matthias was gone most of the evening. Rosalind heard him enter the room that adjoined hers long after she had already retired for the evening, and she forced herself to fall into a fitful sleep rather than doing what she wanted to do. Which was go to him, confront him, and force him to explain his actions.

Perhaps it would take a gentler approach with this man. She had learned years ago to tame her reactions, to be cautious, to never let the strength within overwhelm the masculine pride that so surrounded her, from her uncle to the clergyman at the parish church to acquaintances in ballrooms. Besides, usually there was more strength in being gentle.

Timothy had always been different. He'd listened to her, and it had not bothered him one bit when their opinions varied. There had been discussion then, and respect, and she'd never feared he might think that she was unwomanly due to her outspoken opinions. She'd thought Matthias was cut of the same strong cloth. Yet here he was, refusing to even face her.

Had he thought her too bold? She had not felt bold, but perhaps she had acted it. That was often the case. Her "impertinence" often went unnoticed by her until the punishment for the action came around. Her uncle caned her for actions too far outside the realm of womanhood.

Yet Timothy had understood her. Though she did not love Timothy and had not considered him nearly as dashing a figure as Matthias—despite knowing that it was wrong to do so, despite having been filled with shame for this preference that she believed would slacken as the years went by—she certainly missed Timothy.

She missed his steady, quiet care and the way he always looked to her for advice regardless of having no real cause to do that. Growing up, he had always included her, though she had never known if Matthias had appreciated that—or not.

The next morning, she woke to a maid pulling back the curtains. Sitting up and rubbing her eyes, Rosalind sighed. Had she slept a wink? She must have, yet heaviness weighed down her limbs as if she'd spent the night at work rather than resting in this bedchamber.

By herself. Two days after her wedding.

"Henny, have you heard if Mr. Emmet has risen yet?" she asked as a tray with tea and breakfast was brought to her. Perhaps she ought to spend the day chasing him about as she had as a child, being firmer with the servants who dared try to block her from her rightful place at her husband's side. It was Matthias, after all. Surely he would listen to her, even if the war had changed him. Even if he … Well, James had written her horrible things that he'd experienced before he died. Perhaps Matthias had experienced much the same.

"Oh, I thought you might have discussed it yesterday, ma'am." The maid turned from Rosalind's closet with wide eyes. "He's gone."

Rosalind froze, her teacup halfway to her lips. "Gone?"

"Yes, ma'am. There's a note on the tray." The maid's expression indicated that she had expected the note to be something unimportant, or she would have told Rosalind about it sooner.

Rosalind indeed did find a folded slip of paper tucked under a plate. She moved the tray to the side and began to read.

Dear Mrs. Emmet,

I'm sorry for my distance, and sorrier still to admit that I am leaving on a trip with several of my friends, including Graham Jones, for at least two weeks. I hope you find everything to your liking at Willard Place. Please feel free to do whatever you want with it. I leave everything at the estate in your complete care, and I trust you to do as you will with this property, which always should've been yours, along with my brother's. I'm only sorry it couldn't have been the two of you managing it. You are more than qualified, of course. The war changed so many things, myself included. Please forgive me.

The trip in question is to conduct some hunting. I am hopeful that I shall return with a clearer mind than the one I currently possess. Perhaps at that point, I will be more qualified to be the husband of a woman such as you. I know I have fallen far, far short of the mark. It is not fair that a woman of your quality should have to marry second best, much less a man like me. But I am so lost in my own mind at present that it may take some considerable work for me to even begin working toward being worthy of your esteem.

I am ever yours, and hopeful to be dear to you someday,

Matthias Emmet

Rosalind allowed the letter to drift down to the bedsheet as she thought. He couldn't be sincere. What did he mean? Unworthy of her esteem? There was nothing about Matthias Emmet that was any lesser than his brother. If he would try, he would find her easy to win. She already had considerably tender feelings toward him. It would take little to rekindle her girlhood infatuation.

How did he not realize that? She thought she had made it clear enough that she desired a relationship with him.

Yet he apparently had not grasped that fact.

She snatched the note up once more. What was that he spoke of? His mind was not clear? Could he mean ...?

Again, Rosalind set the note down, failing to heed the concerned words of the maid, who now watched her closely. Could he mean what her brother had spoken of in his last few letters? He had described men staring at nothing, their eyes distant. That sounded like Matthias. James had described nightmares and visions—men screaming in the night, hearing the sound of gunfire even when no such sound existed, living a horror-filled existence both of their own making and entirely out of their control.

This all rather sounded like Matthias—or at least sounded like something Matthias could be afraid to tell her about himself.

That would explain the changes in his demeanor and personality, too. But could it really be that simple—and yet so entirely complicated? Could his claims of love be true, and this, the dread curse that kept him from her? Did they still have a chance?

She picked up the letter again, searching for further clues. By now, her maid had given up on her and was searching for a day dress for Rosalind to wear.

Yet Rosalind's thoughts continued racing.

If Matthias really were in such a vulnerable state, it would be insanity for him to go on a hunting trip. Further, knowing him, he had likely not told his friends about his fragile condition. If that were the case, wouldn't his hunting trip only serve to worsen his condition?

What if he was hurt? Or killed?

Rosalind's stomach twisted. She couldn't allow that to happen. She couldn't.

There was only one true solution. She had to protect Matthias from himself. Somehow, she had to step in where he would not, or *could* not, and keep him safe. After all, wasn't that her principal duty as his wife, to aid him wherever she could?

But how?

She could guess based on knowledge of Timothy's and his childhood trips with Graham Jones and their other schoolmates where they'd be heading first. There was a forest that began at Graham's estate and extended to the north. They would go there— they must go there, for she knew not where else they might go. But could she, as a woman, truly make a trip into those woods alone? The lands were not owned by anyone she knew, and they were haunted by poachers and other ruffians. There were reports that the worst scum of the earth, those hiding from the law, were there. As a woman, she dared not enter those woods alone, even if she hoped to soon discover her husband and his companions.

So what, then? She had no one left who might assist her. She did not feel confident enough yet to command Matthias's servants to accompany her or to go on their own.

Yet what if she weren't a woman?

She pressed her lips together. Would it be possible? Yes, she was slim and hardly noticeable, but could she do it?

She might not have a choice.

"Henny, bring me my brother's trunk—and have my horse saddled and food for a day packed. I'm going on an adventure."

The men had arrived at the camp not an hour ago and had just stopped arguing about the proper placement of their tent and the fireplace and all other accouterments. It was just like old days. Only entirely different, for Matthias was afraid that, at any moment, they would discern that he was different than he once had been.

He'd left early that morning without saying good-bye to Rosalind, but at least he'd left her a note. He could soothe his conscience in this manner, telling himself that it was all right to abandon his bride days after their wedding. After all, he was doing this for her—so that she might have a hope of a happy life.

If his presence ruined her life, he could not be in her presence. He refused to be. After all, didn't he love her better than any other creature on this earth?

Exposure would help. He would hold and fire a musket again, he would sleep under the stars again, and he would convince himself that at least here in England, he was safe.

Though, what of when he had to return to duty in two months? What would he do then? If he could not control this strange, new side of him before he returned, he would surely be shot for cowardice.

In some ways, that would be good. Rosalind could go on to live a perfectly respectful life. Of course, she would not be able to retain the estate in the long run. A distant cousin would become the inheritor—and what if the man in question didn't take good care of her? Yes, Matthias must live long enough to get her with child. Hopefully God would be merciful, and it would be a son.

Then why was he off running about in the woods when he had only a few weeks in which to do that? He sighed as he gave the peg holding up the edge of their somewhat lopsided tent a last firm tap with a mallet. He would be able to control himself now so he could be perfectly distant and perfectly kind in their bedchambers, so he could return to her after the war and resume said relations until she became with child. *Seamless.* It was seamless.

"Hallo! Who's there?" Graham's voice broke the relative silence the men had been working in.

Moments later, the crackling of brush as a horse approached their small campsite told the other three men why Graham had cried out as he did.

"Good morn." A voice that sounded familiar came from the other side of the tent, and Matthias ducked his head around to see a chestnut horse remarkably similar to one that lived in his stables. Seated on top of it was someone who must be a young lad, based on the voice, wearing cream-colored breeches. The rest of him was covered by a long cloak that draped him from head to mid-thigh.

Matthias squinted suspiciously. Was that really a lad? Why ... it *couldn't* be.

The lad spoke again. "I am in search of Mr. Matthias Emmet."

Graham, also squinting curiously, gestured toward Matthias, and he stepped forward.

The lad turned his head ...

And Matthias met his wife's lioness eyes over the length of the camp.

He swiftly jogged forward. What on earth was she thinking? She wore a man's clothing that fitted her surprisingly well, and she had done something to disguise the length of her hair. From a distance, she did look like a young boy of fourteen or fifteen, and she had a talent for imitating the voice of one, granted. Yet he could've picked her out from a crowd. Why, Graham must see—!

"Who is this lad, Matthias?" Graham's voice held some confusion but not indication that he had realized this person was not a "lad."

Was it really that good of a disguise to anyone who didn't know the woman in question? She had a boyish face and form, when not in a dress with her hair done up as women did. Matthias had always known this. He'd seen her in trousers more than anyone else—she'd always donned her twin brother's clothing and ridden like a boy whenever her uncle didn't catch her. Throughout their young adulthood, she had looked almost like a boy from a distance; in fact, she had looked just like her twin brother.

So she'd pulled that trick again, had she?

"This is ... this is ..." Yet he had no reasonable explanation.

"I'm Leander," she supplied. A fanciful name, and just of the type that she would choose. "I'm a friend of Mr. Emmet's brother." A slight arch of her eyebrows indicated that she intended it to sting.

He wondered if she knew how much it did.

She continued without pause. "I heard you had come back from war, but you didn't give me a chance to see you. You were hardly back before you flew away!"

He narrowed his eyes, as much to brush off the hurt that reverberated through his chest at those words. She surely knew that he had not intended to abandon her.

"Why don't you come over here and state your business." There was no chance on earth that he would reveal the truth of her identity in front of his friends. He would have to saddle his own horse and take her home and then return in the evening. But convincing Rosalind of this fact—for it was a fact; there was no other option—might be difficult.

She probably just intended to take him home, but her expression was inscrutable. And why make up an identity? Why do *any* of this? She could've sent a footman with a missive calling him home.

"Very well." She dismounted, and to her credit, she moved like a man. Of course, she had always imitated her twin brother perfectly in every way. The four of them had run about like any good chums might've, her never failing to keep up with them.

But they had always understood, instinctively, that though Rosalind might look like a boy and act like a boy and in every way behave herself like one of their schoolmates, she was not. Matthias hated to see her abandoning the last of her femininity, for that was the best part of her, at least in his opinion.

Graham obligingly took her horse's reins, and Rosalind followed Matthias to the tent he had been working on, just out of hearing distance of his friends.

He turned to her and let the mask drop. Her face immediately seemed to soften upon seeing his anger—becoming more feminine like some defensive method to keep him from being too harsh.

Yet he felt harsh. "What are you doing here? What were you thinking? You could've been stopped on the road, hurt, killed! And now I'll have to take you all the way back home. It's three hours' ride, Rosalind. What were you thinking?"

Her eyebrows raised, nonplussed by his fury. "I was thinking that you're likely to get killed, and I couldn't let that happen."

"What are you t-talking about?" Yet his voice stuttered at the end. How had she known?

"You are suffering from something terrible within your mind, Matthias. I'm not about to let you run around these woods. You ..." Her voice dropped. "You are my husband. I couldn't let anything happen to you. I couldn't. Not when I have already lost so much. You must come home with me."

Ah. There it was. "I will deliver you back home, then I will return to my friends."

Her jaw clenched. "No. If you will not agree to stay away from here, then I will remain here to take care of you."

"Take care of me?" What was he, a child? "Nonsense. You cannot and will not stay. You must return home at once. Why ... this whole situation is none of your business."

Her brow dropped. "Who else's business might it be, may I ask, if not mine?"

"That's ridiculous. It is none of yours. I am just fine, and even were I not, I could mind myself. I am no child."

"No, but I want you alive, even if you are not a child." She folded her arms across her chest. She must've bound herself in some sort of way, for there was little in terms of curvature to be discerned there, even as her heavy cloak fell back. He could see now that a cap under the cloak hid the rest of her hair, which she must've put into some clever arrangement to keep hidden any save a boyish flop of it across her forehead.

It was a thorough disguise indeed. She looked just like her twin had—uncannily so. Yet it was Rosalind. Everything about him was drawn to her in such a unique way that he could not fail to see her through the disguise, clever though it might be.

Yet a clever disguise did not grant her the ability to feign being a man out here in the woods for long. She might be a strong woman, but she could not stand being out in the woods for long. He must get her out of here posthaste. Before she was discovered.

"Matthias?" It was Graham's voice. "We can hear your voices rising but not what you're saying, but if you're insisting there is not room for the lad on this hunt, like the grouch you always are, please tell him that he's welcome to stay. As long as he'd like."

Matthias's brow pinched as Rosalind's face blossomed in triumph.

He couldn't let her stay. He couldn't. His friends would quickly disagree and force her to leave even as this "Leander." That would leave her with no choice, for she could not remain if the sentiment of the party was that she ought not to, correct? Besides, he could not let her stay. She would only get in the way, only cause his anxieties to rise, and he could not allow for that to happen.

Matthias wheeled from around the tent and stepped forward. "Oh, you know me. I would not protest his staying, but he is not up for the task, I'm afraid! Leander knows little of hunting. He would not do well with us, so he must go home. I'll ride with him back to my estate and see him comfortable there, then return to you."

"What a shame!" Hugh exclaimed. "There is no need for it. Why, we could give him a chance, couldn't we? We'd soon see how the lad handled himself."

"Give him a chance, Matthias!" Tacitus said, looking up from the fire he was attempting to light with little to no success.

"Oh, that's a bad idea." Matthias affected an at-ease smile. "Leander is incapable of it. Why, he's even powerfully afraid of the sound of gunshots!"

"He is?"

Rosalind's eyes narrowed. "I'm afraid Matthias is incorrect."

He narrowed his eyes in response. "I know I am not."

Without another word, she turned, and with a deliberately wide stride, she walked to his saddlebags and withdrew his musket from a sheath. To her credit, she handled it full well as any man he'd ever seen. In moments, she had loaded it competently. She marched back toward the trees and pointed. "See that squirrel?"

Matthias glanced in the direction she pointed and wanted to laugh. She could never make that shot. It was a hundred yards to the north and already scampering this way and that all over the trunk of a tree. It would take a champion marksman to hit the creature. "I do."

The gun went off.

There was a round of cheers, but Matthias stood still, the gunshot ringing in his ears. Before his eyes flashed the fearful but determined face of his brother, right before that final charge.

As he began to recover, Rosalind's eyes, concerned but firm, met his. "That was a good enough shot, now, wasn't it?"

"More than good enough!" Graham's voice interrupted Matthias's thoughts once more. "Let him stay, Matthias! He's a crack shot, and I'd hate to see him gone."

Eyes narrowed once more, Matthias turned to "Leander." "He" was particularly pleased with himself, of course.

Matthias nodded. "Aye. I suppose he can stay."

Though he was determined that she should be scared and on her way back home within the day.

Chapter Four

She'd won. Or practically. It wouldn't be long until he saw the good sense of her suggestions and returned home with her—for good.

Until then, all Rosalind had to do was keep Matthias from becoming seriously injured while they were on this trip together. That couldn't be so hard.

She'd seen the expression on his face when she fired the gun. Though none of his friends had discerned it—at least, they had not reacted if they had—he had been shaken. No, more than shaken—barely within the bounds of self-control.

She couldn't let him expose himself to such a dangerous situation again. Why, if this happened while he was supposed to be moving fast—and more than that, cautious of the other bullets flying around him—horrible things could happen. Matthias needed to admit to himself that he was suffering—and remove himself from situations where he could suffer further still. It was impossible to expect a war run by men to be understanding of something within one's own mind. He would be seen as a coward—and cowards were shot. That much, she knew.

She wondered vaguely if there was healing to be found for such an ailment, but regardless of what the end of the story might bring, in this moment, she was determined to aid him in any way she could. Especially if that meant protecting him from himself.

The men were sprawled around the campsite, cleaning their guns and preparing to go on a "scouting mission." If she knew men well, which she was fairly certain she did, there was likely to be some target practice at some point.

How could she get Matthias out of it?

He helped her tie up her horse and established a position for her inside one of the tents, presumably that she would share with him, but she knew he expected her to leave before the end of the day. There were still a few hours before sunset. She wondered if the men intended to hunt for something for their dinner—that was generally the way these expeditions went, if she remembered correctly from reports by her brother. They had packed food, in case the hunting proved unsuccessful, but they would want to live off the land as much as they could.

Matthias couldn't be a part of that. Or he shouldn't.

The other three men were preparing to go off.

"I suppose one of us had best stay behind and tend to the fire," Graham, apparently the leader of the group, said.

"That can be Leander," Matthias said swiftly. He had clearly been waiting for the opportunity to leave her behind, probably hoping she would become bored and want to go home.

No such thing.

"I think it'd be far better if we both stayed," she offered. She'd rather leave him behind and go on with the other men than allow him to go by himself, or else one of the other three could stay, but she would not let Matthias venture off by himself. Not when, apparently, none of these men knew what was truly happening within Matthias's damaged mind.

Matthias squinted at her. "That's hardly practical. There's no reason why I need to stay with you."

"Matthias, be hospitable." Graham's glare was enough to cause Matthias to straighten—Rosalind tucked that information away for later—but she doubted it would be enough for him to change his mind.

So what could she do? What would make him stay here?

Well, if nothing else, he was a gentleman. That meant she had one sure advantage on him.

"Perhaps I will stay behind," she said, maintaining her best "young man" voice, an imitation of her brother's boyish squeak. "I admit I am tired from the long ride, and I had best sit still for a time before joining you on this hunt."

Instantly, she felt a new kind of tension in Matthias's body, and her soul soared in triumph. Even if he did not love her, he certainly would not abandon her alone in the forest, knowing that she might be ill.

"I'll stay with you," he said. "We might as well talk." If there was a hint of a threat to that statement, then he kept it subtle. Good for him. He was starting to catch on.

"Very well." Graham shot an odd look between the two of them. "Tacitus, Hugh, let's go."

As the other men disappeared into the woods, Matthias turned to her with a frown. "Why are you making this so difficult? Let me take you home. You shouldn't be here. Any moment, they will realize it's *you*."

"They don't know me," she said, despite knowing exactly what he meant.

"I mean, they will realize you're a woman, of course." He grunted in annoyance. "This is insanity, Rosalind. It's not safe out here."

"All the more reason for the two of us to stay close to each other. Other than the obvious reason—our vows, for instance." She placed her hands on her hips. "Matthias, if you must know, I *do* agree that this is insanity. It's insanity that you would separate yourself from me, your wife, practically the day after our marriage. We need *time*. We both need time, and if you are here, there is no possibility that we can take that time."

He rolled his eyes. "I'll be home in two weeks."

"I know you will, but after that, we will only have a scant month and a half together to renew our acquaintance before you're back at war. Further, you are not well."

"I am quite well."

"I saw your face when that gun went off."

He turned and marched back toward the tent. "Let's pack your things. I'll leave a note for the men, and we can get you home before sunset."

"I won't be going home, Matthias."

"Yes you will."

"No I will not."

He whirled back to her, face twisted with anger. "Don't you see that this is for the best? You can't be here, and I must stay. I have to *prove* that I can be here. Don't you see that? I have to *prove* that I can survive in a situation like this. This is easy, all right? Compared to a battlefield, we might as well be sitting in a parlor at Willard Place right now. But if I can't handle this, I will not be able to survive the war. All right?"

Shocked by his honesty, she nonetheless remained on her feet. "Matthias, there is no reason why you should have to survive any more of the war. Why, you're a hero! You don't have to go back. It is not expected of you. Surely your commanders would be understanding that a man with a new bride, a new estate ..."

"It doesn't matter what others expect. I must do this, as much for Timothy as anyone."

Her brow wrinkled. "What does Timothy have to do with this?"

"Everything." He tossed his hands up in the air, but they flopped swiftly to his sides, defeated. "He never would've even gone to war if it wasn't for me. We agreed to go together, but he wanted to stay home. He never was supposed to be there, Rosalind. He was *never* supposed to ... Of course, my father preferred him to me." He turned from her once more.

She followed close on his heels, determined not to let this moment of vulnerability within him slip by without a conversation. "Matthias, I didn't realize."

"Of course he did." He continued as if he had not heard her at all. "Timothy was all a man ought to be. Gentlemanly, soft, easy to get along with."

"But he wasn't ... he wasn't what one would call ... heroic," she supposed.

"He was far more heroic than I ever will be." His voice spoke of a soul-deep defeat, one that she longed to comfort away, but he moved far from her touch once more.

Why did he always do that?

Never mind it. She would plainly have to wait for him to open up to her, even if that took a while to happen.

"I suppose you'll be sleeping under the stars, not in the tent," she said. That seemed to be the general consensus amongst the men—that the tents were more to protect the supplies than themselves. "Do you think they'll mind if I sleep in one of those tents? Perhaps they could take it as a young man not familiar with the ways of the forest, not as someone trying to hide ... well, feminine attributes."

He mumbled something under his breath about her "attributes" but did not protest this logic, so she took it as sound.

Nevertheless, it would be a long night to come.

Chapter Five

The next morning, all the men were up bright and early at dawn. Matthias had slept but fitfully, often waking himself in fear that the nightmares would come—or that his wild surroundings would trigger further fears. Thankfully, he had experienced nothing but a restless night, but he got up feeling more exhausted than he had when he lay down.

Somehow, Rosalind had gotten up even earlier, slipped past them to a nearby brook while they slept, and was just returning, her disguise still donned, as they arose. He gave her one thing—she was good at what she did, even if it were an entirely unnecessary skill to have for a woman of her station.

Matthias was beginning to wish he could go back in time and forbid her from joining Timothy, James, and him on their adventures. Certainly, he had not had the foresight to anticipate that those childhood romps could lead here, but he should've known involving a girl in boys' play would only turn disastrous in the long run.

What he didn't like most was that his brother and hers had always pushed her so far. She'd always ended up bruised, and once she'd even broken an arm, but never once had she faltered. She didn't let herself—she never had.

Now it would be better if she hadn't had that experience, if within her, there was some small part that shied away from the rigors of hunting, of tramping through the forest, of being away from the safety and cleanliness of a house.

Yet of course, Rosalind couldn't be that simple. Not that he wanted her to be, truly, but her complexities could be confusing at times. Further, he didn't want her to feel like it was her fault he wasn't home right now—it wasn't about her. She wasn't responsible for this need to run off to the woods and face his demons. He just needed her to understand that he couldn't be there for a while.

They all shared a meal of sorts—mostly bread and cheese—and then packed up a few things to start out on their search for game.

Graham was hopeful, and this raised the spirits of the rest of the men to a high degree. Even Rosalind seemed cheerier than she had the day before, though he could detect a slowness in her movements that indicated she had not slept well. He didn't blame her, for he had hardly slept a wink all the night long for worrying about her.

He lingered back from the other men, with even Rosalind walking in front of him, as they set out. He wasn't surprised that she waded through brambles and scrambled over rocks and fallen logs with the best of them. If Matthias weren't watching her so closely, he wouldn't have discerned her womanhood but, rather, thought her a somewhat effeminate young lad who was doing his best to prove himself to the older men. Her walk and, in truth, everything about her was so womanly that when faced with the knowledge he had, he had not the slightest idea how any of the men thought anything but the truth. Yet none of them had seemed to discern what was truly happening, really.

Tacitus slowed his pace and jostled Matthias's shoulder.

He winced but stayed still.

"Good chap," Tacitus said in somewhat of an undertone. "Your countenance is like a cloud, and I cannot help but think it must be due to the sad news that has so oft beset your family recently."

Matthias shrugged. "That is weighing heavily on me." Not as heavily as the slight of a thing walking in front of him, constantly distracting and always worrying, but the deaths of his father and brother were certainly fresh sources of grief.

"My deepest apologies, Matthias." He placed a hand over his heart, and though his dramatics never faded, his eyes were sincere as only Tacitus's could be. "Please don't hesitate to let me know if my assistance is required in any matter, small or large."

"Of course. Now, if you'll excuse me, I ... I want a word with ... with Leander."

Matthias allowed himself to catch up to Rosalind. She had a satchel over her shoulder containing food for the day, and it must be heavy. She'd not taken one of the guns, at least—he'd known she'd been willing to, but of course she didn't bring her own. All the more reason the men should be suspicious, as it was, after all, a hunting trip, but perhaps they thought it was all a matter of immaturity and youth.

"Are you all right?" he asked. "This may be too much for you."

"You know that it's not."

"Well." He lowered his voice still further. "You are doing well. Better than I could've imagined."

She glanced up then, beaming, her steps slowing. If one of the men had chanced to look back, surely they would've known in an instant that she was a woman. "Thank you. I am determined to stay for as long as you need me—or until we can go home together."

He winced. "I have things I want to accomplish here."

"I understand that, but surely it would be better to accomplish them at home." She settled back into a steady pace once more. "I've always liked you, and I think we could work through this. But we'd have to be together. We can't build a marriage if we're always separated."

"I understand that. But you must understand—you were never mine to wed." He frowned. "That should've been Timothy. Much as I do like you, too, I know we never should've been married."

If hurt crossed her face, he chose to ignore it. In her heart of hearts, she had to know it was true, even if it would take some time for her to acknowledge it. She was such an optimist, but even optimism must wane in the face of reality.

They rested at a brook for a time. Like the wee sprite she could sometimes be, Rosalind slipped away and then returned a few minutes later and sat on a rock by the stream. Again, she chose a deliberately masculine way of resting, but how could any man with eyes not see the curve of her hip when she sat there, her cloak thrown back, her cap over her ears?

Unfortunately, based on the slight narrowing of his eyes, Tacitus had caught on to this, too.

Tacitus stood from where he had been washing his face and approached Rosalind. Matthias didn't dare jump up and run to her side, but how he longed to. Instead, every muscle tensed. He pretended to be taking a deep sip of the water from his cupped hands as Graham and Hugh picked up their packs and continued on down the half-hidden path through the forest.

"Good day, young Leander," Tacitus called in a deliberately exaggerated tone reminiscent of a stage actor's. He splashed his way up the stream, taking large steps in the icy cold water. Matthias winced, but Tacitus would do anything to gain a smile from a friend—even if it meant soaking his boots. "Thou seems quite the fresh-faced youth. But fear not, for we shall soon turn thee into a seasoned hunter, capable of wrestling with the most ferocious beasts. Else they shall eat thee, cloak and all!"

Rosalind smiled, and brief though it might be, it was in that moment that Matthias's heart began to race. Tacitus must know now. Yet he remained still, waiting to see her response.

"I'm sure I can manage. I'm used to this area—and I doubt there are all that many ferocious beasts here, at any rate."

If Tacitus had doubted before, surely he did not now. Oh, she had disguised her voice—and yes, she had endeavored to express herself as a man would, as James would have. That said, the life of her voice—and more than that, of her shoulders—was decidedly feminine. There was a kind of pluck that was masculine and a kind uniquely belonging to the opposite sex. Whether Rosalind knew it or not, she was surely a woman.

"I'm sure you're more than competent." And even if Tacitus had not intended to immediately let on that he knew the truth, his voice had softened. He'd always had a weak spot for women; it was no surprise that he had met and betrothed himself to his lady in London.

"I'm sure I am."

"We ought to rejoin the others," Tacitus said, straightening.

Rosalind followed suit and scrambled her way back over the rocks, making her way back to the main path. Tacitus chose instead to splash his way up the stream again ... right in front of Matthias.

"We shall speak more of this anon, friend Matthias." Tacitus grinned. "But *that* is no lad."

Matthias pressed his lips together. "I don't want to talk about it."

Tacitus shrugged. "Fine. Tonight, then."

Chapter Six

The rest of the day was much of the same as the beginning of it. They trudged about the woods, occasionally setting up in a certain area in hopes that an unlucky roe would wander through their path. Unfortunately, they saw no game.

Of all the members of the party, Hugh Turner was perhaps the most private. Tacitus Ward spouted off Shakespearean English and poked fun at his friends, and Graham Jones offered pearls of wisdom. Matthias's silence was more broken than Mr. Turner's.

However, Mr. Turner was unnaturally quiet. More than that, he often scrambled off for a few minutes through the woods only to return looking grouchier than ever. Perhaps he was searching for game and, unlike the other men, failing to find good humor in the absence of it.

Unfortunately, this also meant that, at times, he popped out of nowhere beside Rosalind. On one such occasion, she had separated herself again from the group to relieve herself. Fortunately, when the taciturn Mr. Turner appeared out of a bush, she had already taken care of business and was dressed and on her way to catching up.

"You've lost the group," he observed. That was the most she had heard him talk all day, and though she was tempted to turn her efforts toward befriending him, that would be unwise, given her current plan.

Instead, she simply nodded.

As they walked through the forest, they were met with rougher terrain than they had found previously. An abundance of roots, rocks, and patches of grass inhabited even the well-worn path, and Rosalind found herself out of breath from scrambling over them.

Oh, she was accustomed to long hikes in the woods; that much was true. Yet it had been over a year now of sitting on sofas pretending to embroider. She had thought her hunting days over, much more her days of chasing James, Timothy, and Matthias about.

Her boot, so ungainly compared to the slippers she had become accustomed to, caught on a branch, and she stumbled.

In a second, Mr. Turner's hand was out, catching her arm. "Are you all right, lad?"

Rosalind felt her face grow warm. "Yes, I'm fine."

Yet he didn't let go of her arm. Instead, he stood there, giving her an inscrutable look, and held on to her forearm. She instinctively jerked away, then struggled more fiercely when he refused to release his grip.

It was only as the panic faded in face of his lack of reaction that she realized how unlike a man the gasp she had released must have been.

"You're a woman," Mr. Turner murmured. "How did I fail to see it? And you look as much like James Daniels as anyone I've ever seen. Are you his sister?"

Rosalind's eyes slammed shut. How could she have let on! She should've been more careful. Yet it was a surprise that none of the men had accused her of being like James beforehand. "Yes. I'm Rosalind ... Rosalind *Emmet.*"

"Oh." Mr. Turner's tone held the first hint of interest since she'd met him. "So Matthias did marry you after all. We'd heard rumors but assumed they were untrue when he agreed to join us."

She opened her eyes and reached out to place her hand over his. "Please, Mr. Turner." If her tone of voice was desperate, she didn't care. "Don't tell the others. If they find out, Matthias will never forgive me for revealing this to his friends. He wants me to go home, to Willard Place—but I can't go without taking him back. He's not well, Mr. Turner, though he won't admit it."

"He's ill? Granted, he does seem a bit strange, but I'd have thought that was due to your presence." He pressed his lips together in a thin line. "Or at least due to getting married. Can't say I recommend the business."

"No, he's ... he's not really ill, I suppose." How could she explain it? "It's an ailment of the mind. Oh, he's not mad, but he ... he is suffering. From the war. From all he's seen. I think he saw something when ... when Timothy and James died."

"Ah. I see." He rubbed his chin, then nodded. "Very well. I'll keep your secret, for now. But you must speak with Matthias. Make him come home with you. That's what he ought to do, I suppose, now that he's started this whole marriage charade, like the rest of these fools."

Rosalind was too relieved to protest, though she ought to be offended. Yet there was an ominous note to Mr. Turner's warning. *I only have so much time left. Lord, help me bring my husband home.*

Matthias's nerves were stretched as taut as a drumhead. Tacitus knew, and somehow, Hugh seemed as if he had an inkling of it, too, though Matthias couldn't imagine why. As often as the man tended to disappear and reappear from the group—too restless and too quiet to stay with even his dearest friends for hours at a time—he couldn't have had as much time to observe Rosalind as the others.

Further, failing to sleep had Matthias's eyes drooping and his limbs shaking. He was on a dangerously short tether, said tether fraying like an overused piece of rope. Yet he could hold it together. He could. He'd gotten this far, hadn't he?

Rosalind appeared next to him, and he flinched away from her, holding back a gasp of fear. Yet she didn't move for a moment, eventually pressed against his side. With all three of his friends discussing the possibility of heading back to camp or sleeping under the stars that night and trying for better hunting terrain in the morning, it was a safe, stolen moment for her to take—and yet he couldn't let himself sink into the comfort of a human being who cared—and apparently, *knew*—despite the soul-deep longing to do so.

He pulled away from her and walked over to the other men. "I say we strike back to the camp while we have light and try toward the east. Besides, I need to escort Leander back to the edge of the forest tomorrow at daybreak."

"Oh? He's leaving so soon?" Graham said, looking over Matthias's shoulder toward "Leander." "I thought he was doing a splendid job keeping up."

The other two men made various mumbling noises. Yes, Tacitus was not the only one who had figured it out; Hugh certainly knew, too. Yet as they harrumphed their way to an explanation, Graham stilled and grabbed Matthias's shoulder.

Matthias managed not to strike Graham, but he did jerk back.

"Easy there." His eyes were now trained to the left, over Matthias's other shoulder. As Matthias moved to the side, Graham raised his musket. "There's a pheasant standing in the path. None of you move."

Matthias watched, motionless, as Graham put his gun against his shoulder, aimed carefully down the path, and pulled the trigger.

The sudden crack of the shot echoed across the countryside, and Matthias felt a bolt of fear shoot through him. His muscles tensed, and his hands shook uncontrollably. The world around him blurred, and he was plunged into the past.

He was back in France, crouched in a ditch with Timothy and James. The scent of gunpowder and smoke filled the air, and the screams of dying men and horses were deafening. He could feel the tremors of the earth beneath him as the French army advanced.

Timothy and James rushed forward, ready to fight, but Matthias remained petrified in the ditch. This feeling of helplessness, which invaded his bones, making them heavy and light all at once, overwhelmed him. Where before he had always pushed it aside and continued on, he could no longer do so.

Shots were fired in the distance, and men screamed. One of the screams was his brother's. He ought to get up, run to him, drag him back to safety.

But he couldn't. He was frozen, more a statue than a man.

There was nothing he could do. Nothing.

Matthias felt a cold sweat break out on his forehead, and his heart pounded in his chest. The feeling of defenselessness washed over him like a tidal wave, and everything shook. The air, the ground, his hands, his stomach.

Yet there was a pressure on his shoulders, forcing him to the ground, though he fought it—and then a soft, warm body was pressed against his, and a hand was in his hair, and a soothing voice was repeating his name again and again.

"Matthias. It's all right. Matthias, you're here; you're with me. Do you feel my hand? Hear my voice? Matthias, come back to me." And the edge of desperation to the tone, despite the calmness, had his eyes focusing back on Rosalind's face. "Breathe," she whispered, lower still. "Breathe, my darling. I'm here."

He took a few shallow breaths and eventually managed to get his traitorous lungs to expand enough to make the spinning stop.

"You don't have to talk. Just sit here for a moment. All right?"

"Aye, we didn't shove you to the ground for nothing. Can't have you falling and hitting your head." Tacitus's voice was slightly less soothing than Rosalind's, and yet it was real and of the earth and the moment.

Hugh's reply, a grunt, was also a sound of the present.

Graham, meanwhile, stared with wide eyes both at Matthias and Rosalind.

Matthias ducked his head. How to explain this to his old friend, who couldn't fail but dislike this new side of Matthias now that he'd seen it—and further, be ashamed of him for abandoning his wife and forcing her to follow him to the forest.

"What happened?" Graham said at last. "And why did none of you see fit to inform me, as you are clearly all aware, that Leander is, in fact, a female and Matthias is … is … What is Matthias?"

Matthias pressed his eyes shut. Of course. Graham couldn't even think of a word to describe him.

"It's from the war," Hugh mumbled. "Not like you to judge a man."

"I'm not judging anyone," Graham snapped. "I just want to understand. And who is Leander?"

"Leander is Rosalind," Hugh supplied. "Rosalind Emmet, of late Daniels, if you must know."

"Oh." Graham's eyebrows hit his hairline. His eyes flicked back to Matthias. "*Your* Rosalind?"

Matthias attempted a shrug, but it felt like all the energy had seeped its way out of his body.

"Though I'd like to explain more," Rosalind said, pushing herself up so she wasn't leaning quite so heavily against Matthias. "I would like to get my husband home. Won't you gentlemen be gracious and see to that happening in the speediest way possible?"

For a moment, all four men froze, then Hugh sprang into action. "We're an hour from our camp, but I can run it and ride back in forty-five minutes."

"Oh, aye. Go." Graham gestured, and Hugh was off at a lope.

Until he returned, the men were silent, and Rosalind didn't pry.

Matthias was thankful. He didn't want to admit to her exactly what had passed through his mind, after all.

He had killed her fiancé—the love of her life—and her brother.

Chapter Seven

Rosalind wasn't sure what she had believed would happen when she arrived back at Willard Place. Perhaps that Matthias would sweep her into his arms and declare his undying love—or perhaps something more subtle, like his agreeing to spend the evening with her.

A part of her had feared that he would be angry at her for dragging him back from the hunting trip, though he had returned willingly when he could've continued the farce far longer.

Yet none of that happened. Instead, little seemed to have changed. They were still painfully awkward around each other. He was still distant; she was still upset with him for failing to be anything like what she'd hoped he would be. He was still going back to war in a few short weeks, at which time she might never see him again.

Matthias had been silent as they rode home, clearly more shaken by the events of the past days than he let on. Yet her mind couldn't help but mull over and over an exchange she had had with Tacitus as he bid her farewell.

"I am sorry you must leave so soon, young Leander," Tacitus had said, a twinkle in his eyes. "But I trust you will take care of our Matthias while I am not in his company."

"Of course I will," she'd replied. If he would let her, at any rate.

"Matthias is a good man, but he has suffered greatly. You have the power to help him heal, to show him love and kindness."

Rosalind had felt a warmth in her chest at Tacitus's words. She knew that she could help Matthias, that she could be there for him in a way that no one else could. Of course, convincing him of that fact might be the more difficult task, but if one person believed in her, it might be more possible than she thought. "Thank you."

Tacitus had smiled at her. "And one more thing, young Leander. Remember that Matthias has always been a bit of a hopeless romantic. He may not show it, but he cares deeply for you."

She'd blushed, but Matthias had arrived far too soon, before she could question Tacitus's words. "I'll keep that in mind," she had replied simply before mounting her horse and preparing to follow Matthias out of the woods—and back home.

That night, in her own bed, she lay awake far longer than her exhausted bones demanded—simply wondering.

Matthias sat alone in his study, the only light coming from the flickering candles scattered around the room. He sipped his port, the taste bitter on his tongue.

Over the past two weeks, he had been distant from Rosalind, which was both a relief and the cause of a constant ache in his heart. *It is the right decision,* he told himself for the fourth or fifth time in so many minutes. The clock would never tick so many times between the weaker of his thoughts, unfortunately. The ones that screamed, "Go to her. Find her. Tell her you love her. Risk it all, risk everything—for her."

Yet there were too many risks. Great and mighty, they sought to overwhelm him—and they usually repressed even his wildest thoughts.

Of course. He took another sip of the port. *My reaction to the gunshot did not scare her.* She had been as strong as he'd known she would be—and she provided him great comfort. But it would be different at night—or if it were unexpected. Not all of his responses were obvious. Sometimes, out of nowhere, he'd be struck with memories and sensations, his mind and body both acting out of his control. And what if he hurt her? He couldn't bear the thought of that.

No, it was best that they remain distant. The hunting trip had proven that he could never fully recover—not really. Even in the bosom of his friends, he had still had the same reaction—and he always would. It would be best if he went back to war and just *died*, rather than risking hurting Rosalind. He took another sip of port, the liquid burning down his throat.

He set the glass down on the table with a heavy sigh. He leaned back on his chair, staring off into the darkness. He didn't know what to do next other than wait out the next few weeks until he was called to the front. All he knew was that he was lost and didn't know how to find his way back.

His head snapped up at the sound of his name, his body jerked uncomfortably, and his heart began to race at once. Why should the simple act of someone's calling out for him cause such a reaction? Yet it did every time, even when it was simply his valet reminding him that he hadn't eaten or slept for three days.

This voice wasn't his valet's. When he regained sufficient control, he turned to face the ever-constant focus of his thoughts—his wife, Mrs. Rosalind Emmet.

She took a step toward him, tenderness apparent in her soft eyes, the comfort of a warm sun shining behind them. He wanted to sink into that light and never come up for air. "Matthias. Please. Come to bed."

A siren she was not, but appealing, she ever was. "You know I can't do that."

"Let me help you." She took another step toward him, playing with the tie of her wrap, unintentionally cinching it tighter about her slim waist.

He dragged his eyes to her face with noble intent. Her face was far too pretty for her own good.

"Let me … let me be with you. I know you've been struggling. I don't even know if you have slept. Let me be the one who is awake tonight. Stay with me and let me wake you if I see you are … are having a nightmare. I'll watch—if you'll just rest."

His teeth gritted, but he shook his head resolutely. "No. I won't. You'd be safer alone—and certainly more well rested."

Her eyebrows lowered. Stubborn creature. "Matthias, I'm not afraid."

"You're never afraid. 'Tis your worst attribute."

A slight upwards quirk flickered over her lips—which had far too briefly touched his own, he remembered. "I've never had much to be afraid of. Why should I—who had once the hearts and the hands of the best, strongest men in Surrey?" She placed a hand on her hip, regarding him with mock seriousness. "A woman need not fear much when she has always had Sir James and Sir Timothy and Sir Matthias at her beck and call." Here, the smile softened—yet never faded. "Even if I have but one of my fearsome knights still, somehow I feel as brave as I ever have—or perhaps braver."

He pressed his lips together. "I'm not much of a knight, Rosalind. I never was."

"I always thought you were." She hesitated then, clasping her hands in front of her. "I always thought you were the most dashing of them all. Though, I suppose that could be on account of one of them being my brother and one … Timothy. He was never quite as much an attraction to a growing girl, as you doubtless know."

Despite the weariness in his bones, he couldn't help but perk up with curiosity. "Timothy was always the charmer."

She laughed—really laughed, as if there were anything silly about that honest statement. "Timothy was always the charmer of old women and fathers. I liked him, of course, very much, but you— faults and all—had the smile and impudence to appeal to a young girl. Surely you knew that."

Matthias frowned. "I wouldn't have said I was impudent."

"You were certainly outspoken."

"More than you?"

"Oh, never more than me." She winked. "I cannot allow that."

He realized then how relaxed his posture had become, how he had leaned back on his chair as casually as he might have in the old days. She made him feel so at ease in his own skin.

Yet he couldn't allow that.

He stood, rolling his shoulders. "To address your earlier point, I'm afraid I won't be joining you tonight. I … I'm afraid I'm not that boy anymore."

She pouted as much as an adult woman could without looking terribly undignified. "I don't want you to be that boy. I'm rather more interested in knowing the man."

"I'm afraid that is not possible." He was determined to prove this to be a fact. Getting to know him would just allow her to become more attached, and if she became attached, it would hurt all the more when he inevitably left—presumably never to return to her again.

"Goodness, you're insufferable sometimes," she mumbled, then disappeared down the hall before he could reply.

Chapter Eight

There comes a time in every woman's life when she must run into the arms of the nearest creature of her own sex and sob out her problems with a man. If it is done over a cup of tea, it is twice as effective, and if the creature in question is older and bosomy and in the habit of calling one "dear" and "poor thing," then the situation may very well resolve itself.

Unfortunately, a woman of any sort of rank cannot turn to the nearest creature of her own sex, as that person is usually a servant—and that is not done. This had been drilled into Rosalind's mind by her brother when she'd developed a "too-close" relationship with a stable boy at the tender age of nine years old, though it was not until she'd become a little older that she'd seen the true cause of his concern. At the time, the stable boy in question had simply been a playmate—and yet it had been unacceptable, and it still was.

Therefore, Rosalind was left in a difficult situation, for in Surrey, she had no true acquaintances, and due to the assumption by some that she didn't exist and by others that her husband and she were enjoying a blissful, private honeymoon, there had been no callers.

Until one day, she returned from her morning ride to discover that a card had been left for her by a Mrs. Graham Jones of Grimsby Court, with a small note on the back in curling script, reading:

Come see me if you need to talk or cuddle a baby boy who is very fat and has the most charming of smiles.
~Sophie

Being in the state of unrest she was, Rosalind dressed herself to go calling, ordered the carriage, and left behind the dim halls of Willard Place to venture out into the brightness of Grimsby Court.

Despite its name, the estate of the Joneses was full of green grass and colorful flowers. The parlor Rosalind was ushered into was also brimming with fresh blooms—every flat surface and even a few corners of the floor held a vase or a pot of fragrant blossoms.

It was a welcome change and had Rosalind wondering why she—with a rose in her name, no less—had not managed to bring more color into Willard Place. She'd been distracted—especially the last week, as situations progressed in a somewhat unfamiliar way, leading to great distresses and doubts in her mind.

Just as Rosalind began to wonder if she shouldn't turn tail and run—she had never had a female friend, not truly, and she was not sure how to begin—Mrs. Graham Jones entered the room, a rosy-cheeked little fellow smothered in lace in her arms, upright but the most comforting amount of floppy.

"I'd hoped you would come." She smiled, and her expression was so sincere that Rosalind couldn't help but smile back. "And as promised, I have brought my baby."

Rosalind gave her full attention then to the little fellow in Sophie's arms. He had his father's red curls, but his eyes were his mother's, dark and full of life. "Oh, he's just precious! How old is he?"

"He's almost four months now," Mrs. Jones replied, beaming with pride. "His name is Jonathan."

"Jonathan," Rosalind repeated, rolling the name around on her tongue. "That's a lovely name. It means 'gift of God,' doesn't it, Mrs. Jones?"

Sophie nodded. "Yes, that's exactly right. We feel so blessed to have him. And please, call me Sophie. But how did you know?"

"Oh, my brother, James, and I—before he went to war, I mean—he and I used to find out all the meanings of the names in the Bible. His means 'he takes the heel,' if I remember correctly, which wasn't at all what happened when we were born—but it was near to it, if I understand it." Her heart lightened talking about him—no one ever talked about those happy days with her brother anymore, not even those who had known him as well as she had. Not even Matthias. "Mother always said we came one after the other in quick succession."

"Oh, you were a twin? I think Graham mentioned that, come to think of it. Here. You must sit down and hold Jonathan. He has been passed from man to man for weeks on end now, what with our recently-departed guests, and I think the touch of a woman will not be unwelcome."

Rosalind hesitated. Her heart clenched, and that little tremor of uncertainty she always worked so hard to hide when it came to babies made its way into her voice. "Oh, I don't know. I'm not good with babies."

"I'm sure that's not true! At least, not of Jonathan. And you seem like the type of woman who could handle a baby, of all things. For heaven's sake, be brave, or I'll doubt your reputation."

Her chin trembled, but she sat, nonetheless, on the sofa she had arisen from and was handed a warm bundle of squirming limbs that swiftly adjusted, with a helpful nudge or two from his mother, into a warm but comforting weight that caused an immediate slowing of her heart—and a lump in her throat that she wasn't at all sure what to do with.

"See, it's true," Sophie said, a hint of triumph in her tone. "I think you and Jonathan are getting along famously. Now." She, too, sat on the sofa. "You must tell me how it happened that you were traipsing about the forest in men's clothes with my husband returning to me convinced you were some wild harridan—and here I meet a woman of great taste."

Rosalind raised her eyebrows. What about her poorly arranged hair and simple gown had indicated "woman of great taste"?

"By which I mean," Sophie said, "you like Jonathan."

Rosalind laughed softly. "Oh, anyone would like Jonathan. Didn't you say he was being passed from man to man for weeks on end?"

"Oh yes, and Jonathan is hardy—but not always appreciative of such behavior. Men are, after all, anything but motherly, and for a baby of his age, some rather rough games were played. That said, I am protective of him." Sophie lifted her slim shoulders in a delicate shrug, ringlets of dark hair dancing about her rounded cheeks. "Still, I must know the story, or else we cannot be great friends. You must forgive me my curiosity."

At first, Rosalind was not likely to forgive her—for she didn't want to talk about it, truly, when faced with the ever-remaining lump in her throat and the stinging behind her eyes. Yet a few words were said softly of her marriage, and then the rest came tumbling out.

Her engagement to Timothy. Learning that he had been lost—and with him, her brother. Her uncle's insistence that she still wed into the Emmet family. Matthias's coldness—so unlike his former self, as even Sophie must know.

Rosalind spoke for, perhaps, an uncomfortable amount of time, given that her new friend was very near to a stranger. To her credit, Sophie Jones was all understanding and simply sat pensively for a time once Rosalind, slightly tearful and certainly rather wrung out, had finished.

"You need to pull him out of this." Sophie smiled, but it was a rather grim expression. "It may not lie in your power, but you must do your utmost—for if anyone can, it is you."

Rosalind shuddered. "I'm afraid of losing him."

"Any whole-hearted woman would be."

"And there's something more."

Sophie's eyebrows arched. "That you have yet to tell me? My, my."

"I think I might be with child."

Chapter Nine

In the five weeks since their marriage, Rosalind had done a lot to surprise Matthias, but nothing had been more surprising than her sudden insistence upon holding a dinner party.

All he knew was, she had disappeared for a morning and returned with the information that Graham's wife was helping her host a few couples from about the county.

The plans progressed with stunning speed, and before Matthias knew what had happened, it was the night of the affair.

He ought to be happy. This was a good sign, wasn't it? Rosalind was embracing her role as mistress of Willard Place. She would thrive here without him. Wouldn't she?

If only he could be at her side forever. If only.

Yet he wanted this dinner party to be as much of a success as she clearly wanted it to be, so he forced a smile and greeted their guests kindly as they arrived promptly at seven o'clock.

Rosalind was a stunning hostess, as he had known she would be. She welcomed each of them with a warm smile and a curtsy, sincere and a little awkward but utterly charming. In no time, they had all made their way to the dining room, where a sumptuous feast awaited them.

Graham was in good spirits, but he didn't speak alone with Matthias—and that was probably for the best.

Matthias had nothing good to report.

The room was decorated with fresh flowers and candles, and the table was set with fine china and silver. The conversation flowed easily about Matthias, but all he could do was stare at his bride. She was resplendent in her evening gown. He wanted to get her away from everyone and keep her all to himself, but that was hardly fair. Around him, his guests discussed the latest news from London, the state of the economy, and the prospects for the upcoming hunting season. Everyone else was continuing on with their lives, as if there were no war. Matthias no longer belonged to that world.

Yet elements of his world remained. Colonel Whitmore, still an active member of the militia, was seated across from him at the table. How did the man, who had seen so much action, remain so calm? So *normal*?

Why was Matthias so weak?

Colonel Whitmore's eyes locked with Matthias's, and his heart stuttered. Was he going to be subjected to still more questions about his former or upcoming service?

Yet instead of directly addressing Matthias, Colonel Whitmore did something worse. He raised his glass in his direction and said to the whole table, "I must say, Emmet, the reports I've heard from your time in France have impressed me greatly. Your bravery was unmatched. All the papers have reported tales of your heroism, and I'm sure we are all grateful for your service."

A murmur of agreement circled around the table, but Matthias stiffened. Unbidden, despite his attempts to focus on anything but his out-of-control thoughts, memories of that fateful day flooded back to him. The sound of gunfire, the screams of dying men and horses, the smell of death. His nostrils flared as he attempted to control his breathing, but his breath came in short pants.

He felt a hand on his arm and looked up to see Rosalind. She had come to his side—of course. Ever the martyr for his failing cause.

Mindless of the other members of their dinner party, he locked eyes with her. "I killed them both."

Her eyes widened. For a moment, she hesitated, then her head shook—she did not believe him. "It's not your fault," she whispered, her words only for him. "I know you were there when it happened, but it couldn't have been your fault."

"No. *No.*" He rose, his napkin falling from his lap and the table rattling and clinking with his sudden movement as his legs bumped into the edge. "You don't understand. I should've been at their side—I should've gone before them. This is my punishment for—for everything I never did right."

He turned and stumbled out of the dining room, careless of the guests and what was presumably their stunned silence. He heard Rosalind call his name but ignored her.

After all, what could she do against the naked truth?

Rosalind found him in the garden, pacing back and forth, tears in his eyes, and hands shaking once more. She had never seen him so affected in all the years she had known him, though at least he seemed in control of his faculties.

"I had no idea," she said softly, standing what she hoped was an appropriate distance away. She longed to comfort him but only if it would not bring him more distress.

Matthias looked at her, his eyes wide and fearful. "How could you have?"

"I'm so sorry you've suffered. Tell me the story. Perhaps it would help for me to know. You think you were responsible for Timothy's and James's deaths? Oh, Matthias, surely during a war, there can be no blaming you."

He shook his head. "You don't understand these things."

"Make me understand! Please. I had hoped … I had hoped seeing Colonel Whitmore might help you. He is a great advocate of … of men like you. Did you know that? Oh, Matthias, let me stand by your side. I want to be your wife. I *must* be."

He slammed his eyes shut. "That can never be. I'm sorry." He turned as if to leave her.

She couldn't stand his walking away—again. She couldn't. Perhaps, as Sophie had suggested, she held more cards than she believed. In a moment, faced with his leaving, the decision was made. "Matthias," she called out, her voice shaking. "I need to tell you something, and I'm not at all sure how you'll react."

Matthias turned back to her, his face lined with worry. "What is it, Rosalind?"

She took a deep breath and placed a hand on her stomach. "I think I'm with child. You … you're going to be a father."

He froze, staring at her as if she'd grown a second head.

At once, she wondered if she had made a misstep, but she pushed through. "I'm happy about it, darling." She took a hesitant step toward him, then another. "I was unsure at first, but Sophie—Mrs. Jones, of course—gave me the courage I needed. We can raise our baby together—this can be the start of our family. I … I think I love you. I might have always, though I'd hoped it was just a childhood infatuation—because of Timothy. But he's not here now—and you are. I need you. I can't properly do this alone—no woman can. After all, it did take the two of us to … to begin this life."

He cast his eyes down. "I'm so sorry. I … I'm so sorry." He turned and ran, leaving Rosalind alone in the garden—and this time she didn't try to chase him. There was a hole in her chest now, but she couldn't let that hold her here. She took a deep breath and let it out slowly. She could control herself. She must.

Wiping her tears away, Rosalind made her way back inside the estate. She was grateful for the dark hallways, which provided her with a moment to compose herself before facing her guests. But as she reached the drawing room, Sophie appeared—eyes full of concern.

"Rosalind, my dear. What happened?"

She pressed her eyes closed. "I told him, and he ran. He always runs. If he would just stay—and talk about it. It's … it's this dark cloud in his mind holding him down, making it impossible for him to see … to see how beautiful this could be. The baby, our life together, *everything.*"

"Oh, my dear." She drew Rosalind into an embrace, as if she'd known her all her life instead of a little over a week. "Be patient with him! Though I know little of this ailment, I do know that war is hell. He's been through so much—and watching his brother and yours die couldn't have been easy. Does he carry some guilt?"

Rosalind nodded. "He says he killed them, though he wouldn't tell me what he meant by that."

"Hmm. You'll have to find that out, too." Sophie stepped back. "Let's go wash your face and send everyone home. I'll make Graham go home and be with Jonathan so I can stay—and we'll pray. All right?"

Rosalind nodded. Perhaps just now, all she could do was plead with God to offer Matthias some degree of comfort—and bring him back to her.

Chapter Ten

Matthias stumbled into his study, then locked the door behind him. He was still reeling from his outburst at Rosalind. He shouldn't have left her—but he couldn't have stayed either.

When before it had seemed like his only alternative, now he deeply regretted having given her the child.

After some time, he drew out a pen and paper and began to write. He wrote of his hopes and dreams for his child, of the love he had for Rosalind, and the deep sense of responsibility he felt as a husband and father. But as he wrote, his despair crept in, overshadowing all else.

Still, he wrote of his fear of returning to war, of the nightmares that haunted him every night, of the overwhelming sense of dread that consumed him. He wrote of his belief that he was a coward, that he would never be able to face the battlefield again, and that he would die in shame.

Tears streamed down his face as he finished the letter, his pen trembling in his hand. He signed the note, folded it, and left it on his desk.

He needed to clear his head, so he went for a walk outside. The cool evening air filled his lungs, and he breathed deeply, trying to calm himself. He couldn't be a blubbering fool all the rest of his life; he must find a way to rise above this.

What if he couldn't?

He walked until he was too tired to go on, then he sat down on a bench and looked up at the stars. In that moment, he felt small and insignificant, just a speck in the vast universe.

A forgotten memory from his childhood, a verse of the Book that he had so often failed to read these days, came to mind. He repeated it aloud: "'When I consider Thy heavens, the work of Thy fingers, the moon and the stars, which Thou hast ordained; What is man, that Thou art mindful of him? and the son of man, that Thou visitest him? For Thou hast made him a little lower than the angels, and hast crowned him with glory and honour.'"

"An excellent verse, Lt. Emmet."

Matthias turned to face Colonel Whitmore. "Oh. I—"

Colonel Whitmore held up his hand. "I hope I am not disturbing you, but I came to apologize. That was thoughtless of me; I should have known better. I did know better, but some strange impulse took over me."

"I'm the one who should apologize." Matthias scrambled to his feet. "My reaction was ... beyond anything it should have been."

The older man shook his head. "No. Don't apologize. War leaves scars on us all that never fully heal—and your time was so fresh. Would you walk with me? I came to Willard Place with a question for you, though I had intended to bring it up to you after dinner in private. I'm sorry that I didn't."

Matthias tilted his head. "Of course."

They walked together through the dim garden, lit only by the moonlight. It was a cool spring evening but certainly not uncomfortable, and the air smelled of fresh flowers and grass and dew.

"I shall keep it simple, Lt. Emmet. The Crown had been wanting to reward you for your service—and I had a strong impulse that you would be further suited for a position that I have long had in mind. Simply put, how would you feel about running a home for convalescing soldiers here in Surrey? Specifically, a place for men who no longer feel suited for war or for peacetime to rest. I thought, at first, that perhaps it was strange that your name came at once to my mind for this project—but now I wonder if God hasn't created you for just such a purpose. You would, of course, not return to war—and the place could be managed from your home, allowing you to be with your bride."

Matthias stopped walking and stood, a little breathless and confused. "I ... I don't know what to say, sir. I don't believe I am capable of such a thing."

Colonel Whitmore smiled. "I believe you are. I have faith that this is something you could do quite well."

"I … I would need to discuss this with my wife."

"Of course, of course. Well, you know I live but a town over, and you are more than welcome to contact me when you arrive at a decision." He held out his hand. "Just be sure to thoroughly consider it."

Matthias hesitated, then reached out to shake the colonel's hand. "I will."

Matthias's study was cast in gloom, and despite the fact that he usually kept it in a similar condition, Rosalind swiftly determined that he was not in the room. She crept forward, glancing around, hoping to discern where he might have gone.

They had much to discuss, and she was unwilling to wait. Surely he'd have calmed down enough by now that they could have a conversation on the topics he had put off again and again.

As she progressed into the room, her eye caught upon a sheet of white paper resting on the desk. She meant to leave it—she did—but she happened to read her own name and could not resist picking it up to read it.

> *My darling Rosalind,*
>
> *As I sit here, pen in hand, I find myself overwhelmed by the emotions that have been swirling inside me since our conversation earlier this evening. You have always been the light of my life, a steady force of cheeriness, even against my least agreeable days. From our childhood, I found myself drawn to you—finding you at once a worthy companion and friend. As you blossomed into womanhood, and as I became a man, I saw more to admire in your strength and beauty, both in person and in character.*

You have always been the one I love. Now, with the news of our child, I find myself even more filled with desire for a future together.

And yet, alongside that hope, there is a deep and unrelenting despair. I cannot shake the feeling that I am a broken man, unworthy of your love and of the honor you have bestowed upon me in both allowing our marriage to take place and in giving me this child. My time on the battlefield has left me scarred, physically and mentally, and I fear that I will never be able to shake the demons that haunt me.

But as I write these words, I know that I must try. For you, for our child, for the future we might have together. I pray that you can forgive me for my outburst earlier and for any pain I may have caused you. I want nothing more than to be the husband and father that you deserve.

I love you, my darling Rosalind, and I promise to do all that I can to be the man that you deserve. I'm not sure there's a way—I fear there is not. But I will do all I can to change that.

With all my heart,
Matthias

Every word wept of the anguish she now knew Matthias to feel—even so, there was such shining hope in the letter, hope Rosalind wasn't sure Matthias could see himself.

If she could show him, if she could drag him back to the light of hope, it would be worth it. It would all be worth it.

She dropped the letter and flew out of the house.

She passed Colonel Whitmore on the way out, but given that Sophie had promised to take care of things, she felt free to ignore him and go find her husband.

He was sitting alone on a bench in the garden, but he straightened when he saw her coming and gestured for her to sit next to him.

"Rosalind."

"Matthias. I … I read your letter."

His eyebrows rose. "My letter?"

"The one you left in the office." She swallowed. "Perhaps ... perhaps you hadn't intended me to read it. But, darling, I'm glad I did. I want ... I want everything in the world with you. This home. A child. But even if we had none of it, I would want to be with you— don't you see that? Even in spite of ... of not knowing what the future may bring. I want to help you get better—and even if I can't, I want to be at your side during your worst."

He stared at her. "I ... I don't understand why."

"Matthias, I ... I was mad about you when we were young. I never told you because of Timothy, but I was ... I was almost relieved when I learned we might be together. Now, I don't think Timothy would hesitate for a moment in wishing us well, and I don't think he would blame you for his death or for James's. I don't. I *love* you. Now, as you are, with any mistake you've made or injury you've gained. Even if you have changed, I want to be with that changed man." She placed her hands on his arms, and he met her eyes, his own brimming with a tremulous hope. "Don't you see that?"

He blinked rapidly. "Do you mean it?" His voice struggled for control over every word.

"Of course! Did you mean it when you said you loved me?"

"Rosalind, I love you more than I have ever loved any other. And if I could live for you, I would. Do you think we could be given a second chance?"

In response, she leaned over and kissed him.

When she drew back, he kept hold of her and looked in her eyes. "Colonel Whitmore offered to let me run a convalescing home for soldiers—here in Surrey. He said ... he said I was owed it—for my service. I think, mostly, he wanted to get me out of the war—and allow me time to heal. It would be a place suited to rest and regain a sense of peace. And, Rosalind, that's exactly what I need. And if I could offer it to others ..."

"I could help with that!" It would be a welcome change from the life of leisure she'd been living in these last few years, without any kind of activity. "I'd love to, in fact."

"That's what I thought. And then we would have something to work on—together." He swallowed. "It's a lot to ask of you, though, with me being how I am."

"Yet it's a commitment I made when I married you." She leaned her head against his shoulder. "I was never afraid of what that might bring me, and I'm not now."

"I'm glad."

She moved back slightly, bracing her hands on his arms. "Will you stay with me tonight? I understand why you don't want to, but it's important to me, and I don't care ... I don't care about anything." She pressed her lips together, trying wildly to think through what might convince him. "Darling, it would mean all the world to me."

Matthias closed his eyes for a moment. "I'd just worry about the baby."

"The baby will be fine. And no matter what happens, I want to be with you. After all, it's 'for better or for worse.'"

He kissed her forehead. "Then I'll stay."

A Note from Kellyn Roth

This was the novella I put off writing … and put off writing … and put off writing … and then when I did finally write it, I will admit, I was unimpressed. It took several rounds of revisions for me to begin liking the story you just read—but once I did like it, I fell in love.

Rosalind (named for the Shakespeare heroine) is certainly not my first foray into a spunky historical female, but she has become one of my favorites. I was slower to accept Matthias, but once I did, I loved his sweet nature and his desire to do right by his bride. (By the way, Matthias was named for one of my best friends in the world, a young man with Down Syndrome who I am delighted to support and teach a few days a week, as well as spend time with his family).

As for thank-yous, the first one goes to you, the reader. You make this story come alive as you read it and imagine it and hopefully enjoy it!

The second goes to Janelle, for loaning me her sons (Matthias especially, but Rosh and Gil, too) and making my days that much cheerier both with their company and with hers! Thank you for all the light and hope you've poured into me.

The third goes to my husband, Matthew, who has had to deal with more than one sleepless night, more than one stress-induced sobbing session, and more than one rant about how nothing is ever easy for me. Though some of that may not be entirely logical, it's also not entirely logical how much you choose to love and support me through all my woes and worries, all my mental health struggles and heartbreaks, and all my pleas for coffee at 10 PM. In this season of fear and confusion, I appreciate your courage, baby. I'm undeserving.

The fourth is to God, Who should have gone first—but I am ever thankful for His sustaining influence on my life. I am such an "unholy mess of a girl" (to quote the esteemed Grace Kelly, or rather her character in *High Society*)—I am blessed with a great and powerful God Who only cares about the woman I can become through Him.

Lastly, I'd like to thank my beta readers: Michaela Bush, Abby Johansen, Addie Grace Putnam, and Catherine Thompson. I deeply appreciate you all reading my messy third draft and helping turn it into a final draft. You all rock!

For my readers, if you would like to connect with me on a personal level, I'd suggest following me on Instagram (@kellynrothauthor) or subscribe to my newsletter:

https://kellynrothauthor.com/newsletter/

I also have a writers-only newsletter, if that's your thing!

With that, I leave you. Thank you again for all your splendiferous support in the reading of this collection!

TTFN!

~Kellyn Roth~

About Wild Blue Wonder Press

Wild Blue Wonder Press was established in January 2016 by Kellyn Roth for the purpose of independently publishing her historical women's fiction series, The Chronicles of Alice and Ivy.

Based on a special location on her family's property and a childhood stumbling over phrases, Kellyn chose the name to evoke feelings of wonder in a world full of dark valleys. After all, where there is snow and ice, there will be chickadees, and in the midst of the darkest woods, you can often find a cozy cabin.

As of January 2023, Wild Blue Wonder Press is beginning working with other creatives to expand its outreach and help other independent writers achieve their dreams in a professional manner.

Wild Blue Wonder Press's mission is to share fictional stories full of grace and truth. Our goal is to create stories that matter, to delve into the deepest and sometimes the saddest parts of life, and to return from the darkest valleys resplendent in the light of hope and the fullness of joy.

At present, we are specifically focusing on women's fiction aimed at a "new adult" Christian audience. Our ideal reader is a young woman navigating life as an adult and asking big questions along the way. We tackle topics such as mental health, sexual sins, past trauma, and more in godly light while also showing the positive hope that comes from healing through Jesus Christ.

If you'd like to support us, consider following our newsletter, which you can subscribe to on our website:

https://wildbluewonderpress.com/

Wild Blue Wonder PRESS

Made in the USA
Columbia, SC
14 February 2024

31534417R00288